# Cross-Country
## CHRISTMAS

OTHER COVENANT BOOKS AND
AUDIOBOOKS BY LAURIE LEWIS

**Women's fiction, romance, and suspense
written as Laurie Lewis**
*Unspoken*
*The Dragons of Alsace Farm*
*Sweet Water*
*Love on a Limb*
*Awakening Avery*
*Love on the Line*
*Secrets Never Die*

**Historical romance, under the pen name L. C. Lewis**
FREE MEN AND DREAMERS series
*Dark Sky at Dawn*
*Twilight's Last Gleaming*
*Dawn's Early Light*
*Oh, Say Can You See?*
*In God is Our Trust*

# Cross-Country CHRISTMAS

## A SILVER-BUCKLE BRIDES ROMANCE

# LAURIE LEWIS

Covenant Communications, Inc.

Cover images: *A Couple Sitting on a Pier above a Frozen Lake* © Katie Martynova / iStock; *Panorama of the Foggy Winter Mountains* © Andrew Mayovskyy / iStock. Interior image: *Plaid Pattern Background* © ZillaDigital / iStock.

Cover design copyright © 2021 by Covenant Communications, Inc.
Cover and interior design by Kimberly Kay

Published by Covenant Communications, Inc.
American Fork, Utah

Printed in the United States of America
First Printing: October 2021

27 26 25 24 23 22 21    10 9 8 7 6 5 4 3 2 1

ISBN: 978-1-52441-886-1

*To my husband, Tom,*
*whose heart,*
*like these characters',*
*always seeks ways to serve*

# AUTHOR'S NOTE AND ACKNOWLEDGMENTS

CROSS-COUNTRY CHRISTMAS WAS INSPIRED BY an adventure I'll always cherish. My oldest son, Tom, invited me to go on a long drive with him from Salt Lake County to St. George. Any one-on-one time with an adult child is a rare treat, so I jumped at the chance, and off we went—in his new Tesla. The car was both a marvel and a fright to me, coming when he summoned it, like a remote-controlled toy. It self-corrected when he neared another lane, it looked like half its parts were missing, and instead of filling the tank, we stopped to charge its batteries several times along our journey. As we drove, I browsed the internet for articles about drivers rigging the automated car to drive solo and found some crazy tales. Thus, this story was born. Thanks, Tom!

This was a two-state write. It was inspired by Utah, born in Maryland as I tapped out the first half amid packing boxes, and completed in Utah when we arrived after making a life-changing move. Many thanks to Beth Bentley, Lisa Swinton, Elizabeth Royal, Lisa Rector, Sarah Lee, and Olivia Aycock, my dearly missed critique group back in Maryland. Their feedback shaped the early pages and these characters.

I've been awed by a dear friend whose adopted children have fetal alcohol syndrome. I was not aware of the unique challenges affected children face until I watched her struggles to help them move into adulthood. I am so awed by her and her family for their dedication to one another despite challenges. I thought of them often as I wrote Nora's story.

Grateful thanks to Covenant Communications for selecting Cross-Country Christmas for their 2021 Christmas lineup. It was exciting to get that news. I owe them my heartfelt thanks for wise counsel, support, and hand-holding during the book's production. No book is born without the tireless efforts of a talented, dedicated, behind-the-scenes army, and I gratefully acknowledge Amy Parker and her creative team for their marketing support. Many thanks to all of Covenant's staff for the many parts they played in getting this book to market.

I always strive to uplift and entertain my readers, but writing for Covenant amplifies that challenge to lift readers on an emotional and spiritual level. I hope you, the reader, feel I hit that mark with *Cross-Country Christmas*. Thank you for trusting me with your time and heart.

A writer's own feelings permeate their work. This book was written during the COVID-19 pandemic, amidst shutdowns and chaos. My sense of loss and isolation during these months fueled CC and Reese's story. I hope life will be more normalized when you read this, but when we look back on 2020, I hope we'll find cause to count our blessings, to see how we grew through adversity, and to see how our individual relationships with and faith in Christ were strengthened.

Much love,
Laurie

# CHAPTER ONE

THE DISCOMFORT OF SKIN-PRICKLING COLD was CC's first cognitive feeling, followed by fear and panic at the inky darkness that surrounded her. One of her flailing hands smacked against icy glass. The other found the steering wheel. She was in a car. And then she remembered driving south through Utah on her way to Las Vegas when the call came through. *What an idiot,* she told herself. The pain of the call was nothing considering her immediate concerns. And all because of him?

*Why is it so dark and cold?*

She reached blindly for the dash, her fingers scraping to find something familiar—the light switch or her phone—anything to end the terrifying darkness. She found nothing but smooth surfaces, the wheel, and a monitor mounted before her and a little to the right.

More recent familiarity sank in.

"The Tesla," she whispered. She'd enjoyed the four-wheeled rocket's unique features when it shot down the open highway, going from a dead stop to one hundred miles per hour in under seven seconds. But not now.

"Where am I, and why can't I see anything?" she whimpered as she beat upon the windows, the doors, the steering wheel, and last of all, the monitor that controlled the car's functions—lights, speed, windshield wipers, heat, and sound—but it remained unresponsive.

Reminders of the car's physical elements returned to her, and she felt along the door panel until her fingers found the release button. She pressed it and threw her entire 127 pounds against the door and felt it give, but it didn't open. Her door was blocked. Frantic, she searched the cupholder and found the key, a credit-card-looking plastic rectangle, which she tapped against the center console. No engine revved. She tapped the brake with her foot to initiate the startup, but still, there was no response. As fear and panic rose in her, CC cursed the electric car's silent start, craving any sign of engine life over dead silence.

She needed light. And fresh air. And heat.

At least she'd been smart enough to wear a sweater, but the leather seats were freezing against her blue-jeaned bottom. Her coat! She remembered tossing it into the back seat. She retrieved it and put it on, hoping to at least delay her freezing to death. Her fingers were nearly numb before she found her gloves on the passenger seat. Her discount boots were cute but poorly insulated against these temperatures. Even her hair was cold to the touch. She gathered it up in a yellow mass and tucked it into the neckline of her coat so she could pull the collar up and over her head. She pulled the zipper up tight until only her blue eyes were visible, but claustrophobia gripped her. She fought back by slamming her palms against the windows again.

Another idea hit her. She felt along the passenger seat for the shoulder strap of her purse and followed it until her fingers found the bag with her phone inside. The battery was weak but sufficient to power up the flashlight app, which she used to scan the glass roof and windows barricading her in. What she saw was even more frightening than the darkness—snow. She was encased in snow! But how? And where was the car sitting? In a parking lot? Or a field? Or on the shoulder of the last highway she remembered?

She grabbed her head and tried to recall her last clear memory. She'd been driving down the empty road when she noticed the dark band in the wide-open sky about a million miles away to the west. The approaching storm clearly moved in faster than she'd imagined it would. And then she remembered the stupid thing she did. The act of foolishness that might now cost her life.

She hunkered down and tried to tell herself that the shaking of her body was from fear, not from life-sucking cold. The phone's screen read 6:38 p.m. "Just ride it out," she told herself. "Morning will come eventually, and someone will find you." She didn't believe her own argument.

And then she heard an approaching engine. Hope filled her, until other sounds, like the riddle of small bullets hitting her car, sent her hurtling across the front seats in a scream. Moments passed. She assessed herself. No pain. She ran her hands over her body, afraid she would see red when she pulled them back, but there was no blood. She used the flashlight to check the car's interior, but there were no bullet holes . . . no interior damage at all.

Then there was a thump.

The car lurched, and she yelped, jerking away from the intrusion. The noise came again, followed by an animal sound and a gooey pink mass that swiped across her window, clearing a swath of snow. CC screamed again and laid across the seat. The pink thing, which she identified as a tongue, took another slimy lick at the door window, revealing a huge, scary cow with horns. Behind the beast, CC could see the dim light of dusk and white in every direction.

Two more tongues and various cow bodies jostled the car. She felt a slam to the rear corner as new worries, shaped like dollar signs, haunted her.

"Stop it!" she shouted at the animals as she slapped her hands against the glass. "Get away from this car!" More pounding and hollering caused one animal to bawl in protest and push back against the vehicle's body. CC felt sick as she imagined the $70,000 car slowly turning into a trash can.

She grabbed her phone to call 911 and then realized she had no idea where she was. *Maybe they can trace my phone's signal,* she thought. She dialed the three numbers as her phone's battery drained to zero and the screen went dark.

She heard a new sound, like a rumble, and then a light pierced through the blanket of snow in her rear windshield, illuminating the car's interior and bathing her in the hope of rescue.

*Rescue?* She didn't see the pulsing lights of a police car or a tow truck. Just ordinary headlights that held no guarantee that the driver was someone she could trust. She didn't have mace, but she fished in her bag for a travel-sized hair spray and hoped the intruder would assume the worst.

A soft male voice, layered with worry and annoyance, called to the cows. "Get along. Yes, I know you're innocent. Dale Earnhardt here broke the fence this time."

CC groaned. She'd broken a fence. That explained the arrival of the bawling, jostling animals who cried louder and pushed the car with greater intensity since the man's arrival.

"All right . . . you've had your fun. Now, get back in the pasture."

Something about the man's strong voice calmed CC as he called out a few encouraging hyahs to the animals. Another male voice, this one with a Hispanic accent, called similarly to the cows. Two men were outside the car. She tensed again over that realization.

The jostling of the car ceased, and when the animals' cries grew more distant, a gloved hand wiped the remaining snow from the window, revealing a ski-masked face. CC startled, curling into a ball by the far door while extending her hair-spray weapon toward the unidentifiable intruder. The man's eyes widened in a flash of concern, and he jutted his hand forward as he stepped back and pulled the lower section of his knitted mask down. His nose, mouth, and chin, all surrounded by brown whiskers, were visible now. The man's face was ruggedly attractive, but she reminded herself that serial murderer Ted Bundy had reportedly been handsome also, so she kept her guard up.

The same concern she'd heard as he addressed his stock was evident in his eyes as he peered into the car, but she focused on something more trustworthy than looks—his voice.

"Sorry for scaring you," he shouted slowly through the glass. "Are you all right?"

CC's heart rate slowed and her breathing steadied as she relaxed and sat up.

He drew close to the glass and repeated, "Are you all right, ma'am?"

CC held on to her can of hair spray and nodded. "I can't open the door!"

The man nodded back and studied the car's position while she studied him. His tan insulated overalls and jacket covered a solid, strong frame. What she could see of his dark hair appeared thick with no signs of gray. Lines that spoke of harsh weather, worry, or both creased the outside edges of his clear, brown eyes that, along with his strength and vigor, left CC with the impression that he was in his early to midthirties and not only willing but able to help her.

He said, "Hold on a minute. I'll have to dig you out a bit." He turned and walked away from her car.

Despite his scruffy facial hair, his overall demeanor gave her a positive vibe that left her feeling safe enough in his care to relax her grip on the can of hair spray. The door to the man's vehicle opened and then closed. Based on the height of his headlights, she presumed it was a truck. After a few moments, she heard the huff of the man's breath as he heaved shovelfuls of snow. She pulled the door handle from her side and moved near the glass, prepared to point to the Tesla's embedded door handle on the outside, a sleek feature she thought might confuse the rancher, but to her surprise, he found the handle's location with ease and opened the door without her awkward instructions.

She got her first good look at him, though it was difficult to determine how much of his bulk was him and how much was his thermal overalls and jacket. He reached a leather-gloved hand in, barely giving her a quick glance before his eyes fell on the plastic bag tied to the steering wheel with a scarf.

His eyes narrowed and pinched. "Is this a self-driving model?"

"Yes . . ."

Disappointment filled those eyes she'd found winsome a moment earlier. "You violated the safety protocols by weighting the wheel so the car's computer would think you were still steering manually."

CC didn't answer.

"That's illegal. What was the bag filled with? Nuts? Bolts? Change?"

"Makeup."

"Maaaa—?"

"Okay," she confessed with her hands poised forward. "It was a dumb thing to do. I needed a minute. I-I-I got a call . . ."

*The call.* The message that had sent her crying until she could barely see the road ahead.

"You didn't need to rig your car to take a call. This four-wheeled computer will tee up your call and make you a sandwich while you pick up."

She didn't pay attention to his joke, because she was gawking at the hundred-foot wall of snow-covered dirt standing a few hundred yards in front of her. Her last conscious memory had been of an open range fringed by mountains, yet she now appeared to be in the actual foothills. How long had the car driven itself, and how long had she been asleep? She felt her eyes begin to burn over her negligence.

The man reached into his coat pocket and pulled out a stack of neatly folded tissues, from which he withdrew one. "Are you sure you're okay? You don't need to cry. It's just a car, and cars can be fixed. I'm sure you have insurance."

His assumption left her feeling sick. "I'm sorry," she whimpered. "I woke up disoriented, in the dark, with what sounded like bullets hitting my car. And then cows were licking my windshield. It's just been a really awful day."

"Bullets? Must've been the salt, but it probably saved you. My neighbor saw me dropping off feed for my animals while driving his salt truck and assumed this snow-covered lump was a hay roll until he heard the salt hit something solid. He called and asked me to check things out. And the salt likely drew the cattle. Once your fancy car was embedded in the snow, it was just a big salt lick."

She thought she might be sick, so she bent sideways in her seat to find a spot in the snow, just in case. Her body kept tipping forward until the man's hands slid under her shoulders to support her weight. The sick feeling passed, but not this new embarrassment. When the man sat her back in her seat, he leaned close, and worry lined his face.

"Did you bump your head? Nausea can be a sign of a concussion."

"It's not that. I'm just . . ."

He hovered close until he was sure she was stable. "Just stay inside, out of the falling snow." His gestures were more medical than grand, but no one had made her feel that safe and watched over since her father, and that realization brought new tears to her eyes.

CC looked through the snow-streaked glass at the brand-new $70,000 Tesla wrapped in barbed wire and perched against a wildly leaning fence post. A smeared windshield and some salt scratches were the least of that car's worries. She let about a dozen more tears fall as she thought about the men she had let down by wrecking it. The list included her father, who was the reason she'd set off in the first place—to honor him.

She was barely holding it together. How would she pay for the damages? Maybe she would end up in jail or debtors' prison, if they still had those. She felt like her six-year-old self the time she tried to pour her own milk and ended up dropping the heavy jug on top of her father's prized accomplishment, a balsa-wood model of a B-52 bomber.

She apologized again. "I'm sorry about the crash and about rigging the wheel. I didn't think. I-I-I just reacted to some hard news."

The truck's headlights and fog lights bathed the bent rancher in a yellowish glow. He scratched a spot on his head and said, "And you thought the car could do fine on its own, so you sat back and fell asleep?"

*More like cried myself to sleep.*

"I didn't consciously choose to shirk my responsibility. Mine was the only car on the road at the time, and no snow was falling then. My nerves were shot, and . . . let's just say I figured this smart car could manage better than I could at the moment, when I was rummaging through my purse for tissues and trying to pull myself together. I settled back to collect myself, and *then* I must have . . . I must have fallen asleep." Her version didn't sound any more responsible than his. "I guess the car rode on until it ran out of battery charge. I'm still learning about this Tesla. I'm not used to stopping for electricity instead of gas. And I *am* truly, truly sorry."

"First trip in this car?"

CC nodded, though the real answer was a bit more complicated.

The man pressed his gloved thumb and index finger against his temples before speaking in a voice that was measured and tutorial, as if he were addressing a delinquent student. "These cars don't veer off-lane when they run out of charge. They veer because they can't see the lines on the road anymore. The snow obscured the lines, and *because there was no one to guide the vehicle*"—he waved his hand at the broken fence and the meandering cows—"it busted through my fencing wire and sent a dozen head of cattle off on a holiday."

"You have every right to be upset about your cows. How many wandered off?"

"There's too many to count tonight. And they're *cattle*. Prize Angus, to be exact. Each of them represents two thousand plus pounds of prime beef, and they've been wandering loose so any hee-haw with a truck could have hauled one home for a free barbecue."

CC felt like a peg being pounded into the ground. "I don't know what else to say besides I'm sorry. I'll help look for them until a tow truck comes or the cops arrive to lock me up."

"Neither one is likely tonight," the young Hispanic man called out as he trudged up to the car. "You're lucky our local hero here decided to distribute hay when he did. There's no telling how long you'd've been stranded otherwise."

"What? Could I have frozen to death?"

"It's been known to happen." The Hispanic man's cheerful manner turned dramatic and somber.

CC sighed and dropped her forehead to the wheel.

"Oh no," the rancher said. "Let's not add a new bump to your problems." Again she felt the rancher's strong hands latch on to her arm to set her back in her seat. "You're not helping, Carlos."

"See? A hero, and modest to boot," Carlos said. "When help is needed quick, Reese fills in, whether it's as an impromptu sheriff, a nurse, or a local preacher."

"It's very kind of you," CC said, "but rescuing wayward drivers shouldn't be your responsibility."

"Most of the time, there is no one else," Carlos said. "There's nothing but Brockbank land and Bureau of Land Management acreage for miles in any direction." He gestured to the land with a sweep of his hand.

The rancher CC now knew as Reese Brockbank, judging from the information she'd just received from Carlos, picked up his shovel and walked toward his truck, the back of which was filled with hay bales. On the way, he tossed a comment over his shoulder. "Your car decided to take a nap on government grazing land."

"*What?*"

When Reese didn't answer, Carlos filled in. "Afraid so. Pretty much all you can do on it is take pretty walks and graze cattle if you have a permit.

Unfortunately, your car broke the fence that divides Reese's permitted land from about a hundred thousand acres of government open range."

CC's stomach dropped at the news as a few strays moved through the broken fence line to nibble on the tall grass poking through the snow beyond. "I imagine that's really bad, isn't it?" she asked quietly, afraid of the response.

"Maybe . . . maybe not." Carlos's attempt to sugarcoat the answer failed.

"What's the worst-case scenario?" CC choked out.

"The more grazing land you have, the better," Reese explained as he returned to coax two strays back through the downed fence. "Especially in the summer, when sweet grass gets scarce."

Carlos nodded. "Reese's permit gives him access to a little stream-fed valley where the grass stays green almost year-round. If his cattle are caught on unpermitted acreage, he could lose his permit."

Breaking one man's Tesla and losing another man's cattle were terrible but measurable things. However, losing Reese's grazing rights sounded like an irrecoverable loss. How could CC ever fix that?

She estimated the damage and how many years she'd have to work to repay all the harm she'd caused everyone. Maybe she'd just set up shop in a prison salon and spend the rest of her life sending people reimbursement checks from behind bars.

She called ahead to Reese and joked, "I suppose you'd like to know who crashed into your fence." Reese apparently didn't hear her, or he was too mad to laugh or smile or even look back, so CC extended her hand to Carlos instead. "Sorry for all this. I'm CC Cippolini, from Chicago."

"Cippolini, like tortellini. Got it. I'm Carlos Barraza. Nice to meet you."

"You too, although I'd have preferred it to be under different circumstances. Are you two neighbors?"

"You could say that. I live two doors down the same hall. My wife and I are boarding with Reese while he teaches me the ropes of ranching. And don't worry about his temper. We've been best friends for over ten years. He's more bark than bite." He gave her hand a final shake and said, "I'd better go help him."

In a flash, he took off toward the truck as well. CC called out in the direction of the vehicle's blinding headlights, "Can I help with anything?"

Again, there was no reply. She assumed Reese was ignoring her because he was angry, and she couldn't blame him.

He unexpectedly reappeared in front of her car, holding a heavy roll of wire. A long-handled tool with hooks and a pulley hung over his shoulder.

She had seen such a device before, and after a few moments of racking her brain, she remembered its name and what it was used for.

"That's a come-along, right? For fixing fences?"

A hint of respect showed on his face. "Where'd you learn that? I figured you for a city girl."

"My dad worked in a hardware store. I hung out with him there after school." CC tried to conceal the emotional tug on her heart whenever she thought of her father.

Reese pressed his lips tightly as he stretched his hand out to her, his eyes focused on her face, with no hint of anger this time. She wondered if he had accepted her sincere remorse. "Forgive my manners," he said. "CC, was it?"

She nodded, shook his hand, and offered him an apologetic smile. Carlos arrived carrying more tools CC recognized—a post hole digger and some wire cutters with a hammerlike head for pounding nails and large fencing staples. "I'll . . . gladly help you patch your fence," she said.

Reese looked at Carlos, and his moustache wriggled like he was chuckling over CC's proposal. "Thanks for the offer, but I don't have an extra set of work gloves on me. Carlos and I can knock this repair out in no time."

She gave the man points for gracious tact. "Then, may I ask another favor? My phone battery is dead. Could I possibly use yours to call a tow truck? If the next town is as far away as Carlos said, I need to call for help right away."

"We barely have a signal on this point of the mountain, even in good weather," Reese said. "You'll never reach anyone from here in this mess."

Panic slammed her again at the thought of how vulnerable she was in the middle of nowhere, in a snowstorm, with a dead electric car. "I . . . where can I . . . ?"

"We'll take you back to the cattle shack with us," Reese said.

*Cattle shack?* "I-I-I . . . There's no way I'm . . ."

"Neither are we, ma'am. Carlos's wife, Emmie, will be there too."

She looked at Carlos, who seemed to be a nice enough fellow, and even Reese had grown less chilly by the minute. She had no other options at this point, so she remained cautiously agreeable for the moment. "In that case, thank you."

While the men got to work resetting the downed post a few feet from the Tesla and inside the fence line, CC's need to assess the car's damage overwhelmed her. Disregarding Reese's advice to stay in the car, she exited and closed the door to get to the hood. It was worse than she imagined. The hood and front bumper had deep gouges that went all the way into the metal. Her pity party had caused more than a mere setback to her plans. This was a full-blown disaster. She bit her lip hard and returned to the car, but when she attempted to open the door to get her things, the door wouldn't budge. She pulled again and again, cursing the powerless electric car whose doors could not be opened from the outside without someone on the inside pulling the handle. Defeated, she leaned across the car and beat her fist against the glass.

Reese walked up beside her. "This isn't your Tesla, is it?"

"No." Tears burned her eyes again, but CC didn't care anymore. What were a few embarrassing tears compared to the trouble that lay ahead for her?

He leaned back against the car without uttering a word. His silence unsettled her, but his body language—head down and tilted slightly away from her, his eyes fixed on a spot of snow as if he couldn't bear to look at her—was saying plenty. "Just tell me you didn't steal it."

"Of course I didn't steal it!" she roared back. She wanted to smack him for suggesting such a thing. "I might be foolish, naive, and a little emotional, but I'm not a thief or a liar. Everything I own is in this car. Everything."

The hard set of Reese's face slipped into sympathetic kindness. "Okay, then. Look on the bright side. If you can't get the door open, neither can any coyote or rabbit passing by tonight. Your stuff is safe. We'll get it in the morning."

The thought of having nothing—no purse or working phone or clothes or ID of any kind—terrified her. Reese seemed to understand.

"Come on," he said. "I just might know a little trick."

With the men's help, she struggled up the embankment to the shoulder of the road. Reese got in his truck and pulled it as close to the Tesla's front bumper as he could before hitting the downward slope where the car was lodged. The tall stack of hay bales filling the truck bed teetered during the move, causing the truck to rock wildly as well. CC held her breath and prayed she wouldn't become the cause of another accident tonight, but everything settled once Reese parked the truck.

He jumped out with a set of charging cables in hand, opened his truck's hood, and connected the leads to his battery. Then he brushed the snow off a large section of the Tesla's front bumper, revealing a circular hatch, similar to a gas-engine car's refueling door but a third the size. He dug some wires out of the small hole and connected the jumper cables to the ends.

"How does he know so much about Teslas?" she asked Carlos.

"He likes cars, and there's not much to do up here on a winter night except read."

In a moment, the jump start allowed the car doors to open, and Reese gestured for CC to grab her things.

"Thank you, thank you, thank you!" CC gushed, even grabbing his arm in a half hug.

Reese bobbled his head as he fished for a reply. "No problem."

CC grabbed her purse and phone and the small suitcase in the front storage area called the *frunk*. She looked at Reese and then at the back of the car. "I have two more large suitcases in the back. Should I . . . ?" She hoped he'd suggest she grab those as well.

Instead, he walked over and opened the rear trunk, yanking out the two heavy bags with ease. "Let's load up," he called out. "We've still got a few drop-offs to do yet."

CC had no idea what he meant, but she gratefully watched her bags get loaded into the back seat along with the tools, leaving no room for her except in the front seat between the two men.

"You'd better buckle up," Reese said. "We're going off-road in a minute."

The truck groaned and threw muddy snow as it backed up the slope to the road. They drove a few hundred yards and stopped. Carlos jumped out and opened a cattle gate to allow the truck to drive through. CC saw snow-covered tire tracks and assumed this was the way the men had come when they'd found her. Once the gate was closed and Carlos was back inside, Reese drove through the field to a random spot and stopped. CC could hear the excited cries of the steers as the men jumped out. She scooted over and adjusted the mirror in time to see them toss several bales of hay to the ground. They jumped down from the truck bed and tore the bales into what looked like thick sheets, which they scattered in a circle. The feed was quickly surrounded by contented cattle, and then the men returned to the cab, and Reese drove on.

"Can I help?" CC asked. "It's the least I can do, considering."

Reese scanned her lean five-foot-five body. "Those bales weigh upwards of seventy-five pounds each."

"I'm stronger than I look."

"Maybe," Carlos said, "but those steers weigh over a ton each."

"They have nearly the same weight advantage over you, and you're not afraid."

Carlos chuckled. "You've got to admit it, Reese. She has guts."

"Which I'd like to keep right where they are." He glanced at CC. "How about I carve out a few for you to feed?"

CC checked his face for any sign of condescension. What she saw was delight. "Fine."

A few minutes later, she was walking by Reese, extending a thick sheet of hay to a black steer who stood shoulder high to her. "Does he have a name?"

Reese checked the tag on the steer's ear. "Number 13276."

"Catchy. Why not a name like Bubba or Ferdinand? Too many?"

"Yes, but a name also implies attachment, and I don't get attached to what will eventually leave."

CC got the veiled message and felt him pull away from her in that moment, without him moving at all. Reese was a solitary man, and he wanted to keep it that way. She wanted to tell him she seconded that position, but that might require her to answer more questions. Questions she had no interest in exploring with this man.

# CHAPTER TWO

THE SCENE REPLAYED A DOZEN or so times. Reese would find a pocket of cattle and stop the truck, and he and Carlos would drop a few bales to the ground while CC found a friendly one to feed or scratch. The game was cute initially, but Reese found it less so the longer they played; she was already growing comfortable in his world, and that was unacceptable.

She was really pretty, in an unpretentious way—long loose hair, just a little makeup, and a style that implied that she didn't know or care that she was a looker. She appeared to be in her midtwenties, and from what he'd seen of her, she was kind—he'd give her that—but she was also reckless, irresponsible, vulnerable, and in need. Those first two characteristics had been thrillers when he was younger, before Iraq and Afghanistan. The last two were issues he'd always found difficult to resist, but his last experience with such a woman had ended poorly for him, leaving his heart dried up like salted beef. He wouldn't make that mistake again.

When they had accounted for most of the cattle grazing on the permitted land, he drove his truck to exit the final cattle gate and headed back down the road. He drove slowly, concentrating on the treacherous path ahead, but CC's worried posture, forward leaning with eyes darting left and right, made it impossible to ignore the woman.

"You don't need to worry, miss. This truck can practically find its own way home."

"Does it snow this hard very often down here?"

As distracting as it was, he understood her concern. The lanes had become completely obscured by snow. Only the guardrails and lumps formed by snow-covered weeds indicated where the pavement ended.

"We get a half dozen or so of these squalls every year because of the elevation," Carlos chimed in. "Even in this weather, you'll see our turnoff. It's just ahead, past the first section of guardrail."

Reese drove a hundred yards to a turn lane and headed back up the other direction to the first lane that broke to the east. This was his land. A thousand prime acres that ran up into a little valley. He'd bought it from his family by surrendering a portion of his holdings in the family business. They'd offered to let him lease the land from the Brockbank trust for a dollar a year, but he wanted to own it outright, to be able to pass it on to his children someday. That plan had become less likely, yet he held fast to this land and the way of life he loved.

He felt uneasy about revealing too much information about the family or its corporate interests, though he had no reason to assume that allowing CC to know the nature of the business would matter in the long run. Opportunist or not, she would get her car fixed, and she'd be out of here soon enough. Still, he devised a plan to distract her from seeing the sign for the Silver Buckle Mine long before his headlights reached the turnoff. As they approached, he asked her, "Would you mind checking on your bags? It feels like they're falling against my headrest."

The obliging young woman turned around and spent a minute shifting a few things. By the time she faced forward again, they were past the sign and heading into the valley.

CC pressed her hands over her face and whimpered. "Shouldn't you slow down? You're heading straight into that mountain."

Carlos laughed. "Don't worry. It's a lot farther away than it looks. Watch. This zigzag section of the road is my favorite."

The headlights revealed sharp left and right turns obscured by rock formations and scrub oak. Reese didn't admit it, but it was also one of his favorite parts of the property. He'd loved it since he was a child, when his grandfather had taken him along on cattle runs in his battered truck. He'd allow Reese to navigate, saying, "Tell me when to turn, Reese."

If Reese called out, "Turn left" or "Turn right" too soon, his grandfather might slow down, but he'd always obey. Poor navigation of the switchback caused the adventurers to kiss a rock wall on more than one occasion. Reese still missed "the ole man," as his grandfather had referred to himself. His dad was a fine man as well, but while the mine had never been more than a blessed lark to the ole man, it was serious business to Reese's father and brothers. And it would have been to him as well, he imagined, had it not been for that day in Iraq.

"It's like a secret entrance," CC marveled as roads appeared as if by magic after each tight turn.

Her admiration for the property resuscitated Reese's own. And then the house appeared like a bright lantern against the black outline of towering pines. Dusk-to-dawn lights cast a gentle glow on the pond that sat out front like a mirror embedded in the snow. Waterfowl had discovered that they were safe there and made it a regular stop on their flight path north and south. Deer, elk, and range animals also refreshed there. Reese had planned it to be a spectacular setting, a welcome mat at the end of each hard day, and it was nearly perfect. But just nearly.

"This is your *cattle shack*?"

"Not too shabby, right?" Carlos asked.

CC swooned. "It looks like a Christmas card or a calendar page, like the December page my dad always hung on the fridge."

Her enthusiasm revived a spark of the dreams that had inspired the home's construction on this previously barren tract of land, but her use of the past tense when speaking of her father told Reese that beloved and revered man was gone. He felt her loneliness. Reese understood that ache, and though it drew him in, he fought back just as powerfully to remain aloof as she oohed and aahed, narrating her view of the home's exterior as if she were her own tour guide. Reese longed to point out the copper cupola he'd made from ore his grandfather had mined and draw her attention to the front porch and the wooden sled leaning there. It was the very sled his father had used to pull his wife and newborn son home when the truck couldn't make it down the snowy lane.

That was in the days when only one home sat on this lane. Now there were three—the old farmhouse where Reese and his brothers grew up, his parents' sprawling new home set on a hill behind the tree line, and this house he had designed and built for a future he'd probably never know. A piece of his life was lived in each home, and instinct told him CC would listen intently to and relish every family story he told about each one. And that's exactly why he didn't tell them.

He would help this woman, and then she needed to go.

# CHAPTER THREE

CC's FIRST GLANCE OF REESE's "cattle shack" was worth every bone-jarring bump and turn. A large pond spread before it, and CC could see a little dock with something tethered to it. The "shack" itself was a high-peaked log cabin, like those featured in catalogs on a rack at the old hardware store. A wide porch spread across the front with four rocking chairs, a sled, and a porch swing at the end. Pine trees from the mountain behind towered above the roofline like stern sentinels while the whimsical string of multicolored Christmas lights strung along the rail issued a warm welcome home. It was still only November 27, but Thanksgiving was past and people were in full Christmas mode.

She turned to Reese. "Your home could have been designed by Currier and Ives."

"That's what I thought when I first saw the architect's rendering."

"It feels like a hug."

"Not to everyone."

Before CC could respond to that comment, Reese drove along the house to the back, following the wraparound porch that opened into a sprawling deck that overlooked a barn, two small outbuildings, and a fenced paddock. The wide driveway ended in front of an attached four-bay garage with expensive wood-look paneled doors.

CC struggled to take it all in—the gorgeous home, the dramatic exterior lighting that illuminated the falling snow, making the atmosphere welcoming and festive. "It's beautiful," CC said.

Reese muttered "thank you" and hit a button on his visor that opened one of the garage doors, revealing polished brick floors. The garage's interior was as finished and clean as most homes.

After parking, Reese said, "Carlos, can you help our guest with her things while I put the tools away?"

"Sure, sure," Carlos replied. He opened his door, offering CC a hand down to the ground.

As he unloaded the bags, a sturdy, fair-complected, freckled young woman opened the elegantly carved, oversized back door to the house. Her thick frame was covered in baggy overalls, a flannel shirt, and a bulky sweater. Her wild mop of curly red hair seemed ablaze when backlit by the home's interior light.

"I see we have an unexpected guest," she called out in a hearty welcome. "Carlos, I hope this pretty lady's the reason you men are late for supper, and not some emergency that's going to take you back out into this mess tonight." She hurried down the steps toward CC. Her smile radiated into beautiful gray-green eyes that were framed by thick brown eyebrows that nearly met in the middle. "Hi! I'm Carlos's wife, Emmie. Welcome."

"Thank you." CC liked her immediately and extended her hand. "I'm CC."

"Nice to meet you. Was it an accident or a breakdown?"

"A wind-down through a fence," Reese said sarcastically from the bed of the truck.

"Ohhh," Emmie said as she picked up one of CC's bags. Then she scrunched her face and turned to Reese. "What did you say?"

"She drives an electric car," Carlos said as he placed a kiss on his wife's cheek. "CC is going to spend the night with us."

"If the weather report's accurate, we might have her for a few days."

Reese jumped down and slammed the gate on the truck. "I had a feeling. In that case, tidy up my room for her, will you, Emmie? I'll bunk on the sofa."

"No, no, no," CC argued, taking hold of Reese's arm. "I don't want to inconvenience you any further. I'll take the sofa."

His tone changed again, from all-business to a shy, almost apologetic mood. "The spare rooms are used for storage now. You'll have more privacy in the master than in the living room. Besides . . . I tend to meander at night. I might forget you're on the sofa and sit on you."

"Got it."

The back door led into an alcove to the left, where an arched doorway offered a glimpse of the home's state-of-the-art kitchen and gleaming cherry cabinets. The outdoor lighting poured through arched windows over the sink, setting ablaze the colorful veins in the black granite countertops and large island. A carved wooden door stood to the right. Reese opened it and welcomed CC into the mudroom, a narrow but ingeniously planned space designed with cupboards and organizers to neatly store work gear. He invited CC to hang her coat on the rack and store her boots in one of the chests that lined the floor. Work overalls, rain slickers, and two fancy overcoats hung on that rack. Likewise, a variety of footwear was visible in the other two chests, where Carlos and Reese stowed their wet boots.

Another door stood at the end of the mudroom. Reese opened it, revealing a laundry and utility room. CC could also see a utility sink and a shower, and beyond that, another elegant door.

"We come home pretty muddy most days," Reese said. "This space helps control the mess."

"Did your wife design this?"

Reese pulled his head to the right and away from CC. "No. My mother struggled to keep up with a load of dirt-loving boys. When my father built their new home, she designed it this way. I stole her idea."

He pointed to the farthest door. "This ends up in the master, where you'll eventually bunk, but why don't you head on into the house now. Emmie will get you settled. I'm going to toss these work clothes into the washer before I shower and change in the utility bathroom."

He spread his arm toward the alcove that led to the kitchen and a spacious open floor plan. CC entered and saw Carlos and Emmie leaning on the granite island, waiting for her. She looked back at Reese, who said, "I'll see you at dinner in a few."

"All right. Thank you again. For everything."

Reese nodded and disappeared as the door closed.

The smell of food reminded CC how famished she was, but the glow and scent of a wood fire in the fireplace drew her into the main room, a huge space divided into two parts—the kitchen, which was situated against the back wall, and a spacious family room that also served as the foyer. Exposed pine beams and hand-scraped floors gave it a rustic feel, but everything was luxurious, as if outfitted at the cowboy version of Neiman Marcus.

"Some cattle shack," she teased as she turned back to Emmie.

"For all its elegance, it's still just a man cave. Reese likes clean lines."

CC could see that. The large black island and its six barstools served as the divider between the two rooms. A long table and ten chairs sat off to the right as she faced the kitchen. The great room used up more than half the space, accommodating the large leather sofa, a love seat, and two matching recliners, all angled toward the massive stone fireplace, above which a large flat screen was mounted. A magnificent reddish wood door with stained-glass sidelights and an arched transom window centered the front wall. The fireplace sat to the right of it while the curved wooden staircase to the left led to a loft that looked down over the lower floor. CC couldn't see past the railings to determine that area's use. Everything was simple and pristine. No adornments other than necessary lighting, a gray rug under the furniture, and a few paintings of western landscape. Clean lines, little texture. It was a man cave, but the most beautiful cave she'd ever seen.

"If Emmie had her way, we'd be drowning in knitted afghans and doilies. Reese did agree to let her place two Christmas pillows on the sofa."

"And one string of twinkling lights. A lean holiday victory," Emmie conceded.

"Reese isn't into Christmas?" CC asked.

"I wouldn't say that," Carlos said. "We all work hard most days. Simple is easier to maintain. And speaking of maintenance, I'm going to leave you ladies and head to our room to shower." He placed a kiss on Emmie's cheek and headed to a hall to the right of the kitchen.

CC noted how Emmie's eyes followed Carlos until he disappeared behind a door.

The wind howled outside, causing CC to shiver at the memory of awakening in that dark, cold car. "I can't thank all of you enough for your kindness. I could have frozen to death. The men quite literally may have saved my life."

Emmie's almost permanent smile dimmed. "How long were you stuck in that snow?"

CC looked at her watch and tried to remember the time when the dreaded call had come through. "I'm not sure. Long enough for the snow to bury my car. The cattle found me, and they led Reese and your husband to me."

"Ohhh . . ." Emmie shivered too, as if she were channeling the cold. "You're safe now." Her smile ramped back up in wattage. "Dinner's almost ready. Why don't you take a seat and relax while I grab some clean linen for Reese's room. I'll be back in a minute."

CC moved to the fireplace to enjoy its warmth. Her father's boss had taken all his employees on a ski trip near Galena once. She'd thought the lodge there was the most beautiful place she'd ever seen. After that ski trip, she'd spent hours perusing log-cabin catalogues at the hardware store, reliving that memory. She had also learned a thing or two about the design of these wood-built homes, but Reese's home exceeded that lodge in every way. She estimated this home's interior to be around six thousand square feet, four thousand on the main floor, including the sprawling, open living area and what appeared to be two wings. One broke left from the living space to where Reese had indicated was the master suite, and one broke right to where Carlos had disappeared.

Emmie reappeared from that direction with an armful of clean linen. "Follow me. I'll get you settled in Reese's room." CC reached for her suitcases, but Emmie quickly said, "They can wait. Just come. Let's chat."

Emmie's now-unpinned and shoulder-length red curls bounced around her pink, freckled face. Her once-fuzzy blue slippers, now matted and holey, scuffed along the wooden floors. She led CC down the hall to the left, where they passed an open door. CC saw a heavy wooden desk, where a computer sat. She assumed this was Reese's office, efficiently placed near his room. Emmie opened the door at the end of the hall, giving CC a glimpse into Reese's room and world. Like the rest of the house, it was exquisite and Spartan, devoid of photos or anything personal. It reminded CC of a hotel suite or a house on a home tour.

The two women set about changing the bed linen, and CC asked, "So how long have you and Carlos been married?"

"Three years, give or take, but we met almost eight years ago. I left home in Nebraska to attend Dixie College. We met in a freshman English class. Carlos already worked for Reese during breaks and summers, and when Reese needed an accountant, Carlos put in a plug for me. I started right after graduation, and we were married a year later."

"You all get along like family. Did Reese and Carlos grow up together?"

Emmie shifted all her attention to smoothing a wrinkle from the sheet. "Listen to me." She chuckled. "It's so nice to have another woman in the house that I just ramble on like an old hen. Winters are hard here. Lonely too. There's plenty to keep us busy and plenty more things to help us pass the time, but a good hen party is a refreshing pleasure."

CC noted how openly Emmie chatted about her own life while deftly diverting away from discussions about Reese. She got the message. Don't pry about Mr. Brockbank.

Once the linen was freshened and CC's bags were dragged in, the women returned to the kitchen. CC plugged in her phone, still unsure if she would need it to place an emergency call for rescue or to leave a last text before her body was found somewhere under a scrub oak.

"Do you like chili?" Emmie asked.

"I love it, though, to be honest, I'd gratefully chew on a table leg about now."

Emmie paled. "I'm so sorry. You're probably thirsty too." She pulled out a glass and filled it from the beverage sink. "I should have offered you something before worrying about your bed."

"No, no. Really, I'm fine. Perhaps a little melodramatic. Sorry if I gave you the impression I was going to drop dead on the floor."

Emmie chuckled. "Hallelujah for another woman in the house! Carlos thinks I'm overly dramatic too. He's learning how to read me, but Reese is never sure if I need a hug or a Valium. He says I make him crazy, but I think deep down inside, he welcomes having a woman in the house again, despite my estrogen tsunamis."

CC laughed, nearly spitting a mouthful of water onto the floor. She longed to pursue Emmie's comment about Reese having a woman in the house *again*, but she didn't out of respect for her rescuers. Emmie's unpretentiousness was refreshing, and every minute spent with her proved she was also trustworthy and loyal. This woman was real, and she made CC feel safe.

Carlos emerged freshly showered and smiling, and then Reese came through the mudroom door, also freshly showered. He, too, had a hint of a smile—a mix of shyness and discomfort, like a wounded pet approaching and retreating and making little forward progress. CC couldn't stop studying him without the camouflage of heavy work clothes, hats, and masks.

He had killer looks, as she had suspected through the snow and darkness. Not the polished handsomeness of cologne models. Instead, he was a rugged man who accepted who and what he was. CC's profession had taught her to assess facial structure and angles. The man had great facial bones, but his cheeks and chin appeared bumpy and pocked as if from severe acne when he was a teen. She had a feeling he didn't know he was still handsome despite the scars, and she wondered whether that was the reason he seemed standoffish.

She understood the wish to simply blend in. She had been blessed with a pretty face and a figure that had brought unwanted attention when she was a teen. Time and experience had taught her how to silence a man's unwanted come-on with a single look, but in her youth, she had simply wanted to blend in. Maybe she and Reese had more in common than she realized.

His thick moustache was established and neat, but his beard was simply the outgrowth of a few day's neglect, and she noted that he'd made no attempt to shave on her account. His scruffy beard matched his wavy dark hair that had grown out to her favorite length—the point where men knew they needed a trim but held off because they didn't rank their appearance as the highest priority on their agenda. Reese was tall—over six feet in his now-stockinged feet. Contoured muscles in his shoulders and thighs showed under his Henley top and sweatpants, but his chiseled face and his eyes revealed the hard work, pain, and disappointments in his life. CC knew she could stare at him forever and never feel she had fully explored who he was.

He peered at her through a veil of hair that had fallen across his eyes. She felt her cheeks flush as she realized he was also studying her as she stood before him without the disguise of snow gear and her hair tucked into her coat. She couldn't read his assessment, but for a moment, she forgot they weren't the only people in the room.

"Who's hungry?" Emmie called out with a nervous yelp. Carlos's anxious smile mirrored his wife's, as the couple's eyes darted back and forth between CC and Reese, testifying to how uncomfortable the moment had become for them.

CC blinked as the eye-bond between her and Reese abruptly broke. Her attempt to segue out of the intense moment went rogue as she replied with a loud and crisp, "Me!" as if she were cheering at an NFL game.

Reese's reply was just as artificial—a head-nodding, eyebrow-raising, "Sounds great!" followed by a rambling account of how famished he was. He bowed his head and offered a succinct blessing on the food. The moment felt familiar and yet strange, as CC realized she hadn't heard a prayer uttered since she was fifteen.

She quickly slapped butter on a biscuit and made a point to chew every kidney bean in her chili until it was pulp. She hoped keeping her mouth fully engaged would make her appear too occupied to chat. But still, the questions came.

Emmie, who sat directly across from her at the table, held a buttered biscuit in midair and asked, "What does CC stand for?"

CC attempted to deflect further inquiry by simply saying, "Just my initials," but Emmie held on with a silent smile, awaiting clarification until CC surrendered the information. "My first name is dumb. I hate even saying it."

Emmie's biscuit dropped from her fingers as she leaned in. "Now I'm really intrigued."

CC stared at her plate and said, "Cedar. My mother named me Cedar."

The other three people at the table softly repeated the word as if approaching a bite of something potentially unpalatable. Nods and assents were followed with the kind platitudes she often heard. "Nice . . . unique . . ."

"I like it," Emmie said.

"I bet you were the only one of those in school." Carlos swept at a disobedient hunk of dark hair that fell into his eyes every time he leaned forward to eat from his spoon. He turned to his wife and said, "Did she tell you she's from Chicago?"

Emmie's adoring eyes met his as if just the sound of his voice was a thrill. CC saw Carlos's affection for Emmie, but it lacked Emmie's immediacy. CC wondered if couples ever got it right—if love and affection were ever equal in a relationship or if one partner always worked harder and took the greater risk to keep the union alive.

CC was so deep in thought that she wasn't aware Emmie had asked her a question until all eyes at the table were focused on the newcomer.

She regained focus. "I'm sorry. Did you ask me something?"

"I was just wondering what it was like to grow up in a big city like Chicago."

There had been too much kindness shown CC for her to avoid her hosts' questions. She stirred her chili and decided to give just enough information to satisfy everyone's curiosity. "I didn't actually grow up in Chicago. I was raised in a little town in the suburbs called Trout Valley; then we relocated to the Far North Side during high school. I didn't move to Central, Chicago, until after I graduated. The city was scary in some ways and exciting in others. You have to use your wits and be smart."

Emmie buttered another biscuit. "What brings you our way?"

Reese wasn't asking questions, but CC knew he was listening to every word as he broke the last bite of his biscuit into tiny pieces and stirred them into his chili. Like Carlos, Reese was sweeping errant hairs away from his face so he could eat, and CC knew how she could redirect the topic. "Did I mention that I'm a cosmetologist?"

Emmie's face lit up. "You do hair?"

CC sat forward and nodded. "Cuts, dyes, highlights . . . you name it, plus makeup, nails, and eyebrows. My tools are in that little suitcase of mine." She got an idea. "I owe you all so much. I rattled off the ladies' list, but I also do men's grooming—I trim moustaches and beards. I hope you'll let me offer my services to all of you as a thank-you before I leave."

"Sign me up!" Emmie said. She placed a hand on Carlos's arm. "And Carlos too!"

"Not tonight, I hope. I've been dreaming of bed for hours."

"Tomorrow's fine, Carlos." CC looked at Reese. "That's assuming the car requires another day to get back on the road."

"I'll make a few phone calls and see what I can find out." Reese stood and gathered his dishes. "Thanks for the dinner, Emmie. The biscuits were top-notch." He walked his dishes to the sink, rinsed them, and set them in the dishwasher before exiting toward the office down the hall.

Carlos stood and cleared his space as well. "It's my turn to wash."

"You've had a long day," Emmie said. "I'll wash. You go rest."

He placed a kiss on his wife's head and said, "Thanks, babe. You're the best."

CC watched Emmie's gaze follow him until the door to their room clicked shut.

"Emmie, please let me do these dishes so you can go be with your husband. It sounds like you've hardly seen each other today. It's the least I can do."

For a brief moment, CC thought the young wife might take her up on her offer, but Emmie's puppy-dog longing visibly turned to apprehension before her eyes. Emmie rose and turned for the sink, shaking her head. "Thanks for the offer, but I imagine the last thing Carlos needs is to hear me chatter on about my statistical analysis class or how long it took me to muck the stalls."

"I bet he'd appreciate how hard you worked today too."

"Actually . . . yes, he would," Emmie said as she turned on the water. "He's kind that way. It's not him. It's me."

"You? Anyone can see how much you adore him."

"I do, and I miss him, but I've been sending Carlos off to bed alone for weeks while I stay up watching online lectures or typing up assignments. Reese has been so good to us, but we want to start our own ranch, and it takes more money than we can make here. Carlos is learning the hands-on aspects of ranching from Reese, and I committed to handling the financial stuff and managing the house. On top of that, I convinced Carlos that I'd serve us best by taking an accelerated course load so I can get my MBA faster and support us by doing accounting work while we get our own ranch started. These late nights are killers, but hopefully, I'll finish by the end of December and we'll be back to normal by the start of the New Year."

"Wow. I've never even attended college, and you're working full time for Reese and completing your MBA? You're amazing."

"Don't get too impressed by me." Emmie turned and leaned back against the sink. "My choices have cost me plenty."

"What do you mean?"

She dug her toe into the wooden floor and continued. "Truthfully, I'm drowning. I bit off too much, and the further behind I get with school, the more nights I spend with Carlos's number-one rival"—she pointed to the three-section armoire that sat against the kitchen wall— "and fewer with my husband."

She walked to the armoire and opened the doors. When closed, it was simply a piece of beautiful furniture that concealed a complete computer workstation with remote monitor and printer. CC now understood that this portable office was where Emmie spent her evenings.

"We both know why Reese works as hard as he does. The ranch is all he has, but he warned Carlos and me never to put work ahead of our marriage, and we kept that promise, until this semester. At first it was just a few late nights here and there, but now it's assumed that I'll be at the computer all night. I barely have the stamina to throw my hair into an elastic band, so that ought to tell you something about the energy I've been putting into my marriage lately. Carlos never complains. He just works late too and matches Reese's hours." She tugged on a tangled lock of hair. "Something had to give, and sadly, it was the promise we made to each other." Everything from her eyebrows to her mouth and shoulders slid southward during the conversation.

CC was impressed by Reese's advice to the couple. Maybe she could help as well.

"For what it's worth, all I hear is lots of ways you're showing how much you love your husband. You're tired, but that's understandable considering all you do. You're also really beautiful, inside and out. You just need a little you time. Let me help with that."

"Like a makeover?"

"Sure. Just leave it all to me, starting with right now." She straightened and turned Emmie until she was facing down the hall. "Go be with Carlos. I've got the dishes. I might not know where to put them once they're clean and dry, but I can sure get them washed."

Emmie shrugged and headed down the hall, leaving CC in charge of the kitchen.

CC was wiping the table when Reese returned. He meandered to a stack of mail on a counter and on to the fridge, where he chose nothing. During some moments, she felt welcome. During others, she felt very much like an intruder. She straightened and attempted to assess his mood, but the discomfort of feeling as if she were walking on eggshells unnerved her. No matter the condition of the car, hiding here from the owner wasn't going to help matters. She needed to get to Vegas, face John Torino, and see what options were open to her.

Reese grabbed the back of a chair and leaned over it. "I alerted the neighboring sheriff about your car so he'd know you're all right and that you're staying here for the night. I didn't want him hearing reports of a car found off the road. Knowing Marcus, he'd head down to check it out with no thought for his own safety. I also called the nearest autobody shop. The guy who runs it is an auto savant. He thinks the smaller battery will need to be replaced. He's ordering one just in case, and he'll assess the body damage as soon as the weather breaks."

The news was crushing, but CC forced a smile. "Thanks for all your help. Hopefully, the car will be running well enough by tomorrow to get me to Vegas. I'll figure everything else out there."

"I wouldn't count on seeing Vegas tomorrow. How did you land here if that's where you were heading? There's no direct path from Chicago to here and on to Vegas."

"I . . . came a different way. I . . . had . . . other stops to make."

"I see."

His tone assured her he didn't.

"Have you been able to reach your family so they don't worry about you?" he asked.

"No. Not yet."

One of Reese's eyebrows arched. "The cell signal isn't good tonight. Feel free to use the landline. I'm sure you've got people who are worried about you."

"Thanks." CC returned to wiping the table and headed back to the sink.

"Please, call whoever you need." Reese brought her a phone and set it down on the counter beside her. "I'll do the dishes."

His eyes kept moving from the phone to CC and back again until she turned to toss the rag into the sink and spun on him. "Let's be honest with each other. You don't trust me. When you look at me, you see a reckless, irresponsible woman driving an expensive car that isn't hers—a woman who's in no rush to notify her people about her whereabouts or troubles—and you'd like to know who the heck you've brought into your home. Am I right?"

Her abruptness clearly caught Reese off guard. He sat on the edge of the island and waved for her to continue.

"Let me put your mind at ease. I'm not on the run, and as I've already said, I'm not a thief." CC turned back to the sink and grabbed the dishrag, grateful for the stack of dishes that gave her an excuse to keep her back to her host. "I had a bad day, and I made a huge mistake with the Tesla." She turned back around and challenged Reese. "Generally, I'm very responsible, and I always own up to my mistakes. I've worked multiple jobs since I was fifteen. I have some savings, and if they're not enough to cover the damages, I'll work until I fully compensate you and the owner of the car. And as for not calling my *people*, I don't have any. I'm on my own."

The words came easier after crossing the first painful admission. "I have been since I was eighteen, but don't feel sorry for me. I don't want or need your pity. I do all right."

"I don't pity you. You're clearly a strong woman. I can see that now."

"Thank you. My dad raised me that way."

"Your dad? Where was your mom?"

"She left us when I was a baby."

"I'm . . . so sorry."

CC absentmindedly folded the dishrag and set it on the counter as she explained. "He was deployed overseas, and when he came home on a surprise leave, I was in the care of a teenage neighbor and my mother was gone. Maybe that's why I hate surprises."

"Me too."

She glanced up at him, surprised by his admission, and added, "I like knowing who or what is up ahead."

"I hate the feeling of losing control."

CC's voice grew quiet. "Or of unfulfilled expectations."

"We circled back to your mom, didn't we?"

CC picked up a dish towel and started drying the glasses. "My dad found her and gave her the choice to come home. She didn't choose us." She paused a took a deep breath. "I dreamed of her, that she really wanted to come home to us, but she never did."

"I'm sorry. That's brutal."

"I got over it. My father was everything to me—my soccer coach, my cooking buddy, my best friend. And I always knew I was his everything too. Then one day, we hugged and said, 'I love you' to each other as he dropped me off at school and drove away. A few hours later I was called to the principal's office, where an officer and the owner of the hardware store were waiting. They told me Dad died suddenly of an apparent heart attack. That was the worst surprise of my life."

Reese's jaw fell open. "Of anyone's life. How old were you?"

"Fifteen. I spent the first few days with my dad's former boss and his wife, but they were older and not up to handling a teenager."

"Did they try to find your mother?"

"I haven't seen her since the day she left. I know nothing about my mother's family, and Dad was an only child. A hair-salon owner named Nora Stubbert lived in a neighboring community. When she read about me in the paper, she offered to take me in as a foster child."

"How'd that work out?"

"She was fine. She encouraged me to take cosmetology in high school so I'd graduate with a skill. Other than that, we basically lived like roommates. We split the chores. She went to work, and I went to school. I spent nights and weekends as her shampoo girl. I was a pretty easy teenager. My primary goal was to never do anything to make my father ashamed of me. I worked hard to keep that promise . . . until tonight."

Reese shrank like warm gelatin; then he folded and unfolded his arms as if he couldn't get comfortable in that moment. "It's not like you robbed a bank or murdered someone."

"Thank you for at least recognizing that," she said drily.

His head slipped into his neck. "You know what I meant."

"Yeah. I do." CC leaned her elbows on the island and dropped her chin onto her hands.

"Your foster mom . . . won't she be worried about you?"

CC shook her head. "I burned that bridge. It might be the one choice I most regret."

"You can mend a burned bridge."

"I'm not sure it would be worth the effort. I had my car packed the morning of high school graduation with a vow to stay if she came to the ceremony, like a real mom who cared, or to drive away if she didn't."

"I take it she was a no-show."

"I had no reason to expect she'd come. She provided a stable home for me, but that was it. She never came to a parent-teacher conference or a concert or a hair show I was in. I figured it would hurt less to stop hoping we'd be a real family, so I headed to Chicago with my cosmetology license, my savings account, and whatever talent I had. It worked out just fine."

Reese slid off the island and leaned back. "You don't need to tell me anything more."

"Yes, I do." CC straightened. "Carlos told me I might have put your Bureau of Land Management grazing rights at risk if your cattle wander onto unpermitted land. For that reason alone, you deserve to know why I wasn't paying proper attention to the road tonight."

She started and stopped, struggling to find the words she needed. "I've had one relationship that mattered in the past few years, and I ended it recently. So . . . I decided to reinvent myself and make another fresh start."

"In Las Vegas?"

"It was Dad's dream. He talked about retiring there." She laughed sadly. "He said Vegas was a working man's New York City, filled with good shows, endless buffets, and a cheap cost of living. It all sounded really good to me at that moment."

"And the Tesla?"

"It belongs to a nice family guy, a Las Vegas restauranteur named John Torino. He comes to Chicago a couple of times a year on buying trips. He strolled into my shop a few years ago for a haircut and became a regular whenever he came to town. Anyway, he tossed his business card into a raffle and won the grand prize—the Tesla."

"Lucky guy."

"Except there were strings . . . expensive ones. The car wouldn't be ready to ship for two weeks, and John was responsible for the taxes, title fees, and two thousand dollars in shipping costs and insurance to get the car to Vegas. As wonderful a surprise as this would be for his wife, he's just a working guy and needed to trim the costs back, so he asked me if I knew anyone who could pick up and haul or drive the car to Vegas by Christmas Eve for a thousand dollars."

"And you volunteered."

"I wish it were that simple. I recommended someone, but John overheard that guy two-timing his girlfriend. He came back to me and told me he couldn't trust a person like that, so he fired the guy and offered the opportunity to me. He'd heard me go on and on about wanting to go to Vegas someday, and he knew circumstances in my life made it a good time for a change, so he gave me his sales guy's card and told me to call him and get some training on the car."

Reese chuckled.

"What?"

"Nothing . . . it's just that, judging from this evening, he wasn't much of a teacher."

"No, he wasn't." The angry tone of her voice caused Reese to raise an eyebrow. She explained, "The guy was more interested in getting to know me than he was in helping me get to know the car, if you know what I mean, so I tolerated him long enough to learn how to drive the car off the lot and watched a dozen YouTube videos about all things Tesla back in my apartment.

I was naive enough to think that was enough, that I knew what I was doing. And things were going fine the first day. I drove a few hours off course to take care of something personal, and then I headed straight for Vegas. The battery was at half charge when I got a call from a coworker telling me to check my Instagram feed."

"Don't tell me someone screwed up your life using social media." Reese dropped his head forward and growled. "I hate all of it."

"Me too."

He glanced up at her. "What did you find?"

"Something intended to hurt me. I needed time to pull myself together. I should have just pulled over, but here was this self-driving car I'd watched videos of people rigging so they could go completely hands-free, and—"

"And the rest is history."

"Pretty much. And, speaking of pretty much, any estimates on what it's going to cost me to make that car look like new?"

Reese rubbed a hand across his face. "I'll get some rough figures for you tomorrow. The real issue is the delivery time of the parts."

"Just as long as I can have it in Vegas by Christmas Eve night, all wrapped in a big red ribbon."

"Surprise."

Reese hadn't felt this defensive since Fallujah, where the threats had been people with guns and bombs. It was hard to tell the innocent from the enemies back then also, and even though CC seemed innocent enough, he couldn't risk another emotional downing because of sentiment. He had to know.

He helped with the last of the dishes and then fabricated a reason to head to the barn. He needed an exit to clear his head. As much as he hated to admit it, the woman and her hard-luck story had gotten to him. After saying goodnight to her, he spent thirty minutes checking on the animals and peeking out of the barn door every few minutes until the light in his bedroom went off, hopefully signaling that she'd gone to sleep. Then he moved to his office and emailed Sheriff Marcus Rucker, his friend in Brisbane, Utah, the next town over.

> *Marcus,*
>
> *Can you run that Tesla's plates and verify the place of sale and the owner, John Torino's, address? Also, the driver, Miss*

*Cedar Cippolini from the Chicago area, says she doesn't have any next of kin. Any chance you can come up with a reason to verify that in case we need to reach someone? (She may have bumped her head during that crash.) Just saying . . .*
   *Thanks.*
   *Reese*


Reese stared at the screen for several minutes, reading, rereading, then editing the email until it sounded more caring than suspicious, which of course was its actual intent. He hit send and, in seconds, received a reply.

*Reese,*
   *Yeah . . . against my better judgment, I can make that happen, but just for the record, not every woman is a Marissa.*
   *Just saying . . .*
   *Marcus*

# CHAPTER FOUR

CC COULDN'T SLEEP. SHE TRIED to deflect the smothering worry over the Tesla by playing Christmas music from her playlist, but instead of visions of sugar plums and angels dancing through her head, she saw her client's angry face, her father's disappointment, and visions of endless bills and orange jumpsuits. Jail wasn't even her biggest concern. Guilt was. What if she couldn't repay the damages immediately? She'd not only ruin John's Christmas gift for his wife, but he'd have to wait for repayment. And what about Reese's losses?

She moved around the bedroom until she got enough of a phone signal to do a Google search of Tesla drivers being prosecuted for hands-free driving. She found three. One had resulted in the driver's death. As troubled as she was by guilt and worry, CC was still alive, and she counted herself blessed.

Reese evidently slept no better. True to his word, his footsteps creaked on the wooden floors at various times of the night. She wished she'd had the courage to open the door and talk to him. Instead, she got back into bed, pulled the covers up more tightly under her chin, and recalled her dreams for Vegas about the salon she hoped to open and the good she wanted to do with her talents.

She prayed that God in heaven, about whom her father had taught her, would find a way to make everything work out. She didn't care how long it took to pay back her debt. She just didn't want to cause harm to someone else.

The cries of animals drew her out of bed again and to the window. Pulling the curtain back, she saw snow geese on the dimly lit pond situated in front of the house. The snow appeared to have stopped, leaving an almost virgin field of white spread to the cattle fence. The view again reminded her of the Christmas print her father had hung each year, the December page of the 1996 calendar. It wasn't until she was decorating the house for her fourteenth Christmas that she'd realized the page represented the very month and year her mother had left. She assumed her father's decision to keep it had had more to do with the woman who'd left than it had with Christmas.

She missed him so much. She longed to hear his soothing voice tell her that everything would work out all right. It wouldn't even matter if he scolded her. He'd loved her through baseball-broken windows, ditching school on the first snowfall, and embarrassing talks about puberty and hygiene, and they'd loved each other even more deeply for it. Somehow, he would have loved her through this.

The clock read 4:40 a.m. More exhausted from the failed attempts at sleeping than from the lack of sleep itself, CC dressed, determined not to waste a minute of her time in this paradisiacal place. The door opened without a squeak, and she tiptoed down the hall, past a sleeping Reese, to the mud-room, where her boots and coat were stored. Once ready, she slipped through the back door, which she closed, entering the pristine world spread before her.

She walked through calf-deep snow to the front porch and sat on one of the rockers, but the decking squeaked each time she moved. Try as she might, her slightly hyperactive self just could not sit still. She thought about pulling a Goldilocks and trying out the other three chairs, but that fairy-tale girl's nosiness had not worked out well for her, and with a potentially grumpy bear sleeping nearby, CC opted for a seat on the stairs.

The snow was powdery soft and easily moved with her hands. She cleared the top step of snow and perched herself there, mentally recording every sight and sound, from the calls of geese to the bawling cries of cattle around the farm. Rabbits hopped across the yard, leaving oblong-dotted tracks. Horses whinnied, and though she longed to find them, CC became lost in the view and in her thoughts.

As dawn rose, three deer cautiously picked their way across the snow to the water to drink. She pursed her lips and made kissing sounds, unsure what result her calls would have. No animals came to meet her, but she enjoyed watching how every ear flicked and tuned to her voice.

She heard the door open behind her and turned to find Reese wrapped in a red quilt. His mussed hair went every which way, and his eyes were still puffy slits.

"Couldn't sleep?" he asked.

"No. I'm sorry if I woke you."

"You didn't," he said as he sat in the squeaky rocker.

It seemed too weird to make kissy sounds at the animals with a witness present, so CC sat quietly until the awkward silence became unnerving, and she stood and turned for the door.

"I've spent many a night in this chair looking over that view," Reese said.

CC turned back at the yellow-gray scene. "It's beautiful and peaceful and painful, all at the same time."

Reese gave a thoughtful "Hmm . . ." as if he were giving her comment serious consideration. "Tell me why you think so."

"Because the stillness makes you think and remember."

"What's it saying to you? Happy or sad things?"

"Both." CC leaned against a post and continued to stare out at the pond. "I suppose that's why I've felt so at home in the city. It's noisy and busy and filled with people to see and things to do. Somehow, you don't feel as alone in the bustle."

"What about the saying 'lost in a crowd'? Ever feel that way?"

She turned back to him. "Sometimes, but I choose not to stay lost for too long."

Reese sat forward and studied her as if she were a book. "How do you do that?"

"No, no, no. That's enough about me. What does the stillness bring to your mind?"

He settled back into his quilt. "Ghosts."

The sorrow in his voice cut CC. She tried to lighten the mood. "Of Christmases past, present, or future?"

He chuckled and ruffled his hair comically. "All of the above."

Even this slight bit of laughter emboldened CC. She took a step closer and smiled. "You know, Ebenezer, this place, as beautiful as it is, could do with some Christmas cheer."

He leaned his head back and eyed her as he pointed to the anemic strand of lights dangling along the rail. "Ta-da!"

"You're not seriously leaving it at that, are you?"

"It's more than we put up last Christmas."

"Really? With Emmie here?"

"She and Carlos weren't here last Christmas. They left the second week of December for Nebraska. In her defense, she attempted to deck my halls before she left, but I declined."

"Why? Because you were alone for Christmas?"

"No. My parents and family live just up the canyon. I had dinner with them. But what about you? If you have no family, who did you spend Christmas with?"

A smile spread across CC's lips at the memory. "About a hundred men."

Reese shot her a look of complete incredulity. "I don't even want to know."

She headed for the door, but Reese caught her hand as it landed on the handle, sending warm ripples up her arm. His sleepy eyes closed slightly more. "I have something I'd like to show you."

"Not a surprise, right?"

"How about a reveal?"

She tipped her head sideways. "How can I turn down that offer?"

Reese grabbed his boots, jacket, and a Stetson from the house and led her down to the driveway and into the barn. CC scratched and patted all four horses she passed and found Reese kneeling in the doorway a few stalls down. When she looked in, she found a doe and a tiny speckled fawn.

CC sighed until there was no air left in her lungs. "They're the most delicate, beautiful things I've ever seen," she whispered. "Where did they come from?"

"A bow hunter nicked the doe in the hind quarters. She made it to the pine trees, where Carlos found her. He brought her home, and we've been nursing her back to health, but she keeps pulling her bandages off. Two nights ago, she delivered this little fawn."

"I thought fawns were born in the spring."

"Generally. This little doe matured late. Babies born in winter don't usually survive."

"Will she let us touch her?"

"Not anymore. She did when she was too weak to fight us, but she became more wary as she got stronger, and now that she's had her baby, she's more skittish than ever."

"Could I try?"

Reese poured a cup of grain into CC's hand and waved her on. She inched near the stall wall and slid to the floor with her back against the boards as she slowly extended her hand in the direction of the deer. The doe backed up, positioning herself between CC and the fawn. When her head went down, Reese said, "Uh oh. You'd better get out. I think she's going to ram you."

CC gently spilled the grains of feed onto the floor, drew her arms close to herself, and sat back again. To her delight, the doe extended her neck and sniffed the feed. "That's a girl," she whispered. "Come on, little mama."

One of the doe's front feet pawed at the floor, inching closer to the feed. From the corner of her eye, CC saw Reese's smiling face light up with wonder. She tried to ignore the shivers his happiness sent through her. For a moment, at least, he seemed glad she was there.

She focused back on the skittish doe, whose nose was just about to reach the feed. The animal took a tiny nibble, then another. CC slid her hand forward, watching carefully for the doe's response. The animal seemed tolerant of CC's nearness, so she reached a little farther. The doe extended her neck toward CC's hand when the barn door slammed, sending the frightened animal back to the corner in a panic. Her previous mistrust returned, leaving her defensive, skittish, and wary. The moment was lost.

"There you are, Reese. I've been looking for you," Carlos called out.

Reese shot a frustrated scowl at the man, and then he offered CC a sympathetic smile. "I'm sorry. You almost had her trust."

"Almost." She was touched by his disappointment. Still, it had been amazing. "Thank you for letting me try."

Reese held out his work-worn hand to help CC up. It was strong and steady as he brought her mere inches from his welcoming face, as if he wanted to say something more to her, perhaps another expression of regret. She wondered if he knew she was like that doe, wanting to trust but still so fearful. She saw the same mix of want and fear in Reese's eyes, and then Carlos called out again as he sauntered their way, carrying Reese's cell phone.

"It's the sheriff . . . about the email you sent him last night."

The color drained from Reese's face as he released CC's hand and stepped back.

"What is it?" she muttered. "Something's wrong. Is it about me and the Tesla?" She turned to Carlos. "It's the sheriff?" She looked back at Reese. "Am I in trouble?"

Reese raised a finger near his lips to hush her panic. His near-whispered reply was filled with urgency. "No, no . . . it's . . . it's not like that. I promise. He's a friend."

He took the phone from Carlos and said, "Hold on a second, Marcus, will you?"

CC watched him mute the phone, and then her words came fast and furious. "Why do you look panicked if he's a friend? Oh my gosh. That makeup bag is still hanging from the wheel. He knows I rigged the car, doesn't he? Did you tell him what I did?"

"I never told him anything about that."

"Then, why do you look so worried?"

"Listen to me. He's not calling to arrest you. And if you're worried about the weighted steering wheel, we'll ride over and fix it as soon as I get off this call, okay? Just . . . just give me a minute to talk to him. Get dressed warm enough to be outside in the snow for a while. Carlos, have Emmie give her some breakfast, will you? I'll talk to him, CC. Don't worry. I'll take care of it. Okay?"

# CHAPTER FIVE

*HOW TO FIX THIS . . . HOW to fix this . . .* The situation reminded Reese of his time in Iraq.

He'd spent weeks cultivating the trust of a female Iraqi informant he believed could lead him to a tribal leader converting hungry ideologues into rebels. The effort was a failure, and that's how he saw himself—as a skeptic and a failure.

He thought his discharge from the military would help him leave those feelings of mistrust behind, but had it? Here he was, so many years later, still suspicious of everyone new. Now *he* was the informant. The rat. And CC? He'd soon know if she could be trusted, but would she trust him?

He waited to take the call until CC was almost in the house and well out of earshot. "Hey, Marcus. Sorry about that. What's up?"

"Her story appears to check out."

The news made Reese feel better about CC and worse about himself. "That was fast."

"The plates belong to a car ordered from a Chicago dealership by a John Torino in Vegas. It was picked up four days ago. Everything looks legit. I plan to run by and check it out this afternoon when the tow truck arrives. I hear Rudy's hauling it to his shop."

"Yeah. He's going to give her a repair estimate. So Cedar Cippolini is on the up and up?"

"As far as I can tell. I don't know her blood type or shoe size, but she appears to be a nice, hard-working woman from Chicago with two jobs. She works at a spa called *Restoration* and moonlights as a cosmetologist at some thirties-themed nightclub where people get dolled up like gangsters for glamour shots. Not my kind of place, but to each his own, right?"

"Right. . . right. Hey, thanks, and thank your deputy for me, or whoever did the legwork."

Marcus called out, "Delilah, Mr. Reese says thank you for helping him out with that Facebook search."

"What? Delilah was your investigator? On Facebook?"

"She investigated the personal stuff. I can't use government resources to check up on every yahoo some suspicious friend asks to know about. But dangle twenty minutes of extra video-game time and a chance to guide Dad through the murky waters of social media, and a ten-year-old turns into a darn fine Inspector Cujo."

"Clouseau."

"What?"

"Never mind." The report of CC's social media presence sent another red flare up. "Has she been posting anything since she arrived here? Please tell me she hasn't posted photos of my home on her page."

"She hasn't posted anything in months, and she only posted about work and community service events. She shows no family connections and only a few friends, most of whom seem to work with her. Most of the traffic on her page is from other people to her. Delilah noticed one guy doing something . . . hold on."

Marcus's voice became muffled, but Reese could still hear his friend talking to his daughter. "Delilah, what did you call what that guy was doing on that pretty lady's page?"

When Marcus returned, he had a smug tone to his voice, as if he'd cracked a big case. "Trolling. Delilah thinks some guy is trolling Miss Cippolini's account. She also checked this guy's account, and evidently, he and your guest were once an item. Now he's posting things on her page that seem intended to get a rise out of her, photos of himself with another woman. The guy's pond scum."

Reese recalled CC saying something about an upsetting post on Instagram. "Did your supersleuthing daughter happen to check CC's Instagram account?"

"You bet she did! She's got her daddy's intuition for tracking a lead."

"What did she find there?"

"Same kind of stuff—more comments from that dirtbag. My little super sniffer also went to his account, where he posted pictures of his new fiancée's honking big diamond, and guess who he tagged?"

"CC."

"Yep, he's a real prince."

"Yeah." Reese flexed his fingers, thinking how great it would be to wrap them around the jerk's neck.

"And then there's that last matter of yours. You asked about CC's *emergency contacts*?"

Incredulity dripped from Marcus's words. "Delilah pulled up an obit for a man named Paulo Cippolini, who died about eleven years ago, leaving a daughter named CC. There was a mention of an ex-wife named Eleanor Anderson, but she's not on social media, and I can't go tracking down people without cause, so that's about all I can tell you."

"Thanks, Marcus. What time is Rudy coming for the car?"

"He said around noon."

"Great. Thanks. Bye, then."

Reese ended the call and shoved the phone into his pocket with more force than the task required. He was angry at himself for surrendering to the mistrust that had grown like a scab over his heart, and he was angry at the jerk whose intentions were to cause CC pain. He was angry that she had come into his life when she was wounded and vulnerable, so like himself. It was still a bad situation. Terrible timing.

Carlos returned to feed the stock and muck the stalls at an opportune moment.

"Saddle up Admiral and Nutmeg, will you?"

"I'm not riding Nutmeg."

"You're not the one I'm taking riding today," Reese said.

A smile spread across Carlos's face. "Gotcha. Glad to hear it."

"Don't get any ideas."

"Who, me? I'm just smiling because you're going to be out of my hair today."

"Oh . . . speaking of hair, CC was going to do Emmie's today."

"Oh yes! The girls are inside making big plans. I think I need to get off work early tonight, Reese. And from what I'm hearing"—his eyebrows arched as if he were revealing a secret—"I might need to come in late tomorrow. I might even need to ask you for a raise!"

Reese laughed out loud for the first time in recent memory and shook his head at Carlos, the friend he loved as a brother. He pulled his hat off and pointed it Carlos's way. "CC is stirring things up around here. I'm going to have to have a talk with that woman."

"I'd say it's all for the better and long overdue."

"Maybe so, Carlos." Reese smacked his hat across his thigh. "Maybe so."

He returned to the house and drew in the welcoming smell of sautéed onions before he opened the back door. Women's chatter filled the place as he entered. For the first time in a very long time, the big house felt cozy and warm. It felt like a home.

CC and Emmie were leaning over the counter, oohing and aahing over magazines. Reese stood on the toes of his boots and looked over their shoulders to catch a peek at what they were so excited about. They were discussing the hairstyles and makeup of the women featured on the pages. He smiled for several quiet moments before clearing his voice. "What's got you ladies all fired up?"

CC spun the swivel stool around at the sound of his voice. The fingers of both hands flew to her mouth, from which she asked, "What's the verdict?"

Reese picked through his conversation with Marcus to avoid revealing information he wasn't supposed to know. "The sheriff and the tow truck are heading to the car around noon."

CC shot to her feet. "And?" She drifted two steps closer to Reese.

"You're fine."

"I'm fine? Fine as in 'not going to Alcatraz' or fine as in 'I'm free to go to Vegas'?"

"Definitely no Alcatraz, so long as we take care of that little issue we discussed, before noon."

CC fisted her hands and shot them skyward in a cheer of relief. Reese soaked up her happiness until it filled him as well. She moved to him and wrapped her arms around him unabashedly. "Thank you so much. You're my hero."

When her head landed on his shoulder, his first instinct was to pull back and keep his distance, but he felt the tussle between his heart and his head and chose to put a hold on the defensive strategies that had so far rendered him lonely and bitter. He breathed in the sweet scent of her hair, responding to the soft warmness of her body against his. He placed his hands on her shoulders, and when she lifted her head to look at him, their mouths were mere inches away. The potential of the moment shot through his brain like fireworks, but instead, he drew his neck back to offer a comical segue out of the situation.

"I'm not your hero. I'm just protecting my interests."

CC slid back until they were holding one another's shoulders. "What interests?" she asked in a voice that left a horizon-worth of room for interpretation.

"You still owe me one of those fancy city haircuts."

She pushed back and laughed out loud. "So now you want a fancy city haircut, do you?"

"Sure. The cattle have been complaining about me letting myself go." He wandered back to the magazines and leafed through a few pages. "Just don't give me one of those . . . what do you call them? Rat tails . . . or mohawks."

CC chuckled, and Reese noticed Emmie's wide eyes and open-mouthed stare, as if he had grown horns.

"But first we've got an errand to run," he reminded CC.

"I'm dressed warm and ready to go. How long do you think we'll be?" She turned back and gave Emmie an excited little dance. "I'm giving Emmie a makeover today."

"Not long." Reese looked at the wagon-wheel clock on the wall. "What if I have you back by eleven? Will that give you enough time to do whatever it is you girls are about to do?"

"Sounds perfect."

"But I don't think that puffy little coat of yours will be enough to keep you warm. Grab the key card to the car, and let's find you something warmer to wear."

After CC retrieved the card, Reese crooked his finger, bidding her to follow him as he led her to the mudroom coat closet hidden behind three wood-paneled doors. They contained an array of outerwear in a variety of sizes and styles. In the last closet, among the decidedly masculine garb, were two small-sized women's coats. One was a long oiled black coat split down the back from the seat to the hem. The other was a thin liner with a similar split back but made of some high-tech thermal fabric.

CC didn't ask any questions about the women's attire, and Reese offered no explanation as he helped her into the liner and stepped back to check the fit. The arms were a little long, and when she lifted them, they both noticed the store tag was still attached to the garment. Reese glanced at CC, then at the tag, removing it with a quick tug.

"That'll do," he said flatly, but a haunted look replaced the previous whimsy in his eyes a few minutes earlier.

CC ached to know the thoughts and feelings the garment had dredged up. She slipped her arms into the outer coat while Reese held it up. Its tag was also still attached, but CC quickly ripped it off and tucked it into the pocket when Reese turned to find gloves and a scarf. As the finishing touch, he plopped a gray felt cowboy hat onto her head.

"Passable, for a city girl?"

A hint of a smile returned to Reese's face. "I'd be seen in public with you."

CC rolled her eyes and gave a little snort that carved a smile into his scarred face, but when he dressed in a second coat that matched hers exactly, she knew she'd intruded into a story written for someone else.

Reese opened the door and held it so she could walk through. She headed to the garage, where Reese had parked the truck the night before, but he kept walking toward the barn, so she followed along, assuming another truck must be hidden back there. Instead, he opened the door to the barn, where Carlos stood with two saddled horses—a small brown mare and a taller black stallion packed with deep saddlebags holding a shovel. CC stopped cold, hoping against hope that what she was thinking was not accurate.

"Ever ridden?" Reese asked.

"Sure," CC replied sarcastically. "In a car, in a plane, on a skateboard."

"On a horse?"

"Only if it had a pole sticking through it and it went up and down."

Reese laughed and bent over beside the mare with his hand cupped like a step. "Lesson one. You sit on top."

CC backed up. "Don't I need something first . . . like a learner's permit or a written exam? Putting a novice on a living machine with relatives capable of doing the Derby at under two minutes seems irresponsible. Can't we take the truck?"

"There's a giant snowdrift across the lane. It'll take time to plow, and we're in a bit of a time crunch here. We can cross the fields if you'd be comfortable riding double with me."

"Slow and smooth?"

"Like butter."

There wasn't enough room on the stallion's back to carry both riders and the packs with the shovels, so the men transferred the packs from the stallion named Admiral onto Nutmeg, the mare. Then Reese mounted, and Carlos helped CC climb up behind him on the stallion. She quickly saw the wisdom in the split coats that flared over the horse's haunches, and she felt the animal's powerful flanks twitch beneath her. She didn't notice the cold, though the breeze whipped snow past them. Admiral's body heat radiated through her legs, but it was the man sitting in front of her who stirred the greatest warmth within her.

Reese glanced back approvingly. "You look like a natural. Now, wrap your arms around me to steady yourself."

CC was tentative, clutching the folds of his coat for support, but when Reese urged Admiral forward and the horse moved, the fabric failed to steady her, and she nearly fell off. Reese twisted and caught her arm, looking as frightened as she felt. He straightened her and said, "Squeeze your legs against Admiral's body and wrap your arms around my waist. I won't break."

CC was certain of that as she slid her arms around Reese's muscled mid-section and clasped her hands in front. She leaned back, keeping a friendly inch or two between her body and the back of the man anchoring her. She tried to think of him as a seat belt and nothing more, but it was a hard comparison to accept. Reese moved with a confidence that made her feel safe and secure in a way no seat belt ever had. In a way Devon never had, for that matter. She wondered why it had taken her so long to realize that lack in their relationship.

She wondered again about the woman the matching coat had been purchased for, a woman who had clearly meant something to Reese. He had secrets—that was apparent—and sharp wounds that lay deep beneath a practiced layer of indifference, but however wounded he was, CC couldn't imagine him casually breaking promises or thoughtlessly breaking a woman's heart. Reese was solid and gentle, a man CC somehow knew she could trust.

She looked back as the house disappeared behind a bend, and then she saw a sign she hadn't seen the night before. "Look at that. *The Silver-Buckle Mine.*" She felt Reese's body stiffen under her arms at the mention of the place, and when he didn't respond, she asked, "What is that?"

"What, the Buckle?" he replied. "It's . . . it's just . . . an old silver mine."

"Wow. A real silver mine? Like in old Westerns?"

"Something like that."

"My father would have loved seeing a real piece of the old West."

"He would've, would he?" He chuckled. "Then, he would've loved the story behind it. My great-great-grandfather opened it with a pickaxe. He was quite a character. The mine has been passed down ever since, so the entire family has a little stake in our ancestor's dream."

"Does it really have silver?"

"Some. Let's just say that some family members have had better luck digging in there than others."

"Did you ever dig in there?"

"Oh . . . sure, but the best treasure was the hours of childhood memories I made exploring those tunnels and shafts with my grandpa."

CC smiled as his body relaxed and his voice returned to that easygoing tone that made her feel comfortable and welcome. "Sounds like he enjoyed your company."

"We had the best family Halloweens there. Grandpa would turn those jagged, dark tunnels into the best haunted house ever. And then he'd build a big bonfire in the open area and tell us stories."

"Tell me one of your grandpa's stories."

"All right. Give me a minute to think of one . . . oh yeah. I haven't thought about this one for a while. My great-great-grandpa Henry was a single man, but his mining partner, Oswald Simmons, was a married man with his first child on the way. When they discovered that first silver vein, Oswald dreamed of giving Mary and their coming child a fine house instead of a soddy. After that, he all but lived in that mine, determined to have his treasure before the babe was born. Weeks passed, and when their supplies and luck both ran out, Oswald trudged home to tell Mary he had failed. But when he arrived, he found his little cabin empty with Mary gone and only a final note in her journal: *I left Tuesday to fetch Oswald home.* Oswald feared she fell into a mine shaft while searching for him. The neighbors figured the Indians got her."

CC gasped over the news. "No one ever found Mary?"

"Nope. Some say her ghost still wanders through that mine to this day, carrying her little baby and looking for her husband."

"That's not a true story . . . is it?"

"My grandfather swore it was. He said Oswald was so guilt-ridden over neglecting Mary that he wanted nothing to do with the mine after that. He sold it to Henry for a dollar."

The tale of love, loss, and regret weighed on CC. She rested her head against Reese's back and closed her eyes.

After a moment, Reese said, "You're awful quiet back there. Sorry if I scared you."

"The story isn't frightening. It's sad. I'm just wondering what's sadder— wasting a love you had or the elusive search for a love you can't find."

"Hmm . . . that's a pretty deep examination of a campfire story."

"Overthinking things is my forte. I think Mary and Oswald had the real treasure all the time, but Oswald threw it all away looking for more. In my experience, wanting more often turns into ending up with less."

Reese turned his head to the side to glance back at CC. "Like phone-call guy?"

"I'd like to think he's had a regret or two about his choices."

"I think you can bank on that."

"Thank you." The compliment, whether hollow or real, filled a need in CC.

"You're welcome." A more thoughtful tone, bordering on melancholic, filled Reese's voice as he spoke next. "And thanks for opening my eyes about Oswald and Mary's story. I never saw what you saw until today. Maybe a person has to get up close and personal with their own pain to understand someone else's."

"As in the story behind this coat?"

CC could feel Reese hitch in the saddle, and she regretted probing a topic that so clearly pained the man. The eighteen seconds it took him to reply felt like an eternity.

"I already told a story. It's your turn."

"All right," she agreed readily, grateful she hadn't completely offended her gracious host. "Give me a topic."

"The phone call that triggered the crash."

Reese touched a point as painful as CC had touched in him. She deserved it, but she needed a moment to gather her thoughts, so she relaxed her arms and sat back to catch her breath while Reese guided Admiral and Nutmeg around a snowdrift.

"I'll tell you my story if you share something personal about yourself."

The horses walked on a bit farther before Reese said, "Deal. You said you ended the one relationship that mattered to you. Was that the person who called?"

"No." She was glad Reese couldn't see her. It made the painful story easier to share, and the breeze seemed to carry the words away to the open sky, where they couldn't hurt her anymore. "It was *about* him. A former coworker saw his Instagram post announcing his engagement."

"How long had it been since you two broke up?"

"Less than three weeks."

"Ouch. I'm sorry. I take it he and the new fiancée hadn't just met."

"No. I broke off our engagement when I found out he'd been cheating on me."

"With the woman he's engaged to now?"

"Someone else entirely."

"He sounds like a real peach. Two women on the side? How long were you two together?"

"We dated on and off for three years, but we got engaged six months ago."

CC heard Reese huff over that disclosure.

"He tried to excuse his cheating by saying he didn't care about the other woman." She drew in a deep breath. "Why would a man compound his cheating with a lie?"

Reese shook his head as if the very question irritated him. "Why let a man like that occupy another minute of your time?"

"This might not make any sense to another man, but no matter how rotten he is, when a man who's promised himself to one woman looks at another woman, his intended never stops asking herself why she wasn't enough."

They rode on, listening only to the sounds of the horses' breathing and the squeak of the leather saddles until they reached the car. CC thought how sad it looked piled under all that drifted snow.

Reese guided Admiral near the car, slipped a leg over the animal's head, and dropped to his feet on the ground so he could lower CC. He brought her down in front of him, sliding her inch by inch until their eyes met. She placed her hands on his shoulders to steady herself, and he held her there for a few seconds, his gaze moving over her face. The lines in his brow softened, and his eyelids half-closed. When his lips parted, a chill zipped through CC at the thought that he might attempt to kiss her, but words came instead. Words as tender as a kiss.

"Men ask themselves the same questions, CC . . . whether they're enough."

"Not all men."

"Any man who doesn't isn't for you."

A hundred replies passed through her mind. She wanted to ask, "Are you the type of man who wonders whether he's enough?" but she already knew the answer. It explained his solitude, the matching coats, the denied want in his eyes. She would have enjoyed exploring that question with him had she met him a year ago, but she had enough pain in her own life right now. She didn't need to explore anyone else's.

Reese stepped back to search Nutmeg's saddlebag. He pulled the folded camp shovel from the bag, along with a battery and cables. CC took the shovel and cleared enough snow to allow the door to swing open while Reese rigged the battery up like he'd done last night.

"Try your key," he called out, and in a moment, the door obliged and was open. "Don't touch a thing. I want to see your felonious invention in the light of day."

CC slid into the driver's seat, and Reese peeked over the open door and chuckled at the rigged wheel. A gallon-sized food bag with pencils and bottles and tubes of makeup straddled the wheel, with its contents balanced evenly in the front and back. A scarf was tied below the wheel to secure the weight so the car registered what it believed was a hand controlling the steering.

"I'd give you an 8.7 for ingenious use of raw materials and a 9 for willful disregard of the law."

"What do we get for evidence tampering?"

"We?" His hands tapped his chest as he backed away. "I'm just packing a horse. What you do in the privacy of someone else's Tesla is completely up to you."

CC laughed as she removed her gloves to untie the scarf and release the bag of makeup. Snow moved on the windshield, and through the cleared glass she saw Reese examining the damage to the car. She bit her lip as the suffocating financial and legal implications of her foolishness pressed down on her again. "How bad is it?" she called.

His expression was serious. Not a good sign. "Are you ready?" he asked.

CC climbed out and closed the car door. "What do you think about the car?"

"Let's wait and see what the mechanic says once it gets towed to the shop."

She was relieved to have another delay before she would know her fate, but she needed to call John and tell him the truth about his vehicle. He had insurance, so the car could be repaired, but that didn't feel right. She'd have to replace the vehicle with a new one. Hot tears burned behind her lids again. She'd never qualify for such a loan. And what would she do with the damaged Tesla? She was more than happy to live in ignorance for a few more hours.

Reese mounted Admiral and pulled her up behind him, and then they were on their way, leading Nutmeg as before. When they reached the ranch's long lane, they met Carlos, who waved as he passed them on the tractor with a plow mounted to the front. He had already cleared an eight-foot-wide swath down the lane, making the return trip much easier. The castanet-like sound of horseshoes on the pavement calmed CC's racing mind. Even Reese's shoulders seemed to relax, but then they squared again.

"Her name was Marissa."

CC picked up on his thoughts immediately, appreciating how long he had been considering her earlier question about the owner of the coat she wore. "Were you married?"

"Legally."

CC let Reese's blunt answer percolate without asking for more information.

"I special-ordered these matching coats with the idea that I'd present them on our sixth wedding anniversary, the first one shared here on the ranch. I wanted her to see that this place was as much hers as mine, but she was gone before the coats arrived."

"I'm sorry."

"Yeah . . . we're full of all kinds of sorry, you and me."

His voice was soft and sad and magnetically boyish. It pulled on CC's heartstrings, leaving her vulnerable. Once again, she felt like the doe, timidly sticking her neck out of the protected, dark corner she called her life, knowing full well she could get destroyed. Even so, she found herself unable to resist the chance to share a moment of human comfort.

His openness gave her courage. She laid her cheek against his back and tightened her arms around his waist. He wrapped Nutmeg's lead around the pommel of Admiral's saddle, freeing up his left hand, which he now laid over CC's. Neither of them attempted to explain the shift. CC simply drank in the feel of Reese's gloved hand moving over hers. Whatever it was—the touch of two loners momentarily defying their self-imposed barriers or two star-crossed strangers exploring the possibilities they'd been given—CC was grateful for it.

When they arrived at the house, Reese gently lowered CC to the ground without making noticeable eye contact. She felt him pulling back again.

"Thanks for the ride and your help at the car."

"Of course." He nodded toward the barn. "I'll tend to these horses. You and Emmie have plans."

She had all but forgotten. "Yes. I should get to it."

She entered the house and hung the coat and its liner in the mudroom.

Emmie jumped up from the computer station when CC opened the door that led to the kitchen. An old plastic shower curtain was spread across the floor, and three towels sat stacked on the island.

"Looks like you're ready," CC said.

"I'm so excited, but do you need some time to unwind?"

"Nope, I'm excited too. Let's get this party started."

Reese came in through the back door about an hour later, when Emmie was in midprocess. Some hair was plastered to her head with dye while other strands were captured between small sheets of foil. CC glanced his way and caught his amused smile. He headed down the hall to his office, where he closed the door, and she turned back to her work.

She tried not to overthink the past few hours, to simply enjoy them for what they were and nothing more, but that was getting harder to do.

She needed to claim the Tesla and get back on the road as soon as possible.

# CHAPTER SIX

IT WAS FOOLISH AND RISKY, and CC would probably be madder than a wet cat if he tried it, but just thinking about his potential plan brought Reese more pleasure than he'd known in a long time. And if he decided to execute the plan and she did get mad, well . . . he figured it would only justify his estimation of her.

First, he needed more information, so he began by calling Rudy to check on the car's status. "Hey, Rudy, did you get the Tesla into the shop yet?" he said.

"She's loaded, and we're on the way now. Wow, what a car! I almost cried when I saw her stranded there, tangled up in the fencing. Lucky for you, Tesla chassis are strong. Best safety record on the road. That sweet car just rolled up and gave that rotted fence post a sweet little kiss is all. I don't suspect any frame damage, but that barbed wire did a number on her."

"So . . . what do you think? Can you give me a rough estimate of the damage?"

"Not until I go over the body with a fine-toothed comb to determine what parts I need to order. And I'll need the insurance information. Some of these parts will be pricey."

Reese didn't bother explaining that there'd be no insurance money. "Just order what you need. I'm good for it."

"I know you are, Reese, but be aware that worst-case scenario could mean we're talking upwards of twenty grand."

"Ouch. Don't you have a coupon or something for locals?"

"No insurance, huh?"

"The owner'd rather not submit a claim on this."

"What's the story there?"

"I can't say, Rudy. Not this time."

"Aah . . . I gotcha. I smelled some nice perfume on that headrest. I know the driver was a woman."

Rudy delivered *woman* in a teasing, singsong voice that made Reese chuckle. His friend thought he was back in the happy lane, part of the man club, bait for date jokes again, for the first time in seven years. Maybe, if his loquacious friend spread the word around, people would finally stop pitying Reese and offering to fix him up with increasingly older and more desperate candidates drawn from the decreasing pool of marriageable local women.

"She's just a really kind lady who's all alone," he said.

"Uh-huh. All right. Cost of the parts plus twenty percent."

"Thanks."

"But I do have to file a report."

"I understand. And what time frame are we talking about? Can you have it ready for delivery to Vegas by Christmas Eve?"

"Probably. My son could drive it down. He'll be home for Christmas break, and I'm sure he could use some pocket change, but I won't be able to guarantee that delivery date until I get confirmation on the shipment of the parts."

"I hear ya. When will you know?"

"A few days."

That meant CC would be his guest for at least a few more days. Reese absorbed that information with mixed feelings of excitement and stress. "Great. That's great. Hey . . . I was just wondering how much value a custom paint job could add to the car?"

"That's hard to say. It depends on what it's worth to a potential buyer. What did you have in mind?"

"What if, instead of making this one look exactly as it did before the crash, you made it a custom-painted dream car?"

"Are you implying I'd have a free hand on the paint job?"

"Yep. Could you make it so elegant people would forget it's used?"

"In my sleep while holding the paint gun between my toes, but is this what the owner wants?"

"Maybe. I'm just considering a few things; that's all." Reese's hands began to sweat.

"Reese, my friend, this all sounds a little crazy for you. Like you're going too deep too soon with this lady."

"It would be strictly a business proposition." Reese doubled down. "I have confidence that you and one of your sweet paint jobs could increase that repaired car's resale value enough to cover the repair costs. Are you saying I'm wrong?"

"Uh . . . uh . . . no," Rudy sputtered.

"Okay, then. Trust me. I know what I'm doing."

He ended the call, but his last words kept echoing in his mind. *I know what I'm doing.* Reese wished he were certain of that. It pleased him to have Rudy think he was throwing everything in for a woman again. He wished he really were that brave or open or trusting. In truth, he was just an honest man. He couldn't bear to sneak a repaired car to a man who expected to give his wife a once-in-a-lifetime gift for Christmas. He knew CC was worried sick waiting for the repair estimate. She didn't have the means to fix the damaged car, let alone replace it with a new one. He could afford to eat the loss if the repaired car didn't cover the new car's invoice. But was he ready to get that involved with CC or her problems? Not yet he wasn't.

He felt chilled, so he checked the thermostat in his office—seventy degrees. Why had he felt warmer out in the snow? And then he knew why—CC. The feel of her body resting against his own had brought a deep inner heat that had warmed him to his core. He enjoyed the feeling of sheltering her, of being her hero, when in truth, he knew she had been comforting him after his disclosure about Marissa. CC had her own hurts she guarded, and yet she'd reached out to him. He could almost feel her hand under his and the weight of her head on his back. He missed her already. She was down the hall, a hundred feet away, yet here he stood, missing her.

He was a disaster.

He'd sworn he'd never allow himself to be this vulnerable again, and yet here he was, because of CC.

The phone rang, pulling him back to safer thoughts, to things he understood. "Hey, Marcus. What's up?"

"A news chopper flying over those acres you're leasing from the Bureau of Land Management reported three steers stranded in deep snow under the bluff."

"They're probably mine."

"That's what I figured too."

Reese remembered Carlos and Emmie's big date night. "Carlos and I'll get out there first thing tomorrow."

"Today'd be better. Three black steers stranded in white snow wouldn't look good on the six o'clock news."

It was too risky to head out alone, but he dreaded telling Carlos and Emmie that he was about to ruin the young couple's romantic plans. He ran a hand over his face. "You're right. We'll head out in the hour."

His next call was to Carlos to break Emmie's heart.

"I'm not telling her," Carlos said. "You are. And CC's going to be miffed too. She's as excited about Emmie's makeover and our date as Emmie is."

"Fine. Come on up to the house, and we'll tell them together."

CC had done makeup for entire bridal parties, and she'd turned frumpy guests into cover models for the glamour photographer at the club, but no makeover she'd done before pleased her as much as Emmie's did now.

She'd shaped Emmie's hair into a sassy layered cut and added a few highlights to soften the roundness of her face. The biggest change had come from plucking and shaping Emmie's thick brows, which now framed her big hazel eyes beautifully and made them pop. She kept her busy friend's makeup minimal—just a swipe of blush, eyeliner, mascara, and lip gloss. CC handed her a mirror.

The glow emanating from Emmie came from inside as her confidence returned. She sat speechless as she studied every curve and change. "It's me again, CC. I almost forgot who I was. How did you do this?"

"I just bring out what's already in a person."

"Thank you! Thank you so much!" Emmie set the mirror down and stood to hug her new friend.

The women heard the doors creak, and CC gestured for Emmie to sit back down for the grand unveiling. Carlos entered first, nudging Reese forward. Both men carried their hats in their hands, looking like two guilty little boys.

CC moved from in front of Emmie saying, "May I introduce you to the very beautiful Mrs. Emmeline Barraza!"

Emmie stood and held her arms out as she did a little turn.

"Oh, Momma!" Carlos whooped. "Emmie! You've always been beautiful, but . . . whoa. Today you look like my bride again." He swooped over and wrapped her in his arms. When he pulled back to gaze at her some more, he framed her face in his hands and placed a sweet kiss on her lips.

"I feel like myself again, Carlos. I can't wait to show you the new outfit I've been saving for a special occasion like tonight."

Carlos's expression went flat. Keeping one arm wrapped around his wife, he turned toward Reese. "Tell her."

"Tell me what?" Emmie asked as CC scowled.

Reese twisted the brim of his hat in his hands. "A helicopter pilot found three steers stranded on Bureau of Land Management land. We've got to rescue them right away."

CC sucked in so much air that the other three people turned toward her. "Did they get out because of the crash?" Everyone's silence assured her she was right. "Oh, Emmie, I caused this. I'm so sorry."

Emmie shrank for a second. "It's all right." She pulled her shoulders back and looked at Carlos. "I'm disappointed, but I understand. It's got to be done."

"Can't it wait one day?" CC begged.

Laying a hand on CC's arm, Emmie said, "No, it can't."

"I'm truly sorry, Emmie," Reese said. "I'd go alone if they weren't so far out."

"No, no. Of course you can't risk going alone. I know that."

"I'll make it up to you guys. I promise."

"I know you will, Reese." She blinked and pasted on a smile for Carlos, who beamed at her with pride.

"You're amazing, babe. My number one."

She kissed her husband again. "I'm just doing what I need to do because someday I'm going to be a rancher's wife."

"Yes, you are," Carlos said.

"You'll be a great *rancher* yourself," Reese corrected. "What you do is just as important as what we do."

Emmie blinked back tears again. "Thank you. So how long do you think you'll be gone?"

Carlos looked at Reese and wiggled his fingers as if counting the time on them. "Two days . . . maybe three."

"The cattle are under the bluff where the drifts are deep," Reese added. "Once we get them moving, they'll be pushing through chest-deep snow, so the going will be slow."

"You're getting a late start. I'll pack provisions for four days, just in case."

"Thanks, Emmie. You're the best. And, by the way, you do look beautiful." Reese glanced CC's way, and the two locked eyes.

"My wife is one of a kind," Carlos said. He framed Emmie's face in his hands again and gave her a kiss that made even CC tingle from three feet away. "We've taken you for granted, babe. We owe CC a big thanks for showing us what idiots we've been. What an idiot *I've* been. Forgive me?"

Emmie's cheeks warmed bright red. She touched them and ducked her head shyly.

CC now recognized that Carlos's adoration for Emmie was equal to Emmie's for him. She chided herself for not seeing it before. Their devotion was more than doe-eyed looks. It was visible in their step-for-step matched goals, their willingness to sacrifice for each other, and their quick ability to forgive and start fresh. CC realized in that moment how shallow her relationship with Devon had been and how glad she was to end that chapter and move forward.

When she glanced at Reese, his pride-filled eyes remained fixed on her as he offered her a wink, rewarding her for her part in the Barrazas' happiness. She felt she was one of them, part of a team of people willing to set aside their own happy plans for the good of the ranch.

As the men turned for the door, Emmie gave a final sigh, but her smile lingered.

CC placed a hand on her shoulder. "I'm really sorry, Emmie. I'm to blame for your plans being cancelled."

Emmie's smile went lopsided, and she shrugged. "It doesn't even matter. Did you hear what Carlos said?"

"That you're beautiful?"

"More than that. He called me his number one. I've been so worried that he was upset with me for neglecting him, and instead, he said *he's* the one who's been taking *me* for granted. And he leans on me, CC. Those things are all that really matter."

CC nodded. "You're right. You're absolutely right. So how can I help?"

"Come to the pantry with me. I'll give you a lesson in Ranching 101."

A long, narrow storage room sat off the opposite side of the kitchen from the mudroom. This room, stocked with food and gear, looked like some outdoor store whose commercials played on TV. Dried food, water containers, propane stoves, and camp cookware lined the shelves, along with canvas packs, plastic totes, and leather saddlebags to carry the goods, whether in a truck or on horseback. CC also saw sleeping bags, tarps, and tents, along with things she didn't even recognize.

Emmie pointed to a laminated chart on the wall. It was organized by number of cowboys and days on the trail. Beneath it ran a list of items and the amounts of each that would be needed.

"Grab what's listed and mark it off with a dry-erase marker," she said. "The goods are labeled and sitting on the shelves."

CC pulled the equipment and left the food to Emmie. Within thirty minutes, everything was gathered on the table.

"The men will pack everything on the horses. We'll pull clothes next," Emmie said. "They don't need much: a set of dry clothes and lots of thick socks." She had Carlos packed in under five minutes. Then they headed into Reese's room, where CC slept. She hadn't opened a drawer or closet, but when Emmie did, the order and tidiness of his things was impressive. His shirts were hung together by sleeve length and fabric weight, from T-shirts to sweaters. Pants also hung together so the cuffs made an even line across the bottom. It reminded her of her dad's way of organizing things. Military order.

A few items seemed out of character for the relatively quiet man—a fringed leather coat detailed with a blinding amount of silver and a jewelry tray filled with silver and gold rings, cufflinks, watches, and other adornments like hatbands and business-card holders. The most surprisingly garish item was a belt with a silver buckle the size of CC's fist, engraved with the words, *Silver Buckle Mine.*

CC asked no questions, but Emmie quickly explained. "This is Reese's parade stuff. The family does put on a good show when they dress up."

The women carried the bags of packed clothes to the kitchen and dropped them onto the floor by the island, where the men were packing the food goods.

Reese looked up and smiled at CC. "Thanks for helping Emmie."

"My pleasure."

"Rudy has the Tesla. He's giving it a good once-over before figuring out a repair estimate. I'll do my best to stay in touch with him while I'm away to make sure he's hurrying things along."

CC waved her hands. "You don't need to worry about that. You've done more than enough. I can follow up with this Rudy guy. I need to get word to John."

"I know you can handle it, but maybe hold off a day or two more. Rudy's giving me a fat discount."

CC chuckled. "In that case, I'll defer."

"Good. Make yourself at home while we're away. I'm sure you ladies will manage to keep one another well entertained."

"Thanks for letting me stay here."

Reese wore a pack over his shoulder and held the straps of two others in his hands. He set them down and extended a hand to CC. "I'd like to show you something before I go."

CC placed her hand in his, and he led her outside to the front porch overlooking the pond.

"I've been doing a lot of thinking about what you said this morning, about wondering why you weren't enough for your fiancé." He pointed to the right of the pond, where the snow was washed away by a running stream. "That creek feeds the pond and keeps it fresh." He moved his hand to the left, where a similar but larger washed-out area was evident. "When the pond level gets too high, it runs off over there and flows away and downstream."

CC nodded, not sure what point he was trying to make.

"That stream pours more sweet water into that pond than it can hold, and the pond runs it off as waste because it's too small to hold all the goodness the stream wants to bring it. You're like that stream, CC, fresh and full of life. If a man treats you as less, it's because he can't handle all you try to bring to him. The lack is his, not yours."

CC's throat felt thick and tight. She wiped a tear from her eye and squeezed Reese's hand while keeping her eyes fixed on the water. "Thank you. That's the greatest kindness I've ever received."

The sheriff's car drove up the lane then, and Reese dropped her hand. "That's Marcus Rucker."

CC wrapped her arms around her waist. "The sheriff? What do you think he wants?"

"I don't know, but I'm sure going to find out." Reese started walking to the car.

The sheriff tipped his hat Reese's way and then to CC, who followed close behind. "I thought you and Carlos would be on your way by now."

"We're ready to pull out. What brings you here?"

The sheriff addressed CC directly. "I need some information from Miss Cippolini for my paperwork. I need to see your driver's license, miss."

Relief flooded over her that he'd come for her ID and not to arrest her. She hurried to grab her wallet and returned. When she handed her license to the officer, Reese impatiently tapped his foot as his friend read it, turned it over, and then returned it with a smile.

"Is there something else?" CC asked.

The sheriff glanced at Reese, who glared back, before saying, "Ma'am, did you tell anyone you were leaving Chicago? Parents? Friends?"

"I wasn't aware I needed to tell anyone other than my employers."

"A woman named Nora Stubbert filed a missing person's report on you."

"Nora? Why would she be looking for me? I haven't seen her in eight years."

"I called the station where the report was filed. It seems a man named Devon Peters showed up drunk at her place the other night, banging on her door and calling your name. He thought you might be there. When he found out you weren't, he told this Stubbert woman that you were missing, and he said he was worried about you, that you might be hurt or in danger."

"That's ridiculous. I left of my own volition. And how did he find Nora?"

"This guy has friends on the Chicago PD, and he got one of them to run the name. He told them she was your mother."

Reese's head cocked sideways, and CC quickly corrected the error. "*Foster* mother."

"This Peters fellow told them he pulled some fool stunt to make you jealous. He said he got worried when your employers told him you'd left town." The sheriff leaned in closer and studied CC's face. "Miss, he reported that he might have driven you to do something drastic. In view of the accident the other night, I felt I needed to check things out."

CC covered her face with a hand. "Please tell me you didn't tell him where I am."

"No, but I do need you to explain that accident in further detail."

CC panicked, and Reese jumped in. "He wants to know if you were trying to hurt yourself."

"No! Of course not."

Reese stepped in front of CC. "I think that answers your questions, Marcus. Let those people know she's fine and that she'll contact them if and when she chooses."

"Reese."

But Reese stood firm and unmovable until the sheriff turned back toward his vehicle. When the car started, Reese headed for the house, taking long, rushed steps. CC didn't want to appear to be chasing after him, but neither did she want him to leave for three days without clearing up a few things.

"Are you angry with me?" she called to his back.

Reese stopped on the porch and turned to watch the sheriff's car disappear down the lane. "I take it Devon Peters is the ex. So is this a game you two play, where he makes you jealous, you run away, and he comes chasing after you?"

"Are you really asking me that?"

He rubbed his fingers into his eyes and shook his head. "I'm sorry. I was just surprised to hear that his engagement was fake and that he hasn't moved on like you thought."

"It doesn't change anything. He's still the same cheating, self-absorbed egotist I put in my rearview mirror."

"And your sadness over his phone call?"

"It was never because I wanted him back."

"Maybe you should call your foster mother."

"I'll think about it."

His gaze bored into her, delivering more than a casual *See ya soon* but leaving the actual words unsaid.

Before the sheriff's arrival, they had shared a tender, unforgettable moment. CC didn't know if that had all changed. "Is it still okay for me to stay here?"

His expression registered a flash of surprise. "Of course."

"Just checking. Okay, then. I'll see you soon." They stood still for a moment, until Reese slowly stepped away and turned for the door. CC slumped against the porch post. "I'm sorry my personal baggage landed at your doorstep."

"Forget it," Reese said as he turned the knob and held the door open. "I hardly notice yours with all the baggage I've piled there over the years."

He studied her, lassoing her with his stare until she felt pulled in by something she saw there. His mouth pulled to the right, as if he were fighting words he longed to say, and then, in a nearly inaudible voice, he said, "I think this trip will be good for me . . . a chance to fight some of the dragons I've been avoiding for too long."

"Then, I hope you find your answers."

"Me too. Me too."

# CHAPTER SEVEN

"You've checked that same strap four times, Reese. Let's go save the cattle so we can get back home again."

But every saddle strap Reese buckled felt like a goodbye. He ran his hands over Admiral's haunches and felt his old friend flinch with excitement. The stallion was ready for a good ride, not the gentle walk of yesterday but a hard run on open snow-swept range. Today, what Admiral needed and what Reese needed were not the same.

Carlos chuckled. "Just go in there and let her know you're glad she's staying around." Carlos fluttered his eyes and raised his voice an octave. "Or you could tell her that you won't be able to breathe until you return to her."

Reese issued him a sarcastic, one-eyed glance. "You're enjoying this, aren't you?"

"Yes . . . yes, I am," Carlos teased. The twinkle in his eyes and the way his smile drew his cheeks up into two happy lumps attested to how much. "I'd rather see you care for someone, even if that caring makes you struggle, than to see that bitter fog you've been living in."

Reese huffed and mounted Admiral. With a gentle nudge, the horse happily headed down the lane for the open terrain ahead. "The ex-fiancé is looking for her."

"Is that why Marcus stopped by?"

"Yup. The guy put out police reports. He's not giving up easily."

"Reminds me of someone else I know. That's why he scares you. You know how hard you fought to hold on to Marissa, but she'd made her decision and so has CC. The ex will see that."

"Maybe this story will have a different ending."

"Don't be a pessimist, Reese. Why not hope this one will end better?"

Reese looked back at the house. It took everything in him not to turn Admiral around and gallop up the lane and straight onto the porch. He imagined CC opening the door to see what the ruckus was and finding him there. He dreamed of sweeping her into his arms and planting a kiss on her pink lips, one filled with all the hope and hunger his loneliness had pushed deep down in his gut for years. Instead, he squeezed his knees more tightly around Admiral and hastened his departure from the place that now represented the most frightening risk of his life.

The packs jostled on the backs of Nutmeg and Spot, a little paint pony. The two were ferrying the supplies. Carlos ran Warrior ahead and then brought the big brown gelding to a stop. "Go back and leave her with a proper goodbye. You're going to be miserable company if you don't."

Reese gave another glance toward the house. He remembered buying the plans for the home when Marissa was stuck in Germany awaiting her visa. He'd hand-carried them across the ocean to her and come home with her long list of structural changes—a large nursery suite near the master, which now served as his office; another suite on the other side of the house, where her parents would live; and extra bedrooms for children or for when her family members came to visit. She'd requested a space with an east-facing window. Reese knew it was to be a gift for her father, so he'd designed a loft that had far exceeded Marissa's expectations. He'd so wanted to make her happy. He'd emailed photos of the home's progress and visited her when he could, but he'd withheld the secret of the loft. It was to be the grand surprise. A peace offering for her family.

Looking back, he remembered the struggle between staying here to build up their ranch and moving there to build their marriage. She'd encouraged him to stay here, and he'd told himself that decision was the reason everything between them had fallen apart. Deep down, he knew the cause was more fundamental. They'd married for all the wrong reasons, and they'd stayed together for over five years out of pride. He'd been an idiot, and he'd nearly ruined his family in the mix.

And now there was CC, who had little, wanted nothing, and needed help but was too proud to accept it. She was beautiful and gentle, like the doe, and giving and filled with life, like the stream.

He could not, would not, mess this up.

"Let's just hurry along so we can get back," he said.

# CHAPTER EIGHT

THE MEN HAD BEEN GONE for only an hour when Emmie's eyes drifted longingly toward the computer. CC got it. Emmie wanted to use Carlos's absence to focus on her classwork and free her schedule for when he returned home. It became apparent that the three days were going to be interminably long if CC didn't find something constructive to do.

"Give me a list of what you'd be doing if you weren't studying," CC said.

"I'd have to teach you everything."

"Just once. I promise I'm a fast learner. Besides, I owe you."

Emmie took CC to the barn and taught her how to muck and clean a stall, who ate what, and where the feed and tools were housed. Back at the house, Emmie showed her where the mops and buckets were stowed, gave her a tour of the kitchen cupboards, and showed her where the Christmas decorations, meager as they were, were kept. CC made a plan and dug in.

She started in the barn, mucking out the stalls for the four horses who were all out on the trail. When the stalls were clean and readied with fresh bedding, she attended to the chickens, whose coop was across from the deer. She had a hoot collecting eggs and freshening the bedding in the nesting boxes. Next were the doe and her fawn. CC slowed down and took her time with them, holding out a handful of grain in the hope that the offering would be enough to lure the doe near. After twenty minutes, CC surrendered the cause and poured the grain into a pail, setting it on the floor as she exited. Emmie would check the animal's wound later in the day.

CC moved into the house, determined to add some holiday cheer to the Spartan decor. The one box of Christmas decorations included a pitiful assortment of unmatched plastic drugstore ornaments that would barely fill a four-foot tree, which they didn't have. With no transportation of her own, and with Emmie studying and too busy to go shopping in whatever stores they could even reach, CC knew she was on her own.

She thought back to the Christmases she and her father used to make, with silver chains and paper snowflakes and cranberries strung on string. There were beautiful glass balls and an angel on top, but it wouldn't have been Christmas without those homemade chains.

"Emmie, do you have aluminum foil? Lots of it?"

"Anything we have we probably have in duplicate so we don't run out." Emmie opened a drawer and pulled out two heavy boxes of foot-wide foil. "Here you go. Whatcha making?"

"Foil chains. They're really pretty. And does Amazon deliver here?"

Emmie laughed. "Of course they do. We're remote, but we're still on the planet."

"Okay, okay." CC chuckled and tore the foil into 9" x 12" lengths. When she had a big stack ready, she took a single sheet and rolled it around the end of her index finger, forming a tube. Next, she crimped one end and folded it into the other end, forming a circle. She crimped the connection point, securing the first link. Now to make about a hundred or so more.

She took her supplies out onto the front porch to work where she could listen to the ranch's sounds and ponder what Reese had said about her being like the water in the stream, refreshing and full of life. She wanted to remember that forever.

The trail of the men and their four horses was written in the path of hoof-prints and muddy snow. She felt the chill burning into her legs and hands and wondered how cold Reese and Carlos would be as they slept on a bed of snow. The thought made her shiver, but she'd sensed a certain excitement in the men as they'd prepared for their winter campout. Life was different here, where work and play merged into one grand adventure. She could see that it required a certain type of personality to find joy in the hard work and solitude of ranching.

She wondered why Marissa left. Had she not been happy as a rancher's wife? Had she been unable to adjust to the lifestyle it demanded? CC wondered if she could.

Her fingers were nearly numb by the time the chain was finished. She measured it out at twenty-two feet and carried it proudly inside, where Emmie was at the stove stirring something that smelled delicious. "What's cooking?"

"Spaghetti sauce. How's Italian sound?"

"I'm a Cippolini. Spaghetti sounds great!"

"I needed a break from the computer before I get cataracts. The chain looks beautiful. Where did you want to hang it?"

CC held it up near the mantel. "What do you think?"

"Nice but naked. We need greenery. Fortunately, we have a pine forest behind the house."

"I know what tomorrow's project will be."

The girls relaxed for an hour after cleaning up the kitchen, chatting about cookie recipes and the limited shopping available in the nearest small town. Out of the blue, CC asked, "Was it hard for Marissa to live so far from other people?"

Emmie's eyes bulged out as if she were about to choke. "Did Reese tell you about Marissa?"

"Just a mention."

"That's huge!" Emmie scooted forward in her seat. "He almost never mentions her, not even to us." Her eyes rolled into her head as she thought. "He trusts you. That's really good."

"I wouldn't say that. Sometimes I think he does, and then other times . . ." She thought back to the wild reversal between the closeness they'd shared on the horse and his coolness and comments after the sheriff left.

"He's just cautious with people."

CC looked down and fiddled with the buttons on her sweater. "I get that."

"Then, you'll both take things slow and be careful with one another's feelings."

"What? No, no, no, Emmie." CC shook her head and shoved her hands forward. "Reese has been kind to me—kinder than I deserved under the circumstances—but that's all. He's got issues. I've got issues. Putting two people like us together would be a recipe for disaster, and neither of us can handle another one of those. I'm leaving here as soon as that car's fixed. End of story."

"Love is risky, CC. It's not for cowards."

"Is that the voice of experience talking?"

Emmie grabbed a throw pillow and hugged it close. "Carlos didn't think he was the marrying kind. He had a hard life in Arizona—a broken home, a juvenile record, some gang ties. His mom got remarried to a soldier who convinced Carlos to join the army. It probably saved his life, but when he got out and started college, he met this innocent church-going girl from a big Nebraska farming family"—she gestured to herself—"and he thought he had nothing in common with me and nothing worthwhile to offer me. He couldn't see what others saw in him. It took years to convince him he'd become the man he is now. I had to fight for our relationship, and I give thanks every day that I did."

Maybe she was right. Maybe, more than perfect timing or perfect people, love required courage—the courage to risk getting hurt again in exchange for a chance at something that could be wonderful.

"That's good advice. Thank you. I'll tuck that bit of wisdom away for the future."

"You're welcome, but I'm not the one who deserves the thanks. Someone else gave me that advice—Reese."

"Reese?"

"Does that surprise you?"

CC nodded. She still didn't know much about Reese's past or how low his heartbreak had plunged him, but he was like a rabbit, hopping forward and then retreating. That inconsistency was paralyzing. Even so, she couldn't forget the little kindnesses he's shown her, like the doe and her fawn, the shared horseback ride, and the metaphor about how she was like the stream. And she couldn't deny how affected he'd seemed by the thought that Devon had not gone away. Maybe all his kind efforts had taken more courage than she understood. Maybe it was her turn to be brave.

Emmie shuffled off to bed, yawning all the way. CC felt unsettled, so she stayed up staring at her phone, watching video tutorials on how to make pine garlands. After a restless night's sleep, she was at the barn at first light. The horses' stalls were fresh and clean, so she spent an hour sitting quietly with the deer, hoping they'd get comfortable with her scent. She fed them and freshened their stall, and then she gathered eleven eggs, freshened the nesting boxes again, and carried the eggs inside, where six of them became two lovely omelets.

"What's on the agenda for today?" Emmie asked when she joined CC in the kitchen.

"I want to cut pine boughs and make garlands for the fireplace."

"That sounds ambitious."

"Do you have anything else you need me to do?"

"Nope, but you'll have a hard time hauling the boughs in the snow."

"Can I get a truck out there?"

"Hmm . . . probably not with the drifts . . . but . . ." Emmie's eyebrows wriggled as if she had a whopper of an idea.

"I like whatever you're thinking," CC said as she rubbed her hands together. "What *are* you thinking?"

"Snowmobile!"

"Perfect!"

"Have you ridden one?"

"Absolutely not. But I'm game!"

"I think I might play hooky with you for an hour and run you up to the pines."

After dressing in snow gear, Emmie hooked CC up with work gloves and all the tools she'd need. CC packed the tools into a canvas tote and followed Emmie to the barn. She passed by the deer stall, and while the doe didn't welcome CC, neither did she race back to the corner as she had earlier. She seemed more comfortable with her near, and CC took that as a minor win.

Emmie led the way to a smaller outbuilding with wide barn doors that opened to reveal two snowmobiles and a black sled made of heavy plastic material. She hitched the sled to the back of a snowmobile and tossed CC a helmet.

CC tossed the pack of tools into the sled and slid into the back seat of the snowmobile while Emmie climbed in front. Moments later, the engine came to life, and the two women inched out onto the snow-covered yard.

"Hold on!" Emmie called over her shoulder, and they were off, leaving a spray of flying snow behind them.

The stand of pine trees was farther behind the barn than it looked. Emmie made the ride even longer by driving around every outbuilding and obstacle she could find. Reaching the trees, the very reason for the trip, seemed anticlimactic compared to the ride to get there, but the girls set to work, cutting boughs and loading them into the sled.

They were preparing to leave when they heard another engine off to their left. They looked at one another and returned to their work, tying the boughs down until giggling voices piqued their interest, sending them off on an entirely new adventure. Wide-eyed and curious, they followed the sounds on foot. Emmie pulled back a pine bough, revealing a slightly younger version of Reese dressed in a Neil Barrett suede-and-shearling-lined designer jacket and sporting a stylish cut to match. CC didn't have money, but she recognized money and style from the clientele who frequented the club. Reese downplayed his wealth, while his younger doppelganger embraced his. The man held a long pair of pruning shears in his calfskin-gloved hands while a dark-haired beauty nuzzled his neck, completely distracting him from the task at hand.

"Morning, Reynolds!" Emmie called in a playful "gotcha" voice.

Reynolds jumped and dropped the shears, which landed mere inches from his designer boot. "Emmie! You nearly cost me a toe!"

Her laughter filled the space with friendship and fun. "You should never mix pruning and pleasure."

Reynolds blushed, while the attractive brunette shot the women a smile that crossed easily into scowl territory.

He tried to step over the hedge of scrub growth between them and where Emmie and CC stood, but he soon abandoned the effort with a friendly shrug. "Emmie Barraza, allow me to introduce Gwinnie Smithfield. Gwinnie, this is Emmie. She and her husband work for Reese." He glanced at CC, adding, "Emmie, you'll have to make the introductions for your friend."

"Nice to meet you, Gwinnie." Emmie returned Gwinnie's welcome-scowl. "This is CC Cippolini, a friend from Chicago."

"Nice to meet you, CC," Reynolds said.

CC returned the greeting, and Emmie continued. "It seems we all had the same brilliant idea today. We're cutting boughs to decorate the cattle shack."

CC still got a kick out of the nickname of Reese's gorgeous log house.

"Reese is letting you decorate?" Reynolds asked. "Way to go, Emmie. Mom's decorator is coming tomorrow to begin decking her halls for the holidays. She needs a pile of fresh boughs for her swags, so we volunteered."

"Then, we'd better let you two get back to your work."

"We'll see you and Carlos at Mother's annual bash in two weeks, won't we?"

Emmie nodded. "Wouldn't miss it."

"Make sure to drag my brother along, will you?"

"*Drag* is the operative word."

"I know." Reynolds laughed and turned to CC. "Will you still be in town on the tenth?"

Today was Monday, November 29. She had no idea what tomorrow held, let alone where she'd be in eleven days. It all depended on . . .

"I think we can convince her to stay," Emmie chimed in, adding a smile and a wink.

"Wonderful! I called Reese, and he said he was out on the range today. Have you met him yet, CC? He's a great guy. You'd like him."

Emmie snagged CC's arm and started walking while tossing over her shoulder, "Gotta run, Reynolds! Great seeing you! You too, Grinnie."

"You called Gwinnie *Grinnie* by mistake," CC said quietly as she stumbled along under Emmie's tug, heading for the snowmobile.

Emmie snorted a laugh. "No, I didn't."

"Oh, yes you did." And then she saw Emmie's smile and the devilish look in her eye. "Oh, so it wasn't a mistake."

Emmie wriggled her eyebrows in a nonconfession, and CC laughed right along with her.

"Sorry for giving you the bum's rush," Emmie said, "but the last thing Reese would want would be for his family to assume you and he were a thing and start asking a ton of questions."

"Agreed," CC said, not knowing what to make of that. "His brother seemed very nice."

"Oh, he is. The Brockbanks are all nice people, but there are seven sons, and none of them are married yet."

"Reese was."

"Yeah . . . that debacle is probably why everyone else is still single."

"Are you saying the Brockbanks are the reason their sons aren't married?"

"Only that Mr. and Mrs. Brockbank tend to be a bit . . ."

"Overprotective?"

"Let's just say Reese is not the kind of man to speak ill of anyone, but he lives a stone's throw from his parents, yet almost never visits them or their family compound."

"Compound?"

"As in gated, guarded, magnificent family-owned opulence."

"Seriously?" CC felt her heart rate increase and her oxygen level plummet.

"Don't worry about them. You've met Reese. He's different. Levelheaded. Real."

"And yet his marriage failed. Are you saying the Brockbanks are why Marissa left?"

Emmie bit her bottom lip. "What happened between Reese and Marissa isn't my story to tell. Reese will tell you when he's ready. We just want him to be happy. For whatever reason, his family seems to add to his stress, but you? You make him happy, CC."

"No one just marries a person. You marry their entire family. I want a man whose family is as ready to welcome and love me as he is. Not someone whose family will divide us."

"Reese would never let that happen." Emmie's expression was dead serious. "Okay?"

CC nodded, but she wasn't really okay. No amount of being brave or sticking her neck out could make people love her if they didn't. She needed to hear the real story about Reese's marriage from him.

"Let's head back. You've got a lot of work ahead of you, and I get to sit in on a prerecorded online lecture about statistical analysis. Doesn't that sound peachy?"

"Thanks for this adventure. I needed to laugh and be crazy for a little while."

On second thought, she considered that she'd had nothing but crazy since setting the Tesla to autopilot. Living under the roof of a pining, divorced heir to a silver mine whose wealthy family lived in a compound? Crazy was all around her. What she really needed was some normal.

# CHAPTER NINE

AFTER MAKING CAMP FOR THE night, Reese set out early the next morning with Carlos, anxious to find the animals and head home. He twisted in his saddle to stretch out his sore back muscles. Camping in the snow proved less exciting than he remembered.

The winter trips with his grandpa had been the ultimate man-thrill. He remembered the clinking sound of tin pots as they hung from a packhorse's saddle and how delicious whatever concoction the old man threw together and warmed over a blazing wood fire tasted. The smell of woodsmoke always made him think of his grandfather. During the days, the men would hunt or hike or round up strays, and the nights would be filled with stories and laughter and off-key singing reserved for just such moments. The side of the body facing the fire was always toasty and comfortable, while the other side was always cold and miserable, so they'd spent the nights flipping like hotdogs on a grill to keep all of them equally roasted.

After Grandpa died, Reese's father had kept up the man-trip tradition with his seven sons. There had been a few modifications. He'd bought new, modern gear like propane stoves and heaters that had made the wood fire little more than ornamental. Still, being together had been fun, with retelling of the old stories and singing of the old, off-key tunes.

And then Reese had gone on his first deployment to Afghanistan, a place with an altogether different kind of cold. The pervading fear of getting sniper-shot had kept his insides chilled while the weather turned his outsides to ice. Afghanistan's cold was not friendly like Utah's. It was an additional enemy.

Admiral's muscles twitched beneath Reese, as if he could sense his master's troubled thoughts. A moment later, the horse began prancing in the snow. Warrior grew restless too, and the men looked at one another, fully aware that the animals knew something they didn't.

Their view was limited by the cloud cover and the barren white palette ahead. Foothills broke to the right, and Reese knew any one of a few hundred different animals could be the cause of the horses' dismay. He took Admiral's reins in his left hand, leaned forward, and patted the horse's neck to calm him. His right hand fingered his rifle in case he needed to pull it from its holster and take a shot at a bobcat or a moose or a bear.

Carlos pulled his binoculars out and raised them to his eyes. He turned his head this way and that, and then his arm went up, pointing to three dark dots against the snow. The pair urged their horses on, and as they drew nearer to the bawling, frightened cattle, they saw how deeply they had become embedded in the snowdrifts that had blown up against the hills. The poor beasts could reach no grass, and they were slamming against the snow more than walking, causing the heavy pack to firm up around them like walls of ice.

The men dismounted and grabbed shovels to dig the cattle out, but the animals thrashed and swung their heads. One came so close to stabbing Carlos with its horns that they decided to calm the animals first by feeding them. Once the animals had eaten, the situation improved, and shoveling commenced.

"Oh, I see. Now you're glad to see us, aren't you?" Carlos said to the cattle as he plunged his shovel into the snow. "Maybe you should have remembered how good you have it before you ran away from home."

Reese rolled his eyes. "You're taking this awfully personally, aren't you?"

"Darn straight I am. These loco steers are cutting into my *personal* time. Did you see how beautiful my Emmie looked last night?"

Reese laughed. "Point taken. You have every right to grumble."

"So do you! You could be making progress with CC. Maybe you'd be sharing a cozy supper for two this very minute if we weren't out here digging an exit for a few runaway longhorns."

"If only it were that easy."

"So you're at least admitting your interest now." Carlos leaned on his shovel.

"I'm plenty interested. I'm just—"

"Scared? Paralyzed? An idiot?"

"Guilty as charged."

"Then, you're as dumb as these cattle. That's actually an insult to the cattle." Carlos turned to the animals. "How can I be angry with you? You're a steer and you've only got a tiny brain, but this man? The boss? He's a little chicken." He bent forward and folded his arms up like wings as he proceeded to cluck and strut in the snow. Reese gave him a playful shove. "All right, all right. You're supposed to be my best friend."

Carlos's clucking turned to a sad smile. "I am. Always will be. That's why I need to remind you of the miracle you received. You cheated death, Reese. When I rolled you over after that blast, I thought I'd lost my most important amigo, but you mended. And except for those scars on your left cheek, God saved you, and I refuse to believe He did that so you could waste the rest of your life."

"I tried, Carlos. Mar—"

"Be done with Marissa, Reese. She's yesterday's excuse. Look forward, bro. And, truth be told, I don't think she broke your heart as much as she hurt your pride."

"She hurt my family."

"*She* didn't hurt them. The rumormongers did. She was as hurt by all that ugliness as you and your family were. And as for your family, they've forgiven you. You need to let it go, bro."

"I should have seen it coming."

"Maybe, but you didn't. Don't repeat that mistake and miss giving a potentially right person a chance to make you happy."

# CHAPTER TEN

CC's HANDS WERE COVERED IN pine tar, cuts, and blisters from chopping pine boughs into small fronds and wiring them into a rope. She couldn't stop herself from making a second chain, which warranted the creation of a second pine swag. She admitted that the results were well worth the sacrifice when she intertwined the garland and the silver chain and hung them the next morning. One section was draped along the twelve-foot-wide mantel. She used the longer piece to deck the railing to the loft and bring another touch of Christmas to the house. The loft had intrigued her since her arrival, and hanging the garland gave her an excuse to explore.

Half of the towering wood beams that formed the open peak of the ceiling had their start in the wall of the loft, which overlooked the great room and kitchen and even gave observers a view of the hall that led to the master suite. Large round windows ringed with narrow stained-glass bevels centered the walls on either end. Morning light and color poured in through the east-facing window. CC timed her visit early to catch the end of the sunrise, when the colors streamed across the room. She was dazzled by this magical space. The wood beams made it feel anchored in elements of the earth while the light gave the room a heavenly feel. So much beauty. So much peace. It felt reverent and holy, as if it were a chapel.

She marveled at the deliberate care taken to set the house and these windows at the precise angle to capture the sun's movement so perfectly. Reese had done that.

For Marissa.

CC expected to find a library and a comfy chair for reading or a stereo and chaise for relaxing. She could also imagine children playing here, in full sight of parents below, yet it stood absolutely empty, as if the place were grieving—for Marissa and for the children that had never come.

The emptiness of the great room below was also more apparent from this angle. CC's efforts to brighten the house now seemed trivial, like attempting to sweep back a sea of sorrow with a pine bough. What was she doing? Why was she here, where Marissa still loomed? She thought about calling an Uber, no matter how much it cost, to ferry her away from Reese's sorrow, which seemed to be compounding her own.

And then Emmie entered the kitchen like a burst of fresh air. She was dressed in red-and-white fleece, wearing slippers that made her feet look like bear paws. Her red mop of hair flopped over the band of headphones through which CC assumed a lecture or podcast on statistics was likely playing. Then Emmie started dancing awkwardly and singing off-key. The sight cheered CC's heart, and she went down the stairs, anxious to feed off Emmie's good mood.

Emmie beamed her trademark smile and pulled the headphones off. "Good morning."

"To what do we attribute this burst of jubilance?"

Emmie shook her headphones CC's way. "Do you know how long it's been since I listened to something besides assigned online lessons? I'm listening to music just for fun, CC. Imagine that."

"Good for you! It sounds way overdue."

"We've been long overdue on lots of things around here, like sleep, laughter, and relaxation. These past few days have been so fun. So normal. I think you popped the cork on all the secret longings I've kept bottled up. I just hope I can rein myself back in and get a little work done while Carlos is away. What's on your agenda today?"

CC touched her fingers together, and they stuck, even after showering. "I considered making more pine garlands, but I think I'll avoid the sap and visit the chickens and the deer instead."

"I wish I could join you, but I need to shower, and then I've got a date with my computer. I have one paper to write, and then I'm ahead enough to devote myself fully to my husband for the rest of the week!"

"You deserve it." Emmie's happiness washed over CC.

"Thank you. We need this. So enjoy your time with nature."

"Will do, as soon as . . ." She looked at her fingers. "I can't get this pine sap off. It's worse than hair dye. Any ideas?"

Emmie shot her a devilish smile. "I guess you'll just have to stay here until it wears off."

"You're hilarious. Go enjoy your shower."

"See you later."

A deep chime sounded a few minutes later. CC ran to Emmie's bedroom door and knocked, but there was no answer. She knew Emmie was likely already in the shower, and now the task of answering the door fell to her, though she didn't feel it was her place.

She looked at her stained hands and rubbed them on the front of her jeans, but the stains remained. She stalled a moment longer, and then the chime sounded again. With a sigh of resolution, she moved to the heavy door and opened it slightly to find a beautiful middle-aged woman holding something wrapped in a red-checked square of fabric.

The woman eyed CC with as much curiosity as CC knew she was showing her. She was impeccably put together and the epitome of grace and elegance, from her stylishly cut blonde hair to her perfectly chosen outfit and manicured nails. Amazingly, something about her smile-crinkled eyes made CC feel completely comfortable with her.

"Hello," CC said timidly. "The owner of the home isn't here. I'm just a guest."

"Lovely to meet you," the woman said as she stepped forward and slipped past CC and into Reese's home. CC detected a slight German accent as the woman talked on and made her way to the kitchen, surveying the house en route. "I was baking some apple cakes, and I remembered how much Reese loved them, so I whipped one up for all of you. I figured I'd run it over while it's still warm."

The woman set her bundle down on the kitchen island and untied the cloth covering the cake. "The house looks festive and lovely. Like a real home." She moved to the mantel and fingered the chains and garland. "Charming . . . just charming. I've never seen anything like these before."

"My father made a set for our home. We hung them every Christmas."

"And the garlands?"

"Emmie and I . . . we . . ." CC kept fiddling her stained fingers. "Everyone's been so kind to me. I wanted to give them something in return."

The woman looked at CC's hands, and CC blushed and quickly hid them behind her.

"Pine tar?"

CC nodded.

"Don't fret over those stains. They'll wear off, but for now, consider them badges of honor. You got them doing a good turn for someone." Her smile changed from friendly to appreciative, and she looked at CC as if she were peering into her soul. "This house was always beautiful, but it has a warmth and coziness to it now. You did that. And as for those hands, you're so very lovely that no one will notice."

CC was not a stranger to compliments about her looks. Those tributes were phrased in assorted ways and too often from men whose inebriation limited their command of English. She had always been uncomfortable with the attention paid her, but this was different. No one had looked at her this way since her father, with eyes that seemed to tell her they were proud of her, and in that moment, despite the pine tar and faded jeans, this stranger did make CC feel lovely.

The normally loquacious Chicagoan scrambled for words to fill the silence. Instead, it was the woman who spoke. "So . . . you're Emmie's friend?"

CC weighed the question and decided she could answer yes and be truthful.

"And Reese? What do you think of him?"

"Reese? He's . . . he's very nice."

"Yes. Yes, he is. Will you be here long enough to attend the Brockbank's annual Christmas party on the tenth?"

"I . . . I'm not sure yet." CC looked for a quick segue away from the topic of Reese or herself. "I'll be sure to tell Emmie and Reese about your delicious gift, Ms.—"

"Oh, no need for formalities. If he asks, just tell Reese the apple-cake lady came by. He'll know." She took CC's hands and gave them a little squeeze, and then she left as mysteriously and quickly as she'd come.

The entire encounter had spanned little more than a few minutes, but a welcome feeling settled over CC, a feeling of being accepted as an equal. Her little gifts and talents were nothing compared to Reese's home and ranch, but the woman recognized that they had value. CC began to believe it too. No matter what happened between her and Reese, she wanted to remember those feelings.

She took a whiff of the apple cake as she passed the counter on her way out the door. Its aroma filled the kitchen with the smell of Christmas. The day was crisp, but the sun was breaking through the clouds, promising a beautiful winter day. The scent of pine lifted CC's Christmas hunger further as she made her way to the barn. She suddenly longed to hear the old carols she and her father had played at home, so she queued up her music app and selected a channel that played traditional favorites by singers from eras long past.

The first note of "Silent Night," her father's favorite carol, fueled CC's longing for her childhood home and for her father. She sang it softly as she cleaned the chicken coop, pausing to thank the chickens for their donation of nine fresh eggs, which she'd need for the day's cookies. When she turned back around to tend to the deer, she found the doe looking at her and turning her head quizzically, as if entranced by CC's singing; however, the fawn seemed unimpressed and continued to nuzzle its mother.

"So, little mama, is it my singing you like, or are you flirting with the voice on my phone?" CC stopped singing, and the doe seemed equally entranced by the prerecorded singer. Following her hunch, CC stuffed the phone into her pocket and allowed it to play as she opened the stall to care for the deer. The mother backed up a step, then reached her neck out as if searching for the source of the music, without drawing near enough for CC to touch her. The doe's wound was nearly healed. CC knew she and her baby would soon be ready to be released back into their habitat and accepted that she might never win the doe's trust in time.

"Still not quite ready to let me touch you? That's okay. I've enjoyed looking at you and your cute baby. Besides, you're not the only one having trust issues around here."

She thought about Reese and wondered if he'd had success facing his multiple dragons. She knew his ex-wife was still a specter in his life, but what other elements from his past was he fighting? Judging from the buckle in his closet, the Silver Buckle Mine was still active and lucrative, despite Reese's efforts to portray it as little more than his grandfather's lark or a family playground. He really didn't know CC, so she could understand his reluctance to reveal financial matters to her, but she sensed something else. Was he uncomfortable about his wealth? Except for his home, his lifestyle was rather austere, not the lifestyle of parties and interior designers his brother Reynolds had alluded to as being a hallmark of the Brockbank family.

CC and her father had never had more than a few paychecks' worth of money in their savings accounts, but that had never stopped her dad from helping someone he believed needed the money more. Still, CC had never wanted for anything growing up, and that included time with her father, who'd refused to work a second job and farm his daughter out to others. When CC set out on her own, she'd realized that to do good like her father *and* have a nest egg would require her to work at least two jobs, so she did. But she'd never lost sight of her father's philosophy about money, that having simple needs was actually more freeing than wealth.

Perhaps Reese believed that too.

But what about the hurt CC saw in him? Was his wealth gone? Had he traded his portion of the mine for the ranch? Or was it possible that Marissa had married him for his money and left when her settlement was secure? That thought made CC's stomach tighten.

Speculating was worse than not knowing anything. Emmie had cautioned her to be patient. CC looked back at the deer. She was being patient with them, sitting quietly with them for hours to win their trust. Why was it so much harder to wait to hear Reese's story? Hard as it was to admit, she knew. It had always been a given that the deer would be released, that they were just a fleeting pleasure, but despite everything she said, she had allowed herself to hope it would be different with Reese.

He was good for her. Gentle and understanding, astute about her insecurities and strengths. The thought of saying goodbye to him would cut her far more deeply than saying goodbye to Devon had.

She left the barn and paused at the corner of the house, looking over the snow-whitened fields that ran up to the foothills. While searching for some sign of Reese's return, she imagined what it would be like to watch for him from this corner every day, to catch the first glimpse of his shy smile as he came home from checking on his stock. It was a silly dream. One stuffed with the potential of massive disappointment, but regardless of how slim it might be, CC considered being patient and taking that risk, dreaming one day at a time about the happiness it could bring.

Emmie was still at her computer when CC entered with the day's eggs and said, "Could you eat another omelet today?"

"Don't tempt me." Emmie rubbed her temples and shook her head. "I'm a stress eater, and this paper is causing me plenty."

CC laughed and grabbed an apple from the bowl on the counter. "I am going to follow your example and lay off the eggs too before my cholesterol count lands me in the ER, but I'm still going to bake the cookies I planned. How's the paper coming along?"

"I'm committed to staying in this chair until I'm finished."

"You've really got your priorities straight."

"Finally. What are yours?"

"My priorities?" CC felt her face and body go slack. What *were* they? What was she working for? "I hate to admit this, Emmie, but my primary thought has been to simply start fresh. A new start in a new place without the complications of the past."

"So you're not committed to Vegas?"

"Vegas was my father's dream; a retirement there would've been completely different from the life he lived every day. I just wanted to see it . . . for him. Driving a man's Tesla there for a thousand dollars gave me the chance to see a few of the sights along the way that Dad dreamed about, and it gave me some money and time to find a job if I decided to stay." CC stared at the island. "It doesn't sound like much of a life plan, does it?"

Emmie stood and moved to CC.

"My dad died so unexpectedly that we never really talked about my future," CC admitted. "He assumed I'd go to college, but we always felt we had time to figure out where I'd go and what I'd study, and then he was gone. I moved in with a stranger, who made my life plan for me."

"I'm so sorry you didn't have him to guide you." Emmie placed a hand on CC's back.

CC shook her head, astounded by how limp and feeble she and her thinking seemed in that moment. She straightened and said, "You'd have liked him. He was a really good man. If an older person came in to buy a pipe wrench, chances were my dad would be at their house that evening fixing a leaky faucet or repairing a pipe for free. I still have the lessons he taught me."

"I'm sure he's proud of you."

"I hope so. I don't regret my choices, but I can see how many opportunities I've missed. I could probably do more with my life, but I do love to see people's faces when they look in the mirror and feel renewed. That part of my job has value, doesn't it?"

"Of course it does. You did wonders for me. I feel confident again." Emmie plopped onto a barstool and leaned into her fist as her arm rested on the island. "Plus, look at how you've transformed the house."

"You hung lights."

"One pathetic strand, but you've brought warmth and beauty and hope to it. You can't leave now. Does Reese know you have to get that car to Vegas by Christmas Eve?"

"I told him that first night."

"Don't make plans to stay there. It'll ruin everything. Come back here and work your styling magic."

"Where?" CC laughed. "In the barn?"

"There are only four hairdressers within thirty minutes of here, and two of them use their kitchens. We local ladies ache to get pampered in a relaxing salon by an operator with city skills. If making a difference is your aim, you could do it here or in Brisbane. There are shop spaces for rent, and staying close would give you and Reese time to get to know each other."

After CC delivered the Tesla to Vegas, her life was her own. Staying close would give her time to see where things might go, and if things didn't work out, she could always run to Vegas or somewhere else to start again. But everything depended on Reese and what conclusions he'd come to during his days on the range. "I'll think about it."

The doorbell rang, putting an end to the conversation. "I'll get it and leave you to your baking," Emmie said. A minute later she returned with an Amazon box addressed to CC. "It's for you."

Wiping her hands on a dish towel, CC said, "Yes! It's the Christmas lights I ordered!"

"You didn't have to pay for Christmas decorations out of your own pocket."

"I wanted to. Besides, I'm enjoying decorating this house. Think of it as my Christmas gift." She opened the carton and pulled out boxes of twinkle lights, two boxes of candy canes, and removable hooks for hanging garlands and wreaths.

"I see more pine boughs in your future."

The oven timer went off. "The ginger bars are ready." CC got the bars out of the oven and placed them on a cooling rack.

"Between pine sap and cookies, it's beginning to smell a lot like Christmas!" Emmie said.

# CHAPTER ELEVEN

THE GENTLE ROCK AND SWAY in the saddle was restful, and with Carlos listening to his phone's playlist, there was nothing to interrupt Reese's thoughts except the squeak of leather, the snorts of the animals, and the crunch of their hooves as they plowed through the snow.

He had too many thoughts, and regardless of where they began, they always meandered back to CC.

*What is she doing?*

*What is she wearing?*

*What was I thinking, getting involved with a total stranger?*

*What if she isn't there when I get home?*

That thought brought a new level of cold.

Carlos and Warrior pulled up beside Reese. Headphones were now hanging loosely around Carlos's neck, and he eyed Reese with incredulity.

Reese eyed him right back. "What?"

"Are you trying to ruin *my* marriage now?"

"What's your problem?" Reese growled.

Carlos raised his hands in defense. "Whoa! I was just kidding about how slow we're poking along. Sorry."

Reese shook his head over suddenly being so sensitive over his failed marriage, especially when he'd snapped at the very guy who'd pulled him through his darkest days. "No, I'm the one who's sorry."

"My timing could use some work. What's your excuse, brother?"

Reese stared off at the white vistas ahead without answering.

"It's CC, isn't it? Listen, if you've got this many reservations about her, trust your gut. Let her go. I'm just glad you felt something for her. Maybe the next girl will be the one."

"It's not about her."

"So you do like her."

"Of course. Only . . . I wish I liked myself."

Carlos winced and whined, "Oh, man, Reese. Don't go back there again. Don't do it."

"I know I can't change the past. I just wish I'd met CC before all that."

"This moment, right here . . . this is the moment you two were intended to meet. You've got to trust God on that."

"I'm trying, but I can't help but wish we'd met before I became a head case."

"What if wishing that means you're wishing away the very things that made you ready to meet her?"

"Like what?"

"I was a gang-running player before the military, and Emmie was an innocent country girl. The day I met her, her scarf got all tangled up in her bike wheel, and she went down hard on the sidewalk, fifty yards ahead of me. The old Carlos would have taken one look at that goody-good country chica and passed on by 'cause I had game all over the place. But I was home, fresh from combat, and the war had changed me. I had been taught how to help, and I couldn't see a person in need and walk by anymore."

Reese nodded. He knew about his friend's past.

"Now, take Emmie," he continued. "She was the youngest child of a preacher and went to school on a scholarship. That semester was her first time away from home. She was a shy, lonely freshman on campus whose only close male friend was the son of her father's friend. Never in a million years would she have spoken to a jerk like me, let alone gone on a date with me. But she had received her first D on a test that morning, followed by a meeting with her academic advisor. Completely overwhelmed, she decided her next stop was the registrars' office to withdraw from school before going to the airport to run home to Nebraska. And then she crashed her bike."

"I didn't know any of that."

"That accident was a blessing for both of us. A bunch of girls rushed over to help her, and then I came by. I knelt down and smiled and offered my help." He pressed his lips tightly together, and Reese knew his friend's emotions were running high over the memory. "She looked up at me with those trusting hazel eyes, and in one moment, her belief in me made me feel like a superhero. I would have carried her through enemy fire to keep her safe, and she still makes me feel that way. I try to be a better man every day for her."

"You two have a great story."

"You're missing the point, bro. We met *after* the bad things happened to us. Those things made us ready for each other. All that hurt and ugliness and pain and sadness—it changed us. I'll never know for sure, but I don't think we would have met if she hadn't hit a low enough point to put her trust in a stranger and if I hadn't been broken enough to need someone to believe in me. So don't regret your past. Every minute of it shaped you, changed you and your priorities. It made you who you are, and contrary to all common sense, CC seems pretty crazy about you."

Reese offered his friend a backhand for that last barb. "All right, all right. You're very persuasive."

"We promised to always have one another's back. I'm just keeping up my end."

They plowed on slowly. Short stretches of forward progress were often blocked by thick, deep drifts requiring Reese and Carlos to dismount and shovel a path through the mounded snow to keep the steers moving along. Two more nights and another half day passed in slow, white monotony. The snow and the provisions thinned out when a happy landmark came into view.

Carlos gave a whoop and Reese said, "You'd better start making plans for that getaway."

He urged Admiral along, and soon the horse and the packhorse behind him set off at a gallop, pushing the steers along. Carlos smacked his hat against Warrior's haunches until his team caught up with Reese. He pulled out his phone and tried to make a call. "No signal yet."

"We'll have one once we get around this bend."

"So . . . you know you and CC will have the house to yourselves when we go."

New worries creased Reese's brow. "Do you think that'll scare her off?"

"You weren't planning anything more than a friendly evening, were you?"

Reese's mouth gaped open. "Of course not. But what do you think she'll think I'm thinking?"

"That you're overthinking everything."

Reese slouched in his saddle. "I'm not good at this."

"You'll be fine. Just pull out a board game."

"That's a good idea."

"And grill up some burgers."

"Yeah . . . I could do that."

"And then relax on the sofa with a romantic show . . ."

"Sure . . ."

"Like an episode or two of *Saved by the Bell*. The ladies love that."

It took a moment or two for Reese to register that Carlos was issuing him another dig. "Oh, you're hilarious. I'm coming to you for advice, and you're mocking my ineptitude?"

"I'm just joshin' you, man. You're a gentleman. Just be yourself."

"This is going to be a catastrophe."

"Or it could be the start of something amazing."

"That seems highly doubtful. How would you feel about staying another day or two before you and Emmie take off together? To give CC and me time to get comfortable with each other again?"

Carlos rolled his eyes, and then pings began sounding on the men's phones.

"And we have a signal, ladies and gentlemen!" Carlos said as he dialed Emmie's phone.

Reese looked down at his phone as text messages and missed phone-call alerts appeared on the screen. One from his brother Reynolds, urging him to reply to their mother's text messages about the Christmas party—he would have to call his brother later. He opened his mother's texts. One contained an attachment—a duplicate invitation to the party with the date and time circled along with the words, *Semiformal attire requested*. The blank space beside the words *Plus one* was also circled, glaringly awaiting a check to indicate that he was bringing a date. *Well*, he thought, *maybe I'll actually go this year.*

There was a voicemail from Rudy at the body shop. Reese returned that call. The estimated cost to repair the Tesla confirmed his original plan. He was more anxious than ever to get home and put it all into action.

The last item he needed to attend to was the sheriff's message. That call worried him. He regretted ever asking Marcus to check up on CC. He listened to the voicemail twice to be sure he'd heard it correctly, and then he called Marcus, growing increasingly unsettled with every word the man spoke.

"Set this up for me again. What happened in Chicago?" Reese asked.

"That Devon Peters guy refused to accept my word that CC was okay. He's stirring up all kinds of interest in finding her."

"CC doesn't want to see him. Doesn't that count for something?"

"Yes, but I'm just giving you a heads up. Guys like this, with cozy alliances with cops, have a way of getting what they want. If he wants to find CC, chances are he'll show up on your doorstep one day."

"Yeah? Well, let him come. There's no way on earth I'm letting him see her unless she says okay."

"Just be careful. You don't need more trouble, Reese, and whether innocently or not, this lady comes with more than a little."

Reese hated how Marcus was undoing the fragile peace Carlos had just restored. He wanted to hurl the phone and Marcus's advice as far away as possible. "Are we done here?"

"Sorry, Reese. I just felt you should know."

"Forget I ever asked you to check up on her. I'm a big boy, Marcus. I'll handle things myself from here on out."

"It's not that simple anymore."

Reese pressed the phone into his cheek, needing to hear every hated word.

"Once that ex filed the first missing person's report, detectives started digging into CC's life to find any place or person who might have information on her. That's how they found Nora Stubbert."

"So?"

"So other information might come forward also, and if something crosses my desk that makes me worry, I'm going to tell you, whether you like it or not."

Reese hung up, shoved the phone into his pocket, and kicked Admiral, sending the horse forward in a shot that jerked Nutmeg's neck, causing her to cry out. Gasping, he looked back and saw the poor mare stumbling and straining to catch her footing. He pulled Admiral to a halt, dismounted, and ran to the loyal mare as Carlos pulled up close on Warrior, with Spot tethered behind him.

"Is she all right?" Carlos asked, his voice worried with a critical edge.

Reese ran his hand over Nutmeg's neck and legs, and when he was sure nothing was broken, he wrapped his arms around the horse, burying his face in her neck. He was ashamed of himself for hurting the innocent animal and for asking Marcus to spy on CC. He wanted to strangle Devon, the cretin who refused to let her go.

Reese avoided Carlos's glare until he was finally back in the saddle, holding Nutmeg's lead in his hand instead of tied to his pommel.

"Wanna tell me what that was about?" Carlos said. "You nearly broke her neck."

"I know. I'm sorry." Reese couldn't stop seeing her stumble. "For a moment, I forgot she was tethered behind me. It was stupid."

"What's got you so knotted up? I haven't seen you like that since—"

Reese shot him a glance that stopped Carlos from mentioning the worst event of Reese's life. He was tired of being reminded of his greatest failures.

"Was it that phone call?"

"I don't want to talk about it." Reese settled Admiral and Nutmeg back into a steady gait. "I just want to get home as quickly as we can. And hold off on scheduling that getaway."

Carlos studied him until Reese surrendered a partial explanation. "I wish things were as simple as you made them seem, but they're just not. They're just not."

Reese heard CC's Christmas carols before he found her where Emmie told Carlos she'd be. He tethered the horses to the fence outside and carefully opened the back door, revealing CC sitting cross-legged in the deer stall, hands on her blue-jeaned knees with her back against the gate. Her blonde hair was plaited into two long pig tails that fell over her shoulders. The pan of feed was placed close before her, luring the doe near while CC softly sang "The First Noel." Reese marveled as the doe nibbled from the pan. She occasionally stretched her neck forward to sniff CC's hand and even lick her finger, while the fawn adjusted its footing to continue to nurse.

Reese was as entranced with CC as she was with the doe. The unscripted, private moment was a glimpse into her pure, gentle soul, and he felt both privileged and guilty for intruding. No report or muddled past with an ex-boyfriend could alter what the moment witnessed to him. She'd quickly wrangled his heart, leaving him schoolboy shy and ready to whoop at the same time. He'd never felt this way about Marissa or any other woman, and that realization felt like a lightning flash of clarity. He was falling for this woman he barely knew. He wanted to hop the gate, scoop her lanky frame into his arms, carry her inside his home, and kiss her. *Home.* Not a cattle shack or a corporate office. It had felt like home since CC's arrival.

He watched the doe stretch and sniff CC's hand. A tortured smile spread across the pigtailed beauty's face, garbling her carol. A smile carved Reese's own face as CC resisted the urge to laugh, as if knowing it would cause her to jiggle and likely end the precious moment. Her self-control paid off as the doe explored CC's hand, then her arm, and then her shoulder, ending near her chin with a sniff and a lick. That's when CC lost the fight to remain still. Her excitement broke loose in a giggle that sent the doe scurrying back several steps with her fawn leaping in its own skittering retreat. CC pushed the pan forward. "You earned it," she said, still smiling but now with a look of pure wonder and awe. "Thanks for trusting me, Noel."

"You named her Noel?"

CC turned with a start. "When did you get back? We were starting to worry. It's been four days."

"We hit some slow stretches."

"I'm glad you're back."

He saw pleasure in her eyes over his return, boosting his confidence. "Carlos called Emmie about a half an hour ago. She told him you were out here with the deer so we wouldn't bust in with the horses and ruin the moment."

"I did that on my own, but did you see how close she came?"

Her eyes lit up like a child's, and he knew that even though he could give her treasures from across the world, they'd hold little more value to her than this simple joy. "I did. It was amazing."

"And Dasher is starting to trust me as well."

"Dasher? I take it that's the fawn's name?"

"As of today." CC stood and tilted her head to the side as she leaned over the gate, eyeing Reese. "Exactly how long were you spying on me?"

He squished his face comically to diffuse the notion that his listening was spying. "Hmm . . . three carols ago?"

She blushed and covered her face with her hand.

"It was great!" Reese insisted with a laugh. "Really." He took one of her stained hands and rubbed his thumb over the chain she wore as a bracelet, enjoying how small yet strong her hand felt in his own. "Pretty. It goes well with the pine tar on your fingers."

CC chuckled. "Noel may have cozied up to me because I smell like her habitat."

"Then you've brought a little extra sense of home into two worlds. I saw what you've done to the house. It's beautiful. You've got a real eye for decorating."

"Thank you. It's one of my favorite parts of the holidays."

Reese knew he was studying her too intensely, paying more attention to the way her blue eyes dipped whenever the tiniest compliment was paid to her than to her response. He realized there was a lag in their conversation. He still held her hand. The last thing he wanted was to let it go, but he sensed a shift was required, either forward into greater closeness or back to the friend zone. Fortunately, CC provided a comfortable segue into the former.

"Did you accomplish everything you hoped to on your trip?"

"The steers are in the lower pasture, safe and sound."

"And your dragons?"

He did a quick search of the corners of his heart and found no glaring reservations there. "If not fully slain, they're at least in retreat."

She acknowledged his assessment with a thoughtful smile and a series of tiny nods. "Are Carlos and Emmie heading out on their trip tonight?"

"Uh . . . not right away. We've been gone longer than expected, so we've got to ride through the fields and check on the rest of the stock."

"I see."

"I didn't want to keep Carlos and Emmie apart any longer, so I told them I'd settled the horses in. I could use some help, and then we could work on getting this tar off your fingers."

"I'd like that."

He maintained his hold on her hand, pretending to steady her through the precarious terrain of the deer's straw-strewn pen and the dangerous walk down the sloshy sidewalk to where the horses were tethered. "I suppose you're going to need your hand back to lead the horses."

"I suppose so." CC blushed.

"I thought about you a lot on the trail ride. I imagined coming back home, knowing you were here."

She blushed again and tipped her head down as she gazed up at him from the corners of her eyes. "Did you imagine a girl who smelled of pine tar and straw?"

"Can't say that I did." He pushed his Stetson back and smiled at her. "Those were unexpected benefits."

They shared a nervous laugh that went on until it ran out of the restless energy fueling it. Reese noticed the bit of straw wedged into the strand of lumber-colored hair sweeping over her eye. He leaned closer to work the almost invisible bit out and found himself hovering an inch above CC's face. A list of clever lines passed through his mind, but all he wanted to ask was whether she'd mind if he kissed her. Wrestling over the moment became easier as she tilted her head up, placing her glossed lips so close he could smell their peppermint scent. He felt the sweet warmth of her breath and imagined the press of her lips, but as he calculated the slow descent to her mouth, the floodlights blazed on and the back door banged open.

Reese growled under his breath and jerked back as he and CC shielded their eyes from the blinding light. His free hand grabbed his hat and slapped it against his thigh. "Are you kidding me, Carlos?" he grumbled.

"Reese?" Carlos called out as he squinted into the darkness.

CC leaned her forehead against Reese's chest. He watched her shoulders shake and knew she was enjoying the agonizing humor of Carlos's timing.

He wrapped his arms around her and replied, "Yesss" without camouflaging his frustration.

"Is CC with you there by the horses?"

"I'm here," she called.

"Oh, man. Sorry. My apologies. Just forget I said anything."

Reese ran his hand over his face and groaned, knowing the mood and the moment were shot. "No. What did you need?"

"John Bigsby's on the phone. He wants to know if you're going to make it to the grange meeting tonight."

He closed his eyes and shook his head. "I forgot about that meeting." He groaned again and stroked CC's hair. "I'd cancel, but we're discussing the state's changes to the grazing rights. I need to be there."

CC looked up at Reese and shrugged. "Honoring your responsibilities is a very attractive quality in a man."

"Yeah?"

"Yeah."

He slid his Stetson back on his head and winked. "Okay, then," he said with renewed swagger.

"I mastered egg-gathering and stall-mucking this week. I'm still willing to expand my knowledge to horse-settling, if that would help."

"You're hired."

They spent the next hour rubbing the horses down and attending to their needs. CC didn't balk over the tedium and smells; rather, she took to the work as if she were born to ranching. Nothing could have pleased Reese more. Their conversation was limited because Reese preferred listening to the way CC cooed to the animals as she tended to them. From time to time, she'd catch him studying her over the back of one of the animals and she'd blush and smile back. The impact of those simple gestures sent waves of warmth through him, and he wondered if his face revealed what he was still unready to say. When the last horse was under a blanket and fed, Reese checked his watch and sighed.

"Is it time to go?" CC asked.

"Yep."

CC tugged on Nutmeg's blanket and left her hand there. "Will you be late?"

"Probably." Reese settled his own hand over hers. "We know what we need, but we can't seem to admit it without first spending an hour fighting about it."

CC chuckled over his explanation, and Reese wondered if she saw a similarity between the ranchers' dilemma and theirs, that knowing what they needed and admitting to it were two very different things.

A silent moment passed between them. CC pulled away until her hand slipped from Reese's. With a parting smile and a wave, she headed for the door. Reese wrapped his empty arms across Nutmeg's saddle and rested his chin in the center as he watched CC make her way. They had been so close . . . so close to seeing what might come from their crossed paths. But that would have to wait a little longer.

# CHAPTER TWELVE

CC LOOKED BACK AT REESE before closing the barn door. His puppy-dog eyes and lost-boy lean into Nutmeg added tender assurance that their almost-kiss had not been just a momentary whim. It and she mattered to Reese in some as-yet-undefined way. She tried not to overthink the moment or make more of the advance than it was, knowing that it may or may not be followed by a second. Oddly enough, the almost-kiss hadn't left her shaking or nervous. It had felt natural, comfortable, leaving her the happiest she'd felt in a very long time.

Emmie and Carlos were nowhere to be found, but a supper plate remained on the table, presumably for her, and she figured the couple were back in their suite and down for the night. She smiled at the thought of them being together without the crushing weight of Emmie's course load stressing her out. The house was peaceful and happy, and though CC considered waiting up for Reese's return, she decided against it and headed to bed to savor the memory of the evening's almost-kiss.

When she awoke and stretched, her first glimpse was of the annoying pine-tar stains on her hands. After a fifteen-minute internet search, she found several tips on removing the sticky brown stains. She headed for the kitchen and noticed that Reese was already up and out of the house. *All the better*, she thought as she pulled a jar of peanut butter and a canister of salt from the cupboard, along with a mixing bowl, in which she planned to mix portions of the ingredients to her online remedy. She scooped a big spoonful of peanut butter out as Reese appeared, six plus feet of swarthy, unapologetic cowboy dressed in jeans and a T-shirt, with his face still unshaven and his hair tousled and wet. CC felt a shiver zip through her, and for a moment, she forgot what she was doing.

"What are you up to?" Reese asked as he sauntered to her side.

Her nerves went on high alert with him so close, as his musky scent and thoughts of the almost-kiss sent possibilities and expectations roaring through her mind. She stumbled through an explanation of the plan. "It's a . . . a kitchen remedy," she said as she beat the spoon on the side of the bowl to get it to surrender the peanut butter. "A scrub to clean this . . . this blasted . . . tar off!"

Reese calmed the hand that slammed the spoon harder with each word. "Can I help? How much salt should I add?"

"Start pouring until I say when."

Reese did as he was told, following the next instruction to stir. A pasty brown goop soon formed, which he scooped up with his fingers and began working into CC's hands. "I've had considerable experience with pine tar. When I was a child, my brothers and I made forts in the hollow under the pine trees. I went home with sap on my hands and clothes and hair most days."

"Your poor mom."

CC noticed how Reese seemed to pause, considering her words. "I never really thought about it, but yeah . . . she had to have been a saint to put up with all of us and our antics."

His smile carried her away again to that soft and cozy place of welcome she loved. His touch was strong yet gentle as he massaged the scrub into her hands in steady circular patterns.

She began to feel as gooey as the paste. "You're very good at this," she said.

"Good enough to redeem me from that total fail last night?"

She glanced up at Reese. "First kisses are notoriously memorable for many reasons."

"I assure you that's not the memory I'd hoped to make."

CC struck a look of wide-eyed innocence, assuming a Southern accent and fluttering her lashes. "In that case, I'm afraid you have me at a disadvantage, kind sir. I have no idea to what you are referring."

"My ego and I appreciate you having our back."

CC felt Reese's warm breath move near her ear. "I could refresh your memory right here and now, but a first kiss should utilize two lips *and* two arms, and considering our current situation . . ." He raised his peanut-butter-goopy hands in the air.

"Uh-huh. Afraid you might have to tell your general practitioner how you got peanut butter in your ears?"

Another long look sent his lips back near her ear. "As fun as that sounds, I'll wait for a moment when kissing you won't require an embarrassing medical procedure."

She shivered and found him pleased by his impact on her. "Then, I suggest a total separation, where we each wash our *own* hands."

He laughed and said, "Understood," and he reached under the sink and pulled out the dish soap.

CC noticed that playful, silly Reese took a back seat to serious, responsible Reese, who returned as they washed their hands side by side.

"You do feel it too, don't you?" he asked. "This . . . this emotional tug between us?"

CC kept her eyes down as she answered, "Yes. I feel it." She worried that his silence implied disapproval. "It's not a bad thing, is it?" she asked.

Reese shoved his damp hands into his pockets. "No, but we've both admitted we're hauling around a lot of baggage. I think we should get to know each other better before this goes any further. I was going to check on the cattle today. Wanna come along?"

"You're on. I'll pack a couple of sandwiches while you ready the horses."

As CC was filling two thermoses, Carlos came out to the kitchen, hopping as he pulled his boots on.

"Did I hear Reese's voice? Oh, man! I overslept. Where is he? We were going to ride out and check the herd."

"I think I'm your replacement today."

His hopping ceased, and a smile spread across his face. "I see."

Her nervous heart took pleasure over his reaction to her news.

"Have him take you up by the falls. It's beautiful."

"Okay. Will you guys check on the deer?"

"We've gotcha covered, CC."

CC turned for the coatroom with her pack, tossing a "Thank you" over her shoulder.

The ride was beautiful and sweet. Their getting-to-know-you was accomplished less by words and more by simply becoming more comfortable with one another. A horn-torn steer turned their pleasant ride into a wrestling match as Reese struggled to cajole the wounded beast home. After patching up the injury, romance was the last thing on either of the exhausted pair's minds. They sank into the sofa like two lazy lumps. Reese gently pulled CC's head over to his shoulder, and he took her hand and brought it to his lips.

Saturday turned into a full cowboy workday requiring the men to hit the trail early and long to finally get around to checking the rest of the herd. By Saturday afternoon, CC heard a whoop from Emmie that preceded her careening into the kitchen.

"Carlos and I are finally cleared to get away! Do you think you can handle things around here for a few days?"

CC placed her hands in prayer position and bowed. "You've taught me well, Master." Then, with a laugh, she added, "Go get packed!"

Carlos burst through the door a few minutes later. "Reese is checking on the steers. He asked me to tell you he'd be up soon."

Emmie arrived, dressed in a black skirt and shimmery blue sweater and pulling a suitcase. She'd become proficient at styling her new cut, and CC stepped back and gave her friend an admiring, "Wow!"

"What did I tell you?" Carlos asked with the punctuated dramatics of a preacher at a pulpit. "My wife is total arm candy now, and I look like a scrub beside her. CC, can you give my hair a quick trim?"

"Isn't he the best?" an almost giddy Emmie asked, lapping up her husband's praise. She handed CC her case of tools and supplies.

"Happy to help, Carlos," CC said. "Have a seat."

Quick as a wink, CC had him seated on a barstool and draped.

"What look are we going for? Do you want me to simply clean up the back and sides, or do you want something new and stupid hot?" The slang her Chicago clients sometimes used to describe the look they wanted seemed ridiculous out here, and CC could barely get through the question without breaking into a laugh. Carlos quickly confirmed that.

"I'll stick with a stylin' clean-up. I was all about my swag fifteen or twenty years ago, when it was just me and my Zona boys tearing up the town, but I'm a respectable, married businessman now. Still young and cool"—he ran an invisible comb through his hair—"but respectable."

"You've still got your swag," Emmie said, sounding a notch above silly with her sweet Midwest voice and innocent manner.

"All that matters is that you think so." He gave Emmie a wink and turned back to CC. "But do something stylin' with this three-day-old beard."

"Got it. I'll dry-cut the sides and back and spritz you good before I work some magic on top."

The cut took under ten minutes, but she worked in some styling paste, which took his respectable haircut up a notch on the youthful scale. She also trimmed his beard. She laid down her clippers and picked up her brush to dust the loose hairs from his neck and collar when she saw Carlos's jagged, stained fingernails. The manicure took another twenty minutes. Reese came through the door as CC set her nail buffer down. When she lifted the drape off Carlos, Reese rolled his lips and nodded appreciatively.

Carlos stood and carried the cloth outside and, with the swagger of a bullfighter, gave it a shake to remove all the hair. When he returned inside, he looked at Reese and pointed to the seat.

"You're next, Reese. And, believe me, you're going to enjoy CC's magic."

Reese caught CC in his glance and raised a flirty eyebrow her way before replying to Carlos. "I'm sure I will, but I think I'll shower off some of this dirt first. You two have a fun trip. See you in a few days?"

"Hmm . . . maybe." Carlos chuckled and took Emmie's hand.

While Reese headed down the hall to the mudroom shower, Carlos picked up the couple's overnight bag with his free hand and leaned toward CC. "I hope you'll give Reese a chance. He's a bit of an odd duck, but he's a keeper."

The door closed behind the couple, and CC suddenly felt chilled by the awkward realization that she and Reese were alone in the house. She busied herself by sweeping the floor and cleaning all her tools. She smelled Reese's musky soap scent before she saw him from the corner of her eye, standing in a corner, fidgeting as if he needed instructions on how to proceed.

CC walked over to the stool Carlos had vacated, picked up her scissors, and waved her free hand toward the seat. "You wanted us to get to know each other better? How about we start with a friendly haircut? A cosmetologist's chair is much like a psychiatrist's couch. People tend to speak freely under my hands." She snipped the scissors three times in the air to punctuate her invitation.

"I talk, you talk?" Reese leaned back against the counter.

"Fifty-fifty."

"Deal." He raised one of his eyebrows. "What look do you suggest for a busted-up cowboy like me?"

With her lips pursed in thought and one eye squeezed half-shut, CC studied the man before her. The skin on her face prickled when she realized he was studying her equally. "I have to say I'm rather partial to your current untailored look. Are you willing to trust me?"

He smirked and raked his fingers through his damp hair, turning it into a wild dark mop as he ambled to the chair and sat down. "So long as we agree that mullets are off-limits."

"You're the boss." CC draped him in the sheet and began combing his hair. The clean scent of his evergreen shampoo floated up to her. She wasn't surprised. Fruity scents and urban colognes didn't fit Reese. He knew who he was and who he wasn't, and he surrounded himself with the essences of his world. She ran her fingers slowly and deliberately through his hair, telling herself she was simply figuring out his natural part and how his hair preferred to lay. It was partially true, but she also enjoyed the closeness to him as she watched how furrows grew between his closed eyes in response to every touch, as if he'd been famished from a lack of it.

"First question," Reese began.

"Make it a simple one. I've got a sharp object near your jugular."

"Easy peasy. Your favorite thing to wear?"

"Leggings and my Chicago Cubs hoodie."

"Okaaay." Reese drew the word out thoughtfully as if he were picturing her in the ensemble. "Did you bring them?"

"I did."

"I'd like to see that ensemble on you."

"That could be arranged. Your turn. Same question."

"Easy peasy," he repeated. "Old jeans, a T-shirt, and my boots."

"That doesn't sound comfortable."

"Didn't say most comfortable. I said favorite."

"Noted. My turn." She moved behind him and used her fingertips to tilt his head forward. Two tracks of muscles bulged along the back of his neck and into his shoulders. When she reached to capture a section of hair, she felt the tautness of those muscles, evidence of how hard he worked on this ranch he loved. "What's one thing you wish you knew more about?"

After a moment's thought, Reese answered, "Juan Ponce de León."

"The explorer?"

"I needed one more right answer to pass a multiple-choice test in fourth grade. I guessed and said that Sir Walter Raleigh was the explorer credited with reaching Florida, and I failed."

"And why has that scarred you?"

"I was held back that year, which caused a blow to my self-confidence while throwing me in with a bunch of younger rowdies who thought I was the coolest thing since sliced bread. That, in turn, caused me to overcompensate by becoming a class clown and overall rodeo-riding, football-spiking, dare-taking show-off, which changed everything in my life. Funny how your life can turn on such a small thing."

"All because of Ponce de León."

"Exactly. How about you?"

"Mine should be self-explanatory. How to drive a Tesla in snow."

Reese's head tipped slightly. "I'm kinda glad about the way things turned out."

The scissors froze in CC's hand, but she quickly returned to snipping away. "I'm not taking too much off—just enough off the ends to clear your collar—and I'm blending each layer into the next so you'll look professional and tidy when you need to." She didn't admit that she was leaving enough length so the wind could still tousle it in that way she loved.

Reese bent his head forward, and when he reached back to feel the length, his hand found hers. He slowly lifted his head to search for her, as if to acknowledge the connection. Their eyes held, consciously or unconsciously, and then he released her hand, cleared his throat, and faced forward again.

His fingers tapped on the chair's armrest in a nervous patter. "Do you like to read?" he asked in a voice that seemed far too weak and small for him.

CC swallowed past the tightness in her throat. Her response had its own curious squeak. "My father read me the classics each night: *Winnie the Pooh, Frog and Toad, Stewart Little*. Once I could read on my own, he picked up his favorites and we read side by side, with his nose buried in Dickens or Melville while mine was stuck in *Charlotte's Web, Anne of Green Gables*, or *The Chronicles of Narnia*."

Holding still, he said, "You can tell a lot about a person by the kind of stories they enjoy."

"What do my choices tell you?" she asked as she trimmed around his ears.

"I'd say that if you love those old classics, you probably love the beauty of words. In those books, good and truth win out over obstacles and injustice, so I'd say you value goodness and justice and loyalty, and you dream of a world where every little creature matters and has a voice."

CC believed he had actually read her soul. She froze in place with her scissors in midair as he turned back to face her.

He continued. "I'm not at all surprised that you'd mount an adventure like driving a Tesla across the Midwest, all to fulfill a loving father's unrealized wish."

She swallowed again. "Thank you."

The room seemed to spin around them, and her scissors felt foreign in her hands, as if she were holding them for the first time. Her mouth went dry, and she realized it was because it was open and drawing shallow breaths across her lips. She moved to the other side to trim around Reese's other ear, and he seemed happy to sit straight forward in silence as she worked.

Moments passed, until CC finally realized she was owed an answer or two. "And what about you? I assume you love books, or you wouldn't have asked me."

"Oh, I loved *stories* all right, but my favorites didn't come from the pages of a book. Don't get me wrong. Mom made us read every day, but she was so grateful to see us read anything that perusing the cereal box counted as reading time. But stories . . . now, that's another topic altogether. I already told you my grandpa told the best stories. He made some up—we loved those best—but some were his own lopsided retellings of *Treasure Island* or *The Swiss Family Robinson*. We were certain the authors' own stories weren't one iota better than Grandpa's."

CC combed a few last errant hairs into place and stepped back, noting a wistfulness to Reese's quiet countenance. He said, "I wish you could have met him."

His want saddened her, and she felt pained to have missed knowing someone of such importance to him. "I feel as though I have . . . through you."

Reese seemed to hang on to those words. "He would have taken to you."

"Why do you say that?"

"Because he was a lot like you. He valued goodness and justice and loyalty too."

Her skin prickled. She moved to stand directly in front of Reese. His knees brushed against her thighs, and she shivered, blaming it on a draft.

She reached for a section of hair that caused her arms to nearly encircle Reese's head. "I-I-I've lost track," she said as she made some cuts and hair fell to Reese's shoulders. "Whose turn is it to ask a question?"

"Yours." Reese leaned toward CC until their faces were mere inches apart, "but I have another topic queued up, if you don't mind." His jaw lowered until his lips parted, and when he finally spoke, his voice was deep and mellow, as if he already had his answer. "Your most life-changing moment."

CC mentally reran the question and knew how she wanted to answer, but she sensed the comment was rhetorical, something Reese was posing to himself as much as to her.

With tiny, almost imperceptible movements of his eyes, Reese studied her face as if he were mapping every freckle and curve and recording the subtle changes in her mood as emotions rose. His tender gaze bored straight into her, past her reservations, which melted away, welcoming him, inviting him to warm her lonely, hungry soul. She saw him swallow, and then she felt his hands slide around her waist. The hairs on her arms rose, and the scissors turned to lead in her hands. She wasn't sure whether she was falling or Reese was rising, and except for the scuff of the stool as he scooted it back, all CC heard was the thundering of her heart that contrasted with the slow draw of

Reese's breaths. She swung her arm to the counter to drop the scissors there, and then Reese lifted her up and set her next to them on the counter, placing her eye to eye with him.

He cradled her face in his large calloused hands and pressed his brow to hers as he completed his earlier thought. "I wasn't looking for this. I'm not even sure I'm ready for it, but I think you . . . this day . . . us here . . . this is my life-changing moment."

CC's eyes closed, and everything progressed by touch rather than by sight. His lips stroked lightly back and forth over her cheek as if he were brushing color on a canvas. The effect turned muscle to putty with each instinct-stirring, resolve-melting pass. CC's mind overloaded as she absorbed every thought and feeling his gentleness harrowed up. She wanted his soft caress to continue forever while also yearning to experience the feel of his lips on hers.

She found the strength to lift her arms. Her fingers found those rock-hard shoulders, inching along until they found his neck and jaw. She cupped her hands there, holding him close. He responded with a contented sigh that heightened her awareness of every sound, every inch of shared touch—her knees against his muscled abs, her forearms on his shoulders, the tips of her fingers riffling through the edges of his hair.

The last pass of his lips over her cheek brought him at last to her mouth, which was parted from the effort required to draw a full breath. He made tiny sweeps now, like the tickle of butterfly wings against her lips. Unable to bear the tease any longer, she pulled him closer, needing to feel the hard press of his mouth on hers. As if awaiting that very invitation, his fingers tightened against her back, pressing her to his chest in a million points of contact like a perfectly fitted puzzle piece. Nothing and no one had ever felt this right, this perfectly paired to her. She melted into him until there was no he or she but only them—one knotted tangle of warmth and gentleness and love.

And then he pulled back, his face flushed, his eyes heavy with passion and something else . . . worry.

And CC's heart burst into innumerable bits, like a piece of brittle crystal on a tile floor.

Reese wished he could turn his mind off, to enjoy the closeness of CC, to simply *feel* without measuring and weighing every word, every sensation, every thought. But he couldn't. The worry was always there, like a yardstick or a scale, measuring every new feeling for CC against his relationship with Marissa.

He couldn't identify the exact reason, whether it was from guilt for marrying a woman he'd never really loved and who'd never really loved him or whether it was the absolute terror that if such an anemic relationship could devastate him so fully for so many years, what could this beautiful, intuitive woman do to him? To his family?

He stepped back from the sweetness of CC's touch and warmth. He could still taste her scented lip gloss that now lined his own lips. Confusion filled her eyes. He had caused that. He longed to return to three seconds ago and fill his arms with the goodness of this soft, deer-loving woman who smelled of straw and peppermint and peanut butter.

He smiled at her and tried to fill the vacuum in his arms with her again, but she stiffened and asked, "What just happened?"

"It's complicated. I'm . . . complicated."

Her expression shifted from confused to stern. She was not ready to accept his lame, vague excuses.

They were microns apart physically but miles apart emotionally, and Reese felt the mounting weight of questions bearing down upon him and, worse, upon her. He again opened his arms to her, and she hopped off the counter and stepped into them timidly, more like that skittish doe than her vibrant, joyful self. She shivered in his arms, and he knew the time had come to get the answers they both needed and deserved.

He kissed her again, but she remained stiff and cool. He pulled back and nodded. "I'm the one with the issues, but you're the one getting hurt. It's time to talk."

CC took Reese's offered hand and followed him to the sofa, where they sat down facing one another. The glow and warmth of the almost-always-burning fire, combined with the twinkling lights strung along the mantel with the chains and pine garlands, should have been a perfect moment, but everything felt dark with her worry over the coming talk.

Reese leaned his elbow on the back of the sofa and said, "Before we bare our souls, you need to know your options. Rudy called about your car."

*The car.* CC braced at the reminder that she was only passing by on her way to deliver a car. She'd been welcomed into Reese's world as if a place had been waiting for her all along, but her original purpose now loomed like a guillotine about to sever her from Reese and all the possibilities she'd begun to imagine with him.

Her hands began to shake, and she clasped them together to still their motion. She had done what she vowed never to do after she left her foster mother's home—she had foolishly allowed herself to become attached—to Reese and to this place—and she'd left herself vulnerable to hurt.

She'd made a concerted effort to keep an emotional distance with Devon. She could see that now. Her hurt over their breakup had not been about getting her heart broken. It was about disruption . . . to her life, to her fragile sense of self, and to another home she'd had to leave because staying and seeing him with someone else would remind her of her aloneness. Devon had never had her heart to break, but she had already fantasized about giving it to Reese, and what had that gotten her? The worry, the fear in Reese's eyes told her he wasn't ready to offer her the same. Not now. Maybe not ever. He was a far better man than Devon, which meant the risk of loving him and not being loved in return was even higher if she held on.

"How much is the damage? When will it be ready for me to leave?"

Reese's face twisted in shock, and he fell back against the sofa. "Is that what you want?"

CC toyed with the silver chain on her wrist to avoid looking at him. "You knew I was expected to deliver the car in Vegas on Christmas Eve."

Reese leaned in again. "Can I at least tell you about an idea I have?"

She braced herself again.

"Rudy can make the car look better than new, but neither of us would feel good about delivering a repaired vehicle to your client. Besides, the accident report would show up if he ever tried to sell the car, and then there'd be all kinds of legal repercussions."

CC drew her head back. "Did you think I wasn't planning to tell him everything?"

"O-o-of course not. If I did, we wouldn't be having this conversation."

"I've done the math," CC said quietly. She thought she might cry right then and there, not just because of her debt but because this transactional conversation to review her "options" was Reese's first thought after shattering her with a pullback from their heart-melting, possibility-filled first kiss. "I know I owe Rudy for the repairs *and* the loss in the car's value."

"I have a plan," he said. "I ordered an exact duplicate of the car. It will be delivered to Rudy by the eighteenth, and he'll have it detailed by the twenty-first and delivered to the owner by the twenty-third. He'll handle all the transfers of titles and Vehicle Identification Numbers."

CC's eyes grew wider with each word until she finally said, "You did what?"

"Hear me out," Reese pled as his hands flew forward to calm CC.

"I have *two* Teslas now?"

"Only for a while. Rudy will make the crashed one so gorgeous that it'll sell for a great price."

CC didn't see a financial escape here, but she could see how the plan would help her deliver a perfect car to John Torino.

"There's one catch," Reese added. "Rudy can't float that kind of debt, so I'll pay him up front."

CC stiffened as the hint of romance she'd imagined moments earlier turned into debt and obligation. "What you're saying is that I'll be in debt to *you*?" Had this been his game all along? She leaned away from Reese. "No way. I pay my own way. I'm not going to be obligated to you or anyone else."

Reese sounded panicked as he rushed, "I-I-It's a loan, CC. Nothing more. A business arrangement to help you out. No strings. Just a loan."

CC's suspicions lessened as she considered the arrangement. She pointed at him with her index finger. "With interest!"

"Okay, if that's what you want. With interest. Awful, horrible interest, if you'd prefer."

He laughed, and her heart calmed. "I'm sorry," she said. "I just . . ."

"No, it was my fault. I'm sorry." He smiled at her, and she saw respect in his eyes, but the entire payoff plan was predicated on her leaving for Vegas. He seemed ready to let her go.

"But I do have a second plan. One I hope you'll find more appealing."

She noticed the nervous twitch at the corner of his mouth. "Rudy's college-age son could deliver the car to the owner and beat it back up here in time for Christmas breakfast with his family. You wouldn't have to go to Vegas at all."

CC's heart leapt at the opening, but she sat back and waited to hear more.

"We'll start calving in late January, and since you love animals so much, I wondered if you'd consider staying on . . . with Carlos and Emmie . . . a-a-and me."

"You want to *hire* me?" Her heart plummeted again.

Reese rubbed his hands over his face and groaned. "I'm totally botching this." He scooted closer and set his hands on his thighs as he leaned toward her. "Let me start again." His next exhale nearly drained his lungs. "The truth is I don't want you to go, CC. I'd do anything to make it possible for you to stay, if you want to, but that's not my call. So the first thing I need to know is . . . are you happy here?"

"As an employee?"

The blood drained from his face, and his shoulders sank. "I swear I can hold my own in a battle of wits with a dozen men, but put me one-on-one with a woman, especially one I care about, and I shut down like a tightwad's purse." He closed his eyes and took another deep breath. "I wasn't trying to interview you for a job. I wanted to give you a stake in staying here . . . in case you feel something between us too."

She finally saw a connection between the discussion of debt and their kiss. The normally stalwart man was a knot of nerves because he wanted her to stay!

He took CC's hands and looked into her face, as if begging her to hear his heart. "The world casually tosses around words like *love*. I don't. That word is sacred to me, one I don't say if I can't back it up with all the other words and promises that should go with it. I tried that once, but I got decimated and ended up dragging my family through the muck as well. I can't afford to be casual with my affections again. I need to truly know the next person I let into my life. What I can say in my behalf is that I try to be an honest gentleman, as old-school as that sounds. A man who owns up to his mistakes with the intent to do better going forward. My gut tells me not to let you leave here without at least asking you to give us a chance. I'd write a check to Rudy without blinking, but I know you're proud and independent, so I figured you'd turn me down flat. That's why I mentioned the job."

CC's fingers moved to the old watch chain on her wrist again. "I'd like to stay and see what might grow between us, but . . ." She paused and bit her lip. "Trust needs to go both ways. I've been more open with you than I've been with anyone besides my dad. I've told you all about my messy past, but I know almost nothing personal about you."

He nodded. "Fair enough, but let's fix something right from the start. You say I know about your messy past. Tell me something about your life that you're proud of."

The question made her self-conscious. "Like what?"

"I'm sure you could name many things." Reese looked down at her wrist. "I've noticed that whenever you're nervous or uncomfortable, you finger that chain. It must be very special to you. Tell me about that."

CC's neck shrank into her shoulders as she considered the request. "It's just an old pocket-watch chain. It's probably weird that I wear it like a piece of jewelry."

"Was it your father's?"

She shook her head as the giver's face returned to her.

"He must have been someone very special to you."

"He was actually a stranger. A man named Rick, who I only spoke to that day we met."

"When he gave you the chain?"

"It was a thank-you because I gave him a free haircut. He was a homeless guy who camped out in an alley near the salon. I probably passed by him a hundred times, never really paying attention to him until that day. Business was slow, and I was staring out the window when one of the other storeowners on the block sent him packing because he was bad for business. He was scrambling to gather his things. I'm embarrassed to admit that's when I finally looked at him . . . really looked at him for the first time, and I recognized him as one of my father's former navy buddies. I wanted to do something, but I didn't know *what*, so I invited him into the salon for a haircut and a shave."

"That was very kind of you."

"It was a simple thing that almost turned into a disaster. Nora was evidently having a really bad day. She took one look at him and turned as white as a ghost, as if he were contagious. I tried to explain his connection to my father so she'd welcome him, but all she saw was a dirty, smelly man standing in her spotless salon. She bolted out of the shop and drove away. I was so ashamed."

The day came back to her with gentle clarity: the way Rick had recognized her as her father's daughter and the pain she'd seen in his face at the connection to his past. She touched the links of the watch chain again. "He didn't say much, but I watched peace come over him as soon as the warm water touched him. A light returned to his face as the dirt fell away. When I was finished, he looked in the mirror and started to cry. He just kept saying, 'It's me . . . it's me,' as if he'd forgotten who he was."

"Like Emmie. That's incredible, CC."

"I took him to the thrift shop to buy him a clean outfit, and then he reached into his pocket and handed me his watch chain. He said it was all he had but he wanted to give me something as a thank-you. Then he said he was going home. I never saw him again."

She caught Reese staring at her as if he were seeing her anew, just as she'd seen that man for the first time. "You changed a life, CC. You may have *saved* his life."

"He just needed someone to help him remember who he really was."

"Is that what the chain does for you?"

She shrugged one shoulder and tipped her head to the right. "None of us should be defined by our last mistake." She lifted her arm and shook her wrist, making the chain jiggle. "It helps me remember that when I forget."

"Thanks for sharing that." Reese sighed. "I hope I remember that myself. You're a pretty amazing woman, CC Cipollini." CC blushed and dipped her head, but Reese tipped her chin up to meet his eyes. "It's my turn to answer a few questions, but could we hold that conversation off until tomorrow? I need tonight to piece my thoughts together, and then there's something I need to do in the morning before we talk. Will you be patient with me a little longer?"

CC gave that a moment's thought and said, "Of course."

"Thank you." He stood and pulled her to her feet. "I also need to get a few things from my closet. Give me a few minutes, and then I think it's best if we both turn in and start fresh in the morning. Thank you for trusting me, CC. Goodnight."

He pulled her close and placed a gentle kiss on her brow. The warmth of it stayed with her as Reese left and headed to the bedroom. She heard a click from the bedroom door that led to the mudroom, and then water began to run. She assumed Reese was in the bathroom cleaning up, and she took that as her own clue to turn in.

The next morning was Sunday. She awoke marveling at how her world had changed in the week since the crash. Reese came immediately to her mind. She heard the garage door open, and as his truck headed down the lane, she wondered over the errand he needed to attend to before their talk.

She dug through her suitcase and pulled out her favorite leggings and her Chicago Cubs hoodie. She made muffins so there'd be something ready for Reese when he returned from wherever he'd gone, and then she headed to the barn to tend to the animals so nothing could distract him from their promised talk.

She heard his truck pull up, and she waited a few minutes so he didn't feel pounced on. When she left the barn, she found him heading her way, handsomely groomed from her cut the night before, but his beard was also groomed, and a new peace radiated from his eyes.

He extended his hand to her, and she took it as he led her back into the house. CC moved into the mudroom to hang her coat and scarf and noted the approving smile that crinkled Reese's eyes as he scanned her leggings and hoodie and retook her hand. Still silent, he moved to the great room and sat in the corner of the sofa, pulling her down and close against him until her back rested against his chest. His arm draped across her, holding her hand, and then he asked, "What do you want to know?"

"Let's start where we left off. Tell me the choice that most impacted your life."

"I don't talk about it much, but since you seem to have a soft spot for the military . . ."

CC turned around. "You're going to tell me about Iraq?"

He nodded and fingered one of her pigtails as she relaxed once more against him. "I don't know about Illinois, but Utah is a land of God, family, and country. Some of my high school friends signed up for a deferred enlistment after graduation. They talked so much smack about being soldiers and how I wasn't. They knew I had a sweet life all teed up and waiting for me."

"You sound bitter about that."

"I was prideful. It would have been a great life . . . college, some sort of community or volunteer service, and then a spot working with my father."

Surprised, she turned back around so she was facing him. "You were planning on doing volunteer service?"

"Yep. Remember I told you how my great-great-grandfather Henry's partner, Oswald, just handed his share of the mine over after his wife died?"

"Yes. Poor Mary."

"That's right. Well, Henry Brockbank was a church-going man, and that day, he promised God that if the mine ever became profitable, he'd show his gratitude to Oswald and to God by serving others wherever he was called, and he kept that promise. After he hit his first vein, he boarded up the mine and had a talk with his bishop about what service he could offer. A few weeks later, he headed to Mexico to serve the people there for two years. Then he returned to Utah, married, and started his own family. He taught his children to give a tithe of their time in gratitude for the good life they'd been blessed to know. Since then most Brockbank men and women have spent a portion of their lives serving others. Some make large cash donations and sit on the boards of charitable organizations across the globe, some have joined the Peace Corps, and many have volunteered to serve across the world."

CC thought she heard a touch of melancholy in Reese's voice. "That's a beautiful legacy. You should be proud of that, not embarrassed by it."

He offered one sad chuckle. "Thank you. I'd like to think time and experience have strengthened my faith. What about you? Do you believe in God?"

"My dad and I were in the right aisle, third pew at Saint Elizabeth's every Sunday."

"And after he died?"

"Not so much, I'm sad to say, but this chat isn't supposed to be about me. It's your turn to talk. What kind of service did you choose?"

Reese's jaw shifted left and right. "That was my first failure. The other boys needed the military to help with college or just to be sure they'd have a future. I felt privileged and out of the club, so one day I drove into Brisbane and enlisted without thinking about the ripple effects my decision would have."

CC turned again and settled back against Reese's chest, awaiting an explanation of the other failure she felt sure was still troubling him.

Reese heaved a sigh. "My mom cried, and my father barreled down to the recruiting office to make them tear up my enlistment until we had time to talk, but I'd waited a week to tell them, and it was already in process. By then their oldest son was already a recruit to the army."

"Military service is noble."

"I think so, and I told God I'd do more when my enlistment was up, but life got more complicated than I expected."

CC looked up into his face. "When you married Marissa. I figured that was the choice that most changed your life."

"That was number two."

"How long were you married?"

"Six years, give or take five." He chuckled, but there was no humor in it. "I swore I'd never get tangled up with another woman, and then you crashed into my world."

"That makes two of us, because I swore I'd never get attached to another man, and then you rushed over in my hour of need . . . because that's what you do. You protect people."

He shook the compliment off. "So where do two crazy-about-each-other people who've sworn off love go from here?"

CC rose to her knees and placed her hands on Reese's shoulders. "Forward. But slowly."

"Are you saying you'll stay?" Reese's hands move around her ribcage.

She leaned in until her lips hovered an inch from Reese's. "At least long enough to see why fate brought two disasters like us together."

"Carlos said on the trail ride that maybe it takes all we go through—the good, the hurts, even the failures—to make us ready when the right person comes along."

Reese drifted closer, and his voice became more gravelly with every word, until CC closed the final distance between them. The initial touch of the intended gentle kiss was like fuel on a fire, deepening the moment and heating up quickly. CC felt her breathing alter into shallow pants and her heart thunder until the blood rushing through her brain seemed to wash away all reason. Reese's fingers tightened around her, pulling her closer, and between kisses, the same wary want she felt clouded his countenance. Their eyes met in a panicked flash, as if each was seeking confirmation from the other before the last thread of sensibility fled. It was all happening too fast and too recklessly. They pulled back simultaneously in a breathless escape.

Reese scrambled off the sofa and paced in a tight circle as his hands raked through his disheveled hair. "What time is it?"

Dazed by the question, CC cleared her mind and glanced at the clock. "Twelve thirty."

Relief brightened his face. "I don't know about you, but I could use some air."

"Definitely."

"Grab your coat. I'll grab my hat. Let's get out of here for a while."

Reese walked her through the stand of pines to a trail that wound deeper into the woods. They walked for hours, breaking the pleasant silence with laughter over CC's work tales from the gangster club where she once worked. They held on to one another and kept the conversation light until they were both famished and ready for food. Reese made a fire in the pit behind the house and grabbed hotdogs, buns, and sticks from inside. They purposely burned through the day and into the night until a good-night kiss was enough to finish off a perfect, slow-and-steady day.

# CHAPTER THIRTEEN

Reese brought CC to an abrupt awakening by banging a pot outside the bedroom door.

"Rise and shine, sleepyhead."

CC cracked the door open and peered at him through the slits of her still-sleepy eyes. "The sun isn't even up."

"Exactly!"

Reese held out a coat for her to put over her T-shirt and sleeping pants and helped slide her heavy arms into the sleeves.

"I know I'm your employee, but don't I have workers' rights or something?" CC argued through smiling lips.

"You have been chosen to be my employee of the month, and this is your reward."

Reese's excitement penetrated CC's fatigue, and she followed along more willingly. The truck was running and warm, and big quilts were packed in back, along with a basket she hoped had a hot thermos. They drove through the darkness to a mountain ridge that overlooked the bowl that was the east valley. The first blazes of sunlight were beginning to stream over the east-facing wall of the Rockies. Reese hurried CC out of the truck and into the vehicle's bed, spread with enough quilts to keep them warm and comfortable. CC scrambled in and sat with her back against the rear window and under the old red quilt. Reese poured steaming cups of hot chocolate, pulled out her previously baked muffins, and sat back beside her to watch nature's light show.

CC grabbed his arm and set her head on his shoulder. "Thank you for this."

"Anything for the employee of the month."

CC tucked the memory into her heart, underscoring it with Reese's excitement over giving her another glimpse of his world. The two returned to the ranch with a day filled with chores ahead. CC didn't mind. This life suited her. Working beside Reese suited her, and being tired was a good diversion from any worries she may have had.

They fixed a simple supper and sat on the sofa, intending to share a movie, but once again, things heated up fast. This time it was CC who leapt off the sofa, asking, "What's the nightlife like around here?" In less than five minutes they were in the truck, headed for Brisbane.

They passed few lights or signs of life on the twenty-minute ride to the ranch's nearest town. CC recognized that the small town was the only hub on a wheel of distant, sprawling farms and ranches. The town boasted a small L-shaped strip center anchored by a small Walmart with a few other local businesses spread left and right, two of which were silver shops. Rudy's Garage, the sheriff's office, a few eateries, and some municipal buildings, like a town hall and library, were the major structures, other than two schools and an urgent care. Christmas banners flew from the light poles down Main Street, and most of the business fronts were decorated with lights, garlands, or both. A large evergreen growing in a tiny plot of land called Vest-Pocket Park was decked out in full Christmas regalia. Every business with a light burning had several cars parked out front.

CC found the place charming.

Reese parked the truck in front of a single structure—a rustic-looking diner called Big Jim's. He got out, walked around the truck, opened CC's door, and offered her his hand.

After gawking at the ancient-looking wood siding and curling cedar shingles on the roof, she pointed to the establishment's sign. "Is Big Jim the owner of this little hovel?"

"I realize the decor looks like a trapper's cabin, but that's because it's named for the famous mountain man Jim Bridger."

"What do they serve here? Buffalo?"

"I didn't bring us here for the food . . . but as a matter of fact . . ."

CC withdrew her hand and slid deeper into the truck cab.

He laughed, extending his hand to her again. "They've got great burgers, but I think what we really need is their entertainment. Big Jim's is a great place to work off stress."

"That's less comforting than the buffalo joke." CC winced until her eyes were nearly closed as she imagined burly, bearded men singing karaoke or, worse, dancing shirtless for the local ladies. "I shudder at the very thought of what local entertainment is featured here."

"Come. You'll see."

They walked into the establishment, and all eyes were on them.

"Hey, Reese!" one young man called. "Who's the filly?"

"Sorry, Rager. This is a woman. Evidently, you need to get into town more."

Laughter erupted throughout the place. Reese tipped his hat to the crowd and proudly led CC to the back of the room, where a cardboard sign that read *Axe Room* hung over the doorway. The table nearest the door was filled by a few thirtyish-year-old men who were not joining in the friendly banter Reese and CC's arrival had stirred. Instead, they seemed perturbed by it.

One of the men rose and shuffled into the doorway of the Axe Room, blocking the entrance as soon as he realized that was where Reese was headed. "I'll throw against you, Reese," he said with an alcohol-induced smirk.

"Another time. I brought my own challenger."

"So I see." He turned to his equally inebriated friends. "Start the clock, boys! Let's see how long this mail-order bride hangs around." The man laughed at his own joke and looked to his friends who were yukking it up as well.

Reese stepped in front of CC, placing himself between her and the man. "That'll be enough, Kernan."

It wounded CC to watch the scene. Reese stood noble and still as he endured the abuse, never raising a hand. It was obvious to anyone with eyes that Reese could pound the guy into the ground, but his petty harasser seemed to know he wouldn't.

Kernan peered around Reese to where CC was standing. "Where'd you find this one? Russia? Syria? North Korea?"

The room grew silent and the mood heavy as all eyes fell on the trio. Reese stepped closer, chest forward, with his hands fisted. "You can jab at me all you want, Kernan, but not her." His tone became menacing, sending chills zipping up and down CC's spine.

The blood drained from the smaller man's face, taking his bravado with it. Reese stood like a stone wall, his superior size and dignified will his only weapons, but they were enough. Kernan returned to his table after sputtering a few final insults.

Reese ushered CC through the doorway, but the altercation had clearly dampened the evening's earlier playful mood. "Sorry you had to witness that."

CC stopped and turned. "What was that all about?"

"Long story. That narrow-minded herd of yahoos thinks harassing me is their patriotic duty. Do you want me to take you home?"

"No way," she protested with a smile. "I'm not letting you off the hook that easily. And what were those guys' names again? Rager? Kernan? I'm feeling much better about my own name now."

The serious set of his mouth relaxed into that playful smile CC loved. "Then, my work here is done."

Reese turned as if he were leaving, but CC grabbed his hand and yanked him back in. "Hardly, sodbuster. I'm intrigued about this de-stressing technique."

Reese hooted. "I'm a cattleman, city girl. That's the exact opposite of a sodbuster."

"Not to these Chicago eyes, country boy."

Reese kept chuckling as he guided her farther into the long dark room shaped like a bowling alley, except instead of having wood floors and pins at the end, each lane's floor was made of packed sawdust and the walls were formed of thick wood planks.

A crosscut slice of a tree with a four-ringed bullseye painted on it hung at the end of each lane. Each ring had a point value from one to four. The red center circle was labeled with a six. CC looked to her left and saw a few dozen axes lying on a table, and she realized the place was a takeoff of the newest date rage. She clapped her hands. "Yes! An axe-throwing place!" She bent her arms to show off her muscles.

"Yeah." He sounded disappointed by her answer. "Don't tell me you've done this before?"

"I haven't, but I've heard about it. I'm excited!"

He bent close and began rolling up his shirt sleeves. "Okay, city girl. Let's see what you've got!"

The game's attendant, a man named Jedd, according to his nametag, sat on a barstool in a corner, behind a counter that held a small cash box and a stack of forms. After saying hello to Reese, he carded CC to verify her age, gave each of them a breathalyzer test to ensure that they were alert enough to handle the equipment safely, and then went over the legal release form and safety precautions, which CC summed up with a succinct, "Don't throw at humans, and don't lop off your own foot. Got it."

The attendant laughed, and Reese gave CC a proud little wink as he led her to their alley. He placed an axe in her hand. "There's a technique to this. If you don't get a good arc and spiral, your blade will just bounce off the target.

I'll demonstrate." He threw the axe one-handed and with perfect precision, but his stellar technique drew CC's attention to elements inconsequential to the art of axe-throwing—how his snugly fit knitted shirt moved across his shoulders, the rugged beauty of his strong work-worn hands, and the intensity of his blue eyes as he willed the blade into the wood.

"Did you see that?" He cheered.

"Uh-huh." This de-stressing plan was having a reverse effect on her.

"Now you try. It's all in the wrist."

Decapitation seemed to be a real threat as CC lifted the axe beside her ear.

"Now, flex your wrist and let it fly."

"Uh-huh," she answered, and with a flick of her wrist, the blade bounced off the very bottom of the target, landing three feet back from the bullseye.

"It's okay," Reese said, though his furrowed brow indicated otherwise. He moved behind her and wrapped one arm around her middle. "Tighten your back and core," he whispered beside her ear. "Let me check your grip." His other hand wrapped over hers as she held the axe. His warm breath caressed her cheek. CC melted into him. She doubted she could hold the axe much longer, let alone find the fortitude to hurl the blasted thing.

She turned and looked at Reese, whose half-closed eyes were fixed on her mouth as if he were measuring the distance from where he was to where he'd like to be. "I don't think it's working," she said.

"What?" he mumbled.

"This de-stress plan."

"No kidding. Maybe we each need our own lane." Reese straightened and unwound his hand from hers, and then he reluctantly slipped his arm from around her waist. Without a word, he picked up an axe and groaned as he hurled the thing so hard that he cracked the bullseye. He sighed deep and low. "Ahh . . . that felt good. You try. Put everything into it. Just let it all go."

CC grabbed the handle with two hands and bent her elbows by her ears. She gave two quick flicks of her wrist, and on the third, she bore down and grunted, throwing the axe with every pound of weight and every ounce of frustration in her. It sailed into the wood and stuck near the outer edge. She jumped for joy, and Reese picked her up and cheered.

"It felt good, right?" He beamed a smile of pure pride and happiness.

"It did! It really did."

He set her down, and she slumped into one hip and said, "You're very good at this. I take it you come here a lot."

"Unfortunately, yes . . ." He drew the word out and gave her a half-smile.

"That's a lot of stress. But did you ever have so much stress that you threw the axe hard enough to split the target before?"

A devilish, crooked smile slowly spread across Reese's face, drawing his right cheek up close to his eye. "Not until tonight."

CC chuckled. "Good."

They ate burgers and threw for about an hour, until Reese's shirt was damp with sweat and CC had a respectable glow from exertion.

"Ready to head back?" Reese asked.

"Yes, but I might need a chiropractor."

Reese set his hands on her shoulders and gave them a little massage. Everything turned to jelly under his touch—her shoulders, her knees, her eyelids that drooped sleepily. "You'd better stop, or you'll be carrying me to the truck."

"I'd be happy to oblige," he said with a wink, "but I don't want to make you wait around while I settle the bill." He clicked buttons on the truck's key fob and handed the keys to CC. "The truck is warming up. Why don't you head out? I'll just be a minute."

"Okay, then. See you outside." With a wave, she headed through the doorway and back into the establishment's main dining area.

Out of the corners of her eyes she saw the evening's earlier nuisances leaving their seats to follow her as she made her way to the front door. All the clever put-downs she'd refined to ward off creepers in Chicago returned to her. She didn't know what history Reese shared with these two Neanderthals that made him willing to suffer their verbal assaults, but she didn't plan to take any of their garbage. She stopped and spun on the two men.

"*Do svidaniya*," Kernan said with a laugh. His words were badly slurred by his drinking.

CC recognized the popular Russian phrase for goodbye and wondered why the jerk was referring to her as if she weren't American. Her ire subdued as she saw his current state. "I'm sorry. What did you say?" she asked as sweetly as she could.

Her kindness appeared to disarm the man, who'd come poised for protest, not thoughtfulness. He looked to his friend, who seemed as momentarily startled as he was, and then regrouped, straightening and saying, "I said goodbye to you in your native tongue, spy."

"My native tongue? Oh, that would be English. See, I'm from Chicago, which is in America. And back there, we say, '*Goodbye.*'" She drew the word out long and slow, exaggerating every letter, as if he were three. She wound up the exercise with another bright smile. "Now you try."

The man turned red and angry as his finger came forward with a jab in her direction. "I know how to say goodbye in English, lady. Are you too stupid to realize that I'm calling you a Soviet spy? Everyone around here knows Reese is partial to the enemy."

CC had no idea what the man was talking about, but she was tired of playing nice. She stepped forward and jutted her chin at the man, addressing him with a snarl. "I don't know why he endures your small-mindedness, but be grateful he does. I feel sorry for you if cutting down a good man like Reese makes you feel less inadequate."

A woman at a nearby table stood and began applauding CC's comment with a slow and steady clap that others joined. When the man felt the tide of support shift away from him, he made a quick exit out the door.

Reese appeared and was by CC's side in several hurried, long strides. "Are you all right?" He headed out the door as if to chase the man down. "If he so much as touched you, I'll—"

"He was all talk," CC interjected quickly, grabbing his arm. "Let's just head home."

"You'd better keep this one, Reese," the clapping woman called out. "She just fried Kernan's bacon for you."

Reese took CC's arms tenderly and peered into her face. "I'm so sorry about all this."

"I'm fine. I promise." She slid her arm around him, and he wrapped his across her shoulders.

"But you need some answers."

"Yes."

"No more sidestepping the truth. I'll answer all your questions when we get home."

He helped her with her coat, and they headed out into the cold. When he turned on the radio, CC was glad to have it fill the silence. He was lost in his own thoughts, and she was busy mulling over everything Kernan had said, figuring it had something to do with Reese's time in the military.

They got home and hung their coats. Without a word, Reese led her back to the sofa and asked her to sit while he stoked the fire. CC studied his face as he poked the smoldering logs that shot red-hot sparks into the air. His face was taut and somber, and she regretted the loss of his playfulness. They were like a pendulum, swinging from serious to silly and back again.

She worried the coming conversation would leave them stuck in that serious place and unable to get back to the joy.

He sat down and began toying with CC's pigtail, as he had earlier.

"So?" CC said tentatively. "What happened back there? Why did Kernan call me a spy?"

"Because that's what he told people Marissa was."

The answer stunned her at first, but she could see that the label still angered Reese.

"It all goes back to Iraq. My commanders in the army realized I was a good shot, good at obeying orders, good at taking initiative—all skills my grandpa taught me, things that made a good leader—so I was promoted in theater. They eventually discovered I also had a knack for languages. So did Carlos. That's how we met, and we became instant brothers. He could pass for a local fairly easily, and I had dark hair and tanned well enough to blend in too, so they taught us enough Afghan Persian to get by and sent us into the villages to gain the trust of the people and establish some informants. A teacher in Fallujah was getting harassed and threatened for teaching young girls. I told her I admired her courage, and I eventually earned her trust. She had gone to Oxford with the hope of coming back to Iraq and lifting her people, but things had gotten so bad there that her first priority shifted to simply saving her family. She became my first informant."

He leaned his head back and stared at the ceiling. "The military told me I could promise her entire family asylum in the US if she identified key insurgents. She jumped at the opportunity initially, until she found out that her brother was on our list of rebels. She defended him and swore he only joined the rebels because allegiance to the insurgents provided the best chance of saving his family. He was the oldest son. Saving his family was his priority, so when he found out that his sister was an informant for the Americans, he was ready to turn her in, willing to sacrifice her in order to prove his loyalty to the rebels and prevent the murder of the rest of his family."

CC watched how the horror of the memory pulled at Reese's mouth. Her own heart pounded as a new realization hit her. "His sister was Marissa?"

Reese pressed his lips together and nodded. "Marissa is the westernized version of her Muslim name." The admission seemed to drain Reese, and he went silent for several long seconds before he continued.

"I got to her brother before he had a chance to turn her in, but the whole scene grew frantic enough to raise a stir. Carlos and I rushed her back to base camp to keep her safe, and then we returned to the city to get her family, but our truck was attacked." He touched his pocked left cheek. "Carlos pulled me to safety. He saved my life."

CC also touched Reese's cheek. "You almost died? Oh, Reese. No wonder you and Carlos are like brothers. What happened to Marissa's family after the accident?"

"Her brother wasn't a rebel by ideology, but regardless of his reasons, that rebel affiliation made the family ineligible for immigration to the US. I could understand the concerns, but without a visa, Marissa was stuck, and staying in Iraq meant she was dead. I lay in a field hospital hating myself because I had failed her . . . lied to her."

"But you didn't know about her brother."

"Neither did she until that day. But I had put her in greater danger, so I did the one thing I could to increase her chances of being cleared."

It all made sense now. "You married her."

"Yes." As soon as the word left Reese's lips, he inhaled long and low in a ragged breath.

CC felt as if the air and light and peace in the room had sucked inward with Reese's breath, like those clips of bombs that implode and then release with devastating force and consequence.

Reese continued. "Culturally, it would have been better for her to die as a martyr than to marry a Christian man. And then there's my dilemma. Like Marissa, my plan was to marry a woman who shared my beliefs, but in that moment, we threw out our playbooks and did what we could to keep her alive."

"Did you love her?"

The ensuing pause said more than his answer. "There are many aspects of love—the desire to protect, to provide, to honor promises. I felt those things powerfully."

"What you did was noble."

"My intent might have been. I was out of my mind with worry for her, but how I handled things? That was all pride. I risked insubordination, even my career, making calls and shaking trees until someone promised to get her and her family out of country."

"How is that about pride?"

"Because . . . call it what you will—intuition, the Holy Spirit, my parents' teachings—I heard a voice screaming in my head, telling me to call my parents for their advice, but I refused to follow that counsel because I wanted to fix my mistake myself."

CC didn't know how to comfort him when he seemed determined to refuse her every attempt. She stared at her hands and waited for him to go on.

"My parents always seem to do the right thing, and they know powerful people. They could have helped me solve the problem or at least helped me see where I was headed. But I didn't want their help. I created the situation, and I thought being a man meant finding my own solution."

"War created that situation. You were a victim too."

"My choices exacerbated our problems. I had no idea what toll our religious and cultural differences would have on us. I forfeited everything that mattered to me. I abandoned the religious principles that had guided my life, and I put Marissa in the untenable position of breaking the sacred promises she'd made to God."

He closed his eyes and ran a hand through his tangled hair. "Germany agreed to take them in as my family members. We were married on a Monday, and she and six of her family members were on a plane to Ramstein two days later. All my screaming managed to get them housing on the American base there."

"Her brother too?"

He swallowed and shook his head. "He never left Iraq. A week later, I was declared partially deaf in my left ear and honorably discharged, but in truth, I think they were glad to be rid of me."

"Did you also go to Germany?" CC asked.

"At first. I was twenty-three, unemployed, and married to a woman I barely knew, who had a family member who had been labeled a terrorist." He gave a sad laugh. "We realized our actions were going to affect everyone we loved. Marissa was willing to do anything to protect her family, so I planned to extricate myself from my own to protect them. I headed to Germany and called my parents from there."

CC remembered the unflattering way Emmie had described the Brockbanks. "How'd that go?"

"They lost it initially, but then they told me they loved me, and they persuaded me to slow down and not make any more impulsive decisions. They begged me to come home so they could help me sort things out."

CC's view of his family changed to admirable. "And you agreed?"

"Not at first, but eventually. I owe them everything for standing by me . . . because things got ugly. I told Marissa I could either go home and build up a little ranch for us or stay in Germany and build a life with her there. She sent me home so I could keep working with Immigration to get her to the US. I bought land from my family and began with a few dozen head of cattle. I lived in a trailer on the property while I worked with an architect to design a home where she and her family and I could be happy. I designed that loft as a prayer space for her father."

Now CC understood. The loft was a gift. A show of respect. Reese continued to amaze her.

"It took nearly six years for their request for immigration to be approved. At first, I was flying to Germany every two months, but it was impossible to care for a ranch and be gone that much. The time between visits grew longer and the calls grew more infrequent and uncomfortable as more change came to her family. Her brothers returned to Iraq, her sister married an Iraqi man who treated her like property, and her parents blamed me for ruining all their lives. By the time Marissa and her parents finally arrived in the states, the house was built and the ranch was thriving, but we were little more than polite strangers moving around in it."

"I'm so sorry."

"A newspaper article about émigrés welcomed the state's newest Americans. Marissa and her family were listed, along with their country of origin and my name. The Brockbank name put a spotlight on Marissa, and that jerk you met tonight, Kernan, saw an opportunity to refuel an old grudge."

"Against you?"

"Against my whole family. His father was once a Silver Buckle shift boss, but decisions he made got men hurt, so my folks let him go years ago. As you can guess, jobs in this area are few, and his family has hated us since. Kernan runs a blog he calls patriotic, but his followers are hate-mongers who wrap themselves in the flag while desecrating everything it stands for. He plastered his social media with innuendoes and accusations that drew some journalist's attention. When the reporter started digging, he found out about Marissa's brother, and horrible rumors began swirling about Marissa, her family, me and my family, and even my family's business. They implied we were using the profits from the mine to fund terrorists."

"I hope you sued him."

"We did, and we won, but the damage was already done. That's why I hate social media. It's trial by keyboard, where people can broadcast lies to a wide audience. Their followers lock onto a lie and accept it as truth without anything but an accusation to back it up."

"And the retraction is never as loud as the lie. I hope you were awarded a big settlement."

"Zero. Dad didn't want to hurt Kernan's parents. He just wanted vindication."

"But Kernan—"

"I know. The loss in court didn't hurt him badly enough to stop him from continuing on with the snide comments and the haranguing. I've had to learn to ignore him."

"And what happened with Marissa?"

"I came home one day, and her bags were packed. She handed me divorce papers drawn up by an Oxford friend of hers living in D.C. She said we needed to face the truth that she married me out of need and I married her out of guilt. That the only real love either of us felt was for our families, and it was time for us to both move on." He puffed his cheeks with air and blew it out. "She left, and I've never heard from her since."

"I'm . . . so sorry."

"She was right. We were never in love. She was as miserable as I was."

CC leaned into Reese. "How are things with your family now?"

He shrugged. "All right."

"Are you close to them again?"

"My parents battened down the hatches a bit on my younger brothers after they saw what a mess I'd made out of my life and theirs. Time and again, they've all proven how much they love me, that they would risk everything to save me. Whatever distance exists between us is on me. I can't forgive myself for what I put them through, and I hang back to keep a buffer between them and any prejudice still aimed my way. That's why I'm so cautious about relationships. I've hardly dated since my divorce, and those few dates were with women I grew up with. And then you arrived, and now I'm rethinking everything."

CC laid her head on Reese's shoulder. "I understand all those feelings. I've pushed people away to protect myself too."

"Like Devon?"

"Everyone. Especially Devon. Although, in his case, I was right not to trust him."

"Any regrets or unfinished business there?"

"Nope. I've never been happier than I am right now."

"Me neither. And if this is the happiest we've ever been, then I suppose neither of us has ever really been in love before."

CC gave that deduction some thought. "Lucky thing, because I hear you never get over your first real love."

Reese laid his cheek beside hers and whispered, "I hope we get the chance to put that theory to the test."

His fingers slid across her jaw in a velvet touch, turning her head as his mouth migrated along her cheek, finding hers. The first kiss spread a love-filled warmth throughout her. It lingered long after the second and third coalesced into one long, delicious burn sustained by every gentle touch and glance that followed. The crash-and-burn abandon of their earlier kiss had wrung them out and left them doubt-filled. They ended this kiss knowing they were becoming a couple with time and endless possibilities.

Reese came back to her for a final long kiss. "We can't ignore the fact that you and I becoming *us* does raise new worries."

"Such as?"

"Let's just say I probably oughta bunk in the barn tonight."

"No need. First of all, you're a good man, and I trust you."

"Thank you. I'm trying to be, but it isn't easy. And second?"

"That bedroom door and lock could hold off a zombie apocalypse."

"Thank heaven for good hardware."

# CHAPTER FOURTEEN

REESE BOLTED UP, THREW HIS arms forward to shield himself from the blast, and then fell back against the couch cushions in a sweat. He was able to clear the memory and return to the present more quickly now, but once awakened by a replay of the blast, all hope of restful sleep was gone.

He stretched to clear a kink from his back. As much as he hated to admit it, he missed his fancy foam mattress. Sharing the bed with CC was not an option. Being near her was like being hotwired, which meant they had to get creative about the time they spent together. So far, he'd kept his promise not to use the word *love* with CC until he was ready and able to promise her an enduring love and commitment, but neither could he be casual with physical intimacy without those same promises. To him, that meant waiting for a loving marriage. This was going to be a challenge. They would have to make other sleeping arrangements if he was going to spare his back.

He stoked the fire and tossed another log on, pausing to finger CC's foil chains and the pine garlands she'd made. Smiling, he padded over to the fridge and pulled a carton of orange juice out. Before guzzling a big drink, he paused. Emmie hated when he and Carlos chugged from the carton, even though the men assured her the paper never touched their lips. Reese's mother's abhorrence over the practice had never deterred her sons from trying it when she wasn't watching, but what would CC think? With less chagrin than he expected, Reese grabbed a glass, poured a drink, and replaced the carton in the fridge.

He headed back to the sofa, glass in hand, and fished his well-worn leather scripture tote from the end-table drawer. The welcome feel of this old volume soothed him, and wrapped in his blanket, he settled in to read. God's word had helped him find and re-center himself many times—during his rebellious high school years, in Iraq, and even after ignoring his faith following his marriage to Marissa. The New Testament spoke most personally to him and to his concerns. He loved that book's powerful promises of redemption. He needed them every day.

He felt a presence behind him several times and ignored the feeling, until he finally looked over his shoulder and saw CC's head peering around the corner.

The shock of actually seeing someone caused him to jump. "Oh, gosh, CC!" He groaned as he turned red and buried his face in his hand. "I wasn't . . . I thought I . . ." he sputtered, and CC backed up with her hands raised apologetically until his garbled complaining turned to laughter. She wore sweatpants and a tee. Last night's pigtails had become frizzy twists that, along with her makeup-free face, made her look like a little girl.

"I heard a noise earlier and came out to see if you were okay. What time is it?"

Reese glanced at the clock and cringed. "Three a.m. Sorry. I couldn't sleep."

She slipped onto the opposite corner of the sofa without kissing or touching him. Reese began overthinking about that.

"Bad dream?" CC asked. "I heard you cry out a while ago."

Ignoring the comment, Reese held up his glass instead. "Juice?"

CC ran her tongue over her teeth and grimaced. "No, thanks." Her eyes finally opened fully. "Are you okay?" She reached a hand to him, and he gladly set his glass down to take it.

"It's just how it is sometimes." He studied her reaction.

"My dad struggled with memories of his time during the first Iraq War."

Reese set his scriptures aside and reached for her other hand as well, sliding her toward him. "You should get back to bed."

She pushed her chin forward and smiled. "I'll keep you company. I saw you reading. Is that your Bible?"

"Mm-hmm." He fanned the marked pages filled with notes in colorful ink.

"Wow . . . all these notes and marks are yours?"

"Yep. I didn't realize how much I needed my Heavenly Father and His Son, Jesus Christ, until I turned my back on them."

CC cocked her head to the side, and her brow furrowed with obvious questions.

"It's a long story," Reese continued, "but this book and my faith in Christ have saved me more times than Carlos has." He instantly regretted going for humor instead of using the tender opportunity to share this aspect of himself.

He turned to a specific page with the header *The Gospel According to St. John* and ran his finger down the page to Chapter 9. The section was filled with notes, underlines, and even verses marked with big question marks. "These verses are some of my favorites. They give me hope and comfort."

"Which story is it?"

"It's where Jesus and the disciples see a man who's been blind from birth, and the disciples assume he's been stricken because someone sinned."

"And Jesus replies that the man's blindness had nothing to do with his or his parents' sins or mistakes."

"Exactly." Reese leaned in closer to CC, anxious to share more with her. "And then this incredibly unexpected and hopeful insight—that sometimes hard experiences come not as a punishment for our bad choices, 'but that the works of God should be made manifest.'"

Her brow creased with the depth of consideration she was giving to those words. She glanced back at the marked page of scripture and touched a verse marked in red with a note written in the margin. "Would you share one of your notes with me?"

He wondered whether she understood the level of trust that simple request, for him to share one of the most painful and private insights into his tortured soul, would require of him.

"I'd have to go back and read these verses first." He read verses 4–7 quietly to her.

> "I must work the works of him that sent me, while it is day: the night cometh, when no man can work.
>
> "As long as I am in the world, I am the light of the world.
>
> "When he had thus spoken, he spat on the ground, and made clay of the spittle, and he anointed the eyes of the blind man with the clay,
>
> "And said unto him, Go, wash in the pool of Siloam, (which is by interpretation, Sent.) He went his way therefore, and washed, and came seeing."

He looked up into CC's thoughtful face. "Those verses really hit me one day. I felt like that man, blind and stumbling through life, and then I wrote this:

> *"I treat every obstacle in my life as a punishment for past mistakes.*
> *Am I being punished? Are You able and willing to turn my trials*

*into blessings? Because I don't want to stumble about like a blind man anymore. I want to see my way clearly and be happy again. Doing things my way hasn't worked out very well. If the key is to trust in You again, then I give You my life. Please help me trust again and make Your works manifest in my life."*

There were tears in CC's eyes when she looked up from the page at him. "What made you feel you were being punished by God?"

His own eyes burned, and he turned away and downed another gulp of juice to pull himself together. "The war. Things I did there, things I saw. Then there was the whole mess with Marissa. All the years I lost trying to build a marriage with someone who never loved me and all the years I took from her as well. I was very angry for a long time."

"Did you find your peace here?" She touched the page.

"It's a daily process. My peace comes from being reminded that God has already forgiven me, and that comes from using all the tools—the scriptures, trusting in Christ's Atonement, lots of prayer, and the strength I get from my ecclesiastical leaders and others like me who are finding faith in Christ. That's where I was Sunday morning. At church. It helped me sort things out so I'd be ready to talk to you about all this. Leaning on Him helps me forgive myself."

The tiniest of smiles graced CC's lips, as if she were feeling Reese's peace wash over her. "I haven't opened a Bible in a long time, probably since Dad died," she said.

Prickles rose on his arms. "There's one in the nightstand by my bed."

"Is it marked up like this one?"

"No, but feel free to make it your own."

She turned and laid back against him, and Reese knew he'd never before experienced such a rush of spiritual joy as he felt in that moment. He wondered if CC had any idea how exciting it was to share not just the romantic part of who he was with someone but also this kind of spiritual closeness. Until this very moment, he'd had no idea how satisfying it could be to open one's soul to another person in this way, to be so vulnerable and simultaneously feel so empowered.

Marissa had urged him to embrace her Muslim faith, and perhaps their marriage would have survived if he had, but something inside him would have died. For all the effort he'd made to resist the tug of the Savior in his life, he wasn't any more able to deny what he knew—that Jesus was the Son of God—than Marissa was able to deny what her faith had taught her, and so the most intimate parts of who they were and what they believed had remained locked to one another, and a wall had gone up between them that had never come down.

Here CC was, exploring the ideas and principles most precious to him, a sharing more exciting and intimate than a kiss, but Reese could find no adequate words to say that, so he simply kissed her head and said, "Thanks for the good talk."

She smiled up at him. Her adorableness was pegging his willpower meter again.

"I sure hope you have a constructive plan for what to do if we stay up together," he said.

"As a matter of fact, I do. I want to bake some more cookies."

"Are you serious? You've already made dozens. And . . ." He went to the kitchen, CC following, and lifted the lid on the glass cake plate. "Did you bake this cake?"

"Oh my gosh! I placed the cake in there and totally forgot to tell you. A woman came by a few days ago and dropped it off."

"What was her name?"

"She didn't say. In fact, she didn't *want* to say. She only mentioned that you'd know who she was if I told you the apple-cake lady came by."

A smile curled the corners of his mouth. "Apple cake? What did she look like?"

"Very elegant and beautiful, with blonde hair and kind eyes. Do you know who she was?"

"That could be any one of several local ladies. I need more information."

"Well . . . she said you loved her cakes when you were little. Does that ring any bells?"

"A few. It seems you liked her."

"Very much," CC said with longing. "She was only here a few minutes, but she treated me like an old friend. And I've been dying to dig into that cake."

Reese slid his arms around CC and gave her a soft kiss. "Then, let's cut this masterpiece."

"Ahh . . ." Her closed eyes opened into dreamy slits. "I think we're back to our original dilemma."

"Which was?"

"How to keep constructively occupied."

"Ah yes . . . so I assume we're back to baking cookies?"

"I think that would be best. Far less fun . . . but best."

Reese wasn't ready to say it out loud, but he knew he was a goner for CC. He felt breathless again, so he retrieved his glass, chugged more juice, and said, "Need a recipe book?"

"Nope. I'm going to bake you something from my world—my grandma Cippolini's traditional Christmas cookies—and you're going to be hands-on. You raid the galley cupboards—that's navy for kitchen cupboards. My dad was a navy cook, and I was his first mate."

"You still miss him."

"Every day."

"Well, you're in luck. This galley is well stocked. We're like a little general store."

CC called out the needed ingredients, and Reese grabbed them and set them on the counter near the mixing bowl she'd found. Once the dough was made, CC placed the bowl in the fridge to chill and called Reese back to duty. "How about you chop the nuts for the filling while I mix the rest of the ingredients?"

When the nuts were chopped to CC's satisfaction, she added them into the filling. Then she preheated the double ovens, checked the time, leaned against the counter, and said, "We've got thirty minutes to kill while the dough chills."

"I suddenly feel hungry, and it just so happens that your cinnamon-scented cookie dough reminds me of a favorite breakfast treat."

"You . . . cook?"

"Do I sense scoffing?" He came at her with his fingers wriggling and a devilish look in his eyes.

CC backed up against the stainless double fridge with her hands smacking air in advance of the expected attack. "No! No tickling!"

"Aha! I have discovered your weakness. Every superhero has one." Reese gathered her into his arms, and the moment slowly mellowed.

"I'm no superhero." CC stepped away.

"You brought my hardened heart back to life. That makes you a superhero in my book."

He wrapped her up in his arms again and held her close, enjoying the feel of her against his beating heart. Yesterday's crazed CC-mania reminded him of his high school romances, when the love of a new girl, a new car, or a new gun sent him equally off the rails. Back then a forever promise had the life expectancy of a goodnight kiss. This was different.

There was an ease between them now, not one degree less impassioned than yesterday's explosive bond but tempered with his surety that she wanted to be with him as badly as he wanted her there. He marveled that she seemed utterly at peace as they stood holding one another, allowing the comfort of the moment to settle in deep. The feeling was new to him. The most extraordinary thing he had ever felt.

An idea struck him, and he called out to his internet assistant, "Stella, play some Christmas music." Familiar lyrics soon began to play, and Reese swayed with CC through that song and four others. Then CC yawned and he remembered the hour. Pulling back, he kissed her softly. "We ought to try to catch some shut-eye."

She smiled up at him, and he thought his heart might burst. "But we have cookies to bake. Besides, I'm too happy to sleep."

"The cookie dough will keep for a few hours, won't it?" He took her hand and led her to a seat at the island. "Mosey on up to the bar, missy," he teased. "I'll fix you up one of my mom's Sleepy-Time Cocktails."

He pulled a gallon of milk from the fridge, gathered honey and some spices from the cupboard, and set everything down near the vanilla still on the counter from the cookie dough. He placed the ingredients in a small saucepan and heated them until the milk was frothy and speckled with spice, then poured the mix into two mugs and squirted whipped cream on top.

"Drink this. It will put you right to sleep."

CC took the offered mug and breathed in the warmth, returning a contented sigh. She walked back to the great room, stopping behind the sofa. Her head tilted back and her shoulders rose with the draw of a deep breath, as if the spices and the pine and wood smoke all combined in irresistible pleasure. Reese reveled in her contentment, and then he saw her hand rise to her eye as if she were wiping away a tear.

He hurried to her, turning her around as he asked, "Why are you crying?"

She tried to beg him off, but he persisted, even taking her mug from her and setting it aside so he could hold her close. "What's wrong?"

She bit her lip. "I'm channeling the Ghost of Christmas Past. It's been a long time since I've shared a real Christmas with anyone."

"Even Devon?"

"He and the other single firemen took the holiday shifts and bunked at the firehouse so the married guys could be with their families, so I did the same, pulling extra shifts at the club."

"That was actually pretty thoughtful," Reese admitted reluctantly.

"Yeah . . . well . . . the guys at the firehouse are his brothers. He loved being with them."

"And where did you fit into that equation?"

"We're very different. I'm the popcorn-stringing, sit-and-enjoy-the-tree kind of person, and he just isn't. On New Year's, he'd have me dress to the nines so he could take me dancing or to dinner with some of his firefighter friends and their dates."

"Carlos would say that you were his arm candy."

CC shrugged. "In his own way, he was totally devoted to me . . . as long as I agreed with him and complied with his every request and never left his line of sight."

"I rescind my compliment."

"It wasn't all his fault, Reese. I never fought for anything different."

"I take it your Christmas past is about your father, then."

"Completely."

"Describe Christmas at the Cippolini house."

A thoughtful look came over CC, which slowly shifted into a childlike smile. "It started the day before Thanksgiving, when a tree farm dropped off the hardware stores' bundles of live trees. I helped Dad get the stands out from the storage room, and we set up the trees that night so they'd be ready for shoppers on Black Friday. We picked out the best one, carried it home, and stuck it in a bucket of water on our porch so it would be ready to trim on Thanksgiving night."

"Thanksgiving night? So soon?"

Her eyes widened, and she nodded unapologetically. "We squeezed every minute of Christmas from the season."

A plan started to form in Reese's mind.

"And lights!" She chuckled as she wiped her eyes. "He hung them from the rooftop and around every window, door, and post. We nearly caused a local blackout. Dad even stuffed lights inside the tree as well as stringing them around the outside. It was glorious."

The word reverberated with its own sense of melancholy glory as it rolled off CC's tongue. "I've always had a place to stay and food to eat, but I haven't had a home or a family to share Christmas with since before Dad died."

Reese didn't know how to respond. He wanted to say something comforting like, "You do now," or, "Let me be your home," but it was too soon for promises that would cut both of them to the quick if unfulfilled, so he simply held her and asked, "What about Nora? How was it there?"

"Sometimes I felt she wanted us to be family, not just roommates, but when I'd try to get close, she'd pull back. She bought a Christmas tablecloth for the

kitchen once. It was bright green with giant red poinsettias. Totally gaudy"—
she laughed—"but still nice. I told her how happy it made me, and then, the
next day, without a word, it was gone. I never saw it again. Things like that
happened all the time."

"I'm sorry."

"I bought a tree one year, and we decorated it together, but she fretted
so much over the falling needles that she hardly came into the room without
grumbling and wringing her hands. I spent weeks alone in that room, growing
more hurt and angry with her every day until I finally took it down and tossed
it out the door."

"She sounds like she had mental issues, CC."

"Maybe. But I'm the common denominator in all these failed
relationships. Maybe I'm the problem."

"No." Reese moved to her and cooed into her ear. "Don't say that."

"Think about it. I pushed Devon away; I was impatient and ungrateful
with Nora. Maybe I'm the one who's not good at loving."

Reese held her at arm's length as he found the courage to ask, "How do
you feel here?"

She looked up at him with tear-filled eyes. "Like I'm home."

Relief swept over him. "See? I don't think you've been the problem,
because it feels like home to me too, for the first time. Because of you."

"But that scares me. We're laying our hearts wide open here. It could be
wonderful, or it could be devastating, and I don't think either of us could
survive that."

"So we go with your plan . . . forward but slowly." He pulled her to him
and kissed her head again, committed to fulfilling his latest plan.

# CHAPTER FIFTEEN

THE SLEEPY-TIME COCKTAIL DID THE trick, buying CC a few hours of additional sleep. The sky was lightening, allowing her to enjoy the final sprinkling of starlight as beams broke through the trees, announcing the rising sun. She rose and dressed and padded down the hall, stealing a peek over the edge of the sofa to find Reese asleep there under a crimson flannel quilt. She was amazed by how normal it felt to begin the day expecting to see his face, as if it were already filed in her psyche under *family*. She watched him sleep for a minute, noticing all the details—the chaotic tangle of his hair, the dark shade of beard covering his lower face like a mask, the relaxed set of his almost-smiling mouth. One arm was propped under his head and pillow. The other lay by his side. His body formed a crescent shape on the sofa, with his backside pressed firmly against the sofa's back and his shoulders and knees situated more forward. She imagined lying in the curve of his body, with that free arm wrapped around her.

*Maybe someday . . .*

She did her best not to clang the pans and bowls, but even the creak of the fridge door seemed unusually loud as she prepared to roll the chilled cookie dough. She tried not to awaken Reese as she searched under the counter cupboards for a rolling pin, when she saw his bare feet appear beside her, shooting her to a standing position with a start. "Sorry! I tried to be quiet."

Reese shrugged, a pinch of raw cookie dough between his fingers, from which he was taking a nibble.

"Sneaking up on me again? How long have you been staring at me this time?"

His flirtatious wink and smile zipped happiness through her. "Not nearly as long as I'd have liked."

With an upward glance, she admitted, "Same here."

"Were you staring at me while I slept?" Reese cocked his head and grinned.

His two-step advance caused CC to also step forward, where he caught her up in his arms. "Not staring," she clarified. "I was checking on you."

"You mean checking me out."

The tickling began again until squeals erupted from CC's lips and she crumpled against him. After one soft kiss, CC pressed her hands to his chest and said, "Back to work."

"On the sugar cookies."

"These, cowboy, are no simple sugar cookies. These are Grandma Cippolini's Cinnamon Christmas Twirls. Or, at least, they will be."

"A Cippolini family tradition?"

"Yes, or so Dad told me. His mom died when I was three, but he carried on the tradition with me."

Reese washed his hands at the sink and dried them on a towel. "After last night, I have a personal investment in these cookies. Put me back to work."

CC divided the dough into eighths and rolled each lump into a ball. She then rolled one ball into a circle of dough that resembled a pie crust.

"Very curious."

"Each ball gets cut into eight thin triangles. Then you top each triangle with a pinch of this sugar, spice, and nut mixture, and you gently roll them up like a crescent roll."

Reese's attempt turned into a broken pile of brown-speckled scraps.

"Gently. Roll it very gently," CC said with an Italian accent. "Here, finish mine off. Sprinkle them with powdered sugar, and they're ready to bake."

Reese picked up a pan and headed for the preheated oven. "How many minutes?"

"About twenty."

He popped his pan into the oven and surveyed the rest of the dough, drawing numbers in the air with his finger as he did the cookie math. "Eight balls of dough at eight cookies per ball means sixty-four cookies. Two pans with fifteen cookies to a pan with a baking time of twenty minutes each . . . we ought to be finished here in under an hour, even with cleanup." He closed one eye and tipped his head her way as if sharing a secret. "Squeeze sixteen cookies to a tray and we cut that time down further."

"In a hurry?"

He raised an eyebrow. "I have plans. Big plans. And they involve the chief baker."

"They do, do they? Well, in that case . . ." She smiled and squished an extra cookie onto each cookie sheet. "So what's up, cowboy?"

"How about I handle the morning feeding while you finish up here? Dress warm between batches and meet me in the barn when you can."

An hour later, the cookies were cooling on the counter, and CC and Reese were mounted on Admiral. They followed a trail that led through a narrow break in the otherwise solid tree line, winding sharply around a bend that followed the outcropping of a foothill. The trail eventually led them to a wide paved road covered in muddy snowmelt. Admiral carried them along at a slow pace. The pair rocked as one in sync with Admiral's gait. Reese's left hand covered hers in front while the right guided the horse.

She moved closer to Reese's ear and said, "I read some passages in the Bible last night before I fell asleep."

He smiled and nodded. "What did you read?"

"I headed for familiar chapters. Luke 2 was sweet and sad. I longed to hear my father's voice reading the Christmas story again. And I kept hearing the familiar strength of our parish priest's voice echoing from the pulpit as I read. I abdicated my religious studies to these men long ago, I suppose, but reading on my own was also very comforting. There's a certain . . . I don't know . . . security to becoming personally familiar with a God who is all-knowing and all-loving. I think that's what my dad was always trying to teach me."

"He sounds like an amazing father."

"He was. His primary concerns were that I love God and know that He loves me in return."

Reese turned, and his smile broadened almost to his ears. "I wasn't raised Catholic, but spiritually, we have a lot in common. Would you like to go to church with me on Sunday?"

"That's quite a commitment. You're planning for me to be here five long days from now?"

He didn't return a snappy comeback. Instead, his voice turned serious. "Will you?"

CC chided herself for making light of what was clearly intended as a tender invitation. "I'll go anywhere with you."

Reese faced forward again and didn't answer for a few seconds, and when he did, his voice was light and fun again. "I'm going to put that promise to the test today. I thought you might like to see where I grew up."

What little CC had heard about the Brockbank family crossed her mind— their wealth, their spectacular annual Christmas party, Emmie's jabs about the control exerted by the patriarch and matriarch of the clan of seven Brockbank sons. The negative opinion she'd begun to form about the family softened when Reese spoke of what they had sacrificed to protect him and what he had done to protect them. She knew it was no small thing that he was bringing her to meet them.

"Tell me more about your parents and brothers."

"All right. My father's name is Richard. My mother's is Mette. She's from Germany. They met there on a Brockbank family vacation the summer my father graduated from high school. Dad was eighteen, and she was just sixteen, but they exchanged more than a hundred letters over the next two years while my father did volunteer service in Tennessee. When he came home, they both attended the University of Utah, and the rest, as they say, is history. They were married after her freshman year, and I was born a year later, in 1986."

She finally had a solid age on Reese. "They were so young."

"Yep. My dad followed in Grandpa's footsteps as a boy, learning to wrangle cattle and work the mine. You've heard the phrase, 'A place for everything and everything in its place'? I think my mom coined that. She's a stickler about order and cleanliness." He laughed. "She had Dad install a hose bibb right outside the back door. If we came home dirty, she'd strip us down and hose us off before we were allowed into the house."

"I take it the showers were cold."

"Frigid."

"Did it deter you guys from diving into adventure?"

"What do you think?"

"Not in the slightest."

"You would be correct." Laughter floated on his words. "Since I was the oldest of all the kids, I had the most time with Grandpa. I was born to love dirt and rocks and cows and horses. Mom and Dad understood that, at least at first, but Dad thought I would grow out of my love of ranching like he did, and once Grandpa passed on, he wanted me to leave the cowboy life behind and follow him into the mining business."

"But you didn't."

"Not really. And that brings us to Lucas, who is two years younger. I was being preened to follow in Dad's footsteps and take the lead in the family business. Lucas didn't feel the same pressure I did, so he dedicated his life to becoming a world-class ski bum."

"Emphasis on the skiing or on the bum?"

"Skiing. He was great. He even skied in an Olympic trial at sixteen. He didn't make that team, but I think he could have made the next one. My choices changed his life."

Reese clicked his tongue at Admiral, and CC felt his legs tighten around the animal, increasing the pace. After a long moment, she dared to ask, "Are you and he okay?"

"I think so. Karma kicked in. He tore his ACL skiing. It would have been a career-ender if he were an Olympic skier, and the accident had nothing to do with me, so that eased the tension between us. He decided to become an Olympic-caliber businessman instead, so he threw himself into school and ended up getting his MBA and becoming second chair to Dad in the company. He's a real bulldog at negotiations."

"And he's single?"

"Are you thinking about switching horses from me to Lucas?"

CC laughed. "Interesting suggestion . . ."

"And the rivalry begins again, folks!" Reese hollered out to the snow and the trees. "We're all single. I think my failure made my brothers skittish about marriage."

CC remembered Emmie telling her something similar. "Who's next on the Brockbank hit parade?"

"That would be Reynolds. He's twenty-eight and Dad's corporate spare heir. Reynolds is second in succession to the chairman's seat after Lucas."

"I met him the day Emmie and I were cutting pine boughs."

"So I heard. Reynolds called me after running into you. It was the first time we'd spoken in a few weeks. We had a good chat, thanks to you."

"I had nothing to do with it. He and a very beautiful girl were gathering boughs too."

"So Gwinnie is already in town." He said her name with a sarcastic lilt.

"Was that a sneer?"

"She's been trying to wrangle a proposal out of Reynolds for a few years."

"Well, he seemed nice. Very polished."

"Mom polished us all up when we were little—table manners, the correct use of all eight utensils and multiple glasses in a formal table setting. Once we passed her dining exam, she eased up and counted on us knowing when to retrieve that information. Gwyneth is stuck in formal mode. That will be her downfall with Reynolds. He's a fun-loving guy when she's not around."

"And how are you two?"

"Pretty close. You can't be a Brockbank and not have some cowboy in you, but Reynolds has the most, next to me."

"Does your mom have some cowgirl in her?"

"Little cowgirl Mette? Oh yeah!" He laughed with joy. "She's a city girl from Berlin, but she took to riding as if she'd been raised on a ranch."

"Wait—the lady who dropped off the cake had an accent. Could that have been your mom?"

"Anything's possible." He squeezed CC's hand.

They rode on for what seemed like another twenty minutes. Once they were around the bend, the trail hit a muddy paved road that split at a guard post. Emmie had told CC of the security around the Brockbanks' "compound," but seeing it for herself made it all the more intimidating. CC swallowed hard, and her eyebrows pinched as she considered that a guard post, guard, and security gate were necessary on the property Reese called home.

As if reading her mind, Reese said, "Things got pretty scary for a while after the newspaper article. Currently, Herb spends most of his days doing crossword puzzles, but it's comforting to my mom to know he's there to ward off protesters and nut jobs like Kernan."

When CC didn't make another comment, Reese jumped back in. "We'll come back to the house after I show you what's up this bend, but when we do, remember that it's big but it's still just a house."

Reese waved to Herb, the uniformed man, who saluted back with a smile and electronically opened the chain-link gate so Reese could nudge Admiral through. Once they passed the gate, the road split left and right, with each entrance marked by handsomely landscaped beds planted with colorful winter cabbages and evergreens wrapped in white lights. Green signs edged in gold with gold letters carved into the wood indicated the names of the lanes. The sign beside the left lane read, *Number 2, Lindy Lane*. The sign to the right read, *Silver Buckle Mining, Incorporated*.

Reese guided Admiral to the right past another thick stand of trees and continued on as if none of what CC was seeing was in any way unusual. The uphill grade increased significantly as they moved on. Admiral leaned into the hill and pranced nervously and snorted when a huge truck with tires as high as Admiral's head roared by, loaded with stone.

CC patted the horse and said, "You and me both, boy." To distract herself from her mounting nervousness, CC said, "You've only told me about two of your brothers. What about the others?"

"Barrett is twenty-six. He recently graduated from law school and is cutting his teeth with a California firm. He'll run the legal side of the business someday.

Finn is twenty-three and quite an artist. Dad convinced him there's greater security in advertising than there is in art, so he paints for joy and is finishing up an internship at an ad agency in New York. He misses the mountains, so he'll return home to run the company's marketing after graduation."

"A son for every department."

"Exactly. And that brings us to Harrison, who is twenty-one and studying geology at Brigham Young University here in Utah. He's very smart. Ryker is nineteen and volunteering in Maryland. Everyone except Ryker comes home for Christmas, but we get weekly updates from him."

CC's attention shifted from Reese's family tree to what lay beyond the muddy road. It split again, with one branch breaking off sharply to the right, where another fenced guard post was situated. Beyond the fence, CC could see an imposing granite facade built into the mountain. It housed two massive arched tunnels that looked like gaping eyes. More gargantuan trucks were parked near or moving through those tunnels, while men moved in and out through a smaller set of doors set into another building with security guards at the doors.

"This is the little mining operation?" she asked. "This is not a few dozen men and some pickaxes."

"Yeah . . . I may have implied that it's smaller than it actually is. That road leads to the actual mine. One tunnel goes in. One leads out. The other building is where the ore is processed. They give tours, but we'll save that for another day. I'll take you to headquarters today."

He urged Admiral on and kept talking. "What I told you was true. It was hit or miss in the early days, more of a lark than a business. When Grandpa took over, he struggled to stay afloat, so he raised cattle to support his wife, Lindy, and their family. But then one day, he hit a big vein. The mine has been very successful since then."

"I had an idea it was bigger than you said. When we opened your closet to pack for you, I noticed you have quite a lot of silver things in trays."

Reese slid off Admiral and helped CC down. "It's not like it was in Grandpa's day, with a few carts on rails and some hand tools. It's a big operation now . . . especially since my father took it over. Besides silver, they're finding copper, gold, garnets, and turquoise. I hope you'll forgive me for not mentioning it before, but it's a complicated topic for me."

"Has your father accepted that you just want to be a rancher?"

"For the most part, but we've finally found a role for me here that suits me."

Reese's mood and bearing had changed upon arriving at this place, as if just being there burdened him. He took CC's hand and led Admiral along the straight fork until they arrived at an imposing three-story yellowish stone building with a fountain out front. The sign over the door read *Corporate Offices of the Silver Buckle Mine*. To the right sat a similarly constructed one-story building with the title *Employee Services*, and to the left was a smaller building with a sign that read, *Education Center*.

They stopped by the fountain and sat. "This complex is where the family goes to work. We get down in the mines from time to time, but the business aspect is run right here. A few uncles, aunts, and cousins work here too, but my father is the CEO. Our family carries the bulk of the operational responsibilities. Most of the other relatives just sit home and wait for the quarterly dividend check as Grandpa laid out in his will."

"Do you have an office in there?"

He bobbed a tentative yes and pointed to a window on the top floor. "I've always seen myself as the black sheep—the golden child who fell from grace and left others to clean up after him. But I finally graduated from college. It was an online university program so I could run the ranch at the same time, but getting that degree made a huge difference to me personally. I finally felt back on track and a little redeemed, if that makes any sense."

CC nodded. She understood those feelings very well.

"Anyway, I serve a different purpose for the company."

"Tell me."

"It took me a while to figure out my place. After the mess my marriage and divorce caused my family, I was ready to extricate myself completely from the business, but my father helped me see that I bring a different kind of value to the group. We're an international company now, but we're a local company first. In one way or another, we impact every family in the area, either because we employ someone in their home or because of how their paychecks affect the local economy. It's a tremendous responsibility, one my family takes very seriously. One I didn't understand when I was an impulsive kid and soldier. I get it now. I feel it. But there are also environmental concerns with an operation this big, and that brings a lot of scrutiny and pressure. My ranch and its success serve a few special purposes I've only recently come to understand. First, I'm helping preserve the natural beauty of the land, and people like that. Second, my healthy animals prove that the mining operation doesn't pose a threat to the other ranchers and their stock. And lastly, the ranchers can relate to me. They talk to me about things they wouldn't mention to others in my family who seem too intimidating, I suppose. That gives me an opportunity to address potential problems before they become bigger concerns."

"That has to make you feel good."

The tension in his face eased a bit. "It does. Especially that last part."

He squeezed her hand. "I wanted you to know this part of me so you could understand that, contrary to what you've seen these last few days, my life isn't just riding horses and chasing steers. I wish it were, but it's a lot more complicated than that. I have responsibilities and obligations . . . to my family, to this business, and to this community, and I take them all very seriously."

A nettle of worry started to form in CC's chest as she wondered if Reese was attempting to discourage her or to draw her further in. She pulled her hand out of his and turned to face him. "Why are you telling me all this now, Reese?"

"I'm trying to be honest with you. Because getting involved with me means me seeing all of me and accepting all this. I'm not just a cowboy whose life and time are his own. I'm also a corporate leader with increasing responsibilities. Up to now, I've only shown you one side of me, but you need to know it all if we're going to move forward, including the fact that I'm hoping to rebuild connections to my family."

CC's head bobbed up and down involuntarily as she processed everything he was saying. He reached for her hands, which had become two fisted balls tucked into her lap as images of security gates, guards and protestors, and a miserable Reese sitting behind a desk passed through her mind.

"CC? CC? What are you thinking right now?" he asked.

"You wanted me to see it all? Let's finish the tour."

Reese took CC's hand and Admiral's reins and started walking away from the buildings and back down the lane. After a few minutes, he asked, "Would you rather walk or ride?"

"Ride," CC said, not mentioning that she chose that option because her legs felt shaky.

Reese mounted the horse and extended his hand to CC. She had become pretty good at her part, stepping into the stirrup and taking Reese's hand so he could hoist her up and behind. She was tentative as she slid her arms around him, wondering again if this ride was a farewell trip or an introduction to a life he was inviting her to share.

He seemed to sense her trepidation. "How are you doing back there?"

"Still here," was all she was willing to say.

His gloved hand cupped over hers in front, and he rubbed his thumb over her fingers in the way she loved, but it couldn't relieve the worries tugging at her. She thought about the chance meeting with his brother Reynolds in the woods, and Reynolds's mention of the annual Christmas party. Even the apple-cake lady and Emmie and Carlos were planning to go, but so far, Reese had made no mention of it to her. She had wrongly interpreted Emmie's comments about his family's dynamics and assumed Reese disliked the Brockbank clan, but she was learning that Reese was more intricately involved with his family, both financially and emotionally, than she initially understood. If he wasn't ready to have her meet them, what was today's show-and-tell all about? Was it a trust exercise to see how she was affected by his family's wealth, or was he measuring her and her simple upbringing against the backdrop of his world? Was she suitable as a date but unsuitable as a Brockbank corporate wife? No matter how hard she tried to dispel all these concerns, one hurtful truth lingered. Reese had still not invited her to meet his family or be his guest at their party. She wondered if he was embarrassed by her.

They returned to the fork in the road, but this time Reese guided Admiral down the other fork, along a lane bordered on both sides by ancient evergreen sentinels whose boughs touched, forming a magical pine tunnel that perfectly followed every curve in the two-lane driveway. The lane slowly rose in elevation, as if funneling arrivers toward the plateau where the grand home sat like a European palace on a hill. CC's skin prickled at the sight. Reese's home was grand and homey, but his parents' home was grand on an entirely different level.

Sculpted shrubbery marked the entrance, where the pavement shifted to a polished brick driveway colored gold, gray, and black. The driveway wound through an iron gate Reese opened with a remote device he'd carried in his pocket and on past a massive fountain that it circled, landing under a roofed portico with four broad columns. The home's light-yellow stone walls rose three tall stories. The first story was festooned with eight large crescent-topped windows, four set on each side of the doorway and each flanked by black wooden shutters whose color matched the primary variegation in the roofing tiles. The second and third stories also boasted eight shutter-flanked windows on the front face, but these were smaller and square. The roof itself was a work of art, with spire-topped turrets and whimsical cupolas, while wide, dark trim outlined every window and doorway and crisscrossed in the peaks of each roofline. Wrought-iron planters installed beneath each window were filled with lighted pine boughs tied with red bows, and similarly decorated wreaths hung in every window, where brass candles were also placed.

After moments of speechless gawking, she finally said, "It looks like a castle."

"A happy castle, I hope."

"This is where you grew up?"

"Not always. The house my parents started out in lies behind this one. A couple who helps run the place lives there now. This house was built when I was twelve. It reminded Mom of home."

As he said it, the entire effect of the place made CC think of photos of Bavaria, and then she remembered that Germany was Mette Brockbank's homeland. She couldn't picture Reese in this house, a home that most certainly needed a staff to maintain it, and yet, unlike his manner at the corporate offices, his body seemed relaxed and at ease here, though when he turned to glance at CC, she saw a twinge of something pull at the corners of his mouth and eyes.

"Dad always promised Mom he'd build her a dream home someday. They'd been working on the plans for years, and then, the year I turned ten, the men hit a lucrative vein. Dad gave each of the miners and the office staff huge bonuses the year of the strike."

CC noticed the unmistakable pride and pleasure the memory brought him.

"Mom ran herself ragged helping Dad adjust to the new responsibilities this level of business required, all while also continuing to serve in the local church and community and managing a home with three busy little boys. Dad decided the time had come to give her a bonus too, so he broke ground on the house's foundation the following year. The house took two years to complete. Before we moved in, they found out Mom was expecting Barrett, so they hired the Millers to maintain the house and grounds so Mom could focus on people things."

"You grew up with a household staff?"

"Hardly." He laughed. "They were more like supervisors, but our friends thought we just laid around all day being served. The Millers are like an extra aunt and uncle to us, and just like Mom and Dad, they put us to work. Even the little ones, as Finn and Harrison and Ryker came along. Between the four adults, they all made sure we learned how to work and serve." He pointed to a thick stand of trees behind the house. "There's an orchard, a garden, and two barns behind those trees. One is a new horse barn, but the older one is used to house all the stock—the horses, the chickens, the goats, and two milk cows. We boys were responsible for tending them all. We were also in charge of helping Mom and Mrs. Miller in the vegetable garden and with harvesting the fruit." He laughed again. "I always knew our house was big, but life here felt normal, and this place never felt less a home than our little house out back."

He chuckled, and CC marveled at how normal this extraordinary life seemed to him. Guilt stung her. She had prejudged this family just like Reese's childhood friends had. "Your parents sound pretty terrific," she said.

Reese scanned the property and nodded silently for several seconds before responding with thoughtful deliberateness. "Yeah, they really are."

CC knew she was venturing into delicate territory with her next question. "Why does Emmie think there's still tension between you and your family?"

"Did she say that?" Reese ran a hand over his face and glanced back at CC. "I probably shouldn't have mentioned it."

"No. I'm ashamed to hear that, but I'm glad you told me. It's time I face what a proud, unappreciative idiot I've been and how my grumbling has soured Emmie and Carlos's opinions toward my family. Please don't let it sour yours, CC. Whatever difficulties exist between my parents and me are my fault. Instead of recognizing that they were trying to support me and Marissa, I took their concern as judgment and lashed out at them. I fell back into that pattern every time my decisions brought pain to my family. Even then, they never stood in my way."

"It's not too late to fix how you think and speak of them."

"You're right, and that apology is long overdue. You've been right about more than you know. You probably didn't even realize it, but it's been your loving memories about your father that have reminded me that I had as sweet a childhood as you, but you cherish yours, and I've been ungrateful for mine. I need to fix so many things. For starters, you were right about the apple-cake lady too. She's my mother."

"Ahh, I knew it!"

"Reynolds must have told her about you. She hasn't brought me a cake in years, so I'm sure she made it as an excuse to rush down and meet you. Did she ask how you and I were getting along?"

"Not in so many words. She asked what I thought of you, and I played it very cool. I said I thought you were very nice."

"More importantly, you liked her, and she liked you."

"That's very important to you, isn't it?"

"More important than I ever realized. I'd like to make this Christmas with my family special. We host an annual Christmas party for the workers and the community. It's a fancy affair everyone looks forward to all year. They always beg me to come, and I usually make a cursory appearance, if any, and then leave as quickly as possible, but I'm actually looking forward to it this time because I'd like you to accompany me, if you're willing."

There it was, the invitation she'd hoped for and the affirmation she needed. But as she sat in front of the imposing home of the hosts, it felt overwhelming and less joyful than she'd imagined it would.

Reese turned in the saddle to look at her. "CC?"

"Your brother mentioned the gala when we saw him in the woods."

Reese pulled up on the reins until Admiral halted, and then he twisted to glance back at CC. "Then, you probably know it's this Friday . . . in three days . . . and you've probably been wondering if and when I was going to mention it."

CC didn't know how best to reply, so she simply tipped her head to the side and scrunched her shoulders in acknowledgement.

The awkward conversation was made more so by their positions on the horse. Reese kicked his leg over Admiral's head and perched uncomfortably sideways on his saddle. "I'm sorry I've waited so long to invite you. I've gone back and forth a dozen times about attending. My father will be ecstatic, and my mother will probably cry, so I've asked myself if I'm ready for that public spectacle or if it would be better to pass on this and just slide back into the family in a more private way."

"I'm fine with not going, but I was a little worried about why you hadn't asked."

"No! No, I want to go now. With you. I want to introduce you to my family, it's just that I've waited so long and it's rude to expect you to pull a party outfit together when the local shopping options are so limited. The event is semiformal dress. Do you have something to wear? If not, we could . . ."

CC didn't hear anything else Reese said. She had imagined this dance since Reynolds had mentioned it a week earlier, when Reese was just a miner's grandson and a successful cowboy chasing wayward steers. When CC believed she was the stylish city girl from Chicago, the more sophisticated of the two. Instead, she felt small today. Naive and foolish.

"CC? CC?"

Reese slipped to the ground and peered up at her. "I've overwhelmed you, haven't I?" He shook his head. "This whole ride, this whole day was planned to help explain those dragons I wrestle and all my crazy, wonderful, blessed baggage, but instead of opening my world to you, I've pushed you into a corner." He took her hands. "I'm the same man you baked cookies with this morning, CC. You already know my heart. I'm just inviting you to know all this."

Now it was her pride that was getting in the way. She tried to recall how vulnerable he'd appeared as he slept on the sofa and how safe she felt pressed into his back as they rode Admiral.

He shook his head. "Forget the party. It's too much too soon. We can stay back at the cattle shack and spend the evening alone together—"

"I-I'd love to go."

The light of hope filled his face. "You would?"

"I'd love to meet your family, and I think I have something suitable to wear."

Reese pulled her down to him. "My family is going to love you, CC. I have a feeling this is going to be the best Christmas either of us has had in a long time."

They walked away from the house, hand in hand, with Reese leading Admiral along. His cell phone beeped, and he checked the call. "It's my mom. I think she saw us from the window." He answered the call, saying, "Hi, Mom" in a singsong voice filled with humor and caring. "Yes, that was me. You saw a girl with me, eh?" He chuckled and arched his eyebrows at CC. "We've got plans for the rest of the day, so I can't bring her by right now, but you might be pleased to know that I'm bringing her to the party." He pulled the phone away from his ear as his mother's excited squeal pierced the air. "I heard you and she have already met, but I'll tell you what. How about we come an hour early so you and Dad can get to know her before the guests arrive? You're going to love her, Mom. Okay. See you Friday at six."

Reese shoved his phone into his pocket and whispered, "I bet you a million dollars she and every member of the family in the house are peeking at us from a window."

The idea of so much family interest in them both cheered CC and terrified her. "What do we do?"

"How about this?" Reese bent down and kissed her and then waved to his family as he led CC away. "We just gave my parents the Christmas wish they've been praying for."

"To see their son smooch a girl?" CC teased.

"To see their oldest son happy again. Thanks to you."

# CHAPTER SIXTEEN

Reese's mother called twice more that day and once early Wednesday morning, begging him to bring CC over for lunch. He was careful to decline the invitation in a loving way, but he was still sorting out old history, determining where he'd pushed back too hard with his parents and where their help had become too intrusive. He didn't want to mess things up this time with them or with CC, so he preferred to take things slow.

"Another time. I promise, okay? I love you, Mom."

Her voice broke over those simple words of affection. It crushed Reese as he considered that she'd probably begun to wonder if it was true anymore. He wondered how a man could reach his age and be so completely inept at relationships. That question brought his thoughts and doubts full circle back to CC.

He'd asked her to dress for another outdoor adventure. Once again, Admiral was prancing and ready to hit the trail, but this time, he was pulling a flat sled loaded with items concealed under a tarp.

"What's all this?" CC asked with excitement in her voice.

Reese wriggled his eyebrows at her and pulled her against him. "A surprise."

"Every day is a surprise with you."

"In good ways, I hope."

"In the very best ways."

He brushed her hair back and saw pure happiness in her eyes. "I never want to take you for granted, CC. I want to make sure you know every day that you're special and loved and safe and valued. Tell me if I fall short. Let's promise to fight for this . . . for what we're building here."

CC tapped his nose and kissed him softly. "Then, buckle up, cowboy, 'cause you're in for the fight of your life."

They confirmed the deal with a kiss that ran long and deep. Reese felt CC's hands on the back of his neck, holding him to her, and when the kiss ended, he could still feel the echo of her touch, still loving him, still keeping him close as his hands slid down her arms to take her hands.

"Ready for today's bout in that 'fight for us' plan?"

"You bet I am. Mount up."

They rode near the site where CC had told him she and Emmie had gathered pine boughs and dropped off the sled. The business of the day was to surprise CC with a Christmas tree. He proposed a contest to her as they neared the border of evergreens that marked the boundary between his acreage and his parents'. "You search left, and I'll search right, and when you think you've found the perfect tree, holler. We'll vote on the best. Deal?"

"What's the motivation for me to kick your trash in this contest?"

Reese hemmed and hawed, pretending to give that question some thought as he pulled Admiral to a halt and dismounted. "How about the winner makes dinner?"

CC scrunched her face up and asked, "*Winner* makes dinner? Don't you think the loser should do that, cowboy?"

Reese knew he had it exactly right. "I know where the best trees are, and I want to make you something special for dinner tonight."

"Ohhh . . . what you're saying is that either way, I win."

He lowered CC to the snowy ground until she stood mere inches in front of him. "That's the idea."

He planted a quick kiss on her lips, savoring it for a few seconds before CC bolted into the thickest section of the growth. Reese wondered if she was competitive enough to try to win even if it meant she'd end up cooking that evening. It didn't take much thought to know that she was exactly that kind of woman, and he chuckled with pleasure at her spunk.

The phone rang again, and he rolled his eyes and smiled at the thought that his mother was so curious and excited by their earlier conversation. Without even looking at the screen, he said, "We really can't make lunch today, Mom."

"Well, tell Mette I'm free if she's making biscuits and sausage gravy."

The voice was Marcus's, and the realization made Reese's jaw tighten. "Sheriff," he said in a stiff greeting.

"*Sheriff?* You sound as if you're mad at me."

"If this call has anything to do with CC, I'm not interested."

"When you were rational, you asked me to keep you informed about her, and I told you I would pass along any information on her that crossed my desk. I'm going to do that, whether you like it or not, either by phone or in an email. What you do with that information is up to you."

Reese cringed at the thought that there was new information at all. For the first time in a long time, he was happy. He looked at the sky, searching for heavenly help, and muttered, "Consider this case closed."

"You can block the news out, but you can't shut the investigation down. Other people are looking for her."

That news turned his legs to jelly. "Who's still digging around in her business, and why, Marcus? Is it that cheating, possessive ex of hers? She doesn't want to see him, and I don't care about anything he has to say to her."

"He's got her mother on his side."

Reese's breathing hitched. "Nora Stubbert isn't CC's mother. She was a guardian."

"The tip I got didn't specify a name. It just said it was the missing person's mother."

"She doesn't know her real mother. The woman walked out on CC's deployed father when CC was a baby, and she never looked back."

"I know that's what she said."

Reese tensed at the implication. "Are you saying she's been lying?"

"Someone has, and I think it'd be worth your while to find out who it is before you have your momma set a place for her at the family table."

Reese tasted blood and realized he'd nervously bitten the inside of his lip. He walked in tight circles until the snow beneath his feet had been pressed into ice. "Fine," he growled. "Send me your stinking email. Are we done here?"

"I take no pleasure in this, Reese. I'm not trying to hurt you. I'm trying to protect you."

"Goodbye, Sheriff."

His hands were quivering when he heard a victory whoop echo through the trees. The sweet joy-filled sound slammed him like a Mack truck. He wanted to run toward the sound and scoop CC up, to savor this season of bliss, but it was tainted now. He wondered if she'd sense his anger at Marcus and his worry over the news. He knew he could blow everything with her if she sensed mistrust. What if Nora was a troubled woman who believed she was CC's real mother? From what CC had said, it seemed likely. Or, more likely, maybe that cretin Devon had coerced Nora into lying just to get a meeting with CC. That was probably it, Reese reasoned. A new worry crept into his mind. What if that dirtbag ex-boyfriend actually had found CC's mother? Would the hope of rekindling a relationship with the woman who'd discarded her be powerful enough to draw the abandoned, family-starved woman back to Chicago?

His hands shook as a challenge call rang out. "Time's up, cowboy! I found the guaranteed winner! Mosey on over and give me a victory kiss!"

He wanted nothing more than to do that very thing, to run to her and carry her home. To lock the doors and love her so fully that no mystery person would ever have the power to lure her away. He loved her. As terrifying as that sacred admission was, he knew it was true, and true though it may be, he was powerless over what fate lay ahead for that love. Once again, a woman's family stood between him and what he wanted.

He bent forward and breathed, trying to calm his heart and settle his voice so CC wouldn't sense that anything was amiss.

She called out again. "Reese? Where are you? If you hopped in your car and drove to a tree lot to select the perfect tree, I'm going to make you fly to Maine for fresh lobster for dinner."

His eyes burned even as he laughed over her joke. *Pull it together, Reese. Pull it together.* He reached into his pocket and pulled out his sunglasses to hide his eyes. CC arrived in a blur, running full speed toward him with the ends of her blonde hair flying wildly from under her knitted cap. He swept her close and matched her laugh.

"Let's see this winning tree," he said with as much enthusiasm as he could muster.

She broke free and put her hands on her hips. "You're exactly where I left you. Where's your entry?"

Reese conducted an instant scan of the perimeter and locked in on the most promising specimen he saw. He walked ten paces and grabbed the top of the fir as if he were holding a shark by the tail. "What do you think?"

CC cocked her head sideways and eyed him as she walked over to inspect the sparse little tree. She gave Reese a hard push and sent him reeling backward into a pile of snow. Piling on top of him, she said, "You totally threw this contest, you loser!"

She squealed when Reese pulled a wrestling move and flipped her over, pinning her in the snow. He smiled down on her, soaking up the wind-burnt rose of her cheeks, the crazy disarray of her yellow hair, and the radiance of her smile that unlocked places long dormant inside him. He refused to accept that she had deceived him, but he choked over the possibility of losing her.

CC's expression filled with concern. "Is everything okay?"

"One hundred percent." He hated lying to her, even if it was to protect her . . . or him.

She surrendered the playful fight and studied him. Her smile and the teasing tone in her voice couldn't deflect him from noticing her pinched brows and tense lips. "Having second thoughts about introducing me to the family?"

"Not a one."

He watched the tension release from her face, but her voice remained mellow and cautious. "Something's bothering you. You can tell me. I'm in your corner, remember? Fighting buddies?"

"I remember. I'll never stop fighting for us," he said, even as Marcus's allusions to secrets and unknown family members picked at his peace. Reese resumed his playful offense. "Did you call my tree a loser?"

The light partially returned to her eyes. "I'm calling you *and* your tree losers," she teased on. "Admit that you threw this contest so my tree would win and I'd make you dinner."

Her banter ignited the fight in him. He was not surrendering any ground to Devon or to any long-lost relative. He loved CC, and though neither of them had voiced those words to the other, he knew beyond the power of words that she loved him too.

He regained his mental footing again and teased her back. "What tree?" he asked. "I don't see your entry."

CC wiggled free, stood up, and crooked a beguiling finger, urging Reese to follow her. This flirty side of her made his heart ache.

"Don't dawdle. Embrace your defeat," she said.

He wished he could dawdle.

Or stop time completely.

To live in this moment forever with her here in this place of peace and beauty, joyful and separate from the rest of the world.

CC stopped by a giant lodgepole pine. "This is it." She wrapped her arms around Reese, and her voice softened. "Isn't it perfect?"

It truly was a perfect Christmas tree that would fill the great room's corner. Reese felt his throat tighten at her overwhelming happiness. "It's a beaut."

"I think you were right."

"About what?"

"This is going to be the best Christmas ever."

He held her close and kissed the top of her head. "It already is for me."

"That is, if we survive felling this tree. Did you bring a saw?"

"It's still on the sled." He blinked rapidly behind his sunglasses and silently thanked her and God for an excuse to slip away for a moment and compose himself. "I'll hitch it up to Admiral and see how close we can get the sled to the tree."

Cutting, securing, and dragging the tree home kept the pair occupied for nearly two more hours. The struggle to get the tree inside and onto a stand required an hour more of laughter and grunting, followed by another hour of recovery time spent flopping on the sofa, gazing at their trophy tree.

Reese gathered what ornaments he could find, and CC slipped away to the bedroom, returning with an Amazon box filled with lights and more ornaments.

"Where did these come from?" Reese asked.

"I ordered them when you and Carlos were on your trail ride. Emmie showed me what you had, and . . ." Her features squished to the center of her face in a clear reaction to the inadequacy of his Christmas decor.

"You bought ornaments for a tree we didn't even have?"

"I had hope."

"You are hope."

She tilted her head to the side and smiled until her eyes crinkled into slits. "A tree this big needs lots of decorations. I'll make more chains."

She pulled out the rolls of aluminum foil and got busy on that task. Reese wanted to put his worries to rest once and for all, so he stole away to check his email. His fingers shook as he scrolled for Marcus's address, hoping the dreaded message hadn't arrived, but as promised, it was waiting in his inbox.

CC's ex, Devon Peters, had relentlessly continued dredging up her past, and he'd shared the basics of his findings with the Chicago police—he'd contacted a woman claiming to be CC's mother. This mystery mother had petitioned Chicago's finest to provide CC's whereabouts so she could speak to CC face-to-face. Thankfully, the police had refused, citing Marcus's eye-witness assurance that she was fine and that she had requested no further contact.

Reese reread Devon's statement. Though the facts were intentionally vague, the allusion to a mother CC claimed not to know still rattled him.

He bit his knuckle and stared at the screen, praying for insight as he debated the ramifications of sharing the report with CC. He concluded that there was no point in telling her unless the information could be verified, and he'd work on that in a few days. In the meantime, he convinced himself that this was just Devon's latest desperate ploy to get her attention, like the fake engagement photos. What else would that cheater do to win CC back? Would he really try to find her? And if he did, would he be CC's hero or her undoing?

# CHAPTER SEVENTEEN

REESE NEEDED A FEW MINUTES before facing CC. When he exited his office, he found her in the same place, listening to Christmas music as she rolled and crimped pieces of aluminum foil.

"So tell me about these," he said, more to open a dialogue than because he had any real interest in the topic.

"Well," CC began, "according to my father, my great-grandparents Aldo and Silvia Cippolini were a young immigrant couple from Italy who arrived in New York City a few years before the war broke out. Aldo got a job as a cook in a restaurant, and the manager allowed him to wrap up a few leftovers in tinfoil and take them home to his wife. Silvia washed and saved every piece and used them to make chains for their tree that year. By the next year, she had enough links to also hang a tinfoil garland over their door, but war was declared before their third Christmas in America, and wanting to be a good citizen to his new country, Aldo enlisted in the army. People began to collect tinfoil for recycling as part of the nation's Win with Tin WWII defense project. My great-grandparents donated all their chains to the war effort . . . all but one link, which Silvia supposedly tucked into Aldo's pocket so, wherever he went, he'd never feel far from her."

Reese swallowed past the lump in his throat. "That's a beautiful story."

"It is, isn't it? Great-Grandmother Silvia made new chains once the war ended and aluminum foil was available. Then my grandma made them for her tree, and my father made them for ours."

"So it's a Cippolini family tradition, like the cinnamon-twirl cookies."

"Yes, but Aldo and Silvia probably didn't invent the idea of foil chains. It must have been something a lot of people used to do. Nora even had a set, except she hung hers in the beauty-shop window. Most of the shops on her block had them too."

"Really? I'd never heard of anything like that." Something about that story picked at his peace. He sat down beside CC and fingered the chain she was making. "Did you make a set for the apartment you shared with Nora?"

"No. She was obsessive compulsive about clutter, and she wasn't the least bit sentimental. Remember the tree incident I told you about?"

Reese remembered. "And yet she hung chains in her shop?"

"It was probably a holiday marketing thing, like the gaudy posters of new hairstyles and seasonal things she hung in the storefront window."

"I see."

CC made more room for Reese. "Wanna help?"

"Sure." He scooted closer, and after a few moments of instruction, his links were passing CC's inspection. The two fell into a link-making rhythm, but he couldn't shake the worry nagging at him, so he asked, "Can I pick up on the game we played the other night and ask you another question?"

"Another getting-to-know-you question?"

"Yeah, something like that." Reese wished he could let it all go, let go of the worry and the doubts and the second-guessing and just enjoy what he and CC had in this moment, but he couldn't ignore contradictions and inconsistencies. He'd gone into one relationship blindly. He couldn't make that mistake again.

"Okay. I'll answer your question as long as I get to ask you one back."

"Agreed." He rolled his dry lips to moisten them. "If you were granted the ability to spend an hour with anyone, living or dead, who would you want to spend it with?"

"That's easy. My father," she said with a slight echo of melancholy.

"I guess I should have figured that. Who would be your second pick?"

CC looked up from her chain work and gazed blankly at the fireplace. After a few moments, she finally said, "I really can't think of anyone else I'd rather be with than you."

"Besides me. Really? No one? No family friend? No other relative?"

She sighed as she gave the idea some thought. "No. We had good friends, but no one I'd need to call back from the dead for a chat." A light came over her. "I suppose it would be fun to meet Aldo or Silvia or my grandmother."

"But not your mom?"

He scrutinized every shift in her features to see what response the question produced, but aside from a slight wrinkling of her brows, there was none.

"I used to wish she'd come back when Dad was alive, but not after he was gone."

"I would have thought that's exactly when you'd have needed her the most."

"Exactly."

The answer was definitive and disappointment-filled, leaving Reese feeling censured for not understanding her reasoning the first time. "I'm sorry. I shouldn't have pried."

"Why did you ask me that?"

"Because this time of year makes us long for family. I wondered who you were missing this year."

She leaned toward Reese and placed her hand on his knee. "I'm so happy things are getting better between you and your family—I really am—but please don't feel bad for me because I don't have family waiting to welcome me home. Enjoy what you have. I'm grateful to share even a little of that with you. And you might be very proud to know that I took your advice and called Nora."

That news physically set Reese back. "You did?"

"Yeah. She's not really family, but she gave me a decent home, and she's the closest thing I have."

Reese's heart thumped in his chest. He wanted to scream out all he knew about someone claiming to be her mother, to give CC a heads-up so she wouldn't get waylaid by Devon and his *investigation*. "Tell me about your conversation with her."

"You don't need to worry. She didn't answer, but I left her a message telling her I was all right and happy. I apologized for leaving the way I did, and I thanked her for all she did for me. I said she could call me if she ever wanted to talk, and I wished her a Merry Christmas. I'm glad I called. Closure is good."

Reese moved sentences and phrases around in his mind, preparing his delivery of the message he needed to give CC. "That door might not be clo—" but before he finished, the back door opened, and in rushed Emmie and Carlos.

"She's still here!" Emmie squealed as she ran to meet CC, who had leapt from the sofa and was making a beeline for her new friend.

Carlos entered right behind with bags in both arms. "That's great! We wondered how you two were getting on." He winked at Reese, who stood to help Carlos with the bags.

"How was the little getaway, you two?" he asked.

"Fabulous! We ate too much, slept too little, and generally need one of these every month." Carlos glanced at the women, who were babbling together on the sofa, and lowered his voice. "So . . . how are you and CC getting along?"

"She's great. Really great."

Carlos studied Reese's eyes, as if he were giving him an exam. "There's something else hiding behind that tepid endorsement."

"We're just worn out from choosing the best Christmas tree ever." Reese pointed to the corner. "What do you think of it?"

The oohs and aahs over the tree and plans for decorating it were superseded by Carlos's request for food. Reese quickly explained about the best-tree bet and how CC's win also relegated her to the role of chef.

"I accept my victory," CC said with her arms raised in the air. "And that means you have to eat whatever I cook."

"Ahhh . . . in that case," Reese said, "I offer myself as substitute chef. Carlos, will you grab four steaks out of the freezer and meet me by the grill?"

"Gladly."

The women threw some sides together, and the group ate and talked and played games until the yawns outnumbered the jokes. Reese and CC found each other's hands once or twice under the table, and they found opportunities to steal mixed-emotion glances that left Reese longing for a return to yesterday's privacy, but neither of them seemed comfortable sharing the shift in their relationship with Emmie and Carlos.

When the last game was won and packed away, everyone stood and stretched before calling it a night. Reese caught CC looking at him as if she were lost and unsure how to proceed. He moved to her and offered her a tentative hand, which she countered with a quick good-night kiss before peeling away to bed. Reese scolded himself for his reticence, noting that CC held back as well. Was she playing off his anemic lead, or was he following hers? What had happened since their morning promise to fight for this relationship? Reese wondered if the magic of their days alone was simply that and whether it was sustainable when the tedium of real life resumed. And whether it would disappear altogether with the coming of a new day.

# CHAPTER EIGHTEEN

THE COMBINED SMELLS OF SAUSAGE and bacon served as CC's call to arise Thursday morning. She pulled her hair back in a ponytail and dressed quickly in jeans and a sweater, finding Reese at the stove, dressed for the day, with a spatula in hand. She walked up beside him and leaned into the counter, keeping twelve inches of question-filled space between them.

"Are we okay?" she asked as her head tilted to the side.

Reese stretched his left arm out, and she stepped into the void. "Do things feel different with Emmie and Carlos here?"

"I think things started feeling different before they arrived."

Emmie shuffled out before the comment could be explored. "You two are so cute. So . . . I take it things went well in our absence." She wiggled her eyebrows while nibbling on a slice of bacon. Aside from a smile, neither CC nor Reese acknowledged the question.

Carlos strolled out, dressed to get back to work. "I'm starving," he said as he stole a sausage.

"Dig in," Reese said as he pushed the plate toward his friend.

Emmie held a hand up. "If you can wait thirty minutes, CC and I can keep the meat warm in the oven and rustle up some pancakes while you two tend to the stock."

With a smile and a touch of ceremonial flair, Reese handed his spatula to CC and exited the kitchen with Carlos.

Emmie bunched up her arms and shook with excitement. "I've never seen him this happy."

CC wanted to say that she'd seen him even happier just a day ago, but she didn't. Things had risen and ebbed between them in a disappointing pattern. After sharing too much, they fell back into their own corners to reflect and evaluate. Each time, they'd found their way to one another again, and she hoped their little dance would move that same way once more.

"To be honest, this makes me happy for selfish reasons too," Emmie continued when CC didn't respond. "Carlos and I were afraid to make our own plans because we were worried about how Reese would do all alone here. But now that he has you—"

"No one has *anyone* yet." CC held up a hand. She couldn't let Emmie's imagination run wild when she was still unsure where she and Reese stood. "We enjoy each other's company. We get along. That's all I'm saying."

Emmie rubbed her palms together until CC wondered if a genie might pop out from between them. "Did he kiss you?"

Heat rose in CC's cheeks until no answer was needed.

"See? He's crazy about you!"

"More importantly, he and his family are not as estranged as you think. We're going to the party. He told his mother two days ago."

CC's effort to redirect the conversation off her romantic life only fueled Emmie's imagination further. "He's taking you to meet his family? That's huge! Don't you see? He almost never *speaks* to them, and now he's taking you to *meet* them?" She squealed and danced in little circles.

"Pancakes, Emmie. Focus on the pancakes."

CC succeeded in directing the conversation to Emmie and Carlos's getaway long enough to get a ten-inch stack of hotcakes ready and the table set. When the men came in, Reese headed for the sink instead of to CC, and though it made sense, she read withdrawal into everything.

"Carlos thinks the doe's wounds are fully healed," Reese said as he washed his hands.

He spoke to everyone, but his eyes shot to CC. She stiffened at the news and then asked, "Does that mean you're going to release her today?"

Reese's mouth twitched, and Carlos delivered the hard news. "The longer we hold her in captivity, the harder it will be for her and her fawn to adjust to the wild."

"So today it is," CC said, feigning nonchalance. "Shall we eat?"

She pushed her food around her plate more than ate, and when the meal appeared to be winding down, she stood and said, "Leave the dishes. I'll get to them in a few minutes. I just need to do something first."

She slipped out the front door, needing to see Noel and Dasher without being obvious about her objective. The view of the pond captured her attention, holding her spellbound as it conjured memories of that day when Reese had made her feel whole and valued with a few words about water. She obscured herself behind a wooden column in case anyone came looking for her, and reran those words through her head, telling herself that if things didn't work out between her and Reese, it was not because she wasn't enough.

The pond welcomed a gaggle of migrating geese and other fowl today. Snow was melting off the trees and rooflines, forming icicles whose attachments were weakening, sending them to the ground in sporadic clinks and crashes. Everything was in movement, coming and going, here for a brief time and then moving on. She closed her eyes and tried to picture this spot from memory so she could retrieve it in case . . .

A breeze blew by, and she wished she'd thought to grab a sweater on the way out, but her emotional retreat had been unplanned. She rubbed her arms to warm them and thought about the doe and the fawn. She'd barely even visited them for days, and today they would be gone. Her fickleness seemed obscene, that a being that had been so important to her one day had barely crossed her mind another. It was so much easier than it should be to forget one love when another came along. The broader implications of that thought struck her with staggering intensity.

The door groaned as it opened. CC knew who was coming by the sound of his boots on the porch. She felt a blanket fall across her shoulders and the comfort of a gentle squeeze before his hands withdrew.

"I know you're upset about the deer," Reese said.

She continued to face forward and stare at the water with Reese standing a step above her.

Then CC handed the blanket back to him. "I should get on those dishes."

"No need. Carlos and Emmie are washing them, and don't beat yourself up about it. They're probably playing the finger equivalent of footsie in the dishwater."

A soft laugh escaped her tight lips. "I'd like to think so."

He stepped down, and their eyes met. His showed the same pain she felt. She replayed every moment from the previous day, trying to identify when the distance first arose between them.

"I know things . . . feel . . . different," he said.

She waited for him to fill in the blanks, but he left the comment hanging in the cold air. Her defenses came up, and she changed the subject. "When are you setting Noel and Dasher free?"

"Emmie was the primary vet until you arrived. We should do it when we're all together."

"I'd like to go sit with them for a few minutes."

"Would you like company?"

CC shook her head. "I'd like to see if they'll come to me once more, if that's all right."

They parted with an understanding nod instead of a kiss. CC found it sadly funny that she was right back where she'd begun, more comfortable in the barn enjoying the company of the other guests and the deer than with the owner of the property.

She entered the barn and stopped by the deer stall to gauge the animals' responses to her arrival. They had just been fed, so CC had nothing with which to entice Noel and Dasher to come to her. Inching her way, she opened the gate, slipped inside, and sat with her back to the wall. She was glad the two had each other. At least they would be sent off to face the world together.

She lost track of time as she sat there, as still as stone, eyes closed, humming softly. Both animals stayed in their corner, picking kernels of corn from the bedding. She questioned the wisdom of teaching the deer to trust humans who would send them away again into the wild, where other humans would try to kill them. A tear stung her at the cruel irony of the situation, and she clicked her tongue to put the animals on alert. Their ears shot straight up, and their bodies froze as they monitored every sound and movement.

"Keep your guard up. You're going to need that," she said as she rose to her feet.

"CC, if we kept every stray or wounded animal that crossed this acreage, we'd be a zoo instead of a cattle ranch."

She wondered when Reese had entered and how long he'd been standing there. She remained facing the deer. "I thought this was about what's best for *them*."

"This is what's best. You said it yourself. They need to keep their guard up. Their instincts will suffer if they stay here too long."

"Instincts or not, the wild nearly killed them once. They're safe here. Maybe being free and loose isn't all it's cracked up to be. Being loved and cared about is its own kind of freedom, isn't it? The freedom not to be hurt or afraid or separated from the ones you love?"

She heard the door latch scrape and the hinge squeak and the scuff of Reese's boots as he came up behind her. He turned her toward him, and she dropped her chin to her chest, unwilling to have him see her cry. She resisted his initial attempts to comfort her, knowing that when her head found his shoulder, the floodgates would fully open. They held each other in silence for a time.

"I didn't come to see them yesterday. I spent nearly half a day with them three days ago, bonding with them, and now I'm a stranger again. It's so much easier to lose trust than to earn it."

"This conversation is really about us, isn't it?"

She looked up at him, needing to see his reaction and needing him to see hers.

"You're not a stranger again, CC. You made magical moments with them and with me. They're not gone because reality returned."

"Despite all we said about going slow and being cautious, we moved too fast."

"Maybe we did. But . . . slowing down is still moving forward."

"Pulling back isn't."

"Pulling back?"

"Ever since you invited me to the party to meet your family."

"I want you to meet them; it's just . . . it's not a small thing. It's a big step, and I want to . . . I'm trying to make sure I'm balancing all my—"

"Responsibilities?" She stepped away from him. "I heard what you said about your past mistakes and your obligations. I get all that. I even respect all that, but I deserve to have some protections in place too. I didn't crash into your fence to land a man, nor was I trying to get Devon's attention. And I don't need hollow attention now." She straightened and poked her finger into his chest. "You spin a great story about sacred words like *family* and *love*, until I started to believe that's where we might be headed, but it's been hot and cold with you. And, for the record, love shouldn't look or feel or hurt like this, so maybe that's not what this is after all."

CC stepped for the open gate, but Reese's hands tightened slightly on her arms. "Wait, please. I have been holding back. I'm . . . sorting through some things."

"What things?"

Her challenge seemed to cow him. "Marcus called while you were searching for your tree. Devon isn't going away."

CC felt equally flummoxed and frustrated. "Is that what this is all about?"

He drew in a breath as if he were preparing to speak, but nothing came out. CC grabbed her head in both hands and groaned. "Why are you still worried about a man I cut from my life weeks before I met you?"

Light burst through the opened door. "Reese? CC?" Emmie called from outside. "I'll just stand out here in case you're midkiss. I just wanted to say that we're ready to trim the tree."

Reese barked back, "We need a minute, Emmie."

She exited in a flash, and immediate regret paled Reese. He released CC's arms and paced in random circles, coming to a stop in front of her and shoving his hands into his pockets. "You say you're finished with Devon." He dipped his head, and when he raised it again, his hands came forward, pleading his case. "But you forgive people who've hurt you. You root for the underdog, and you try to rescue them at all costs."

She wanted to scream or hit something, but she saw how raw his worry was. She walked to him and took his hands. "Hear what I'm saying to you, Reese. I could have run back to him days ago, but I have no interest in being with Devon. Look at me. I'm here . . . with you."

"Yes, you are." He pulled her close once more. "But do something for me. Search your heart, CC. Make sure there's no one from your past you'd rather be with than me."

"You know my entire list of exes—Devon. Period. And I don't want crazy infatuation. I want all those qualities you reserve for your family and town—your loyalty, responsibility, and strength."

"I want to give you all that and more."

"And I can't give you anything more than my word. So where does that leave us?"

"I don't know. It's my problem, not yours . . . and I'm working on it."

"Great. Well . . . let me know what you figure out. I've got a tree to trim."

# CHAPTER NINETEEN

CC NOTICED EMMIE AND CARLOS staring out the window at her and Reese as they made their way from the barn toward the house. Curtains flew shut as they scrambled from the glass once they realized they'd been caught spying.

"CC, wait, please." Reese took her arm and gently pulled her to a stop before she reached the back porch. "Are we okay?"

Her eyes burned. "We've been better."

"I'm sorry." Reese brushed her hair back. "Do you want to take a walk or something? I want to get this right between us."

"How about instead of protecting ourselves, we look out for each other?"

Reese seemed to age a decade in a second. He closed his eyes and groaned. "Oh, CC. How'd I get so lost?" He studied her with love-filled eyes. "You do look out for others. That's your gift. You flood goodness into others, putting their happiness ahead of your own, even when we're too small and petty to receive what you're offering. First Devon, and now me."

He threaded his fingers into her hair, and CC felt her heart would burst.

"I've been acting like a martyr, telling myself I sacrifice what I want to protect the people I love. The truth is I've been a coward. Worse, I've sacrificed your trust to protect my pride." He pressed his forehead to hers and whispered, "Can you forgive me?"

It was all she could do to say the words that needed to be said. "I just need to know that you think I'm enough for you."

His mouth fell open. "You're enough and more. You're everything."

For that moment, everything disappeared—past hurts, the people watching from the house—until all that remained were them and Reese's words. He pulled her to him, resting his cheek against hers. His mouth slid to hers, and the kiss deepened until the background noise of the door opening broke the moment.

Carlos and Emmie cheered while Carlos took the steps two at a time to reach Reese and pat his back. "Nicely done, brother."

Reese glanced up at Carlos. "All right, all right, you two." He led CC to the open door and waited for her and the others to enter first.

Emmie stood next to Carlos, her eyes wide and her fingers pressed against her mouth like a patient awaiting a shot.

Reese closed the door and glanced at CC, then Emmie. "I'm sorry I was short with you out there, Emmie."

"I'm fine . . . but I'm so glad you two made up. I mean, you were both so quiet during dinner, and then things didn't seem very cozy out there in the barn. We were afraid you ruined everything, Reese."

Another glance at CC confirmed for the whole room that Emmie's assessment was spot-on. Reese pulled CC closer to his side. She looked up at him and saw the worry lines still visible around his eyes. When he spoke, it was directly to her, as if they had gone back a day, and they were the only ones in the room. "How about we decorate that tree?"

The words were simple, but the delivery was personal and meaningful. He was fighting for them again. She threaded her fingers in his and nodded as she led him away.

The lights were quickly hung, followed by the chains and the ornaments, which took no time at all with all four people hanging the few balls. When the last one was hung, the group stood back and studied the tree.

"It's still a little bare in places," CC said.

"We can add to it later," Reese said. He gave her a knowing smile. "We have time."

The hum of an engine and the whoosh of tires on the pavement drew everyone's attention to the window. Reese stiffened and glanced quickly at CC.

"Are you expecting someone?" Emmie asked as she and Carlos peeked through the curtain. "Whoever it is drives a sweet car."

Reese headed for the door in long strides. CC picked up on his wary vibe, and she also tensed until his shoulders relaxed and he said, "Hi, Rudy."

Relief flooded over CC, and judging from the color returning to Reese's face, it appeared he, too, had worried that the driver just might be Devon.

"The Tesla's fixed," Carlos announced as everyone headed for Rudy and the car.

CC swooned and ran her hands over the repaired hood. "I can't believe how great it looks! It's prettier than the original. And this paint job is amazing!"

Rudy tipped his baseball cap to her and said, "I got a little creative. I couldn't help myself. I'm glad you're happy with how she turned out. She rides like a dream too."

A truck bearing the lettering *Rudy's Garage* pulled up behind the Tesla. Rudy waved to the driver. "My son's here to give me a ride home. If I hadn't just mailed Junior's college tuition, I'd be real tempted to make you an offer on this baby, Reese." He extended both the invoice and the key card, which dangled from a curly lanyard.

Reese handed the key to CC and asked Rudy, "What about the other car? Is it still scheduled to arrive on time?"

"Yep. Early, in fact. It should arrive here on the eighteenth to give me time to do the detailing. Junior will head down to Vegas with it and have it wrapped with a bow on Christmas Eve, as planned."

CC extended her hand to Rudy. "Thanks a million, Rudy."

"Oh, it didn't cost that much. Almost, but not quite." He laughed as he waved goodbye and strolled to the truck.

Emmie and Carlos headed to the car as soon as father and son were gone. "If I didn't know what this crazy car costs, I'd beg you to let me take it for a spin," Carlos said.

"But you do," Emmie said, "so be happy with double dessert instead."

"Save some for us," Reese said. "We'll join you after we park it in the garage." He turned to CC. "Do you want to do the honors?"

"Sure, but first, what was the final bill? I need to know because I'm calling John today to explain everything, and I'm paying you back every penny."

Reese slid the bill behind himself. "Hear me out before you look at it. We've got options. Just remember that and don't panic over the total."

CC reached for the bill and Reese laid it in her hand. She gave herself a B- for concealing her shock over the final figures. "Thanks for that, but I only need one thing from you. Let's sit down and work out my payment schedule for the repairs. And you should also know that I've changed my mind about staying here on the ranch while I pay off what I owe you. We've hit rough patches already. I don't want either of us to worry that I stayed because of my debt."

"I would never—"

"It's just better this way. If I stay, I'll find a place of my own in Brisbane."

Reese's shoulders rounded. "*If* you stay? But earlier you said—"

"I'm here, Reese, and if it's right . . . if *we're* right, I'll stay, but in my own place. You can't keep sleeping on the sofa, and Emmie thinks the town could use a new cosmetologist. I've done some research online. I have enough savings to open a little salon. I'll pay you back from my earnings, and I'll moonlight as a ranch hand to double my payments."

"If paying off this debt faster is more likely to help you feel comfortable about staying, then I've got a plan to recoup all the costs in a few weeks. Some of our most loyal clients do a New Year's Eve Jewelry Showcase in Vegas. Family members dress themselves and their mounts in silver-studded finery and head down to the strip to promote it. That's what you saw in my closet."

"You go down too?"

Reese frowned and shook his head. "I used to, but not since my enlistment."

"You haven't been back since?"

He shrugged and brushed at a speck of dust on the car. "I . . . I went to Vegas one last time . . . alone . . . after Marissa left. Let's just say it wasn't a good experience, and I opted out of participating in the showcase after that. But this year? I have good incentive to go."

He shot her an overly cheerful smile. "New Years in Vegas is a great gig. The tourists love getting their photos taken with the horses. I think I could raffle off the Tesla that night—a hundred and fifty tickets at one thousand dollars each. We pay the Tesla and the repairs off and give the rest of the money to a charity. What do you think?"

"Is that legal? Could you even sell enough tickets?"

"My attorney has filled out all the paperwork with the Nevada Gaming Commission, so the legal aspect is covered, and as for selling enough tickets . . . after what Rudy did to this car? I don't think that'll be a problem. The city is always filled with high rollers, and more than usual during the holidays."

"You've really given this a lot of thought."

"I've never wanted this car to be an issue between us."

They parked the car in his garage, and when they got out, Reese took CC's hand and led her into the house. Emmie and Carlos were nowhere to be seen, but their voices could be heard coming from their suite down the hall.

Reese walked CC to the Christmas tree and hung the Tesla's key on an empty branch. "I want you to see this every day and understand that this car is just a pretty, fun thing. A giant ornament with an engine. It has no bearing on our lives. Not at all. Whatever decisions we make, to be together or not, have nothing to do with this car, okay?"

CC nodded as tears welled in her eyes. "I like this plan."

Reese laid a finger under her eye to catch the first tear. "I don't want worries about debt or people from our past or anything else to keep you from hearing and believing what I'm about to say." He placed his hands on her shoulders and tightened his fingers, steadying her as he leaned close. His voice dropped in register until it was barely a husky whisper. "Tomorrow is my parents' Christmas party. You're the first woman I've introduced to my family since Marissa. I hope you understand what that means to me. That's the surest admission I have that I love you, and I want the people I love most to love each other too."

CC felt as if she were floating and looking down on someone else's story, someone else's happy moment, and then Reese's words and his shining eyes broke through and assured her this was her love story playing out. Her eyes burned and her throat tightened, and she brought her hand to her breastbone to steady her pounding heart. "I love you, Reese. And I love you all the more for not just offering me your love but for sharing your family with me. Thank you. You've given me everything I've ever wanted."

He swallowed and slid his hands from CC's shoulders to her hands, giving them reassuring little squeezes. "Be patient with me. If I appear to drop back and become defensive, call me out." He smiled down into her face. "But please don't give up on me."

"I won't. I promise. I'm a fighter, remember?"

CC's dreams were sweet that night. She dreamed of a life with Reese, of open arms welcoming her to large family dinners filled with happy, laughing voices. She didn't care about their money and lavish lifestyle. She wanted people—people to love and to be loved by. And, most of all, she wanted Reese.

# CHAPTER TWENTY

THE NEXT MORNING, SHE SETTLED into the passenger seat of Emmie and Carlos's truck and buckled her seat belt. "Thanks for taking me shopping, Emmie."

"Of course. I don't need much. What's on your list?"

"A hostess gift for Reese's mother. What's my chance of finding something nice in Brisbane?"

"That depends. What's your price range?"

"Let's just say I'm leaning more toward sentimental than elegant."

"Then, you might be surprised. There are some talented artists in the area. I'm sure we'll find something worthy of the Brockbanks."

Emmie's sarcasm wasn't lost on CC. "I know you don't care for them, but Reese loves his family. He's sorry he allowed his hurt and guilt to influence your negative opinion of them."

"They're all right, I guess," Emmie said. "They've always been pleasant to Carlos and me. I just know how sad Reese seems whenever they call or stop by."

"Maybe their visits reminded him of old hurts, like Marissa."

"Maybe."

"Did you know her?"

Emmie shook her head slowly, as if she were caught up in a memory. "She was already long gone by the time I arrived. Carlos knew her, but he's almost as close-mouthed about that part of Reese's life as Reese is, probably because of her younger brother's death."

"Wait . . . the brother who joined the rebels?"

Emmie's face paled and then burned red. "I thought you knew. I shouldn't have said anything. Carlos hates when I gossip."

"Please, Emmie. What happened?"

Emmie sighed. "He died in that blast that hurt Reese. He was only sixteen."

When Reese told CC about Marissa and her family, he'd admitted that Marissa's brother hadn't travelled to Germany with the others. CC had assumed it had been because of his rebel ties. Not because he was dead. "What happened?"

"Reese and Carlos had almost arrived at Marissa's home to pick up her family and take them to safety on the American base. Marissa's brother was standing in the street in front of them when the truck blew up."

"What? Was he the bomber?"

"Maybe, or it could have been from a roadside bomb. The team didn't see it coming. What haunts Reese is the possibility that Marissa's brother was there because he planned to turn himself in to the Americans, hoping to provide intel in return for asylum."

"Was that even a reasonable possibility?"

"Marissa's parents evidently said as much."

CC could see the dilemma. "And that's all the stick Reese needed to beat himself with."

"There were other willing hands swinging that stick."

"Marissa's family?"

"Some of them."

CC could only imagine the mounting guilt Reese had heaped upon himself. He had recruited Marissa, and as he likely saw it, that began the spiral that led to the boy's death and the trauma to two families. The wife who didn't love him may have even blamed him for her brother's death. So much hurt. So much pain. CC felt sick—for Reese, for the families, and over the whole situation. "No wonder he has such a hard time opening himself up to anyone."

"Then, you see what a big deal it is for him to want to introduce you to his family?"

"I do now. I hope I make a good first impression."

"No matter what trinket we find today, it's you they'll notice, and how happy you make their son."

"Thanks, Emmie."

They pulled up in front of a small retail strip and a place called the Whittler's Nook Consignment Center. Emmie pointed to it. "About twenty local artisans and a few out-of-towners, all great, showcase their wares here. You can find some amazing pieces."

The shop was stuffed for Christmas with holiday decor items and gifts for every age. Emmie poked around shelves filled with metalwork pieces, but

CC zoned in on the Christmas ornaments, marveling over the variety and beauty of the handmade pieces. Within ten minutes, she found the perfect ornament—a ball of wood, intricately hollowed until it was a thin sphere with four thin teardrop cutouts, separating the ball into four small palettes. A scene from the Christmas story was carved into each, and those carvings were inlaid in gleaming silver. One scene was of an intricate star. The second was of a shepherd. The third showed a Wise Man, and the fourth was a masterfully carved image of the Nativity. It was the most delicately beautiful ornament CC had ever seen. "This is it," she whispered almost reverently. "This is the one."

Emmie confirmed the selection with her own swoon. "It's glorious! But what's it cost?"

CC was almost afraid to look at the tag. When she did, she gave a little shiver, noting that though the price was high, it fairly represented the amount of artistry and work that had gone into the piece. "It's worth every penny."

While one clerk rang up the purchase, another found a box for the ornament and gift wrapped it in red paper with a silver bow. "I do calligraphy," the middle-aged woman said. "For a dollar more, I can create a customized tag for your gift."

"That would make it perfect! Please make it out to Mr. and Mrs. Brockbank, from CC."

"The Brockbanks, eh?" The woman smiled down at CC over the rim of her glasses. "You must be that friend of Reese's I've heard so much about."

A warning shudder skimmed over CC. "Have we met?"

"No, but my son was in Big Jim's the other night." The woman smiled more broadly.

CC felt her cheeks burn, and Emmie's wide-eyed stare only amplified the comment.

The woman's face warmed with tenderness. "He said it appeared that Reese had finally found a woman who truly loved him."

CC didn't know how to respond, so she smiled back and muttered a thank-you.

"I'll go make up this gift tag and be right back."

After the woman's exit, CC silently counted, *Three, two, one* and nailed the amount of time that would elapse before Emmie began interrogating her over the events at Big Jim's. She was barely able to complete the Cliff Notes version of the run-in with Reese's drunken "friend" when the clerk returned with the elegant card lettered in flowing gold. It was, as CC had imagined, perfect.

The woman tied it to the gift and presented the completed package to CC. "I can't tell you how happy I am for you two. Sounds like Reese is his old, happy self again . . . having someone special in his life and inviting other guests to the ranch again."

"I'm sorry. Guests?" CC asked.

"Oh . . . I just assumed they were, what with his parents' party being tonight. There was just that man who stopped by, asking for directions to Reese's place, and that woman he had in the car with him."

CC looked at Emmie, who seemed just as puzzled as she was about the news.

"Looks like you weren't expecting them after all. Don't worry. I didn't give them any information. I told them I was navigationally challenged," the clerk explained.

CC and Emmie thanked the shop clerks again and exited. Once outside, CC questioned Emmie again about the report. "Is it weird that someone was asking for Reese's address?"

"It was probably a guest looking for directions to the party tonight," Emmie reasoned.

"But they asked for directions to *Reese's* house."

"Both houses sit on the same lane, plus Reese lived at the Brockbank house before he built the cattle shack. Not everyone invited to the party knows his entire history."

"That makes sense."

"Now, let's grab whatever else we need and get home so we have plenty of time to set those deer free and get ready for the party. I have a feeling this is going to be a night to remember . . . for both of us."

# CHAPTER TWENTY-ONE

CC AND EMMIE FOUND A black car parked in the driveway when they arrived at Reese's house. The Nevada plates were encased in a frame advertising a rental company out of Las Vegas. They also noticed a thin person sitting at the very edge of one of the rockers on the front porch. The stranger was pitched forward, arms folded under them like wings, as if their primary focus was conducting an intense study of their shoes. Their gender was concealed under a knitted cap and the puffy green coat they wore.

"Any idea who that is?" CC asked.

"No," Emmie said curiously as she drove around the house and entered the garage in back. Carlos must have heard the whir of the garage-door motor announcing their arrival because he appeared in the doorway. Concern showed on his face, though he tried to disguise it with a nervous smile. His mood reminded CC of the owner of the hardware store the day she'd walked into the principal's office to receive the news of her dad's passing. Her skin turned clammy as Carlos beckoned them into the mudroom and closed the door.

Her eyebrows bunched up in concern for Emmie, as she feared something terrible had happened to someone she or Carlos loved. Carlos looked at his wife and placed a hand on the center of her back, and then his somber eyes moved past Emmie to CC.

She froze.

"What's going on, Carlos?" Emmie said. "You're kind of freaking us out."

His wavering emotions settled on just one—sadness. "CC, you have company."

"Me? No one knows where—" She felt the blood drain from her face as she remembered the store clerk's comment. Only one person would care enough where CC was to track her down—Devon—and if it *was* him, he'd come despite her making it clear that she never wanted to see him again. Did Reese still believe that? She was ready and willing to make her point again.

CC scanned the open area for men . . . or bodies. She found a slightly meeker version of Devon than she remembered standing a few yards from the front doorway, dressed in a carefully selected outfit from his ample wardrobe. The shirt and jeans he wore were the ones she'd given him for his recent birthday. His good looks weren't completely lost on her, but the neat cut of his brown hair and the new trim of his beard were styled according to changes she'd proposed. It was a power game. Calculated moves designed to get her attention, perhaps because he actually loved her but more likely because his ego was bruised.

Reese was in front of the fireplace. His angry finger-jabbing halted when he noticed CC barreling out of the mudroom, but what she saw in his eyes stopped her cold. The intimidating cattleman, who a moment earlier had seemed poised to toss Devon out, shrank when CC appeared. Love seemed but a background emotion to the others vacillating across his face. CC blamed Devon for the change.

"What are you doing here?" she spat at the unwanted man.

"We need to talk."

"We're done. Wasn't blocking you from calling or contacting me on social media proof enough of that? Didn't you get the message that I never want to see you again?"

"Loud and clear."

Softer now, more in control, she said, "All right. Then, why are you here?"

She thought she saw Reese straighten a little, as if her dismissal of Devon had assuaged any doubts he may have had about her loyalties.

"I just came to tie up a few loose ends, and then I'll go."

"What loose ends?"

Reese took a step toward Devon, but Devon didn't back down. CC moved like a guardian, stepping in front of Reese and leaning into him with her arms crossed in front. "Say your piece, Devon, and then leave."

His eyes flashed red over CC's move to Reese, and then his mouth pulled to the right. CC had seen it dozens of times, as that wounded look had often been aimed at her if she showed the slightest courtesy to a customer. It generally preceded one of two responses: the isolating cold shoulder that generally lasted until CC apologized for the perceived wrong she knew she hadn't committed, simply to restore peace, or Devon's signature move—the sulking exit. This was his power play, where he'd go dark for days at a time, which she now assumed was when he'd found someone else to massage his fragile, wounded ego. She watched his eyes move from her to Reese, and she was grateful his characteristic sneer raised its ugly head right then, putting every caution within her on high alert.

"You've known each other what, two weeks? And you're already this close? Let me guess. He's a veteran, isn't he?"

CC flinched at having her relationship with Reese so easily dismissed. "The clock is running, Devon."

"You always did have a soft spot for battered heroes."

She glanced back at Reese and saw the steeled set of his jaw replaced by the disquieting curiosity in his eyes. Devon was a master at gamesmanship. Divide and conquer. Well, she was having none of it. "You don't know anything about us. Your time is up." She took a step for the door, and Devon folded.

"Okay, okay. I'm sorry." He smiled and began shaking his head slowly, as if amused by the story he was about to tell. "When you blocked me, I posted that engagement photo knowing your friends would pass the post on to you."

"Don't you mean fake engagement photo?"

"Not fake for long." He smirked again.

CC braced for Devon's next trick.

"I needed to get your attention because you have something I need, and I have a little gift for you."

"I have nothing of yours, and you have nothing I want."

"How about you cut me a little slack? You took off without a word. I was afraid for your safety."

"That's such a lie." She had almost forgotten that it was his insinuations to the police about her mental state that had brought the sheriff here, asking questions about whether she was *really* okay. "My employers and coworkers all knew my plans. All you had to do when you *finally* missed me was ask them. That fictitious police filing and the drama it caused was all about you playing the hero. Well, fine. You solved the case. Go home to the next number on your call list, tell your sad tale, and make some other girl's heart flutter."

His hands unclasped and fell by his sides. "You really have changed since you left Chicago. If you're happy, I'm happy for you. Truly . . . I'm actually impressed by how well you're taking the news about your mother."

"What?" Every nerve seemed to fire simultaneously at the mention of her mother. "What are you talking about?"

Devon's gaze shifted back to Reese, and CC could feel Reese lean away from her. She turned to him, needing desperately to understand the signals being shared between the men. "Do you know what he's talking about?" She tried not to make it sound accusatory, but she could hear that tone in her whispered question.

"He made some statements to the police, and Marcus passed them along to me. I-I-I didn't know what to make of them . . ."

Reese's sheepish reply set CC's nerves further on edge. "But you didn't think to tell me?"

Reese stared down into her face and tried to touch her, but she pulled back and turned on Devon, who was ready with an explanation.

"I wanted to tell you the good news as soon as I found out. I know how much you hate surprises, but I had no way to get ahold of you, so I did the only thing I could do. I passed the news along through the police channels your friend here opened up after your accident."

Her mind was spinning from the prospect of making contact with her real mother, but for the moment, she was processing the latest revelation, that Reese had opened a police investigation about her. She looked back at him and knew it was true. "You? You said you called Marcus so he'd know the driver of the car was safe. You blamed Devon for opening the investigation into my disappearance, but it was you? You were *investigating* me?"

"Just that first night. To verify who you were and who owned the car. It didn't get past Marcus, and I asked him to shut it down the next day, but Devon had reported you missing and possibly in danger. That's what launched the investigation."

Nothing seemed real or solid or true anymore. Reese had kept secrets from her, several secrets, despite the fact that she had asked and asked him if he had reservations or questions about her.

As for Devon, his act was self-serving. She didn't believe anything he said. Did she dare trust the news about her mother?

She walked to him and stopped. "What do you know about my mother?"

He leaned close and cupped her arms in his hands as his face took on a portrayal of concern. "CC, your foster mother, Nora? Her real name is Eleanor. Stubbert was the name of her third husband, but she's not just your foster mother, CC. She's your birth mother."

CC stepped back, almost in revulsion over the idea. "No. No." The second word came out as a whimper. "She would have told me."

"I wanted to," a voice said from the doorway.

CC had missed the opening of the door, but the woman standing there was unmistakably Nora. Her hair was mussed from being under the knitted cap, and her fingers were in constant motion. She looked as if she'd rather leap from a roof than stand there, facing CC, and yet she stood her ground, as if she had more to say.

"I planned to tell you the truth of who I was the day you graduated. I planned it. I figured that once you had your diploma and cosmetology license in your hand, you could choose to stay or leave because you'd be able to make your own way."

"You didn't show up at my graduation."

"I know. I know. I made a mistake."

CC noticed how she repeated herself and avoided making eye contact.

"I was so nervous about my plans that I double-dosed my anxiety meds and fell asleep. When I woke up and saw the clock, I knew I'd missed the ceremony, so I waited for you to come home so I could explain everything, but you never came. You never came."

Nora took a step forward, but CC backed up, registering the attempted advance as another threat, like the secrets and surprises that had already fractured everything she had previously understood.

Nora muttered, "I'm sorry," and halted. Her only motion was her nervous fidgeting with the zipper on her coat, zipping and unzipping it a few inches as she rambled on. "I don't blame you for not coming home. You probably knew I had problems. Lots of problems. If it weren't for your father's help before he died, I'd probably be dead."

"What'dyousay?" CC delivered the one-word challenge sharply, sending Nora back two steps. "Are you saying my father knew where you were all along? That he lied to me about you all my life?"

"He checked up on me from time to time."

"That's a lie!" CC shouted, making no effort to dilute the sting of her words. She'd intended to merely stop Nora, but she far exceeded her goal.

The woman drew her arms close like protective armor. Her entire body seemed to thrum with nervous energy while her fingers tapped erratically against her shoulders. "I knew I shouldn't come. Knew it, knew it. He said I needed to do this. Leave my home and routine. I said no, but he insisted it was important, so I came. But he was wrong. He was wrong."

Nora's rant unleashed Reese, who sidestepped CC and reached Nora in two long strides. His gentle motions and compassionate words to the fragile woman contrasted with both the disappointment he shot CC's way and the fierce anger he seared into Devon. The Chicagoan leaned away and fisted his hands in preparation for expected blows that never came as Reese passed him. Instead of punishing Devon, Reese tended to Nora, taking her outside, then closing the door behind them. Emmie and Carlos had been frozen in their places in the kitchen, but no more. They followed Reese's lead, exiting through the back door.

CC watched through the window as Reese and Nora strolled to the edge of the pond. Nora slowly relaxed until she was her old detached but calmer self in the comforting safety of Reese's care. CC missed that care even as she wondered if she and Reese would ever feel close with one another again after the last few minutes. She didn't know if she even wanted a relationship with another man who hadn't been honest with her, but she knew the topic was likely a moot point. Judging from the glance Reese shot her way, he was equally disillusioned with her over her tirade at Nora.

She tried to let go of those worries and focused instead on Nora, studying the woman through the prism of her new understanding. She had always seen herself as solely a Cippolini, as if her mother's genes had exited CC's body the day her mother departed. She'd always found comfort in seeing her father and his people in her high forehead and cheek bones, but her wheat-colored hair, her turned-up nose, and her long willowy neck were all similar to Nora's. Tears traced down her cheeks as she slowly accepted that this woman was telling the truth. When CC's father died, Nora had not merely offered her a home out of some sense of random compassion. She'd taken her in because she was CC's mother. The woman who had left her for reasons CC still didn't understand.

Devon inched to the window beside CC. She didn't care where he stood or what he did. She was fixed on the scene outside, as she watched Emmie and Carlos join Reese and Nora.

"Maybe it was wrong to bring Nora here, but I didn't think you'd believe the truth unless you heard it from her."

He was right, but CC didn't want to validate his logic. Her attention was focused on the group by the water, peacefully watching the giant fish swim to the edges of the pond, searching for cracked corn.

Devon looked straight ahead and kept talking.

"Nora told me she'd had problems from the beginning of her marriage to your father. She knew things were unravelling. She felt no yearning to write to him during his deployment, and she farmed you out to relatives and neighbors as often as she could. Your father wrote and told her rumors were starting to fly about what she was doing with her free time. When he came home on emergency leave, you were in the care of a neighbor, and she was out on the town."

"With another man?"

"She said she was binge-drinking."

CC's shoulders slumped at the ugly truth. She felt broken, and she longed to shut the door on the past, but doing so wasn't enough to protect the present. The hopeful life she and Reese had discussed was washing away like runoff from the pond.

Reese then said something to Emmie, who nodded and took Nora by the arm, freeing Reese. He looked up at the house as if searching for CC. She didn't know if he saw her in the window as clearly as she could see him, but the happy, light expression he'd shown Nora slipped back into one of worry and weight as he headed toward the back of the house. CC feared he might head to the barn and saddle Admiral to ride away from the drama. She touched the glass and traced his exit until he disappeared from view.

Devon placed his hand on CC's cheek and turned her face toward him. "There's a reason Nora is such a mess, CC. *That's* what you need to understand."

"You didn't come here out of concern for me, Devon. There's always a payoff for you, so just tell me what point you're trying to make or what outcome you're hoping to achieve."

He dropped his hands by his sides and huffed as if she were too stupid to recognize his message. "Nora has a mental illness, CC. She can't make emotional attachments or adapt to change. She stayed in the same general area and married two more times, but those marriages also failed. Your father bumped into her and found her in a bad way. He got her diagnosed and on medication and planned to introduce you to her when she was stable and ready, but . . ."

Devon's matter-of-factness over the most intimately painful details of her life ripped CC raw. "But he died? Is that what you're trying to say? Why did he feel a need to wait to introduce Nora to me?"

"He must have been trying to protect you."

"From Nora?"

"From what meeting her would do to you."

His answer almost seemed caring.

He placed his hands on her shoulders and drilled into her with his eyes. "Your *mother* has attachment issues. Get it?"

CC pushed away from him and fired back. "What are you saying?" But the concern was planted, and it was already taking root in her mind.

"Maybe our issues weren't just mine. You pushed me away, and instead of talking about our problems, I reacted poorly."

"You cheated! And not just once."

"I was lonely. I needed to connect with someone."

His gall was incredible. He was twisting their history, turning it inside out, and placing the blame for his failures on her. She wanted to physically toss him out, but she also couldn't unhear the words he'd said. She walked away from him and back again. "You're unbelievable. This is a new low, even for you."

"And yet a part of you wonders, doesn't it? I asked around about you at a place called Big Jim's. A guy there told me he'd met you, and he told me about Reese's past. That he was a man crushed by a wife who left him. Sounds familiar, doesn't it?"

CC's throat grew tight. She hated Devon at this moment for using her parents' pain to make his point. And he knew some of Reese's story.

"One wife walking away nearly crushed him. What would happen if a second woman did the same?"

Her hands flew to her ears to shut out his words. "I love him. I would never do that."

"How can you be sure? And won't he be asking himself the same thing now that he knows about Nora?"

"Why are you doing this to me?"

"All those things you said to the sheriff about me, making me out to be some cheating loser . . ." Devon spread his arms wide. "I just wanted to set the record straight. The problem wasn't me. It was you, baby. You're just like your mother."

"Get out. Get out!"

"Gladly. Just give me what I came for. I left a diamond ring in the glove box of the Tesla."

"What?"

"Don't worry. It wasn't for you. I took the Tesla to shop for that ring. As expected, that fancy car impressed the jeweler, and he gave me a good deal. And then you ruined everything. Bible-thumping John Torino overheard me telling Julia I was planning to dump you and that I was taking her with me on the trip. You got me fired from driving the Tesla to Vegas. I planned to propose to her there, but I bought her a cheap ring just for the pictures and proposed in Chicago instead. You saw the photo."

CC didn't know when Reese had entered the kitchen, but he suddenly stepped into the great room and squared himself to Devon. "It's time for you to leave."

"Not without that ring. I promised it to her."

"Fine." Reese pulled the key card from the tree. "Follow me . . . now."

As the men left the room, CC closed her eyes and wrapped her arms around her midsection. She knew how much she looked like Nora right now. Maybe Devon was right about her. Maybe she was a mess too. But hadn't she given her relationship with Devon three years? How many times had she planned to leave him, staying only because he'd controlled her? But Nora had stayed with her father for two years before she'd left . . .

The back-and-forth continued as CC examined her feelings for Reese. The emotions he stirred in her were comfortable and deep. She didn't want to run from him. She wanted to stay by his side.

But he hadn't been honest with her either.

Her head hurt. Her stomach cramped.

She wanted it all to stop.

She heard the door open again and was marginally relieved that it wasn't Devon. She felt numb as she watched his rental car race down the driveway, as if her mind and heart had short-circuited, leaving each cut off from the other.

"CC," Reese said, but she shook her head and put her hands forward to prevent any attempt to touch her.

"I'm sorry I didn't tell you that Devon claimed to have found your mother. I planned to wait until after the party so you'd know that whether Nora was your mother or not, and no matter how you felt about her, you had people who loved and . . . and cared about—"

Reese and his explanation withered as he met her blank stare.

"CC? Please. Talk to me." She watched panic darken his face as she turned and headed down the hall for her room . . . for Reese's room.

"Don't let Devon get in your head. Please, CC, let's talk this out. Please don't leave."

The plea so exquisitely summed up her inner wrestle. *Leave now? Leave later?* What if leaving was inevitable? She somehow managed to hold it together until the door clicked shut behind her, and then everything tore loose, thread by fragile thread—her view of herself, the history of her life, the sacred memories of the father she had held as her one true anchor.

She fell onto the bed and sobbed into the pillows to muffle her cries. Every agony in her life had been laid bare. She would at least keep her sorrow as private as possible until she could find a way to leave.

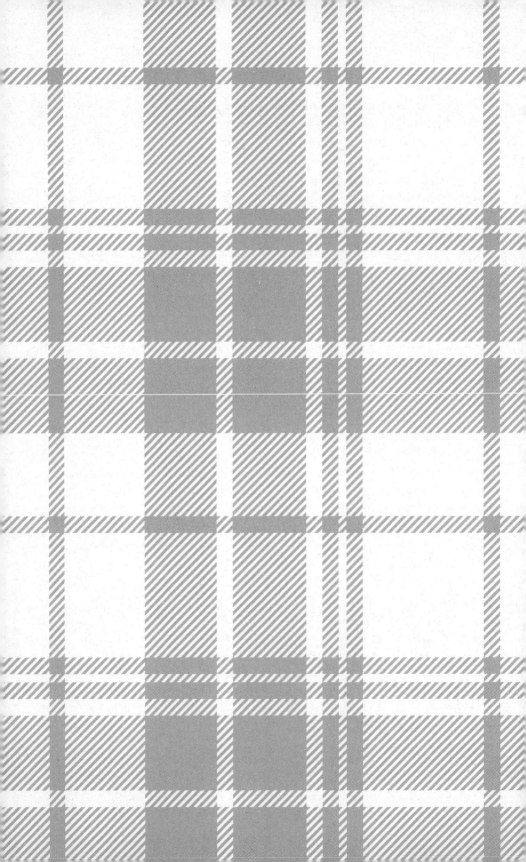

# CHAPTER TWENTY-TWO

REESE WALKED TO THE BEDROOM door a dozen times to listen for sounds that might indicate what CC was doing in there. He prayed she wasn't packing. He heard crying, and though he wanted to plead his case through the heavy door, he hated himself for not knowing what that case was. The innocent beauty of their short romance had become mired in doubts. He'd caused many of them, and yet he knew a part of him would crawl back into a hole and die if CC walked away.

He was so desperate for insight into her plans that he accepted Emmie's offer to reach out. Her text to CC went unanswered, so she knocked on the door. After an hour, CC opened it a crack, and before Emmie said a word to Reese, he knew the outcome.

"Reese, I'm so sorry," Emmie said. "CC asked me to give her a ride to the nearest bus station. What should I do?"

He instinctively clutched the fabric over his heart, which he feared would stop beating. "You . . . you should take her," he answered. He turned for his office. "This house . . . isn't a . . . prison." He dribbled out the word *prison* as his legs began to give out. Though not a piece of furniture or even a pillow had been moved and the sun's light hadn't dimmed a bit in the last hour, everything about the house suddenly felt cold and dark and unwelcoming again, as if it were *his* prison. He felt like the cursed prince from *Beauty and the Beast*, destined to never know lasting love.

He considered banging on the bedroom door and begging CC for another chance, and then he remembered her expression as she'd told Devon to leave. She was in pain. That recognition seared him. He was being selfish, thinking of only *his* wants. *His* loss. *His* needs. He loved CC, no matter what that love cost him. So he made a plan.

After a few deep steadying breaths, he called his attorney and got the ball rolling. Then he moved to the garage to attend to things there. Shortly after he completed his list, CC came down the hall, red-eyed and shaky, a bag in each hand, looking as vulnerable and hopeless as she had the evening of the crash. He swallowed hard, scolding himself for how far she had regressed from that fresh-faced beam of light who'd left the house that morning to prepare for a party. All those dreams and joys were dashed because he'd asked Marcus to investigate her. And what had he found out? That she had been truthful—brutally honest, in fact—about the mother who'd abandoned her and the jerk she had left. Reese's baseless suspicions had led her mother and her ex back to her with news that had shattered her world.

He offered to help with her bags, but she shirked her shoulder away from him. "I've got it."

"You still have two more bags, CC. Please, let me at least take these so you can grab the others."

She dropped the bags as if her strength were giving out, and then she turned, but Emmie was already coming down the hall with similarly red eyes and the other two bags.

Reese glanced at the glowing evergreen that seemed to symbolize everything he was losing. He could barely get his shaking fingers to pull the key card from his pocket and hold it out to CC. "Here. I don't want you to take a bus. Take the car. It's yours."

"No. Absolutely not." CC shook her head forcefully and picked up the bags again.

A shuddering breath escaped Reese. "I figured you'd say that." He pulled a business card from his pocket and extended it to her as well. "You'd be doing me a favor. Please. Take the car to Vegas and park it at the address marked on the back. I've already programmed the GPS with the final address and charging stations along the way so you won't have any more mishaps. My attorney's number is written on the back as well. He'll handle the raffle."

Panic flashed in her eyes. "I forgot about delivering the other car."

"Don't worry. It's still all arranged. Rudy's son will deliver it Christmas Eve, as planned. The auction of this Tesla should cover all the repairs *and* the cost of the new car and still leave plenty for charity."

Her eyes were shining, and she leaned toward him. For a second, he almost thought she might forgive him, and then she stiffened and pulled back. "Thank you. I wish . . ." Her eyes dipped, and when she raised her glance back to Reese, she was resolute once more. "Thank you," she repeated as she stuffed the key into her pocket, hefted the bags, and headed for the garage door.

"Tell me one thing," Reese said, unable to stop himself. "Devon said you had a thing for vets. What did he mean by that?"

She stopped, barely glancing over her shoulder. "It had nothing to do with us. I didn't even know you were a vet when you stopped to help me, but it did confirm my first impression."

"Which was?"

"That you give your all for others. Like you did for me."

His voice broke. "I did that because I knew from the moment I watched you feed the cattle handfuls of hay in a blizzard that I could love you."

"I knew before that."

"Then, what are we doing? I'm sorry I wasn't honest with you, and I'm sorry for screwing everything up. I'm sorry for all of this. Please, CC. Watching you leave is killing me."

His voice shook, and her chin fell against her chest. Reese knew she was crying, and it took everything in him not to go to her, but the moment felt like glass, as if the very floor might shatter if he moved.

"That's why it's better that I leave now instead of later."

"Don't *ever* leave."

CC ignored Reese, as if never leaving was an impossibility. She opened the door to the garage and left the house with Emmie following behind. Reese forced his leaden feet to carry him along as well. He was determined to watch CC's exit, hoping he or she might find a word or a memory powerful enough to buy them more time to work things out.

He pushed the button to open the garage door and found Nora standing in the driveway with an overnight bag by her feet. He'd assumed she had left with Devon to return to Chicago, but there she was, and he prayed she was an answer to the silent prayer running through his mind.

"You're still here," CC said.

The woman was shaking again, but her feet were firmly planted, and she was not letting the car move until she said her piece.

"For the first time in my life, I'm putting someone else's needs ahead of my fears." She closed her eyes for a moment, as if resetting her thoughts, and spoke again. "I'm putting *my daughter's* needs ahead of my fears."

CC leaned her increasingly limp body against the car.

"We need to talk. Alone," Nora said. "So I'm coming with you."

"What about your shop?"

"My employees can handle it. That's how I cope now—I hire people to handle what I can't—but only I can fix things with you."

"Get in the car," CC said as she hefted her bags into the trunk. Nora followed suit with her bag and sat in the passenger seat. Emmie reluctantly added her load, and CC closed the trunk.

Reese held the driver's-side door open, suffering as the trunk slammed shut with finality. He scrambled for the right word or phrase to say to CC before the women pulled out. She kept her gaze downward, avoiding another goodbye, when Reese got an idea. "The deer! We were . . . we were going to set them free today. We should do that now, before . . ."

The comment stopped CC for a moment, and Reese dared hope he'd bought himself a brief delay and one last chance for her to remember how good things had been. Her mouth opened, and then her head lowered and shook, declining his unuttered invitation.

"You'll see to it," she said.

Reese bit the side of his mouth to distract him from the ripping pain in his heart. "You've got my card with my number. Please call me if you need anything or have any problems."

Her tearful eyes glanced up at him, and she nodded.

His chest was so tight he could barely draw a full breath. "At least let me know you got there safely. I can't even call you. We never exchanged phone numbers. Will you—"

"Please stop." CC covered her twisted mouth with a hand and slid into the seat.

Reese held on to the door for a moment before closing it. "I'm not going to say goodbye. I just can't believe this ends before we gave it a real chance."

"Please, Reese. I need to go."

He closed the door and stepped back, hoping the car wouldn't start. He even considered blocking her exit until she agreed to talk. Anything was worth keeping her there a moment longer. Anything but extending her pain. He stepped clear, and with her in control of the wheel, the car pulled out and headed down the driveway.

Carlos came from the barn and placed one arm around his weeping wife and one around Reese. "Let's hope Nora is your Christmas angel."

"You talked Nora into staying behind when Devon left, didn't you?" Reese said.

"Hmm . . . maybe, but whether or not it helps is up to CC now."

The day that began with inestimable promise had become a salvage mission. Reese was determined not to toss away the gifts CC had given him. She'd taught him what mattered. Like love, however brief it might be, and family, as flawed as it certainly was. She'd taught him to cherish traditions and truth and promises, and tonight, no matter how deeply he wanted to curl up in a ball and cry the holidays away, he would not disappoint the people who were counting on him. His fingers could scarcely button his shirt or tie his tie, but he battled through the process of dressing and made sure Emmie and Carlos were coming close behind.

True to his promise, he arrived at his parents' house an hour before the official start of the party. He took a deep breath before opening the door from the attached garage that led to their mudroom and pantry. Pausing, he braced for the welcome awaiting the return of the prodigal son and the pretty stranger who had helped him navigate his way home.

The buzz of caterers and servers eased his expectation-filled entrance with party-prep chaos. He crossed through the kitchen and down the opulent hall bedecked in gold, magenta, and teal, where the musicians were tuning up. He saw his mother first, dressed to the nines in a green hostess dress with adornments that glittered like glass. She looked like a Christmas queen, but it was her smile, her radiant, welcoming smile employing every facial feature, that first caught his eye. She came toward him, arms outstretched, and paused, waiting for Reese to accept or ease back from her hug. Her blue eyes sparkled with welling tears. "You came."

He stepped into her arms and bent down, laying his cheek against hers. "Merry Christmas, Mom."

"Thank you, Reese. You've made my Christmas wish come true."

She framed his face and smiled so brightly that any doubt of his welcome and value disappeared.

"And CC? Where is she?"

Reese saw his father and several of his brothers coming his way. Some were adjusting their ties. Others had their hands outstretched. He felt the quiver begin in his chin and move like an earthquake through his body until he could not camouflage his grief.

His mother's smile turned into worry and then sorrow. "Oh no. She's not coming?"

"She's gone, Mom, and I don't know what to do."

The voices of his family members settled into a nurturing hum as arm after arm wrapped around him. And all he could think was how much CC would have loved these people and how they would have welcomed her in.

# CHAPTER TWENTY-THREE

A THREAD OF CC'S HEART was still attached to Reese and unravelling with every yard that passed between them. She felt certain that at some point there would be so little of her shriveling heart left that it would simply cease to beat, allowing the rest of her to quietly slip away. And then there was Nora, a frazzled being barely a breath away from unraveling herself. The similarities were not lost on CC.

"Half the dashboard is missing from this car," Nora said, her face scrunched up as if in preparation for a collision.

"It's a Tesla. This is just how they're made."

"I can't help you drive this thing."

"I don't need your help, and I didn't ask you to come." CC regretted the words as they left her mouth. She had a right to be angry and hurt, but she was not a cruel person, and she didn't want her anger to make her so. Miles of open land passed with CC's jaw clamped tight to prevent her from spewing out all her hurtful questions. Questions were all she had left of the life she knew, a life that now appeared to have been riddled with deceit.

They passed through a few one-stoplight towns with signs of the season visible in the garland-wrapped streetlamps and store windows plastered in Santas. CC noticed that Nora had settled into her seat and her fidgety fingers had quieted.

After taking a deep breath, she turned to CC and said, "You loved mashed bananas."

It was not the opening CC had expected for their first mother-daughter chat. She turned to Nora with a gape-mouthed stare.

"That's not the only thing I remember," Nora added nervously as her fingers started fidgeting again. "Your smile lit your whole face up every morning when I leaned over your crib to get you. And you had a favorite yellow blanket with satin edging."

That comment brought a sting to CC's eyes. She was glad she was driving a car that could correct itself when tears burned. "My silkie. I dragged that thing around until I was seven. Dad coaxed me into giving it up by promising me a two-wheeler."

Nora smiled, and for the first time, CC felt the woman might be calm enough to answer the question that had haunted her entire life. "Why did you leave us?"

Nora began rocking back and forth. "I was sick."

The thin answer was too small a bandage for the gaping wound opened by her mother's exit. CC needed and deserved more. "What kind of *sick* makes you leave your baby?"

"Ever heard of fetal alcohol syndrome?"

CC did a double take. "Me?"

"No, me."

It required a few moments for the information to settle in. CC hadn't expected this answer. Not from Nora, a grown woman. *It's entirely possible*, she chided herself. Affected babies grew up to be adults. "Your mother drank when she was pregnant with you?"

"She said she tried to cut back when she found out she was expecting, but her boyfriend, my father, was killed in a motorcycle accident when she was four months along. That's when she started drinking heavily. Lucky for me, she was in the second trimester by then, and I was spared the worst of the physical things alcohol can do to a developing baby, but it plays havoc with my reasoning, and it still messes with my emotions. I've also got OCD. I hit the jackpot."

The words rolled out so matter-of-factly that CC didn't know how to respond to the shocking confession. And then a new panic hit her as Devon's insinuation stole her peace. "Did you drink when—"

"No!" Nora was emphatic in her answer. "Never. I couldn't do that to you—or to your father, after all he'd done to get me dry."

CC relaxed her grip on the wheel and felt her shoulders drop. "I'm sorry I judged you so harshly. I didn't know."

"It's all right. I'm glad you didn't know. You had a good life with your father. I only hope living with me for three years didn't undo the love and happiness he gave you."

"You were good to me. I just . . . I didn't understand you."

Nothing CC said seemed to give Nora peace. It was as if the frazzled woman could only vacillate between varying levels of distress. CC couldn't quite bring herself to call her Mother yet. Nora was still the detached foster parent who'd made dinner every night but spent mealtimes fixating on a crumb on the counter or a crack in a plate. She'd never showed up to things that mattered desperately to a kid, like science fairs, school concerts, parent-teacher meetings, and class trips, but she had made sure CC had what she needed: clean clothes, money, a full lunch box, and the best hairstyle in class. It all started to make sense now, and CC could see what abandoning Nora had probably done to the woman who had given the best she had to give.

"Tell me more about you. About how you and Dad met."

Nora clamped her teeth down on her thumbnail and spoke out of the side of her mouth. "I don't see the good in rehashing what's gone and lost. We should be talking about why you walked out on that nice man."

"His name is Reese."

"I know. Now, that Devon, sure—I can see why you'd want to get away from a user like him. But Reese? He reminds me of your father."

That truth hit CC hard and deep, like a blow to her heart. "We were talking about you."

"I can't change my history, but you can still change yours. Call him, Cedar. Please."

The use of her given name irritated her. "My name is CC."

"I guess I got that wrong too." Nora folded her busy hands and glanced down at them until they stilled. She turned to CC. "I didn't mean for your name to be a burden. It holds sweet memories for me, of walks with your father along Lake Michigan. That's where he'd take me to calm my nerves and help me relax. It was so peaceful and serene there. The clean, sweet scent of cedar washed Chicago's exhaust fumes and smoke away. That's how you seemed to me when you were born—fresh and clean and sweet."

"I never knew the why behind my name."

"I never explained my reasoning to your father. He always planned to call you CC, but you were going to be my little Cedar."

Somehow, the name didn't sound as bad to CC that time.

"I've made a lot of mistakes. Let me help you correct this one. Please call Reese."

CC didn't take her mother's advice. She drove on, stopping only when it was time to recharge the car. A little diner sat beside the car wash that hosted the charging station. Giant candy canes were strapped to the front pillars, and plastic sheets bearing gingerbread men were stretched across each door. Christmas music played in the background, and a twinkling tree filled a corner. The women ordered sandwiches and used the restroom while they waited for their order.

The place had a hokey charm. It reminded CC of Big Jim's and the small shopping center with the craft store in Brisbane. She knew Reese would have loved this place.

Everything reminded her of him. She couldn't stop thinking about him or questioning her choices that afternoon. He hadn't been honest with her. She had all but unzipped her soul for him, and still, he had not fully trusted her. But they had known each other only two weeks . . . two glorious, unforgettable weeks, but still only two. Could she truly have fallen in love with him so quickly? The feelings he stirred in her were so confusing. Romance and passion, fun and whimsy, childlike wonder and security and peace. Weren't these things all aspects of love? Facets of caring that answered both the needs of CC the woman and CC the lonely child?

Yes, she knew she loved him, but his refusal to be honest with her had left her vulnerable to all the hurt and confusion that had ridden in with Devon and Nora.

What did that say about Reese's feelings toward her? He said he loved her. He'd certainly gone way out of his comfort zone to make her want to stay, to draw her close to him, but he'd withheld the truth of his worry from her, along with whatever he'd known about Nora. And why? Because he didn't trust her. At least, not completely.

Round and round the debate went in her mind as she grabbed the bags of food and returned to the car. Nora followed after her like a little duck. As CC unplugged the car from the charger, she remembered how Reese had rescued her from the dead car and then jumped the battery to free her suitcases. That memory led to another, of sitting astride Admiral with her arms wrapped around Reese. She could barely separate those happy memories from his deception and her worry over her debt, and one truth became clear. They could build nothing good and lasting as long as she was in debt to Reese, so she set her sights on Vegas with one goal—to get her life back on track.

After buckling her seat belt and starting the car, she almost shared her revelation with Nora, and then she caught herself.

"Did you say something?" Nora asked.

"Just thinking out loud."

"About Reese?"

CC refused to give Nora the satisfaction of being right. "I believe you still owe me some answers."

"I know I do; it's just that hearing them is as likely to hurt you as telling them will hurt me."

"The truth will hurt me less than still wondering."

"Maybe so. Maybe so." Nora drew a deep breath, set her gaze out the window, and began. "There's nothing worth discussing about me before I met your father. My life changed the first day of my sophomore year, when I took the seat next to him in first-period American history."

"I never knew you went to school together."

"All three years of high school. He probably would never have picked me out of a crowd if he were anyone else, but his kind heart took pity on the skinny kid who sat across the aisle. The teacher thought I needed glasses because I couldn't stay awake and I complained of headaches every day. Paulo told his mother I looked poor and that he was worried my family might not have the money to get my eyes checked. His mom met me after school and drove me home so she could speak to my mother about paying for the checkup herself. When my mother stumbled out from the bedroom at three p.m., unwashed and drunk, your grandmother turned and asked me if I drank."

Nora chuckled sadly. "I could never lie to that woman. She correctly identified the cause of my headaches—that I was coming to school hungover. She could have walked away right then and there, but she didn't. Bettina Cippolini looked my mother in the eye and told her she was taking me to her house until I felt better. Then she and Paulo helped me dry out."

It pleased CC to know Nora admired her round, jovial grandma Cippolini.

Nora fiddled with her zipper and chuckled again. After a moment, she wiped away a tear and said, "I was like a wild animal for two days. I called Paulo every name in the book and broke his pinkie fighting him to get out of the room, but he never gave up on me, and I got sober. Afterward, his mother called the school and convinced them to enroll me in the career cosmetology course that year."

Every word made CC miss her father more. Nora seemed to shrink with every mention of his name, and CC suspected they shared a mutual love of her father.

"So Grandma was the one who set you up in business?"

Nora shook her head slowly. "No. That was all Paulo. I struggled in school and work. I had the skills but not the discipline for arriving on time or completing assignments. Somedays, I just couldn't bear the thought of touching a client's hair. I was a mess, so when Paulo turned twenty-one, he asked me to marry him. He thought I'd be all right if I had some steady support, so he enlisted in the navy, and I got pregnant with you right away."

CC stole a nervous glance at Nora to see her reaction to that admission. A hint of a smile appeared and slowly faded.

"We were so happy at first, but as the day of Paulo's departure grew closer, I became a wreck. He set up a little salon chair in a corner of our kitchen so I could book a few clients to keep me busy while he was in basic training. Being able to work on my schedule helped fill the loneliness, and Bettina kept pretty close tabs on me, bringing one friend or another by for a wash and set. I told myself that everything would be fine when Paulo came home—I had you to care for, after all—and it was true for the first few months of your life, but the thought of future deployments and separations was too much for me."

"So you left."

"Not at first. Not really. I needed someone who would understand the chaos in my head. I didn't want to disappoint Bettina or worry Paulo, so I reconnected with my mother."

"Who was still drinking?"

Nora stared at her fingers and nodded.

"Did you start again too?"

The nervous woman turned toward the window and rested her head against the glass, offering a slight nod as her reply.

"Did you love my father when you married him?"

"In every way I was capable of loving him. But part of me was broken. Paulo refused to accept that truth. He believed he could love me into recovery, but it doesn't work like that."

"Were there other men?"

Nora's head shot up. "Not when we were married. Liquor was Paulo's only rival, but that time its hold was too powerful for Paulo or me to break. It was killing both of us. He got a compassionate discharge from the navy, and I finally did the only thing I could to free him—I lied and told him I didn't want him or you anymore, and he finally gave up on me. I didn't see either of you again for nine years."

CC's brain latched on to one phrase. "It was a lie?"

Every muscle in Nora's body seemed to twitch at once as if the confession unleashed a demon tearing at her. "Yes. I couldn't stay. I couldn't stay, but I never wanted to leave."

CC couldn't imagine the agony of Nora's situation, and then the irony of her own decision glared back at her. *I couldn't stay, but I never wanted to leave.*

She was repeating history. Different reasons. Same results. She wanted to scream. Instead, she turned the radio up and drove in silence for a few miles.

Dusk began settling over the landscape as they closed within eighty miles of Vegas. She was getting sleepy, and autopilot was not an option this time. She needed a distraction, so she glanced back to Nora, who was lost in her own thoughts.

"I don't think Dad ever stopped missing the navy."

"I know. That's another thing my leaving cost him."

"He always had a soft spot for veterans. He gave them personal discounts, which meant he paid the rest of their bills at the store. He sought out homeless vets and bought them lunch, and he kept in touch with most of the sailors he served with. He called them on their birthdays. Do you know why I originally decided to go to Vegas?" CC rushed on without waiting for a reply. "For Dad. Because he always wanted to go there. When I was fourteen, we planned our whole trip out. We were going to stop and pick up two of his buddies and take them along. Then we'd eat and see shows and lay by the pool. He died before we got the chance to go, and as the years passed, so did those two friends. I honored his promise and visited both of their graves before I got stranded at Reese's place. I think Dad would have been pleased."

Nora reached a hand across the seat and laid it on CC's knee. "He would have been very pleased. You're definitely his daughter. Do you remember the time you brought a homeless vet into the shop?"

"You ran away as if he disgusted you."

"No, no. You misunderstood. He didn't disgust me; he terrified me. He was a friend of your father's. They enlisted together, and I was afraid he'd recognize me and you'd find out who I really was before I was ready to tell you. So I ran."

CC shook her head and sighed. "I've been wrong all these years. I wonder what Dad would have thought of all our missteps and missed opportunities."

"He was such a kind man. I think he cried for us and then kept cheering us on. He never gave up on the people he loved. I'd probably be lying in a street somewhere if it weren't for him."

"You said you didn't see either of us for nine years. How did he find you?"

"A friend told him he saw me in a bar. Paulo drove over, picked me up, and got me into a hospital and then into treatment. It didn't end there. He helped fund my shop and hired other operators to pull the daily load at the salon. He even promised to float my debt so long as I attended all my meetings."

"I can't help wishing he'd told me the truth about you. I would have understood."

"Maybe. We both thought waiting was the best option at the time. You'd have wanted to meet me, but we couldn't guarantee that I wouldn't relapse and break your heart too."

"Is what Devon said true? That you and Dad were planning to tell me the truth?"

"We were. I was four years sober, my shop was successful, and I'd finally paid off Paulo's loan. I felt ready to meet you, and then your father died."

CC's throat tightened as she lost the fight to withhold her final desperate query. "Why didn't you tell me then? Do you have any idea how alone I felt or how badly I needed my mother?"

Silence hung in the air like thick smoke, choking CC. Nora's body compressed with each passing moment—her ears to her shoulders, her chin to her chest, her body rolling forward until she looked tired and frail and old.

With her head facedown, she shot a quick glance CC's way and said, "I don't have the answers you want or deserve. Paulo's death almost derailed me again. He was my strength. I didn't know if I could be yours, but I did what I could. I offered you a home and us some time to see if what I had to give you was enough. And we were doing pretty good, weren't we? Pretty good. At least, I thought so, but that time you were the one who left, with no warning and no way for me to even know if you were all right." Her voice trembled at the end.

CC no longer questioned Nora's love for her, nor could she deny the pain and worry she had caused.

"That was wrong of me. I'm . . . I'm so sorry. All I wanted was for you to care enough about the biggest moment in my life to show up, and when you didn't . . ."

"Love is powerful. When we give it, love is a gift, and when we withhold it, love is a weapon . . . the only one you had back then. But even though I couldn't say the words out loud, I've always loved you, CC. I tried my very best to show you in small, unspoken ways."

*I've always loved you* were the words CC needed, the magic key that opened her heart to Nora. Her hands shook so badly that she jerked the wheel when she steered the car to the shoulder and parked. She didn't know how to proceed, whether to reach for Nora or to simply offer her own spoken love in return. She felt like the doe, nervous, fearful, hungry to connect yet ready to bolt at the slightest movement. She turned and reached a hand toward Nora, not touching her but showing a willingness to be touched.

"I understand now. I understand you and why you did or didn't do certain things. I can only imagine the panic I caused you. I'm sorry, Nora, and I want you to know what it means to me that when you thought I might be in danger, or that I needed you, you came."

Nora looked like a bobblehead version of herself for several seconds, lifting her left hand and moving it toward the console, where CC's right hand was resting. She patted the air above CC's hand, lowering each motion until her fingers made fleeting contact.

"Maybe I'm finally evolving," she said as she pulled her hand back and rubbed it. "Aside from Paulo, you're the one person I care about enough to try. That might be the best I have to offer you. And this: you love that man you just left, and if you're of any mind to take some motherly advice, hear me now. Follow your father's example. He never gave up on the people he loved. He fought hard to save them and to hold on to the relationship he shared with them. And maybe you can learn something from me too. Don't do what I did. Don't be too proud to accept a good man's love."

"You waited to tell me you were my mother because you wanted to have your own life in order first, to know you were stable and confident and reliable. I need to know those things about myself, and I can't move forward with anyone until I do."

Conversation flowed more easily from that point. The sky darkened as the GPS led them to the home of Charles DeWitte, Reese's attorney. The grand two-story stucco-and-stone home was situated outside the city in a quiet gated neighborhood away from the lights of downtown Vegas. CC had called Mr. DeWitte when the women were a few miles out, and the fortyish man was waiting outside when they arrived.

"You made good time, but Reese has called three times in the last hour to see whether you'd arrived. He'd like you to contact him."

CC handed the key card over and smiled. "It's late. Could you just text him that we arrived safely?"

"Of course. But you will call him, won't you?" The tone in his voice assured CC that the attorney was also Reese's friend and that he knew at least a little about the couple's rocky goodbye.

"I'll contact him, Mr. DeWitte, but first, we need to find a place for the night."

The attorney smiled broadly. "Please, call me Chas. And your accommodations are all arranged. Reese made reservations for you and your mother to stay at the Bellagio for a week. You're also booked for two shows with tickets to the city's finest buffets."

CC's skin prickled. "I . . . we . . . can't."

Chas smiled again. "He knew you'd say that, so he told me to show you this."

The lawyer pulled out his phone and opened a photo of people standing in the midst of what appeared to be a Hollywood Christmas movie set. Gold glittered everywhere, from the twenty-foot tree's trimmings to the pine swags draped from corner to corner. Splashes of teal and magenta gave the decor an upscale twist on Christmas's traditional green and red, while the radiance of candles and twinkle lights softened the glitz and made the room glow with warmth.

"What's this?"

"Look closer."

CC studied the faces and soon knew exactly where the photo was taken. Reese had gone to his family's Christmas party after all. She couldn't have imagined the rustic cowboy in such a grand setting, dressed in a tux, as poised and debonair as a prince and surrounded by faces that each matched a piece of him. His face was closely shaven, as if he no longer felt a need to camouflage his scars, and his hair was combed back, framing the face she had come to love. His tux skimmed over his frame, giving him the look of a fashion model, yet he appeared out of place in the setting, a little stiff, a little sad. Goosebumps rose on her skin at the sight of him.

"Reese said you helped him keep a promise to his parents. He's returning the favor. The room and tickets are to help you keep a promise to your father."

CC's bottom lip began to tremble at the thought that Reese had remembered her father's wish list. "I-I-I appreciate his thoughtfulness . . . I really do . . . but—"

"CC?" Nora's voice came from behind her. "What would your father do?"

She knew the answer instantly. "He'd be gracious and say, 'Thank you very much.'"

"Good," Chas said. "If you ladies would be so kind as to get in my car, I'll drive you to your hotel."

On the ride over, he discussed all the plans to raffle the repaired car and to get the new car delivered. "I've already spoken to John about the accident and the replacement car's arrival," Chas said.

"I planned to do that," CC protested.

"I told him you'd be by."

The lights from towering buildings along the strip glowed like fifty-story lamps against the black sky. CC was no stranger to big cities, but not even the night life of Chicago could prepare her for the glitz of the Las Vegas strip. She audibly swooned with excitement as they neared the world-famous street.

Chas shot her an appreciative smile in the rearview mirror. "It's a sight, isn't it?" he asked.

"Like a working man's New York City," she replied, remembering her father's words.

Illuminated fountains at the entrance of the Bellagio shot golden beams of water and light into the night sky. The hotel itself glowed like a golden lantern—a thirty-six-story paradise wedged into a busy city. "Who needs to pay for a show when you can see all this for free?" CC muttered.

Nora seemed equally transfixed, though she'd settled into her seat as if the experience was too overwhelming.

A bellman was waiting before the car pulled in. The women soaked in every detail of the Bellagio's sumptuous exterior while Chas instructed the bellman and guided the women into the hotel lobby for check-in. CC fretted over her denim-and-sweater appearance until she looked around and saw people attired in everything from sweats to formal wear. Chas returned from the front desk with the bellman close behind.

He handed CC two key cards and said, "You're all set. Room 1222 is your new home until next Friday morning. You have VIP check-in, which gives you access to the lounge, where you can get snacks and beverages at all hours. Shall we head up and see the suite?"

CC shook her head. "You've done enough. Thank you so much for arranging the raffle and for . . . well . . . everything else Reese asked you to do. We can manage from here."

Chas nodded and tipped the bellman. "Please make sure they're settled in and every need is met. Just bill the expenses to the room. They'll be covered."

"By me," CC said, bristling at that final instruction. "I'm not Reese's wife or girlfriend or any other kind of *friend*."

Chas's eyes doubled in size as he bumbled through an apology. "I didn't mean . . . I wasn't trying to imply . . ."

"So long as we're clear on that point."

"Perfectly." He took her hand and groveled further. "The Brockbanks host business associates here. It's standard operating procedure to cover all their needs and expenses."

CC blushed as she realized it was she who had blundered. "I-I-I'm sorry. I thought . . ."

Chas chuckled. "It's actually very sweet. Reese said you were one in a million. I see why. Well, since you don't need anything further from me, I'll leave so this fine gentleman can get you settled in. And, CC, you have my number. Regardless of what happens or happened between you and Reese, please know that I'm just a call away and that I'd count it an honor to help you if I can be of service."

The bellman led the women to their room, filled the ice bucket, opened the blinds to reveal the balcony and view, and turned down the bed. Once he left, Nora made a beeline for one of the suite's two bathrooms, and CC moved to the balcony to soak up the view. She heard the shower begin, followed by a long, contented sigh. Her mother was relaxing, perhaps for the first time since she'd left Chicago. CC had Reese to thank for that.

She gazed down at the fountains of dancing light and across the obscenely illuminated city. This was the wild whimsy she'd set off to enjoy in her father's stead. Reese had made it happen in grand style, altering CC's fairy tale and extending it a few days longer, days when she and Nora would have the chance to bond as mother and daughter. Days that might cause another shift in her plans for the future.

Thoughts of Reese pushed every other thing from her mind. Missing him came easily. Holding herself together was the challenge. She found his business card in her purse. It would be so easy to call and thank him for this gift, but where else would their conversation wander? What more was she ready to say?

She sat at the suite's desk and pulled an envelope and piece of hotel stationery from the drawer. She knew she had a hundred pages' worth of explaining to do about her exit and a hundred more asking if he still wanted her in his life, but she couldn't get the words down. Thirty minutes' worth of agonizing produced nothing but *Dear Reese* and an addressed envelope. Thirty minutes later, she had but a single page written, folded, and in the envelope, ready for mailing.

# CHAPTER TWENTY-FOUR

*FAMILY CAN HELP FILL THE emptiness.*

His mother's parting words provided little immediate comfort as Reese left the party and headed home. *Home.* There was nothing homey about his return. The glow of the freshly cut tree, the tinfoil chains, even the cake stacked on the glass cake plate, mocked his pain.

The worst agony came when he returned to his bedroom, the room CC had occupied during her stay. There hadn't been time to strip the bed, and she was everywhere—her musky body spray on the sheets, the scent of her citrus shampoo on the pillows. He could almost see the curve of her body in the rumpled quilt and linens, and when he found her forgotten T-shirt, he balled it up near his face and breathed her in.

He'd called Chas three times from the party and once when he'd gotten home, hoping for some word from CC. His phone was lying on his chest as he stared at the ceiling, willing it to ring. Around eleven, the call came, not from CC but from his attorney, who assured him that the women had arrived safely, adding that CC had declined the suggestion to call Reese, offering only a weak statement about getting in touch later. Nothing more. At least she'd accepted his gift . . . after a little coaxing from Chas. Reese smiled at her predictable stubbornness and brushed away the tear that slipped from the corner of his eye.

Why hadn't he been forthcoming with CC and told her the news about her mother? Two answers came to mind. One made him feel ashamed; the other made him feel weak. As much as he detested admitting it, a tiny part of him, the part still marred by past pain, had made room to doubt CC's story. That was on him. All him. As incredible as her story was—that she didn't know the woman she'd lived with for three years was actually her own mother—she

had never given him reason to doubt her, and yet he had. Which brought him
to the second soul-scarring truth—that he'd been afraid to tell her about Nora
because he'd feared he might not be important enough to the woman he loved
to hold on to her when family pulled her the other way.

The revelations left him wired. He shot from the bed and stripped it down
to the mattress, as if in removing the linens he could also strip away reminders
of CC. He regretted the move almost instantly as he tried to remake the bed,
but he was too wrung out to complete the effort, so he flopped back onto the
mattress and pulled a mound of fabric over him.

He heard Carlos and Emmie enter the house. Their whispered conversation was couched in worried tones he assumed were about him. One of them
knocked on his door.

"Hey, Reese. Doing okay, bro?" Carlos said through the door.

"Yeah," he eked out as he pulled into a sit and leaned back, staring at the
evidence of his distress gathered all around him.

"Your family was sure happy to see you tonight. You and I didn't get
much of a chance to talk, and Emmie's heading to bed. Wanna sit and hang
out for a while?"

"Thanks . . . but . . . I don't think so. Not tonight."

"I hear ya, buddy. Hey, uh . . . why don't we get up early and saddle
Warrior and Admiral. Let's ride the fence lines and make sure they're all
right. We haven't done that since the snowstorm."

"Yeah. Okay." He leaned his head against the headboard, wondering if
he'd feel like leaving the room by morning. "I need to release the deer first.
I promised CC."

Neither man said a word for several long, awkward seconds, and then
the gaping elephant in the room could be ignored no longer.

"Reese . . . I'm really sorry how that all went down with CC."

"Thanks."

"What's your next move?"

What *was* his next move? He knew where she was tonight—at the Bellagio.
He could call her there. But even his dull instincts told him the timing was
bad for such a move. "I don't have one. I don't even have her number. It's all
up to her now."

"Really? Wow. Well . . . I'm . . . sure she'll call."

"Yeah . . . sure." But Reese wasn't sure at all, and neither was Carlos, judging
from the flat tone of his voice. Wanting desperately to end the discomfort for
them both, Reese said he was tired and wished Carlos a good night, but sleep
didn't come, and he found himself outside in the barn at around two a.m.

The horses snorted when he entered. He gave each one a rub, but when he reached Admiral, he pulled the horse's muzzle to his face and held it there, enjoying the animal's warmth. "You're a good boy, Admiral. I can always count on you, can't I, buddy?"

He saw the deer across the barn in their corner stall. The doe eyed him suspiciously as he approached. "Sorry, it's just me. Not CC. I bet you miss her and her Christmas carols, don't you?"

The doe scrambled to her feet and backed tightly into the corner, with the fawn close behind. "I'm not going to hurt you, Noel. I'm going to open the gate so you can leave." Reese moved slowly, releasing the latch on the gate and swinging it open. He stepped back, but the doe didn't move. "Don't be afraid. I know you don't trust me, but believe me, I can tell you from experience that trust issues keep you from what you want. Don't let that happen to you. But stay or go. It's up to you."

The similarities between this conversation and his goodbye to CC weren't lost on him. He turned the lights out as he left the barn, second-guessing himself and wondering if he'd given up too easily with CC. Had he come off too willing to let her go? Had he not fought hard enough to convince her to stay? If he could just talk to her now that she'd had some time to sort things out . . .

*Call the Bellagio.* Maybe . . .

He couldn't face the bedroom again, so he headed for the sofa, but it was filled with memories of holding CC in his arms by the firelight. Fatigue eventually brought some relief from the constant questions and reevaluations, and then Carlos tapped him on the shoulder, waking him around seven.

He appreciated his friends' entertainment efforts through Saturday. He spent Sunday at church with his family and then at a family supper of exquisite party leftovers. Family dinner on Sundays was a tradition he had observed too infrequently over the past few years. He found comfort without pity around that table as each family member avoided all references to CC. To his surprise, he even found himself laughing a few times at a joke or a story from the past.

He lingered in the kitchen after dinner, packing up leftovers with his mother while his father and Reynolds finished off the last of a cheesecake.

His mother laid a hand on his shoulder and shot him a smile targeted to penetrate his heart. "I love having you around again."

Her eyes held him in place with the same loving gaze she'd given him as she'd tucked him into bed when he was a child. The cost of the distance he'd placed between them became so evident in that moment that his throat grew tight as he spread his arms to let her in. His mother's hug didn't come with the three-count timer attached to men's friendly embraces, and it came without the cautions attached to other women's hugs. It lingered on in the best way, without expectations of any kind. In that moment, he understood how much CC longed for and needed this kind of love. Her mother's love.

What kind of man could be jealous of that?

Later, before Harrison headed back to school, he cajoled the pack of brothers into playing a few hands of a card game they'd played as kids while their mom stacked bags of leftovers on the counter for each exiting son to carry home. The sense of familiarity and warmth of it all compounded Reese's regret over the time they'd lost during his self-imposed pullback from his family. He longed to make the last of the distance disappear, and then his father provided an opening.

He stood behind Reese, bent over, and spread his arms wide, giving a group hug to three of his boys at once. "I hate to see the weekend end," he said. "The Christmas press begins tomorrow."

Though Reese had abdicated from the family's support of their clients' Christmas events, he fully understood the hectic schedule. Various family members attended about a dozen jewelry companies' December dinner parties and board meetings, not to mention the Jewelry Retailers' Showcase. As humiliating as Reese found that spectacle, he knew the event gave the mine's big jewelry wholesalers a stellar opportunity to preview their new designs. The retailers also believed that meeting the family who produced the silver added a touch of romance to the customers' buying experience. Reese's parents had worked hard to rebuild the mining company's great-American reputation after the narrow-minded reporter and idiots like Kernan had slandered the family. Continuing to build on the family heritage and the mine's Western history by showing up on horseback, dressed to showcase the quality of the metal pulled from the Silver Buckle Mine, made these flesh-pressing public demonstrations a necessary evil.

"Finn," their father began, "when does your advertising internship wind up? We could sure use you on a few of these upcoming events."

"I'll be lucky if I make it back for Christmas. The VP handling the interns believes in the Edward Cullen work ethic. He'll suck the last drop of blood out of us before our contract ends."

Their father's face twisted in comic sympathy as he moved on to Barrett. "Any chance that fancy California law firm will let you take another day off to attend the Jewelry Showcase on the twenty-second?"

Barrett pulled out his phone and opened his calendar. "You want me to ask the partners if I can have a day off in the middle of a work week, at the busiest time of the year, to ride a horse in a parade?"

"I suppose not."

Barrett shook his head. "I'm sorry, Dad. We're not kids anymore. We don't have the luxury of long Christmas breaks. We discussed this last year. It's time to hire some locals or actors to round out the group."

"I know. It's just not the same. Your mother and I will tackle all the dinner parties and meetings, but who does that leave to ride with us in the Showcase? Just Lucas, Reynolds, and Harrison?"

A battle commenced within Reese's heart as his father's request for help hung in the air. His pullback from the family had added to the rest of the family's burden. It was another debt he needed to address. The balance sheet of his life showed deficits in nearly every category that really mattered to him—family, love, marriage, closeness, and most of all, peace of mind. Being his own man and doing things *his* way clearly hadn't paid off, and he wondered if it was too late to humble himself and come fully home.

While mentally wrestling over the decision to help at the Jewelry Showcase, his hand raised, and then he stood, pushing his chair back, as if his body had a mind of its own. He stood in silence for a few seconds, then said, "I owe you all an apology. Several, in fact. I know I've apologized for the damage my decisions caused the family and the company, but I also need to apologize for being too proud to accept your help or your forgiveness. I haven't pulled my weight around here in a long time, and that hasn't been fair to the rest of you, who got stuck picking up the slack. I can't fix the past, but I can do better going forward. I don't have any scheduling conflicts, so just fill out my dance card and tell me when and where I need to be, and I'll be happy to help this year."

His father stole a glance at his mother, joy evident in their shining eyes.

"Well," his father said, "that would be great. Thank you, son."

Reese spent an additional hour swapping memories and challenging his brothers to stupid male upmanships like arm wrestling and darts. His face literally ached from smiling as he walked to his car, and then he drove down the hill to where his darkened house sat, and all he could think of was CC.

He gave thanks for her arrival in his life and cursed her departure. In some ways, she had left him a better man, more comfortable in his skin, more anxious to right past wrongs. In other ways, she had left him ruined, because she not only filled his heart's vacancy, she expanded its capacity to love, leaving behind a bigger void in Reese than when she'd found him.

But as he thought of his family, he felt their love ooze into the cracks and crevices of his recently shattered heart, filling it with a contentment that replaced his guilt. And he finally got a decent night's sleep.

Carlos and Emmie continued hovering on Monday morning. Reese smiled, choked down his rising pride, and surrendered to every help they offered. Carlos laid a folder on the table and opened it to page one. "Instead of checking fence lines, I'd like you to look at these numbers Emmie ran last night. I think you'll find them interesting."

A spreadsheet reflected the cash flow of every dollar spent on the ranch, including the sale of every animal and how much each one had brought. Reese had bought the financial software at a cattleman's event, but Emmie had entered and analyzed the data, breaking it down by acreage sections and cattle breed, with a written report that showed which acreage with which grass produced the fattest steers.

"This is great information, Emmie," Reese said as he flipped the pages and marveled over her conclusions.

"You like it?" she asked.

"I love it. It clearly shows that our cattle aren't thriving on some of that government land."

Carlos kissed Emmie's cheek and gushed, "Thanks to my brilliant wife!"

"What do you suggest we do, Carlos?" Reese asked.

"I'd cull the best stock from our herd and place them on the acreage with the best grass. They'd go to market sooner and make a better profit." Carlos turned a page of the report and pointed to spots on a map of the ranch and their permitted Bureau of Land Management land. "Here, here, and here." He pointed to a wide swath of that contracted land and looked at Reese. "No use in letting the land rights go to waste. We could still run a decent herd on this land, but we just need to expect that these animals will take longer to reach auction weight."

Reese turned back to the page of figures and studied Emmie's findings. "Thanks for this report, Emmie. I'm convinced. Carlos, let's make it happen."

The two men headed to the mudroom to grab gear before saddling Admiral and Warrior. This would be a real cowboy day of cutting and roping. Reese watched Carlos's enthusiasm as he forecast the day's excitement to Warrior while cinching up the horse's saddle. The city boy had become a fine rancher and a savvy businessman, and he had a strong partner in his equally smart wife. An idea started formulating in Reese's mind.

The men rode out of the barn and into the back field, headed for the foothills. Reese saw two deer under a tree. Carlos soon saw them as well and said, "Isn't that our doe and fawn?"

"I think so. I opened the pen door before dawn on Saturday. They were gone before breakfast."

"Not far," Carlos said. "They wanted to be free, but they feel safe here. Maybe that means they'll stay close by."

Reese wished that were true for CC.

After six long hours in the saddle, the men came home frozen and stuffed with stories of cowboy suffering. Emmie smiled at their grousing as she dished up bowls of soup to thaw them out. When she passed Reese his bowl with a napkin and a plated slice of bread, an envelope graced the corner of the plate.

"What's this?" he asked.

A mile-wide smile spread across her face.

His heart pounded. "From CC?"

She nodded and laid a hand on Carlos's shoulder.

Reese opened the envelope calmly, warning his heart to limit expectations. And then he read:

> *Dear Reese,*
>
> *I'm sure your attorney has told you that we arrived safely, and let me add that we arrived manually, without risking another hands-free ride. I hope that makes you smile. Thank you for the arrangements at the Bellagio and for the tickets. It was a beautiful gift with deep personal meaning for me. Thank you so much for remembering the original purpose of my trip.*
>
> *My father has been on my mind so much during this drive. I think I'll finally be able to let go of him and my old hurts now. I hope your reunion with family is as sweet a new beginning as my reunion with Nora is proving to be. Still, accepting that she's my mother is a lot to take in.*
>
> *You and I took an amazing leap together. I feel like I'm still flying, all air, and I'm not sure where or who I'll be when I land. No matter how things turn out, I like to think we left each other better than we were. We're not alone anymore. I have family again, and I can't tell you how happy it makes me to picture you at home with yours for Christmas.*
>
> *Think of me when the water overflows the pond. You filled my heart to the brim.*
>
> *Love,*
> *CC*

Emmie's enthusiasm had dimmed severely by the time Reese looked up from the letter. Whisperlike, she asked, "What did she say?"

Reese's hands shook as he struggled to get the letter back into the envelope. "That she arrived safely and that she appreciated the reservation I made for her and her mom."

"That's it?" Emmie's disappointment sounded as personal as Reese's felt. "Nothing about coming back? About how much she loves you?"

Reese set the envelope aside and picked up his soup spoon.

"She used the Bellagio's stationery with the phone number printed on the top," Emmie said hopefully. "Maybe she's signaling for you to call her there."

Reese's first inclination was to reject the idea, but he wasn't about to let his pride get in the way of his happiness again. He grabbed his phone and punched in the numbers. "She wrote this on Friday night . . . three days ago. But the reservation was for a week. She should still be there."

He waited with irritation as the front desk attendant delivered the hotel's elegant, too-long greeting.

"CC Cippolini's room, please," he barked into the phone.

"My pleasure, sir," the voice said. The phone rang again, and apologies and expressions of love were on Reese's tongue, ready to burst out like a racehorse at the gate. He was prepared for a pause, even for a cold reception, but he was completely unprepared for what he got.

"Hello?"

A man was answering the phone in CC's room.

Reese started to hang up, but that's what the old Reese would have done—react and then spend the rest of his life second-guessing and regretting not getting the facts. The new Reese needed answers. Perhaps there was a perfectly logical reason for a youngish-sounding man to be there. Maybe it wasn't even CC's room. He swallowed down the acid creeping up his throat and asked, "Is CC there?"

A hand covered the mouthpiece, but Reese could hear the muffled exchange as the young man notified CC that the call was for her, and he heard CC's voice reply. She was there. In the room. With another man.

He returned to the call and asked, "Who's calling, please?"

Pride won that round. Reese ended the call and tossed the phone onto the table.

"What? What happened?" Emmie asked.

"It doesn't matter. It's over. At least I know."

# CHAPTER TWENTY-FIVE

"Was that another reporter?" CC asked the young man lying back in her bed.

Dan shrugged and shot a smile her way. "He didn't say."

"Just in case, I'll call the front desk and tell them not to put any more calls through tonight."

"I'd appreciate that."

CC stood, and the young man scrambled to a stand as well. "Are you sure about this?"

"Completely. And Nora insists. This suite is too romantic for a mother and daughter. It was made for a couple with something beautiful to celebrate."

Nora picked up her bag and set it by the door. "Are you ready?" she asked CC.

"Yes. I just want to catch one more glimpse of this beautiful baby." CC moved closer to the bed and smiled down at the sleeping mother and the baby curled in her arms. She waved the new father back to bed beside his wife and child. "You need your rest too."

Dan sat on the edge of the bed. "I wish I had some way of showing you how grateful we are. I can't believe you're giving us your suite for the rest of the week. Most people would have written us off as a couple of idiots. It sounded like a good idea at the time—one final hurrah before the baby came and Melanie was nursing-bound to our daughter. We never dreamed she'd go into labor four weeks early and a thousand miles from home."

"Babies come when babies come," Nora said as she leaned against the door.

"Even during a show at the Bellagio."

"Evidently," CC said with a giggle. "I knew Melanie was in some sort of distress, but she had her coat draped over her, so I didn't realize she was expecting." She giggled again. "I was just hoping she wasn't sick and contagious."

Dan ran a finger along his sleeping wife's face. "Melanie was determined to see the end of the show. She kept insisting that she'd read that the first baby takes a while. I was ready to call an ambulance when the curtain went down, but she told me it would do her good to walk through the next few contractions. I can't believe I listened to her when she told me to get the car and meet her out front. Of course her water broke as soon as I left."

"It's a good thing Nora was there. She was a champ," CC said.

Nora shrugged off her daughter's compliment. "She had all the signs of labor. I've seen it plenty of times. When a homeless woman in my town's time comes, they look to me for help."

"Well, we sure needed your help Saturday night. And you too, CC."

While Nora had helped deliver the baby, CC had done her best to fend off the throngs trying to post the birth to their Instagram feeds."

"Glad to help," she said.

"I guess we shouldn't be too hard on the amateur paparazzi," Dan said. "They made our baby an overnight celebrity. The casino owners were so delighted we named Bella after their hotel that they bought her a layette and they're giving us a vacation trip back here next year."

"That's wonderful! Everything worked out perfectly," CC said.

"Except I feel terrible about you giving us your suite. Melanie could barely sleep in that hospital bed, and my back is still achy from that sleeping chair they gave me, but this suite must have cost you a fortune."

"They cost *someone* a fortune," Nora said as she raised her eyebrow CC's way.

"This suite was a gift to me, and now I'm regifting it to you." CC thought about the giver of the gift. Once she left this room, he'd have no way to reach her, and though she had his business card with his number and knew where he lived, she still wasn't sure she could stick her heart out again to reconnect. "We saw a wonderful show, ate great food, and enjoyed two very relaxing nights in this gorgeous suite. Nora is anxious to head back to Chicago, and I've already got an apartment lined up, so please, don't feel bad. Just enjoy it."

"Well, I don't know what we would have done without you two. You're a great team."

"Thank you. The bellman's waiting, so we should go."

Nora opened the door and CC followed, closing it behind her. As the bellman led the way, pushing the loaded luggage cart, the years spent as Nora's foster child flashed through CC's mind. Good memories. Not stellar, but good. She and Nora had been a team, and they had worked well together. It was the denial of the intimate bond of mother and daughter that had haunted her all these years, but perhaps Dan was right. Maybe she was finally leaving past hurts behind.

Nora's eyes darted from her to the floor as they walked out of the hotel together. "Thank you for what you said to Dan."

"I meant it." CC stopped walking and reached for Nora's hand. It dangled in the air between them for seconds until Nora reached out, brushed CC's fingers, and then snatched her hand back against her body. CC smiled at their awkwardness as they started walking again. They had issues. They probably always would.

Nora's eyes again darted to CC, down to the floor, and back again.

"What?" CC asked.

A look of concern twisted Nora's features. She pointed to CC's neck as if a scorpion were crawling there.

"What?" CC repeated as she brushed and slapped at her collar.

Nora's face relaxed and slipped into a calm smile. "It's okay now."

"Was it a bug?"

"No. Your collar needed straightening."

Yes . . . they had issues.

The furnished studio apartment CC had found online was a perfect temporary answer for her as yet undetermined needs. The unit passed Nora's stringent cleanliness check, but she still insisted they head to the nearest department store to buy a new mattress cover, bedding, pillows, and towels. This was one time CC was grateful for her mother's obsession with cleanliness.

They planned to use up Reese's remaining gifts before Nora headed back to Chicago in the morning, and CC treated her mom to an early Christmas present. The two women purchased sparkly tops and black jeans to wear to the Mandalay Bay's stage show. They spent hours doing one another's hair before the show, and amid the combing, braiding, snipping, and styling, CC learned a few more things about herself and Nora. Nora was still a beautiful woman, and when standing side by side, it was impossible not to catch the similarities between the pair. Their old familiarity returned quickly. It was deeper than friendship and had always been, CC admitted. In truth, she knew she had always loved Nora, even when she didn't know Nora was her mom. Hard as it was, she accepted that running away had felt safer than loving someone who appeared not to love her back. That deep, painful admission immediately swung her thoughts to Reese, but before she was able to analyze them, Nora broke in.

"What do you think?" she asked as she stepped back and stared into the mirror at CC.

"About what?" CC asked as she struggled to catch up to the conversation.

Nora pointed to CC's head with the brush in her hand.

"Oh . . . yeah. It's . . . great. Thank you."

"You hate it."

"No, I love it. I was just thinking about something else."

Nora began pulling pieces of CC's hair loose from the clips and pins.

"What are you doing?"

"Making it better."

Manic Nora was back, and CC remembered some of the darker aspects of the woman's psyche. She longed to have the Nora of Saturday night back, the one who was together and strong, the Nora who'd seen a need and capably met it. CC knew rational Nora was in there, but first, she had to calm the woman down. She reached up and held Nora's hands in place. "It's great. I love it," she said, emphasizing every word.

Nora's face turned to stone. "I should go home."

CC crumpled onto the bed in frustration. "Fine. I'll take you to the bus station."

"Do you want me to go?"

While gritting her teeth, CC drew a deep breath and let it out in a high-pitched whine while bobbling her head as she'd seen Nora do.

"What's wrong with you?" Nora asked.

"I want you to fix my hair so we can go to the show."

"Fine."

Five minutes later, they were on their way out the door with designer dos and sparkling tops, but the ragged start to the night had left a cool distance between the pair.

That night, they lay in bed, each hugging her own side. CC was contemplating what she should say or do to mend things with her mother before they parted in the morning. She was about to apologize for losing her temper when Nora said, "Are you awake?"

CC rolled to her other side to face Nora's back and said, "Yeah. I can't sleep."

"What more proof do you need?"

"About what?"

Nora rolled over, and CC could hear her words near her ear. "You said you couldn't move forward with Reese or anyone else until you knew you were stable and confident and reliable. You left your job and everything familiar to you to honor a dream of your father's. You helped a good man reconnect with his family. And you forgave me for all the terrible things I've done. That sure sounds like a stable and reliable person to me. What more proof do you need?"

The question confounded CC for a time. "When I asked you why you left, you said you couldn't stay but you didn't want to leave. What did you mean by that?"

Nora paused for a few seconds before answering. "I guess I didn't feel like I deserved Paulo or you."

"Did you believe my father loved you?" CC asked quietly.

"Always."

"It was you who didn't love you."

"I suppose."

"So it doesn't matter how much Reese may or may not love me. *I* need to love me in a way that makes me never doubt what I deserve."

Nora's voice shook when she said, "Did my leaving do that to you?"

CC took Nora's hand. Whispering gently, she said, "Maybe . . . a little. And Devon."

"I'm sorry, baby girl."

CC gave her mother's hand a squeeze. "You came back, Mom. And that helps more than you know."

"And now I'm leaving again, but I think that's best for both of us right now. Don't you?"

CC rose up on one elbow. "Both of our lives have changed a lot in the past few days."

"For the better for me."

CC sensed worry in her mother's voice. "Oh, for me too. I'm grateful to have you back in my life. Still . . . we probably do need some time to let all of this sink in."

"What will you do?"

"I'm not completely sure yet. I have enough savings to carry me for a while, but I suppose I'll get a job at a salon while I figure things out."

"Figure things out? Are you planning to change careers? I thought you loved being a cosmetologist."

CC rolled onto her back and stared at the ceiling. "I do, but . . . being at Reese's ranch helped me see possibilities I'd never dreamed of before."

"Like?"

"Maybe college? I don't know. I'm not sure what I'd study, but I didn't know until last week that I enjoy being around animals. I think I owe it to myself to broaden my sights."

Nora gave a contented sigh. "That's exactly how I felt when I first met your father, as if he had opened my eyes to a life so much bigger and better than anything I'd dared to dream of."

"What will you do back in Chicago?"

"Same as always," Nora replied in a singsong voice. "I love my community Christmas gift."

*My community Christmas gift.* It was one thing about life with Nora that CC had carried with her to Chicago. "I have to tell you something." Knowing Nora would likely be apprehensive, CC rushed in. "Don't worry. It's a good thing. I've been giving that same gift during my Christmases in Chicago."

"You have?" Nora's voice filled with light and joy. For a moment, CC imagined the happy mother buried inside the emotionally stunted woman. "Was that—"

"Because of you?" CC said. "Yes. And Dad. He always did service for people at Christmas. You both influenced me and my life."

"You did that for me too. You know those Christmas chains Bettina hung in her home? I made a set for us that first Christmas with Paulo, when I found out I was expecting you. And later, I made a set for the shop and for my neighbors' shops to remind me of my happiest time—of being with you and your dad."

Tears burned in CC's eyes. "You made those? I thought Dad did." The hairs rose on CC's arms. "You know what that means? That a piece of you was always with us because of those chains."

Nora's hands flew to her mouth. "You could come back to the shop with me. We could work together like old times."

"I'm not sure I'm ready to return to Chicago, but I'll give it some thought."

"It's all right, because when I get on that plane tomorrow, it won't be goodbye this time."

"No. No, it won't. We won't even say goodbye, because we each know who and where the other is now, so we can stay close. We're a real family now, Mom— wherever we are."

# CHAPTER TWENTY-SIX

REESE FELT LIKE A CYBER stalker as he dialed Chas DeWitte's number. He was embarrassed by what he'd become, but his heart rate still increased with every ring. A man had answered the phone in CC's room mere days after she'd left him. That should've told him all he needed to know about the likelihood or wisdom of getting back with her. A month ago, he would have considered CC a bullet dodged, a crisis averted, but he was not the same man now, nor did he want to be.

"Hey, Chas. How are you?"

He paid less than a modicum of attention to Chas's reply. All he wanted was to get to the real point of his call.

"Good. Good to hear you and Darla are well. Hey . . . I, uh . . . I'm going to be in town next week, from the twenty-second to the twenty-third."

"You're doing the Jewelry Showcase this year?"

Reese heard the shock in his friend's voice. "Yeah. It's time for me to step up."

"I know how you hate the Showcase, but supporting your family is good. Maybe we can grab a bite together while you're in town."

"My evening schedule is pretty packed, but I could do lunch. While I have you on the phone . . . I was wondering"—his palms had become sweaty—"if you'd heard from CC lately."

The pause on the other end of the line told him Chas knew something.

"She's a client now, Reese. I can't talk about her with you."

"A *client*? Is she in trouble? Why does she need an attorney?"

"Reese . . . you know I can't—"

"Okay, okay." He put on the brakes. "Can you just tell me whether she's still in the city?"

"Reese—"

"I'm not asking you to divulge the balance in her checking account, Chas. I love her. You know that's not an easy admission for me, and you also know I'm not some crazy lunatic with psychopathic inclinations. I just want to know if I can see her while I'm there."

"Wherever she is, she has your number, Reese."

"Meaning?"

"I think you know. Listen to someone who cares about you. I'm advising you to step back. Give her some space. Trust her, Reese. If and when she wants to talk to you, she'll call."

"And if she doesn't?" Reese didn't need Chas to weigh in on what that would mean. He ran a hand through his unruly hair and huffed. "You won't even tell me if she's still in Vegas?"

"Reese."

"All right, fine. Chasing her will only push her away."

"Now, there's the rational guy I remember."

"This isn't like it was with Marissa, Chas. It's not about guilt or responsibility. I just love her."

"I can tell. And I'm sorry this is so hard."

"Well, thanks tons for that," Reese said with a sad laugh.

"How about some savvy stock advice or real-estate investment tips?"

"I'll pass."

"Call me when you get into town. Let's try to grab that lunch."

Reese replied with an anemic "Sure" and ended the call before tossing his cell phone onto the edge of the bed. He dropped down beside it, hanging his head as he replayed the wasted conversation, and when he looked up, his first glance was into his closet, where his silver-studded parade gear hung.

He remembered how excited he'd once been to ride his new horse, Admiral, down the strip and how he'd loved posing for photos. He no longer enjoyed that attention. Riding Admiral through that gauntlet of oglers was bad enough, but doing it while looking like a cross between a cowboy and a knight in shining armor? He thought about regrowing a bushy beard to provide some anonymity. He chuckled dryly at the thought of that image, realizing once again how far he'd come from the confident young man he once was.

Still, he had reconnected to his family and was sitting in on meetings at the company to support the business he'd ignored for so long. That was only possible because Carlos and Emmie were picking up his slack on the ranch. He owed them big-time, and payback needed to begin today. He headed for the barn.

The open back barn door and the sound of a pitchfork scraping the floor alerted Reese to Carlos's presence. After stopping to give Admiral's head a rub and feeding his four-legged companion a carrot from the icebox, he headed toward Carlos, but a sight in the back field caught his attention.

"Carlos . . . look," Reese whispered. "The doe and her fawn are here again."

"I know. They've been appearing and disappearing from the tree line since morning."

"Seems they can't decide if they feel safe here or not."

Carlos shot him an understanding smile.

Reese tipped his hat back and sighed. "Then, I suppose the best thing to do would be to give them both the space they need to figure things out."

Carlos parked his pitchfork, laid a hand on Reese's shoulder, and pointed to the fresh bales of bedding waiting on the floor. "Have a seat. Sounds like you need to talk."

Reese sat and gazed up at his friend. "Yeah, but not about CC. About you and me and Emmie."

His friend and war buddy lowered slowly to the neighboring bale. "I love you, man, but you can't have my wife. I'll fight you for her."

Reese chuckled. "No contest. You're the winner. The better and wiser man by far."

Carlos sighed in mock relief. "Glad you see it my way . . . but . . . exactly which topics am I supposedly so dang wise about?"

"About knowing how to love and lean on people."

"Is this about my wife again?" Carlos teased.

"No, I promise. It's about knowing how to love anyone. I finally understand that I was never as independent as I thought. I owed a lot of people for a myriad of things—especially my family but also you and Emmie for picking up the slack around here. And guess what? Owning up to my indebtedness doesn't bother me as much as I thought it might. I'm finally smart enough to realize that needing and being needed is part of loving people. It means people care. It's not rocket science, but that simple truth has just recently become clear to me."

Carlos swung a hand up to receive Reese's open-palmed grasp. "My man Reese is back, folks. He's back!"

"What are you talking about?"

Carlos leaned in and punctuated his words with a finger jab. "Don't you remember giving me a very similar speech soon after we met? We were in theater when you went off on me for being a lone wolf. You told me to lay down my tough-guy image and learn to trust my brothers. Ring any bells?"

"Oh man." Reese leaned his head back against a stall and raised his eyebrows in wonder.

"We've come full circle, bro."

Reese pulled himself forward. "I want to move out of that circle. I want to move forward and accept that my parents and brothers and you and Emmie might be all the family I ever have."

"You don't know that."

"I don't, but I keep hoping CC will call, and she hasn't, and I have no way to reach her."

"As great as she is, CC's not the only woman on the planet, Reese."

"But she's the only woman I love. And unless another miraculous car crash brings her back to me, I need to focus on the family I have. I don't want to just be welcome at my parents' table. I want to claim my place there again. I want to help build the family business *and* this ranch, but I can't do that without you and Emmie, so I'm proposing a change to our work relationship."

Carlos's eyes widened. "I'm listening."

"I want to deed that seven acres in the north corner of the ranch to you and Emmie."

"I can't accept a gift like that. Not even from you."

"It's not a gift. It's an advance payment for the extra load you'll have to carry when we hire on new people. It's not enough land to run an independent ranch, but it'll make a fine homestead."

"But you know our dream is to have our own ranch and herd."

"How about part ownership of this herd?"

"What? How? We don't have the kind of money we'd need to buy into this operation."

"No cash needed. The skills you and Emmie bring are your deposit. I have more than enough land and grazing rights for two herds the size of ours. We'll split the fees and expenses and start you guys out at twenty-five percent owner-ship of the current herd—"

"But—"

"—and you can add to your herd as you're able."

"I can't, Reese. This sounds too much like charity."

"You're going to have to pull seventy-five percent of the load around here. The way I see it, I'm the one getting the bargain."

Carlos pulled on his chin. "You're serious?"

"Completely."

"I'll have to talk it over with Emmie."

"Of course. My mistake was not speaking to you together. And that's exactly why you're smarter than me."

Reese filled the next two weeks with family and work. He watched the sun rise from a saddle and arrived home dressed in a suit long after it set, checking his phone a million times in between. He hoped against hope for some word, some text, anything at all from CC, but there was nothing.

He ate more meals at his parents' table than he had in years, and he crossed an important milestone the day he entered their house and rummaged through the pantry for a snack without feeling like an intruder. His mother's glassy-eyed smile from the doorway as he sat at the table assured him that this was an important milestone for her as well. Her oldest son was fully home.

And yet the ache remained.

Visiting was easy. Accepting advice was still a challenge, but it was next to impossible for a Brockbank to withhold their opinions. Giving advice seemed to be the family's love language. When his gaze locked on his parents' elegant Christmas tree, with its perfect decorations and glistening lights, memories of CC pummeled him again, and within moments, the wisdom began.

"A penny for your thoughts?" his mother asked, breaking the silence.

Reese coughed and choked out, "I was just admiring the tree."

"I don't think the tree makes you that sad," Lucas said. "Hanging out together like when we were kids is great, but as awesome as we are, we can't replace CC. It's clear you miss her. We wish we knew how to help."

"Thanks, but there's nothing anyone can do. I'm miserable company tonight. I should go."

As he stood to leave, Reynolds stood also.

"I'll walk with you to your car."

"I'm fine." Reese bent and kissed his mother and shook his father's hand. "Don't worry. I'm not going dark on you again. I just need time alone."

Reynolds laid a hand on his brother's shoulder and followed him out to his car anyway. Reese leaned back against the door and said, "I haven't asked how things are going for you and Gwinnie. Are you planning on giving her a diamond for Christmas?"

Reynolds shoved his hands deep into his pants pockets. "I'm not ready to make that commitment, so now I have to find a gift that distracts Gwinnie from the fact that there won't be a diamond under her tree."

"That's a high bar, and you're running out of time."

"Don't I know it. Any ideas?"

"To compensate for the lack of a marriage proposal?" Reese laughed out loud. "No."

Reynolds's huff of frustration echoed through the garage. "Love shouldn't be this hard."

"Agreed."

"The only answer is that *we* must be the problem."

"Sadly, I agree again. I was never as happy as I was when things were good between CC and me. Despite my abject failure at marriage the first time around, I believed she was the woman I've been waiting for and that marriage to CC would be amazing."

"I'm so sorry, Reese. I didn't know things had gotten that serious. I'd give anything to feel that way."

"About Gwinnie?"

"About any woman. Do you hear yourself? You have your answer."

Reese scoffed loudly. "But it's hopeless. I ruined everything."

"Maybe it's hopeless for you on your own, but you're not alone anymore."

"If you're referring to God's help, believe me, I've been praying my heart out. I've begged Him to inspire CC to reach out to me because I don't even know if she's still in Vegas."

"Just don't give up hope, okay? For the rest of us as much as for you. It's time we all grow up and stop using you and Mom as our excuses for playing the field and not getting serious about anyone. All Mom wants is to see us happy, and that starts with you finding CC."

Las Vegas's gaudy spectacle was the antithesis of the quiet country life Reese preferred. It was even more garish during the holidays with neon-lit electric Christmas trees and bigger-than-life snow globes erected everywhere. Hordes of people were drawn like mosquitos to the wonder of the strip's bright lights and indulgent promises of fun. Sadly, many would succumb to the decadence lying beneath the glitz and be singed or burned or ruined in days. Reese knew that all too well.

Vegas had been his escape after Marissa left. He'd become invisible here—one more sad, self-destructive man escaping his barren reality, moving between wide-eyed tourists in for a show and those hoping to pull a lever and see their fortunes change. He'd sat down at a card table, hoping to lose himself in a game in a seedy little establishment where no one knew him or his family name, but the dealer had evidently noticed the large silver-and-diamond ring on his hand and had the waitress bring him a complimentary beverage. It was his first and his last, because whatever the bartender slipped into the drink had left Reese impaired and angry. He'd ended up broke and in jail for picking a fight with the dealer. Too embarrassed to call his folks or the family legal firm, he'd used his one call to dial an attorney whose number he'd found in the phone book—Chas—who rescued him in his hour of need. After their initial client-attorney interview, Chas bailed him out and took him to his home, where they'd spent the night sharing tales of Nevada's proud cowboy past. The two had been friends ever since.

Pulling into the city again was surreal. Doing it at night in a fully loaded, customized truck pulling a semisized horse trailer emblazoned with the Silver Buckle Mine logo made him feel as conspicuous as the city's neon Christmas trees. He buried the bitter memories, choked down his discomfort, and tried to enjoy his parents' pleasure at having him along, but he searched in vain for an unlikely, if not impossible, sign of CC.

The sponsors of the Jewelry Showcase had made the regular arrangements for the Brockbank entourage. A fully equipped stable had been erected in a parking lot with twenty-four-hour guards and attendants for the horses, while three lovely suites were reserved for the family's comfort over the next two days. His parents had the grand suite, which was outfitted with a spacious living area, where the family could eat privately while discussing the coming day's events. Lucas and Harrison shared a double-king suite to the right, leaving Reynolds and Reese in accommodations down the hall.

After checking on the horses, Reese and Reynolds headed to their room and found their bags already waiting for them. Reynolds immediately set about unpacking, but Reese wandered over to the window and pulled the curtain back far enough to give him a glimpse of the dazzling city below. He closed his eyes, hoping he'd get some sense of CC, some confirmation that she was at least in the city. Instead, he felt nothing but a deepening ache, knowing she'd fled here because his failure had made being with him unbearable. He was so engrossed in his own thoughts that he barely noticed his brother standing beside him.

"Thinking of CC?"

Reese blinked to ease the burning in his eyes. "I don't know if I can do this, Ren." He pounded a fist against his heart. "It hurts too much to be here."

Reynolds's arm fell loosely across his shoulders. "There's something we didn't want to tell you in case things didn't work out, but maybe it will help for you to know we at least tried."

"What?"

"Family meeting time. In Mom and Dad's room."

Reese followed Reynolds back to his parents' suite. Lucas and Harrison were bent over pages of a ripped-apart phone book, video-chatting with Barrett and Finn online.

"What's up?" Reese asked. "Is there a problem with tomorrow's photo shoot?"

Lucas scowled at Reynolds. "No, it's not that, Reese. We're just working on something."

He felt hurt and frustrated over the realization that if Reynolds hadn't clued him in, he'd have been the only Brockbank son excluded from this strategy session. He was the eldest son, and he'd stepped up this year, so why was he still being treated like an outsider? As much as the city pained him, being considered the weakest family link pained him more, so Reese laid his feelings out on the table. Pointing his thumb at Reynolds, he said, "Your secret agent here already let it slip that your *project* has something to do with me. If you're afraid Admiral and I aren't up for a stroll through the big city—don't be. I think we can handle it."

Their mother threaded her arm through his. "This has nothing to do with that."

"We're not *worried* about you, Reese," Harrison said. "We're trying to *help* you."

Their mother patted her oldest son's arm. "We wanted it to be a secret because we could completely fail."

"Reynolds told us you don't know if CC is still in Vegas," their father said. "Well, if she is here, we're going to do our level best to help you find her."

Barrett, whose 2D face smiled from a laptop screen, added, "She's a licensed cosmetologist, so I've scoured the city business index and compiled a list of every salon or spa or barbershop in the city. We plan to call each one to ask if she works there."

Finn piped in. "We've split the list eight ways, so we ought to be able to call every place in a few hours."

"We know she also worked at a club in Chicago," Barrett said, "so I'm compiling a list of every bar and restaurant in the city limits. It's a much longer list, so let's hope we get a hit on salons first."

Reese felt his body go limp with gratitude. He scanned each loving face smiling at him. "Why would you do all this? Most of you have never even met her."

"Everything we need to know about CC is very evident in your eyes." His mother laid her head on his shoulder. "We love you, Reese. We're your family. We'd do anything for you."

Reese swept the back of his hand across his glistening eyes. "I don't know what to say . . . except thank you."

# CHAPTER TWENTY-SEVEN

CC HAD TURNED HER BACK to the shelter only long enough to accommodate the local news reporter's request for a quick video interview, but when she turned back around, a line had already begun to form. Her own pleasure radiated equally on the faces of her three homeless temps. Each had signed on to be her week-long assistants for the grand sum of ten dollars an hour, a free makeover, and a chance to meet with local employers who were hiring.

A thin young man CC guessed to be about nineteen bounced on his toes as he came toward her. The former panhandler she'd found on a street corner was now dressed in clean jeans, a red pullover, and a baseball cap. CC marveled at the transformation of her first Vegas "client." She was still amazed at how a shower, a clean set of clothes, and a little time in her care could restore the light in a downtrodden person's eyes.

The young man who referred to himself merely as Chip said, "Look at that line, CC! Good news sure travels fast."

She looked at her watch. "It's not even nine. Would you mind alerting Mitch that we're starting early today?"

As Chip headed off, CC paused for a moment to appreciate her good fortune. Determined to recreate her Chicago Christmas gift, she'd found the perfect location on the very day she'd said goodbye to her mother at the airport.

Her phone rang, and Chas's name appeared. She knew the call was intended to make sure she was sticking to the plan Chas had helped make possible. She'd known him for only two weeks, but in that time, he'd become her personal angel. After listening to her ideas, he'd set up appointments for her and cancelled a day's worth of clients to take her to meet with the shelter's manager, Mitch, and the Tesla's owner, John Torino. As a result, Mitch had generously agreed to have the shelter host the event. At the meeting with

John Torino, CC apologized for the complications she'd created, and she forfeited her thousand-dollar car-delivery fee. Once Chas explained CC's project, John agreed to donate the money to cover expenses at the local thrift store. Additionally, he'd lined up licenses and permits and supported her every step of the way. The plan had always been to shut down the enterprise on the evening of the twenty-third, but with all the people still flocking to their location, CC wished she could stay through Christmas.

Her phone rang again, and she finally answered.

"Nice piece in the morning paper, CC. You must be so proud."

"I couldn't have done it without you."

"It was my honor. Are we still on for tonight?"

CC took a deep breath as she considered all the ramifications of her answer. By evening, all the tasks she'd come to Vegas to complete would be finished. The car issues were settled, and she'd faced John and made amends there. Her personal questions were all that remained.

She'd agonized for days to sort out her feelings—about Reese, about her mother, and most importantly, about herself. Running away to Central, Chicago, at eighteen had taken guts and confidence. She'd made a good life for herself there, but her years with Devon had somehow reopened wounds from her childhood and eroded that confidence and courage. Reese had helped her tap back into those strengths. So had Chas. It was time to decide what future this renewed version of herself wanted—whether she wanted to be with Reese or whether her time in Vegas had opened her eyes to other possibilities.

Finally, she answered Chas. "Yes. I'll be ready."

"You close down at six, right? Can you be packed by seven?"

"I'll have items to return to the thrift store, but I'll try."

"Seven, then."

Reese felt as if ants were crawling over his innards during the first evening's formal dinner and speeches. He just wanted to get out of there and see if Barrett and Finn had found any leads on CC. Numerous texts with his brothers proved that there had been none, which was no surprise since most salons were already closed for the day.

The family started early the next morning, calling their lists and pouring every free minute between photo ops and interviews into asking salon and spa workers if they had a technician named CC. Again, all their efforts proved fruitless. As they dressed in their silver-studded parade gear for the evening's final event, Barrett and Finn promised to continue calling from their remote locations.

Reese tucked the item he'd brought from home into his pocket. It would have meaning only to CC, if he found her, but his hopes of that outcome were thin as he headed into the dusk to get Admiral. The bedazzled horse's gear boasted studded silver buckles and silver-tipped straps that gleamed against his black body. His saddle's silver embellishments reflected the city lights like lasers, and Reese marveled that this glorious onyx steed was the hardworking horse who spent most days covered in dirt and sweat as he cut herds and jumped muddy streams.

He looked Admiral in the eye, winked, and whistled at the horse to show his approval. "Well, look at you, buddy. I know how ridiculous I look, but you, my friend, are looking studly. You're gonna drive the mares wild tonight." Another thought struck him, prompting a painful chuckle. "Imagine what CC'd say if she could see us dressed brighter than a couple of strands of twinkle lights." He grasped Admiral's bridle in his hands and pressed his forehead to the horse's.

"Tomorrow we head back to our quiet ranch and life, but tonight is not about us. It's about those camera-toting tourists and their families. We'll give them a grand Christmas show, won't we? Because they're going to think you're the prettiest horse they've ever seen."

He placed a kiss on the warm softness of Admiral's muzzle and patted his neck as his parents and Reynolds arrived in their own silver-studded splendor.

His father laid his hand on Reese's shoulder. "Admiral might rival my Gentry tonight. And you don't look half bad yourself."

Reese snorted at the backhanded compliment. "That's not saying much considering the fact that you look like you pulled your outfit out of Mom's silverware drawer."

"Very funny, but I wouldn't give up your day job," his father retorted.

Reynolds had a good laugh and then noticed their missing member. "Where's Harrison?"

Their mother scanned the path they'd just come from. "He was right behind me when we passed through the hotel lobby. Maybe someone asked him to pose for a photo."

"We've got time," their father said as he checked his watch again. "The hotel set up a little corral in the parking lot, and people are already arriving, so let's take thirty minutes to run through a few patterns right here before we head over. The people know we're a mining company providing photo ops, not Buffalo Bill's Wild West Show, so just take it nice and slow around the fence line for a few rotations so the guests can get great shots. Your mother and I will run through a few simple tricks to get the audience clapping. Join in and follow our lead with your own horses, and then do something individually so we showcase each animal. After that, we'll just be real friendly with the folks so they can pose beside the horses. Sound good?"

Harrison rushed into the tented stable with wide eyes. "Reese, I think I just saw your girl on TV."

Reese caught him by the shoulders. "What?"

"I was passing through the lobby when one of the TVs in the bar showed a local news story. A reporter was interviewing a woman named CC who was giving free haircuts to homeless people in Vegas."

Reese tightened his grasp on his brother. "Was it live? Where is she? How long will she be there?"

"Wait, wait," Reynolds said. "A local station is sending a film crew to cover tonight's event. We could ask them if they know where she is."

"There's more," Harrison cried. "The segment was shot this morning, in front of a homeless shelter. I think the reporter said she'd be back at that location when CC closed up shop at six p.m. because CC is the one drawing the name of the winner of the Tesla being auctioned for charity."

Reese looked at his watch and felt a tsunami of panic crash over him. "It's five thirty now. How many shelters are there in this city, and where are they?"

Everyone pulled cell phones out of their pockets to search for shelters.

Reynolds sighed. "I see at least ten, Reese, and they're scattered all over the city."

Their father looked at their mother with worried eyes. "It would take all of us to hit every shelter in the city by six, even if we left immediately."

"And what would we say to our retailers and their guests?" their mother asked.

"They'll be as angry as hornets," her husband said.

"Are you going to call them, or am I?" she responded.

Reese watched the exchange in wonder. Once again, his parents were willing to lay their own reputations on the line for him. "I can't let you do that."

"It's the only way, Reese," his mom said.

Then Reese saw a familiar sight that caused his heart rate to increase even further. The used Tesla, with its one-of-a-kind custom paint job, was driving down the strip right in front of the hotel, and the driver was none other than Chas DeWitte. "He still has the Tesla!"

"How does that help you?" Reynolds asked.

"Harrison heard CC was going to draw the winning name. Chas has to be headed to wherever she is!" Reese rushed over to his parents, hugged his father, and kissed his mother. "Thank you, but I have to take a chance on this lead."

He jumped on Admiral, prepared to take off across the parking lot as the film crew arrived.

The reporter jumped out of the press van. "We were told the show didn't begin until six!"

Reese's mother called their hosts to share the news while his father approached the press. "I'm sorry. Tonight's show is postponed. There's been a change of plans," he said. "A family emergency."

That was all the press needed. They were back in the van in pursuit of Reese and his horse as they swiftly bolted toward Chas DeWitte and the Tesla.

Reese reached the end of the hotel property when the car stopped at a red light. It was his chance to catch up to the vehicle, but he'd ridden Admiral up to an intersection with traffic moving across his path.

Then he got an idea. He removed his hat and reared Admiral up on his hind legs to create a photo moment that completely stopped the traffic. While the drivers snapped photos of the crazy silver cowboy and his blazing-saddled steed, he guided Admiral through and around the parked vehicles to the other side of the street, and then the two took off toward the Tesla as it started moving once again.

The car turned a corner, so Reese headed Admiral diagonally across a neighboring casino's grassy plaza. He began calculating what laws he was breaking and how much financial damage this wild ride would cost, but the hope of finding CC left him well past the point of reason, so he rode on, jumping Admiral over a little man-made water feature as the horse kicked up grass behind them.

He heard a siren in the distance and caught a glimpse over his shoulder of the press van filming him as they followed. He was closing in on the Tesla as another red light came into view. Reese whipped his hat up and down, hoping to catch Chas's attention in the rearview mirror. His wish was granted when Chas pulled the Tesla to the curb and jumped out in complete disbelief.

"Are you crazy?"

"Probably. And likely about to be arrested. The news station said CC is pulling the winning ticket. Is that where you're headed with the Tesla?"

Chas's hands flew to his hips. "Yes, and I'm in a hurry. The film crew is shooting the drawing in a few minutes."

"Please, Chas," Reese begged. "Take me to her. Please."

Chas rubbed his hand up and down his face. "What do we do with your horse?"

"How far away is she?"

"About seven more blocks."

"We'll follow you."

"Good grief, Reese. Let's at least take the side streets and try to delay your arrest. You know it's nearly Christmas, don't you? I'm going to bill you triple if I end up bailing your sorry hide out of the pokey during the holidays."

Reese kissed his friend's cheek. "Charge me anything you want. Just get me to CC."

The seven blocks became eleven or more as Chas inched their little band away from the strip and down lamplit service alleys to avoid detection. It was nearly six and growing chilly when they reached a shelter run by a local church. Chas parked the car in the corner of the lot, where a single camera and a reporter stood. Reese dismounted and scanned the scene. A small group of people was still sitting on the ground, in line for the last operators whose makeshift stations were still set up outside. A sign on the main door of the shelter read *Showers* with an arrow pointing down a flight of cement steps. Another sign by a dimly lit shelter door read *Apply for work here*. Racks of clothes and shoes were being loaded back into a panel truck with the words *Helping-Hands Thrift Shop* painted along the side. CC was not only cutting hair; she was mobilizing a community and giving people a fresh start.

Reese saw her before she noticed him and Admiral. She was dressed for work in jeans and a sweater. Her makeup was minimal, and her hair was pulled back in a messy ponytail with tendrils escaping everywhere. She looked tired, but her face was alight with contentment and peace. She'd never seemed so beautiful to him, not just because he missed her so but because there was something new about her. A depth and confidence he'd always sensed but hadn't seen before now.

She made her way to the camera crew and endured three takes before pulling the winning ticket. She didn't stick around for the hoopla, but instead, she headed back to her temporary shop to complete her day's work.

Some clients were turning and pointing to the silver-bedazzled cowboy and his matching horse. He laid his hat and coat on Admiral's back and tied his reins to a tree before slipping into the shadows to await a moment alone with CC. As operators finished up with the last few clients, others packed up to leave. CC stayed on, thanking each operator for volunteering to help after they'd read the newspaper article that morning and making sure every client had "new" clothes and the chance to apply for work.

Before she turned back to the shelter, Reese stepped forward. The silver medallion holding his bolo tie caught the light and reflected it back at CC.

"Hello," she called out. "Is someone there? Did you come for a haircut? We're about to close."

Reese stepped out and studied her reaction to his arrival. His first attempt to speak failed in a sputter. He tried again and managed to eke out a yes. She shielded her eyes as if she couldn't identify him, and then he took another step into the light. "Yes," he repeated. "I would like a haircut, if you've got the time."

"Reese? What are you doing here?"

He felt unprepared to answer, like a child called to the blackboard without a clue as to how to solve the problem waiting there. "You . . . you never called."

CC slumped into one hip as the silence brewed around them. "I needed time . . . to think."

"I've done a lot of thinking myself. I'm sorry, CC."

"You're sorry?"

The words implied a challenge to his apology, so he began enumerating the sins he had memorized from castigating himself a thousand times. "I'm sorry I didn't just tell you the first time Marcus mentioned you still had a mother. I'm not proud of that, but—"

"Stop." CC's eyes pinched shut as she raised her hand. "Do you think that's why I left?"

Reese swallowed, afraid to know the answer. "Yes. Because of that and about a dozen other stupid mistakes I made, but—"

"I didn't leave because of anything you did or didn't do. You couldn't fix the reasons I left."

Reese felt like melting jelly, a barely together mass that was slowly disintegrating into an irrecoverable puddle of wasted dreams. He took a shallow breath in, and when it released, his entire body pitched forward, toward CC. "But I love you."

"That's why I left."

Reese found enough backbone to straighten. "I thought . . . I . . . don't . . . understand."

"*You* couldn't fix my issues. Only *I* could. That's why I left. I needed time to figure some things out. To decide who I am and what I want."

Reese licked his dried lips, nearly gasping for breath for any sign of a future with CC. "And?"

She took his hands and led him to a darkened curb where they could sit and talk privately. "I wanted to blame all my issues on Devon, but that would be a lie. Devon picked sores that were already in me, hurts and issues I carried around inside because my mother left and my father died and because the only motherly figure I loved couldn't or wouldn't love me back. Devon made me doubt myself, but I made him my crutch, and that's on me."

"But he cheated on you."

"And that's on him, but despite his cheating, I managed to summon the fight in me, and that gave me the courage to leave him. For that, I'm grateful."

"You said you needed time to decide who you are and what you want."

"Come with me." She stood and offered him her hand, bringing him to his feet. She raised her arms and swept them across the shelter's parking lot, where haircutting stations and the thrift-store truck could be seen. "Chas helped me make the arrangements, but this is what Nora and I did every year we were together, and it's what I did every Christmas in Chicago."

Realization struck Reese as a memory surfaced. "This is what you meant when you said you spent last Christmas with a hundred men?"

"Yes. Nora never forgot her years on the street, so when my father lifted her up, she pledged to lift others when she could. Every Christmas, she'd set a portable shower up in the laundry room of her shop and invite the homeless to come inside for a shower, a cut, a hot beverage, and lunch. She also gave them each a twenty-five-dollar voucher to use at the local thrift shop so they could buy new clothes. Some of her clients told her they left her shop feeling worthy to see their families for the first time in years—she made that big a difference in their lives."

"And she still does this?"

CC nodded. "Yes, sadly, last year was the first I didn't continue the tradition. I let Devon fill my head with horror stories of murdered naive do-gooders. He made me promise not to do it anymore. I gave up what I loved, Reese, because I had become fearful and increasingly dependent on him—until a few weeks ago."

She closed her eyes and sighed. "I was sad but strong and self-assured when I went to Chicago. I missed that strong part of me. I once had dreams—big dreams—not of making lots of money but of doing good like my father and

Nora, but I gave them up and lost myself. And then, when I met you, my heart just seemed to recognize yours immediately, as if it had been waiting for you to make me whole. Your story about how I reminded you of that stream meant more to me than you could possibly know. For the first time in a long while, I believed I was enough just the way I am. You made me feel safe, but you also pushed me to be brave and try new things. Then being here with Nora brought other good memories back to me. The days we spent here together helped me forgive her and let go of my anger. She helped me imagine so many possibilities for my future. Now the only question left is where does all this leave us?"

"I hope there's someplace for me in this new future of yours."

"Well, it might please you to know that Chas was on his way to pick me up . . . to take me to you."

Reese's heart hammered in his chest as he pulled her close. "You were coming to find me?" A smile spread across her face like sunshine that warmed Reese.

"You didn't have to pretend to be a homeless person seeking a haircut to find me."

His voice became gravelly with emotion. "I didn't pretend. I am homeless, CC, because no place—not the ranch or my parents' house or anywhere else—feels like home without you."

"I'm sorry I hurt you. I left because I loved you too much to risk leaving you down the road and hurting you the way Marissa did. I needed to prove to myself that I wasn't like Nora, a person who can't fully commit to anyone."

"You were protecting me? I thought you were furious with me. So furious that you'd found someone new in Vegas."

"Someone new?" CC stepped back and looked completely clueless.

His shoulders rounded, and he tipped his head to the side, eyeing CC with a mixture of embarrassment and hurt. "I called your room at the Bellagio and a man answered the phone. I . . . I . . . ." He took a deep breath. "I just hung up. I figured I'd really lost you. Have I? Have I lost you, CC?"

A smile slowly crept across her face. "I remember that call. And you were still willing to come and find me, even after hearing Dan's voice on the phone?"

"I figured if you could forgive me, I could forgive you."

"It might comfort you to know that Dan is married and the father of a new baby girl. I gave them the room so the mother could recuperate from the birth in style."

Reese's relief was so complete he sank down into her operator's chair.

CC straightened and wagged a scolding finger his way. "Now, that doesn't mean you're off the hook for your other blunders. They were infuriating"—she placed her hands on either side of his face—"but they couldn't make me stop loving you. You are in my heart and in my head, Mr. Brockbank. In every feeling and thought. If I do any good in this world, I want to do it with you."

Reese brushed his lips across hers until they settled down softly in a kiss. It was the one he'd longed for during the past weeks and for years before that. And it came with music in the distance . . . and then Reese realized the music was actually sirens blaring, followed by news cameras and his family in an Uber.

"I'm probably about to get arrested, but before I do . . ." He tipped her chin up and kissed her again. "I need you to know that I love you with all my heart, CC Cippolini."

Reese pounded Chas on the back as they walked from the Las Vegas court-room with Reese's father and brothers. "Chas, you proved your worth today. You pulled off some Olympic-class legal gymnastics in that hearing. How on earth did you locate that ancient law permitting horse riding in the city limits?"

"Aren't you ashamed of the way you've mocked my cowboy fandom?" Chas blew on his nails and polished them against his suit coat. "Most cities still carry a lot of antiquated laws in their books. They don't take the time to clear them until someone points them out or uses them, as we did today. You're just lucky I knew a few I could pull from the dust of Nevada's cowboy past."

"From one ole cowboy fanboy to another, I'm grateful to you," Reese's father said. "I couldn't tell if the judge let Reese off with fines and a tongue-lashing because she was amused, dazzled, or befuddled by your argument, but I'm not going to question it."

"I get some points for throwing myself on the mercy of the court," Reese said. "Instead of tossing me into jail, the judge accepted our invitation to tonight's show, and I'm happy to pay any fines she dishes out."

"My lawyer's instinct tells me she might be coming simply to verify your crazy story." Chas rubbed his fingers together under Reese's nose. "And save a little of that generosity for when you get my bill. Remember my holiday fee schedule?"

"Ouch," Reynolds teased. "On the plus side, the video of your romantic horseback ride to find CC aired on the local news, and it's gone viral on social media."

"Speaking of CC, where did she and Mom go? They peeled out right after the judge gave her ruling."

"Once they knew you weren't being hauled off to jail, they got to work soothing our sponsors' ruffled feathers," Harrison said.

"We can add Finn and Barrett to our list of heroes tonight," their father reminded them.

Finn had tagged Reese, Admiral, and the Jewelry Retailer's Showcase in the video. As a result, the Brockbanks' hosts were getting a big bump in hits on their websites, which bought enough forgiveness to get the Silver-Buckle Mine a reprieve that night.

"Everyone wants to meet your mystery lady," their father said, "so dust off your silver studs one more time, son, and get CC on Admiral. I think we're going to have a record crowd."

As predicted, the audience spilled out beyond the stadium seating and into the streets. With CC riding behind him, Reese and Admiral performed all their tricks. When the performance was over and the photo ops began, a chant grew from the crowd. "Kiss her! Kiss her!"

Reese removed his hat and gave a big whoop as he latched his free arm around CC's waist, pulling her in front of him. He bent over her, giving her a kiss that set the crowd wild and their cameras snapping. Secrets and past hurts no longer separated them, and as public as the moment was, Reese had never felt closer to CC.

He urged Admiral out of the corral and back to the makeshift stables, warmed by CC resting against him. He nuzzled her cheek until she giggled, enjoying the sound of her happy laughter almost as much as he enjoyed the feel of her in his arms. "Have I told you how much I love you?"

CC leaned her head closer to steal a quick kiss. "I'm hard of hearing. You might have to repeat it a thousand times."

"Happy to oblige, or I could show you."

"The audience seemed to enjoy that."

"Miss Cippolini, you make me blush!"

Reese pulled Admiral to a stop and slid down to the ground. As he reached for CC, he couldn't conceal the more tender feelings surfacing in that moment. "Actually, I had another way of showing you in mind."

He lifted her into his arms and kissed her, letting her slip slowly to the ground. When her feet were firmly set, he lowered to one knee and pulled a single aluminum-foil link from his inner coat pocket.

"You remembered! And you brought this from the ranch? Why?" she asked.

"To tell you what I've learned these weeks we've been apart. Your great-grandparents had a beautiful love story, but that was theirs. I don't need a token, like a link, to keep you near my heart. You're in it, CC. I've known that with certainty these past few weeks. Nothing feels right without you. Come home with me."

"Are you saying you want to build a life with me?"

"Every blessed, crazy day."

"Are you asking me to marry you, cowboy?"

"Yes, I am. Evidently doing a terrible job at it, but in my defense, I had dreamed of doing something far more spectacular if I found you, and then something you said yesterday convinced me to wing it."

"What did I say that convinced you to wing it?" CC asked.

"That your heart just seemed to recognize mine from the first moment we met. It was the same for me, as if you were my other half. That's why I felt utterly hopeless without you." He smiled nervously and started again. "Would you do me the honor of marrying me, CC? I admit that we don't know everything about one another. We probably don't know everything about ourselves right now, but we match on the important things, and growing together will be our adventure. If you say yes."

"Any man willing to risk incarceration for me is a keeper." She wrapped her arms around his neck and kissed him softly. "I'd love to grow with you. Yes, Reese, I'd love to be your wife."

They shared another joyful kiss and heard whoops and hollers from his family, who were arriving on their mounts.

"Happy?" Reese asked.

"Deliciously."

"Thanks for taking on a battered cowboy."

"Thanks for making me your personal cosmetologist."

Reese touched his hair. "I didn't know I needed continuous improvement."

She looked at his silver-studded outfit and clamped her lips tight, stifling a smile. "We'll discuss it later. Let's just enjoy the moment. It is our engagement day, after all."

# ABOUT THE AUTHOR

Laurie (L.C.) Lewis is a weather-whining wife, mother, and grandma. She's also crazy about crabs, nesting boxes, twinkle lights, sappy movies, and the sea. It's documented that she's craft-challenged and particularly lethal with a glue gun, so she set her creative juices on writing, which was less likely to burn her fingers.

Born in Baltimore, Laurie will always be a Marylander at heart, but a recent move to a house overlooking Utah Lake makes Utah her new love. Her Maryland years, spent within the exciting and history-rich corridor between Philadelphia, Baltimore, and D.C., made her a history nerd and a political junkie. During Laurie's years as a science-education facilitator, she honed her research skills, eventually turning to writing full time.

*Cross-Country Christmas* is Laurie's thirteenth published novel, and she will be launching *The Letter Carrier* independently in January 2022. She writes in multiple genres, penning her women's fiction and romance novels as Laurie Lewis and her historical fiction novels as L.C. Lewis.

She's a RONE Award Winner (*The Dragons of Alsace Farm*), was twice named a New Apple Literary Award winner in 2017 (*The Dragons of Alsace Farm*), and in 2018 won Best New Fiction (*Love on a Limb*). She is also a BRAGG Medallion honoree and was twice named a Whitney Awards and USA Best Books Awards finalist.

Laurie loves to hear from her readers, and she invites you to join her VIP Readers' Club (https://www.laurielclewis.com/newsletter) or contact her at any of the following:

Website: https://www.laurielclewis.com/

Twitter: https://twitter.com/laurielclewis

Goodreads: https://www.goodreads.com/author/show/1743696 .Laurie_L_C_Lewis

Facebook: https://www.facebook.com/LaurieLCLewis/

Instagram: https://www.instagram.com/laurielclewis/

BookBub: https://www.bookbub.com/profile/laurie-lewis